MW00398433

Where careers are made over lunch and lives are shattered overnight.

THE IMAGEMAKERS

Arthur 'Greg' Gregory: a P.R. whiz kid, he climbed to the top of Communications Unlimited with lightning speed, but he could fall just as quickly.

Maureen Crawford: An ambitious ingenue from the midwest, she knew Greg was her ticket to success, and she'd give anything he asked if it would get her where she wanted.

THE CLIENTS

Mark Ashley: The ruggedly handsome actor lived for cocaine and beautiful women, and he longed to add Maureen to his collection.

H. Leslie Williams: He was a backwoods minister with a shady past until Maureen transformed him into Reverend Jack, TV's hottest evangelist.

Mona Tyson: A fading actress battling old age and drug addiction, she signed her life away to CU for a second chance.

Cyrus Masterson: Respected businessman, hot-shot financier, he harbored a dark secret that could destroy him—and everyone he touched.

ABOUT THE AUTHOR

A former public relations executive for Howard Hughes, Arelo Sederberg has published five books. He has worked as a newspaper columnist, a reporter for the *Los Angeles Times*, and a network television producer, interviewer and commentator for Financial News Network. He is now a freelance writer and media training specialist living in Los Angeles, California.

Critical acclaim for Arelo Sederberg's novel *The Power Players*

"A winner!"—*Publishers Weekly*

"Sederberg understands people and how to write about them . . . Good novels often tell me more than nonfiction does about the intracies of such complex subjects . . . Sederberg's book gives that kind of insight into the machinations of business and their impact on people and nations."

—*The Washington Post*

"Arthur Hailey, move over!"

—*Daily Press*, Newport News

ARELO SEDERBERG

HOLLYWOOD
GRAFFITI

TUDOR PUBLISHING, INC.
NEW YORK CITY

A TUDOR BOOK

March 1990

Published by

Tudor Publishing, Inc.
276 Fifth Avenue
New York, NY 10001

Copyright © 1990 by Arelo Sederberg

This is a work of fiction. The characters, names, incidents, places
and dialogue are products of the author's imagination, and are not
to be construed as real.

All rights reserved. No part of this book may be reproduced or
transmitted in any form or by any electronic or mechanical means,
including photocopying, recording, or by any information storage
and retrieval system, without the written permission of the Publisher, except where permitted by law.

Printed in the United States of America.

It is strange that men, inhabitants for so short a while of an alien and inhuman world, should go out of their way to cause themselves so much unhappiness.
—W. Somerset Maugham

ONE

Maureen met Greg at a good place in a good town on a fine morning: Camden Drive in Beverly Hills during the 7th Diamond Jubilee. It wasn't much of a celebration; Beverly, after all, was sedate, not loud and gaudy. Yellow and purple pennants heralded the Jubilee. Buses shaped like old-fashioned streetcars competed for parking with old Rolls-Royces and new Bentleys. It was April, clear and sunny, and Maureen felt marvelous, even giddy, as she stood before a full-length mirror in the window of a hairstyling shop, admiring herself. She was dressed for business—blue tailored suit with shoulder purse to match, black half-length heels, and a frilly little hat. The hat was distinctive because other women didn't wear them, but now she decided against it. She took it off and folded it into her purse. It was better to dress as others did. She stood out just by being herself, Maureen Crawford. Furbelows were unnecessary.

A tall man in a gray suit appeared in the mirror, standing behind her. He raised his chin and adjusted his tie.

Maureen turned. "Pardon me, but aren't you Mr. Gregory?"

He glanced at her, his brown eyes steady. If he was surprised at being recognized, he didn't show it. "Yes, Arthur Gregory," he said.

"I'm sorry. You don't know me. My name is Maureen Crawford. I was in a public relations class at UCLA. You spoke to the class."

"Did you say Crawford?"

"Oh, no relation," Maureen said.

"I'm flattered you remember I talked to your class. I hope I didn't tell the truth."

"Why do you say that?"

"If I had told the truth, nobody in the class would have gone into PR. There really are PR classes?"

She nodded. She felt slightly foolish. "Are you still with the firm of Piper & Anderson?"

"Yes, but it's called Communications Unlimited now. CU, for short. Mind expanders."

"Actually, I'm applying for a job with your agency," she said quickly. "I didn't realize CU was once Piper & Anderson."

"I won't say good luck and I won't say I pity you. But I will escort you in."

"I'd rather brave it by myself."

He smiled and walked away, disappearing into the crowd. She wasn't sure she liked his bad-mouthing the business and organization she hoped to join. It made her feel apprehensive and somewhat melancholy. But she quickly shook it off. He was an old grouch or perhaps just having a bad day. To hell with him. Looking into the mirror, Maureen felt good again. She was a tall girl with long black hair, a flawless olive complexion, and large, widespread dark eyes. Her eyes were her greatest asset, but men looked first at her body. She didn't mind. She knew what she had in breasts, hips, and legs. Great ass and tits, the crude men said. That was all right. Sex itself was crude, a pushing and writhing and gasping until the man was finished. Yet Maureen felt her sexuality. Warmth flooded through her. She didn't consider herself beautiful, but neither did she demur modestly if someone wanted to call her beautiful. Her face was fine, her body superb. She was always aware of it, feeling its movements inside and touching it outside. She could feel it without touching it, the pump of her heart, movement of pulse, tickle of air in and out. It was the her no one could know. It was secret and wonderful.

Something glinted on the sidewalk, a new penny, heads up. She stooped and picked it up, full of excitement, grasping it tightly. A new penny heads up meant luck, very good luck; now she knew for sure this was her day. She glanced around, totally aware. The others who rushed by took this life for granted, like their jewels and furs, taking their spoiled and sweet-scented Pekingese and dachshunds for strolls, selecting what they wanted at Neiman Marcus or Gucci's and, with a regal sniff, charging it. They did not appreciate it, not at all. She hated and envied them. They didn't see. Maureen did. She window-shopped in Beverly Hills often, envying the regulars yet considering herself superior to them. They were vapid as mannequins, eager to be ripped off in exchange for flattery and pampering. She looked and wanted. No other place compared with it. The streets were cleaner, the cars bigger, the women trimmer, the men handsomer and better dressed. No vulgar price tags were pinned to merchandise or disgraced menus of the good restaurants. If you had to ask how much, you couldn't afford it.

She was early, so she went to Rodeo Drive. Diamonds sparkled at her behind windows, furs seemed to beckon her to touch. She roamed by the galleries, Simic and Browes-Sorokko and Sotheby's, she lingered before displays at Cartier and Elizabeth Arden, Nina Ricci and Ungaro of Paris, Alaïa gowns and Louis Vuitton handbags. It was a huge theater, full with players and actors. A little Chinaman was balanced like a porcelain figure on a stepladder, placidly smoking a cigarette as he

4

lazily polished a jeweler's gold letters. A motorcyclist booted to the knees and trussed in a black leather jacket with zippers and patches like scars and sores and his butchy blonde rider invaded with snarls and sneers, unwelcome aliens. A black meter maid with pillowed buttocks in a crisp starched uniform searched her territory for parking delinquents like a watchful spider. Maureen paused before a jeweler's window, seeing her reflection. A spell had gripped her and now it was broken. She shivered. A cop, one booted leg on his cycle, was eyeing her. Was he suspicious about something or just undressing her mentally? Men often did that, especially cops or cab drivers or construction workers. Maureen shook it all away—the lost feeling, the fear. Her mood changes often were sudden, startling her. Now she was all right again. Walking away, chin high, she gave the cop a decisive and exaggerated wriggle of her behind.

At an insurance building where Camden met Dayton Way and Wilshire, she took the elevator to the twentieth floor and passed through the double glass doors ornamented with silver lettering. She paused to read:

COMMUNICATIONS UNLIMITED
Public Relations Professionals
Los Angeles   Chicago
New York   London   Tokyo

Arelo Sederberg

Vice Presidents
Arthur Gregory
Timothy Harte
Willard Sterne

There were other names, but she stopped reading them. She thought, *Maureen Crawford*. The receptionist, gray and straight-laced, her hair done up in a bun, asked:

"Is it about a position?"

"Yes."

"Fill out this form, please."

"Well, actually you see—"

"Fill it out, please."

Straight Lace slid into her chair at her work station, sniffing and looking away. Maureen jotted on the form and returned it. She smiled. Then she sat demurely, her hands folded, ignoring the magazines. A red-haired office boy wearing a bow tie and yellow suspenders took the form from a wooden basket. The mail arrived, a chubby postman with puffy cheeks who brought in a whiff of outside air; a delivery man with a pencil stub behind his ear placed manila envelopes on the counter; the black hands of the clock moved from 9:30 to 9:45 and then to 10 a.m. A buzzer sounded, Straight Lace spoke quietly into her telephone receiver, and soon a woman entered. Miss Layne, assistant to Mr. Harte, she said. She was young and pink but dressed old, in funereal gray. Maureen was directed to a large paneled office. The walls were covered with photographs and caricature drawings of

6

entertainers, past and present. She recognized a few of them and walked over for a closer look. The drapes were half open, providing a view of a busy Wilshire Boulevard below, jammed with vehicles between buildings and the red girders of construction. A toilet flushed, a door near the windows opened, and a red-faced, balding man appeared.

"Come away from those pictures, please," he said.

Maureen went to a leather guest chair and sat down, crossing her legs.

"I'm Timothy Harte," the man said. He slumped down behind his desk and put on glasses. "You're—?"

"Maureen Crawford," she said.

"Ah, yes, I'm writing a book on your Mom. Hah-hah." His face became redder and beads of perspiration appeared on his forehead. With an effort that seemed exaggerated, he crossed the carpet and drew the drapes together. "That's better," he said. The office was darker, almost foreboding.

He went to a leather sofa and stretched out on it, taking off his half-lens glasses, closing his eyes and fanning himself with Maureen's personnel form. "Forgive me, if you will, but it was a terrible night last night. Premiere, then a party, then *another* party . . ."

Maureen felt cold with repulsion but she had decided that nothing was going to upset or shock her, not even if the man stood up, unzipped his fly, and paraded like a peacock with his dong hanging out. In fact, she felt slightly amused. Harte put his glasses back on and, looking very serious, mumbled:

"Undergraduate major, marketing. Good. Master's in communications? Stanford and UCLA. Why UCLA?"

"Well, frankly, Mr. Harte, I couldn't afford to continue on at Stanford for my master's."

"Honesty," Harte said, raising one pudgy finger. "There's not enough of it. I read a book once that had a chapter in back titled, 'How to Cheat on Your I.Q. Test.' Honest, you could get your I.Q. up like twenty points by *cheating*. It also said, 'If you're honest in your answers you'll get some credit for that, but not very much.'" He squinted at Maureen and laughed. "But I think honesty pays," he continued rapidly. "There's not enough of it."

"I agree."

"Up to a point, that is. Our overriding consideration here, of course, is for the client. A *white lie* now and then never hurt."

"Well, I suppose we've all told a white lie now and then, Mr. Harte."

He returned to the form, squinting behind his glasses. "Worked at Cagle & Harrison. Hummm. Summer at *Times*?" He looked up. "You have newspaper experience?"

"Not exactly, Mr. Harte. I was in the promotion department."

"Good. We get so many applicants with media experience. It seems never to work out.

Somehow, newspapers spoil them. I've found that media is one of the worst backgrounds for a public relations professional."

"Well, I have no media experience."

"Good," Harte said. He stood up laboriously, swayed, and headed unsteadily toward the glassed-in bar. "Drink?"

"No, thank you."

"I'm going to have one. Hair of the dog?" He took the application with him, put it on the bar, and continued to glance at it as he spoke. Ice clicked in a glass. Without turning, watching her in the mirror, Harte said: "You are a very attractive young lady."

"Thank you, Mr. Harte," she said coolly.

"Even beautiful, one might say."

"Thank you."

"We're being honest, so I'll ask you a frank question. Do you have ambitions to become an actress?"

"Absolutely not."

"We get applicants, as you can imagine, who think because we represent entertainment interests we are—what shall I say?—a highroad to success in the business."

"I don't think many of them have degrees in marketing and master's in communications."

He downed his drink. He hadn't turned, still watching her in the mirror. "Quite so," he said. "Or, I should say, touché." He poured another drink, a very liberal one, and dispatched it in a single swallow, head back. "That's better. Much better." He leaned on the bar, his back to her; she could see his face, the piggish eyes and prurient lips. Suddenly she hated him, knowing what was coming, and her mood darkened, anger and depression coming with the hatred. Harte wiped his brow and licked his lips. "Since we are being honest with each other," he said, "I want to say that I would like to go to bed with you."

Her expression didn't change. She hid her anger. "That is the proverbial casting couch, is it?"

He turned. "I'm quite serious. Do I startle you?"

"No, you don't startle me at all. Many men want to go to bed with me. But I didn't come here for that. I came here looking for a job."

"There are no openings here at the present time."

Maureen felt another snap of temper, controlling it before it showed. "But you advertised in *Variety*, an opening for an account executive."

"Filled."

"Why then didn't you say so right away?"

"Besides, you haven't the experience to qualify for an account executive with us."

"I did account work at Cagle & Harrison."

"That was with Cagle & Harrison, not here." Harte advanced ponderously to his desk and sat down. A rush of air escaped from the chair's cushion. "We'll keep your application on file."

"What would happen if I were to tell someone here that you propositioned me?"

Harte belched. "To my mind, it was the other way around. I've been propositioned more than once by job applicants. Both male and female."

Maureen sighed. Now that he'd been rejected, and had in turn rejected her, Harte apparently saw no reason to be nasty, so he began to ramble on in a friendly manner about old movies, declaring himself an authority on the subject. He darted about, moving with extraordinary alacrity for a large man afflicted with a hangover, giving capsule histories of the autographed pictures on his walls. Returning to his desk, he asked Maureen— very seriously—if she was in any way related to Joan Crawford. "Joan of Arc," he said. "The late, great one."

Maureen had given up on the job, so she said playfully: "She was my grandmother."

"You are kidding me."

"Well, actually, I am. I'm not related to her. I'm not related to anybody."

Harte became playful himself, garrulous and childlike. Again he said he was writing a book on Joan Crawford—well, at least a book on her films, *Mildred Pierce* and *A Woman's Face* being his personal favorites.

"I'm sorry I came on strong with you back then," he said. "I was just kidding, you know. I mean, you are a beautiful woman and all, a little like Crawford herself in her younger days, and I just got carried away. When I do the book, it's not going to be your typical movie stuff, none of that crap. Nor will it be one of those anti-Hollywood books, like the one about locusts in Hollywood. It's going to be about living styles in a Hollywood that was and is no more. About values." His telephone buzzed. He pushed a button. "No, I didn't get home until after four," he told the caller, speaking as if Maureen were not there. "Sure the flick is a stinkeroo but with forty mill in it and a big promotion budget there's ways to air it out. Maybe play up the dog part. Sure, go on do the big laugh. But who can you name in the industry that was bigger than Rin Tin Tin in his day or Lassie in hers? Dog day? Get it? Ha-ha. Well, maybe Joan Crawford, only, or the Duke, or like maybe Gable. Among the cunt of the species, Crawford stands by herself."

He spoke earnestly, his features serious.

Maureen rose and with great dignity walked out of the office, surely showing as much poise as Joan Crawford had displayed in *A Woman's Face* or *Mildred Pierce* or in any other of her overrated overemotional outdated films. She strolled past Miss Layne, thrust out her chest at Straight Face, and pushed through the glass doors. But it wasn't helping. She couldn't hold it in. She crossed the marble floor, her heels sending up staccato reverberations, and went into the ladies room. In a cubicle she snapped shut the lock, sat down, and began to weep bitter and angry tears.

After she had cried it out, which didn't take long, she fixed her makeup and left. Arthur Gregory stood leaning against the wall by the elevators, his ankles crossed, his chin lowered, stopping her motionless with his piercing lynx gaze.

TWO

They went downstairs to the parking area. The attendant ran when he saw Arthur Gregory, but brought up a white Mercedes very slowly, careful not to let the tires squeal. He held open the door for Maureen. She leaned back in the deep upholstered seat.

"How about lunch?" he asked.

"Yes, if you'd like that."

"Polo Lounge, Scandia, Bistro Garden? L'Ermitage, L'Escoffier?"

"Stop. Stop, you've impressed me enough."

"Any of those interest you?"

"All of them do." They were in traffic on Wilshire and the sun was bright. Maureen smiled, feeling better. "I think I'd like to go to Hollywood."

15

"Hollywood what? There is no Hollywood anymore."

"How about the Hollywood Brown Derby?"

"Be serious."

"Why do you say that? I'd like to go there. I've never been there."

"The Hollywood Derby it is then."

They didn't talk much on the way. He concentrated on his driving, east on Wilshire and then north on Fairfax, and Maureen enjoyed the sun. She glanced at him. He certainly wore clothes well and his taste was impeccable. He had a good profile and a pleasant, sensual mouth. His hair was dark brown, styled down over his forehead. But his eyes were what got you. They had a way of catching and holding. He was an aggressive driver, taking advantage of any opening, but he didn't honk or intimidate, perhaps assuming a Mercedes had a right-of-way. He seemed confident and assured. But why not? He was under forty, very successful, well-known and respected. He mingled with stars and would-be stars, a part of the glamour and glitter of it all. She had never been to any of the restaurants he'd mentioned. Perhaps she should have leapt at the opportunity. But, no, she'd done the right thing. It had been an instinctive ploy, an act to make him think such matters were unimportant to her, superfluous, that she was blasé about it, not easily impressed. But in fact she was rather easily impressed and considered nuances extremely important.

Because she yearned. She wanted. She yearned and wanted absolutely. She deserved it, clothes and cars and maids and a house with a view, freedom from bills. She had more to offer than most women. She had great looks, carriage, creativity, brains. College was necessary only for purposes of the résumé. Otherwise it was a waste. For too long she'd sat in hot uncomfortable classrooms and listened to dull professors with stained glasses and chalk smears on their clothes expound impractical academic theory, such as competitive equilibrium or relative deprivation; she had digested fat textbooks and underlined paperbacks, sweated at tests, and, yes, hatefully, once or twice screwed her way to a grade, but only when the bastard professor would have it no other way. Others had exercised power over her. Now it was her turn to exercise the power. It was time for the payoff. She was ready. She would use anything she had to get what she wanted. Why not? Others would. She was up against men in the competitive race, and they were favored in the marketplace—something the egghead professors would never admit—so she was entitled to use what she had in any way possible.

At the Brown Derby she ordered Cobb salad. "What else, here?"

"Nothing else is allowed. What would you like to drink?"

"How about some wine? A light white wine."

Greg ordered a bottle so expensive the waiter had to check the stock. Finally bringing it, he opened it reverently. Greg tasted; she sipped. The wine went right to Maureen's head—she never could drink, not even wine —and she felt slightly giddy but content, happy. She peered at him, trying to figure him out. Why had he asked her to lunch? Perhaps he was horny and looking for a quickie nooner at some motel. But, no. A man like him didn't shack up in a sleazy motel. His gaze held her. It came to her that she wanted him, wanted to take him to bed, any bed—soon, today, now. It had never happened like that with her before, and it frightened her. It had to be the wine.

"You weren't offered the job," he said.

"No. But that didn't bother me as much as the way he interviewed me."

"He sat on the john, did he?"

She felt warmth rushing to her cheeks. "On what? The john?"

"Harte read once that Howard Hughes when he had RKO interviewed starlets while sitting on the toilet. He told me he was going to try it with female job applicants. This is a tough business, he said, really no place for women, and his act on the john would test their mettle."

"Now I guess I've heard it all."

"He's proud of his john. It's the only office in the suite with a john. I suppose he also tried to put the make on you."

"I'd rather not discuss it, Mr. Gregory."

"I'm known as Greg."

The waiter, suddenly sourpuss and hurried, brought the salads and moved away, showing a Walter Matthau scowl and shuffle. Maureen looked down, her demure act, and then took out her compact, studied her face in the mirror, and returned the compact to her purse. She tasted her salad. She was hungry— starved, in fact—but of course it wouldn't do to let him know that.

"Not to worry," he said. "Harte tries to put the make on all the girls, but it's the boys he yearns after."

"He's a homosexual?"

"I think so. Latent. But I really don't know him. The New York overlords sent him out. He's a sweet tooth in a candy shop. Movie buff."

"I think he's a child."

"We all are. We play in a playpen on a funny farm. Consider our names. There's the Heavyweight, the Closer, Planter, Great White Father. Harte is called the Lightweight. As for me—"

"Yes?"

He held out his arms. "Behold . . . the Legend!"

"A legend in his own time!" She felt a little

foolish, but it was all right. She'd play his foil, the new green kid. "Tell me why. Why are you the Legend?"

"Because I bring in business. And I keep the biggest fish in the house, Cyrus Masterson and his conglomerate."

"I'm impressed. I've heard of him, of course. What sort of man is he?"

"Company secret," Greg said.

"I read he's looking for a movie studio."

"Company secret."

"Is he really all that secret? I mean, when you get to know him?"

"I don't want to know him. I only want to take a few of his dollars in exchange for making him look legitimate."

"You sound just slightly cynical."

"It's a cynical business."

"Well, I think it's exciting. I'll admit that glamour attracts me."

"What experience have you had? Have you ever been an a.e.? Account executive?"

"Oh, I know what a.e. means. And, no, I never got that far. I've had one job. Two, if you count a summer internship."

"You're young enough so I can ask your age."

"Twenty-six."

"You were raised in the Midwest."

"It shows?"

"That was a guess."

"I came from Des Moines, Iowa. My parents

scrimped and saved and I got through Stanford. It was a scholarship, but only two years. The rest was hard cash. I took a master's at UCLA."

She'd said it too fast, letting it rush out. Maybe he didn't believe her. "Where did you go?" she asked.

"Cal."

"What else? About you, I mean."

"What else? Well, I have a mortgage, a son called Rob, and an ex-wife. I'm more of a homebody than you might think."

"I want to know about your career."

"Oh, that's simple. I wanted to be vice president of something before I was thirty and on my thirtieth birthday I was made CU vice president. I went to work at William Morris, *dressed* Morris, or dressed MCA, got hooked into PR by a headhunter and stepped my way up. I learned lessons, got the idealism out of me. I mean, marriage and war. Those things."

"You paid your dues."

Again his eyes caught and held hers. "Do you want a job?"

"Why, yes," she said, managing to hide her surprise. "Of course I do."

He stood up and walked slowly away. Maureen finished her salad and began to nibble at his. The waiter came by, frowned, and stood watching. She looked away. Outside, at the intersection of Hollywood and Vine, was a liquor store, a bank, and a pizza

21

express. A husky woman with frizzy blonde hair leered at her through the window. Greg returned.

"You're in," he said.

"You mean I have a job?"

"Harte gave you a runaround. Don't ask me why. Maybe to test his power. We have two clients coming into the house and need hand-holders for both. You have your choice between the famous Martin Bradford and the reverend, one H. Leslie Williams, who desires fame—and money."

"D-do I qualify?"

"Do you read? Can you write your name? I notice that you can speak. Therefore you qualify. Pick your victim. As a warning, Bradford wants to go to the Senate although he is a lush, and the Reverend Williams has a past milieu."

"What past milieu?"

"For now, a company secret."

"Why is the famous Martin Bradford famous?"

"You really don't know, do you? Fame doth flee. He was a star. A big star."

Maureen closed her eyes, seeing lights. She was so excited she lost her breath and for a few seconds she couldn't catch it. Glamorous golden visions danced fleetingly before her— the soldierly snap of a headwaiter's heels, ladies in blue formals and men in tuxedoes and she among them, a part of it. The lights were so bright they blinded.

"I don't believe it!" she said. "How did you do it?"

"Piece of cake. I called New York."

"You saved me from certain starvation."

"I noticed how the salads disappeared."

"Why would you do this for me?"

"Because you're a good kid from Des Moines."

She leaned forward and kissed his cheek. "I won't be a disappointment. I swear that. Thank you. Just thank you!"

"Well, I'm not so sure I did you such a big favor."

"Oh, you did me a big favor, all right. Believe me."

"We shall see."

"What does the a.e. do in your agency?"

"The a.e. lies, cheats, steals, begs, steps on others. PR is the art of creative lying and back-stabbing."

"Will you please stop that, running it down?"

"You misunderstand. A lie isn't necessarily bad. Most people live on lies. Who wants to know the truth?"

"You're a philosopher."

"Half. I'm half on everything."

"Tell me more. About the agency, I mean."

"We will represent a snail if the snail has money. We will costume and cosmetic the snail, polish and perfume it, rehearse it, write its scripts, teach it to speak and read if necessary. We render a service, you see. We give dreams, we give hope. Right or wrong is immaterial."

She smiled. "Personally, I like snails. Well cooked."

"That is what we do. Cook and eat them when they have no more money."

"Of course you're putting me on."

He leaned back and regarded her with a serious gaze. "Of course. We're professional putter-oners. In an agency there are two societies—professionals and flunkies. You can read about the professionals, or a.e.'s, in Holt's *History of Red Light Districts*. The job of the a.e., quite simply, is to make clients feel helpless without him. The flunkies run errands for the professionals, and the professionals run errands for the clients."

"Somehow I can't see you as an errand boy for Cyrus Masterson."

"I am Cyrus Masterson's beard," Greg said. "Ready?"

He took her arm. She brushed against him. The sky was bright blue and there was a slight wind. In the hills behind the Capitol Records building she could see the big sign—H O L L Y W O O D—and beyond it the houses nestled among the trees or perched impossibly over cliffs. Cypress trees seemed to thrust from their roofs like stiff rods holding them up.

"Look at the stars on the sidewalk," Greg said. "How many names do you recognize?"

"Hardly any."

"An object lesson."

"Well, at least they once were famous."

His brown eyes gazed at her. She took out her compact, an instinctive reaction. The sunlight danced on the little round mirror. A convertible cruised by, its radio screaming rock sounds, two boys with mohawk haircuts pressed close together like lovers in the front seat. A man in a mime's whiteface pushed a baby buggy containing a dummy with scarlet lips and orange hair. "Heed the coming of the Lord!" he shrieked. Maureen laughed, taking it in. She stopped beside a star containing the name W. C. Fields.

"On the whole, I'd rather be living in Philadelphia," Greg said, glancing at the star.

It was a good imitation and Maureen managed a smile. "He's in front of Le Sex Shoppe. Do you suppose he would have appreciated that?"

"Well, he requested a liquor store. All his life, he sought to live above a liquor store with a perfect wife—a deaf and dumb nymphomaniac who owned the store."

"Frankly I never understood why he was considered so funny."

Debris swept across the sidewalk, flitting contemptuously over the golden stars and gathering in dirty gutter piles. They passed the sights. Woolworth's and Chicken Charles, Mr. Submarine and Bargain Shoes, Mickey Mouse and Marilyn Monroe T-shirts piled in the outside bins of novelty stores. Loiterers

25

slouched languidly in front of the Samuel
Goldwyn library, squinting in the sun. Shreds
of paint peeled in scabby layers from the walls
of a burlesque theater. LIVE GIRLS, TOTAL-
LY NUDE ON STAGE. They turned back, facing a little wind, hurrying. In the parking lot
two young men slouched against the fender of
the Mercedes, smiling.

"Hey, got any money?" one asked.

Greg slipped in front of Maureen. The impression was vivid, indelible. The young men
stood with their thumbs hooked in their front
pockets. They had ponytailed hair and wore
dirty shirts and Levi's. One had new black
boots, highly polished and decorated with
swirling designs. They looked like brothers,
short and dark. One was much younger, hardly more than a boy. Separated, they probably
were no menace, but together they might do
anything. Now they posed in hard-eyed intimi-
dation, their lips curled and their jaws thrust
out. Maureen gasped. Air caught in her throat,
hurting.

Greg's hand slipped into his coat pocket.
"I'd leave it alone," he said.

"He's got a gun," the younger man said.

"You got a gun?" said the other.

Greg looked at them. They looked back,
sizing up. Then they shied. The older one
shrugged, grinned, and threw his arm around
the other. They shuffled away.

"God," Maureen said, too weak to move.

He took her arm, helping her into the

26

Mercedes. "My knees were shaking too. Still are. But they're just street punks. Harmless."

"Oh? Well, I think I see what you meant about Hollywood. I need a stiff drink."

"I have a better idea. How about miniature golf?"

"Did you say miniature golf?"

"Yep. It's good therapy."

He was serious. He actually took her to a miniature golf course. She was too limp to protest. And, what the hell, he'd gotten her a job and probably saved them from a mugging, so if he wanted kid sports, that's what it would be. She even got into it, trying to beat him. She didn't like to lose. Greg won by a stroke.

"I used to take Rob here," he said, trying the video machines. "He grew out of it."

"And you didn't?"

"Well, I do it for a living, game-playing."

"I have to say that I've never had a date like this one before."

"How about a party? Hollywood party."

"All right, but I warn you I can be pretty square."

"It's a party, not an orgy." In the Mercedes he turned garrulous. "Don't hold that against Hollywood, those punks I mean. When I said Hollywood was gone, I didn't mean the real estate. I meant that it's different. A studio boss used to say, 'Let's do it.' Now a committee says, 'Let's take a survey.' It's not creativity, it's copycatting. Everybody wants to fish where the other guy got a bite. Yet good movies still are made."

"Good movies like what?"

"Well, like *The Deer Hunter*."

"You liked *that*?"

"You didn't."

"I prefer happy movies."

"I think *The Deer Hunter* is the best picture ever made in the history of film."

"Oh," she said. It was best to change the subject. "Is Cyrus Masterson interested in film?"

"No, but he *is* interested in buying a studio."

"What did you mean, when you said you were his beard?"

He didn't respond, but she knew full well what beard meant. A beard was a star's personal attendant, a slave who obeyed a temperamental master without protest. He was exaggerating, of course, trying to discourage her. But that was impossible. Even if the job did include some star pampering, what of it? Talent deserved pampering.

She had envisioned a mansion in Holmby Hills with a kidney-shaped swimming pool, but the party instead was at a small Spanish stucco house on Barham above Universal City, an older neighborhood. It had arched doorways, balconies with wrought-iron guardrails, a sunken living room. Flowers were in profusion, cut and in pots, and a rich buffet was served, lavish with desserts. No liquor was in evidence, but cigarette smoke lingered everywhere, and from some areas came the acrid stench of cigars.

"Republican Convention," Maureen remarked.

"Hyde Convention," he said. "Or, rather, ex-Hydes, although a Hyde is a Hyde is a Hyde."

"What do you mean, Hyde?"

"It's my word. Don't ask. Just observe."

The guests were of all ages, including some children. Couples danced to old-fashioned silvery music on a maroon Turkish rug. The furniture was huge—grand piano, sectional couch, pillowed chairs. The party was chatty but not loud, very informal. Greg had removed his tie.

Maureen almost pointed. "Is that man—?"

"Yup," Greg said, Gary Cooperish. "It is Mark Ashley, superstar. If you rid yourself of your Orphan Annie eyes, I'll introduce you."

He did. Mark Ashley kissed her cheek and took her hand, bowing in a gentlemanly and almost courtly manner. Then, stroking his mustache, he exhibited his famous dimpled smile. He wore a prop, a white scarf.

"My compliments, sir," he said to Greg. "Your taste in women, as in other matters, is impeccable."

Maureen was seldom speechless, but her tongue now had thickened to numbness. If she had any vulnerability, she knew, it was awe of famous people. Mark Ashley moved

away, democratically mingling, employing his
magnetic smile and silk scarf elsewhere.

"I guess I need not ask what you thought of
him," Greg said.

"A charmer."

"That line he directed to me was from his
latest movie."

Maureen recognized several others, by face
if not immediately by name. The hostess,
holding away a burning cigarette in a jeweled
holder, hugged Greg. She looked familiar.
Maureen tried to remember. She was a once-
svelte blonde now not quite so svelte yet still
attractive who'd been paired many times with
a Cary Grant or a William Powell, sometimes
as a comic foil against their well-tailored
savoir faire. Her pictures appeared occasionally on late-night television, wide eyes and
moist lips sensual in close-ups, yet she was
more recognizable in person by her gestures
and walk than by her face.

"Mona Tyson," Maureen said, the name
coming to her just before Greg introduced
them. "I just saw you on TV in—"

"Horror flicks," the blonde woman said,
drawing on her cigarette holder. "I haven't
made a picture since the war. The *first* war,
that is."

She laughed. Then the laugh faded and her
nostrils belched smoke, a Dragon Lady pose.
Her eyes were just as wide and her complexion as flawless as in the old movies. The eyes
seemed to pierce, bright blue and burning,

giving Maureen an uncomfortable feeling she was being looked into, or through. Then Mona Tyson was gone with a silken swish, leaving a peculiar mixed scent of perfume and smoke. A stream of guests followed her into the living room. The music had been turned off. A tall, gaunt man with bushy gray eyebrows and a trim white beard held center stage, standing on the Turkish rug. He wore a blue suit without a tie. A locket on a gold chain dangled around his neck. He spoke, his voice sonorous and commanding. There was absolute silence and no eye strayed from him as he told his story.

THREE

1

Nate and I worked the Greyhound depot territory. The city's name isn't important. Areas around bus depots are about the same in most cities. They're usually close to the slum or skid row. One difference, though, is that there is more snow and rain in some depot territories than in others. It was raining the day I died—a cold rain, and thick, like sleet or wet snow.

I've used many names in my life and the one I was using then was Clive. Just Clive, nothing else. And he was just Nate. We didn't need last names, since we were just half-men anyway. So we, Nate and Clive, worked the bus depot territory. I couldn't remember how long we'd been together, but it was a long time and we'd gone through a lot, suffered enough so we knew it would take a lot to get us to split up. We'd both saved each other more than once. And he was on the watch, a protector. The territory was pretty much ours, because no one dared encroach. I'm not exactly a small fellow, as you can see, and Nate . . . well, Nate was a foot taller than me, although skinny as a rail. We were both skinny, of course. We didn't eat much. We didn't need food, only the white stuff a connection gave us in the filthy john of the wino bar across the street. We could see the red light of the bar from the window of our room and we'd watch it get brighter and brighter as we got higher and higher. It was all we needed and we'd do anything for it, just like that fellow in rags creeping in the rain on the sidewalk down below there would do anything for a short dog of Thunderbird.

Of course, since we'd gone through so much together, Nate and I loved each other. Never has a person loved me more and never have I loved another person, man or woman, as much. We were *part* of each other. Separated, we would die. Nate was the suspicious one, and guarded like a hawk. He'd sit and smoke his pipe all night long, crouched by our window overlooking the connection bar and the depot too, watching as an army of red-eyed winos with sticks and clods of dirt shiftily darted closer and closer, hiding behind lampposts and sneaking like snakes on their bellies, determined to destroy us so they could take away our territory. Nate kept them back.

It was a close one last night, he said in the morning.

Eh?

They almost got in.

Oh.

When I was working, between snorting lines of coke, that was about the extent of my vocabulary. It wasn't that I couldn't say more. I didn't want to say more. I had a job to do, a territory to work. Between Nate and me, the habit cost maybe two hundred a day, even at wholesale prices we got from Atari, our connection. So we had some cash flow. We'd pickpocket or con young sailors, go up the street to the department stores and shoplift; we'd beg and dance and sing or I'd recite Shakespeare in the street, anything for a dime to make a dollar and a dollar to make up what we needed. Nate said he'd once been an opera singer, and I believed him. Look at what I'd once been. His voice was gone, but he tried his best; some travelers paid him quarters because they thought his performance was comic. He never intended to be comic.

We had no cash, of course. It all disappeared. But we always dressed as well as we could, kept our clothes clean, bathed and shaved. Our greatest fear—greater even than death—was to be caught and imprisoned, for without our goods we were certain we could not live. On the floor in our room was a rug, one I had preserved from better days. It was our fall-back position. If ever we failed to earn our daily quota from our territory, we could take the rug, which was quite expensive, and hock it with the Greek pawnbroker down the block. The rug had originally cost several thousand dollars, as I remember, and I was sure it would bring at least a hundred and perhaps even more from the Greek, who knew value.

If I die, I should like to be buried in it, I said. A last dignity.

When I die, throw me in a pile of camel's manure, so that I might return from whence I came, Nate said.

And he crouched by the window, eyeing the crafty encroachers below. They would not get in.

But I was the one who died. It was still light when I came home. I emptied my pockets as I always did upon entering and then I cut and sniffed. It was never the same as the first one, but it was all right. I was standing on the rug when I felt a great pain in my chest. It was like my heart was bursting inside of me. Everything turned gray and then black. That's how simple dying is.

2

When Nate came home and saw Clive on the floor he gave a little cry of dismay and,

36

leaning down, he listened for his heart and felt his throat. There was no breath and no beat. He wanted to weep for his dead friend, someone he had loved, but his instincts for survival took over. Last night the encroaching winos from Skid Row had had allies, a group of uniformed policemen with drawn pistols and brandished nightsticks. Now there was a dead man, meaning a possible murder charge. Of course the cops would use any excuse to put him away. Nate sat beside his friend's body and pondered, his eyes rolling. Soon he had a plan.

So it's happened, 'as it? said Princess Isolde, as usual at her post on the third landing, encased in cigarette smoke.

Her name wasn't Princess Isolde, of course. Nate called her that. She liked it, or didn't care. She was a fat old lady who'd been dying of cancer for many years.

What has happened? asked Nate, looking surprised.

You're taking the rug out to be hocked, finally, said Princess Isolde.

I fear so, said Nate, pushing past her.

It was fortunate that in this city the dump was not far from the bus depot. In fact, Nate and Clive could smell it on clear nights. This night was far from clear, with a rain that was nearly snow. Nate struggled against the cold and wind-driven sleet, his burden over his shoulder. But not once did he put it down until he reached his destination, the dump.

Then he laid it down carefully, tucking in the edges, and he said a prayer, on his knees with his face lifted.

Good-bye, my friend, he said to the body in the rug.

3

Noise, or perhaps it was the cold, awakened me. I could not move. Where was I? It was dark and there was a terrible stench, a combination of rot and must. My eyes were open. That much I knew. I couldn't feel my heart but I knew my mind was working.

Surely I must be dead now. I am dead and have been buried. I have passed through a period of darkness and now I am in hell and will be here forever, like Prometheus tied to his rock and Ixion to his wheel.

That was hell, being aware but unable to move.

But there was that scent, the must. It was so familiar. And what was that noise? Put-put-putter; bang, cough, put-put-putter. Like an engine. It was not in my head. It was outside, somewhere close. And the scent. What *was* it?

Then my brain realized that it was the scent of the rug. And, with the realization, came a small shaft of light from one end. I managed with great effort and pain to move my head.

The light was there. It was real. It hurt my eyes. For a long time I lay thinking, and then my brain knew.

I had not died. I'd had a seizure like death. I was inside my rug, bound up by it, the coffin I'd requested. I don't know how much time passed. The sound outside was louder and even louder and I felt the ground around me shaking. With a supreme effort I wriggled my feet and shoulders and moved ever so slightly toward the light shaft. When I turned over I could see outside.

It was a yellow tractor with a scoop in front, and it was moving, cutting wide rows, filling in a deep hole with trash and dirt. It had just dug out a row next to my coffin and was turning to hew another, one that would crush me or send me reeling into the hole, buried alive in an initiatory hell until I suffocated and was sent in agony to my true hell. If you imagine a conscious person in a casket, aware but paralyzed as mourners pass by, hearing them and desperately wanting to speak, then you know the anguish I felt. I could see. I could hear. I knew what was happening. But I could do nothing about it. Of course I could pray, and I did that, promising God I would lead a good and clean life if He released me from this horror.

I was certain I was alive. Perhaps I had been dead, returning to life by some miracle. Most likely I had given every appearance of death, symptoms a severe narcotics seizure sometimes exhibits, and had been taken for dead, trussed up in the rug, and brought to the city dump for burial, like a sailor who has died at sea is sewn into a canvas, the last thrust of the needle driven through his nose to assure the grief therapist his subject no longer lives, and thrown overboard. For me there had been no needle.

The mind cannot explain the will to live to the body, but the body sometimes reacts to this will, obfuscating the brain's ability to function, a force undoubtedly instinctive that refuses to allow the mind to lull the body into the sweetness of surrender. This sweetness says: There is no hell, no punishment; there is nothing but rest without struggle. So, as the noise of the engine again approached, louder and shaking the earth once more, I found my body taking over from my mind. I moved. I kicked. I stretched out my arms and spread the rug enough so that I could crawl out of it, rise from the wet ashes and the stink of the dump, and escape. I wallowed in mud and slime and excrement, tasting it and feeling it on my face and hands. I didn't care. I was free. I stood. I even had the presence of mind to drag the rug out of the way of the tractor and to shake my fist at the astonished driver. I felt born again. I had escaped hell and from this filth I had found cleanliness. I knew then I would never again use.

But there was something I had to do. I was sane now, and thinking clearly, more clearly than in years. I had been let down by a man I trusted absolutely, one I loved, one whom I had more than once rescued in situations similar to what I had just experienced. My keen and stretching mind knew full well why I had been dispatched by Nate at the first opportunity. Every addict, no matter how close to another, hides a surplus store of his balm. I had. Nate, in a state of paranoia as usual, had carried me away to be buried because he'd discovered my hiding place and wanted or needed what was there. I could see the pattern clearly now. When I had had good fortune in our territory, I had always shared with him. But he had seldom shared with me.

I sought him, hating him.

He must die. I chuckled. It was a supreme irony. I would kill him and truss him up in the same rug where he'd placed me, carry him to the dump, and deposit him into the hell from which I had escaped. Then, avenged, I would leave, a clean and free man, to find a new life.

When he returned that night, I was waiting for him. I expected him to scream or turn white at this appearance of a ghost, or to fall on his knees and beg my forgiveness. But he did nothing. He just looked at me.

I knew you were here, he said. Princess Isolde, she told me.

And you didn't run?

No. I know now it's all caught up with me. I'm done in. You can do what you like with me.

Oh, Nate! Why did you do it?

I thought you were dead, Clive! What was I to do?

You didn't think I was dead.

I did! You said you wanted to be buried in that rug.

You wanted my stuff. You knew where it was hidden.

No!

Nate, I don't mind the dying as much as I mind that you had forsaken me.

But I didn't!

You did, Nate. You did.

Nate was a very clever man—how else was he to survive in the world that was his, and mine?—and a clever man, I had decided, cannot be trusted, in particular a clever addict. He could talk his way out of the gallows when the noose was already around his neck. But this time he was up against a man equally as clever. And a clean and sober man, one born again through suffering and a kind of death. He seemed to sense that. I had somehow gone away from him; by a miracle, through *his* doings, at least indirectly, I had been cured. No longer were we blood brothers.

Have at me, he said. If I'm the kind o' man you think, my life isn't important. Have at me.

And maybe I would have, except he said he could prove his innocence. That stopped me.

All right, I said. Then prove it.

Go to your hiding place. See if your stuff isn't still there.

And if it is?

Then we'll destroy it together. We'll be free together.

You want to find my hiding place, that's all.

I'll go outside and wait.

So you can run away from me, eh?

I can't run. Not no more.

I went to my hiding place, a loose board under the sink basin that I'd smoothed over perfectly, and pried it up. It didn't matter if Nate knew about it. I wouldn't need hiding places anymore. It was there, all right, in its plastic sack. I drew it out. I turned and we both looked at it.

Did you have a good day today? I asked Nate.

Rotten, he said. I was thinking about you, you know.

How much did you earn?

Pennies. Dimes. Nothing more.

We don't need it. We don't need this anymore.

I'd tell you a lie that I don't need it anymore if you weren't my friend, Clive. But you're my friend. I can only say the truth. I *do* need it. So do you.

I did. It was a moment of decision. Down the drain? Or up the nose, in the pipe? I'd died and been born again. But that was nonsense. Nate had made a mistake, an honest mistake, thinking I was dead. He'd buried me in the rug that he could pawn for a hundred or so. That was a gesture of friendship, even of love. Anybody could make a mistake. My mouth was dry and my body ached for the stuff. Nate's eyes were wide.

I handed it to him.

Fix us up, I said.

Both of us, Clive?

Both of us, Nate.

A little while later, we were feeling very good. We told each other what great pals we were. We loved each other and we both swore we'd be loyal and stay together, working the territory very hard, successfully.

Nate moved to the window and looked out, guarding.

FOUR

Maureen had been somewhat apprehensive about the party, and the man's story certainly didn't allay her feelings. She considered it embellished and unnecessarily dramatic, even foolish. But after he'd finished, bowing and leaving the premises like an actor leaving the stage, she loosened up and flowed with the stream. The music remained old-fashioned, a reflection of Mona Tyson and her house, but the party became good fun. Stand-up comics performed, an accordion teamed with a harmonica, there were dueling guitars, a ventriloquist tried his best, and a man played country and western music on the piano with his toes. Maureen considered that an offense to the magnificent old grand. But she enjoyed herself. While Greg chatted with the hostess or made telephone calls in response to his pocket page, handsome men paid attention to her, talking and asking her to dance. Some of them wanted her telephone number, which she politely declined to give. If a man wished to reach her later, he could find a way. She asked few questions and gave only vague answers to those asked of her. Some guests left and new ones arrived. Mark Ashley was gone, and for a fleeting second Maureen wondered if he'd really been there, kissing her cheek and holding her hand, smiling hypnotically. But of course he'd been there. And he'd paid attention to her, not that it mattered. She scolded herself mentally for being so naively star struck.

"I'm afraid I'm just a rube from Des Moines," she said later, in the Mercedes heading toward the San Diego Freeway. "I'll confess. When I first got here, I bought a map of the stars' homes and took a Gray Line bus tour."

"Why is that a confession? Many people do that."

"When you said Hollywood party, I half expected to be chased around in bedrooms or get thrown naked in the pool."

"Well, they're sobersides now. They've had their orgies."

"It's disillusioning. Hollywood and drugs and all, I mean."

"It's no worse here than elsewhere. It's just more visible, that's all."

"Mark Ashley! That was a shocker!"

He scowled and stopped by a curb, braking so abruptly it startled a woman walking her dachshund. He turned her to him and kissed her, kissed her hard, his lips parted. The woman looked at them, disapproving, but he glared her away and she retreated, dragging the reluctant dachshund by its leash.

"The rube act doesn't work," he said. "You knew they were addicts right off. You knew it was a Narcotics Anonymous group. You looked down on them as freaks."

"I—I guess I did."

"What counts is that they're clean and sober now."

"How long have you been clean?"

"That's better. Straight question. Straight answer, a long time. I slipped back once. Mr. Hyde always sits waiting. Mona got me clean again. She's cleaned half of Hollywood." He continued to talk about her as he drove on, edging toward the freeway lane. "She wants to make a comeback in films, feels the itch. She asked me to handle her publicity, get her known again."

"Will you?"

"Sure. Mona is a sweetheart."

"Well, she doesn't like me."

"Why do you say that?"

"Women know those things about each other."

He ignored it, probably as woman talk. "A comeback is very important to her. She wants to prove something. Everybody slammed the door on her until she got a chance a few years ago, and then she fainted on the set the first day. She had a needle hooked into her leg. Just pump it when you need it. So that part was gone, her confidence with it. Now she's sober and wants to prove it to herself."

"It's like that?"

"Like that. You have to prove it to yourself."

"Who is Clive?"

"He used to be a well-known Shakespearian actor. One day he showed up on her doorstep, the rug over his shoulder. The joke is Mona cleaned both. Now Clive tends bar."

"Nate interested me. Nate the guarder."

"Cocaine paranoia," Greg said. "I once knew a cokehead who was certain a little man lived under the hood of his car. He'd always stop and look."

Maureen suppressed a shudder. "Interesting people," she said. It was something to say. She regarded them as frightening, far from interesting. But Greg seemed different.

Greg's mind seemed elsewhere. "What I'd really like to do is produce a picture with a cast of oldsters. Actors who can act."

"Then go for it. We have only one life."

"I discussed it with Masterson. He gave me the brush-off."

"Well, it really doesn't sound very commercial to me."

He seemed to stiffen. "Is your car in the office garage?"

"Actually, I don't have a car."

"Then I'll take you home."

"I'm going to be brash. I don't want to go home."

"Where, then?"

"Your place, actually," she said.

He didn't say anything. He just drove. At Sunset he left the freeway and went up the hilly curves past Will Rogers Park and UCLA, turning north on Laurel Canyon. Maureen felt smug. After tonight it didn't matter, as long as he didn't get serious. She hoped he wasn't the kind who fell in love. Love was a complication to be avoided. She had felt it once, or thought she had, the terrible captivity of it—waiting to be called, trying to impress, feeling out of control and jealous, hurting after the breakup.

Greg's house was rustic and paneled, two bedrooms upstairs and a book-crammed den below. It had a brick front, stone fireplace, hardwood floors. A balcony in back extended over a hillside. The city lay below and in the distance was a glint of ocean. Maureen felt soft and warm. Birds chirped. A squirrel perched on the railing, eyeing them with its head cocked.

She felt his hand on her hip, stroking. She wasn't ready yet, but she'd do her best. What men wanted of women had been obvious to her since age ten and she knew how to give it yet she'd never really enjoyed it, never *felt* it. It seemed gross and rather silly. With some men it was a thrust and a groan and then mercifully over, but others went on for what seemed like hours, prolonging it, playing, getting as much as possible out of it. Many were rough and coarse, hurting her. Some were filthy. They expected her to be filthy in return, and sometimes, to please them and help get it over with, she was. She laughed at their dirty jokes and talked dirty when they did. It helped the man get off, and once that happened he was less dangerous and more vulnerable.

But she had made up her mind that it would be different tonight. She had primed herself to enjoy it. She would make love to him and also fuck him, fuck him good. It didn't seem filthy, not now, to call it what it was—cock and cunt and tits and ass. Somehow the clinical penis wouldn't work. Once she'd been to bed with a man, a bank clerk, who called it "junior." It had been awful. But not tonight.

When he kissed her she kissed back, her heartbeat quickening. She moved her hips against him and felt his hands on her breasts. Something was rising in her. His thumbs moved her nipples, pressing and circling. She moaned and rubbed him between the legs. He was hard, big hard. She squeezed.

"Oh God it's big."

"Big for you."

"I'm not going to be shy. I'm going to kiss you all over. There and there."

"Hurry," he said.

In the bedroom they threw their clothes on the floor and she fell into his arms with a little sob. Immediately she was demanding, hammering his back, scratching and forcing him on, big and hard and deep. Soon she lay wet and exhausted. She had felt it, a wonderful flow deep inside. She'd also lost control, which frightened her.

"Des Moines, you're a wonder."

"Please don't call me that, Des Moines."

"I also think you're very lonely."

"Everybody is lonely. Everybody in this city, at any rate. Here, even the crowds are lonely."

"Maybe it's because they really don't know what they want. What do you want to do?"

"I don't understand."

"I told you what I want. To produce a movie. What do you want?"

"A bath. And then some eggs with bacon, I think."

"Be serious. What do you want in life?"

"I don't know. Just a job, I guess."

"I warn you that I can be impulsive."

"So be impulsive. You only go around once."

"I think I'm in love with you. I *know* I am."

She put her hand over his mouth. "You don't mean that. You can't."

"Why can't I?"

"Well, for starters, you don't know me."

"That's the way it happens sometimes, love at first bat. Romeo and Juliet and all that."

"Oh, maybe in storybooks."

He sat up and faced her, naked and cross-legged. He had the kind of body she liked—not fat, not skinny, not too hairy, straight and firm. "Life can be a storybook if you let it. Merry-go-round brass ring, they-lived-happily-ever-after—all that sort of thing. Move in with me."

"Move *in*? Why would you want that?"

"Well, maybe I need a good cook."

"That's not a very good joke. In fact, it's a very bad one. And I was led to understand I have a job, one not as a cook."

"You do, if you want it. I don't think you should take it."

"Not *take* it? Be serious."

"I like you the way you are."

"What is that supposed to mean?"

"The job won't make you happy."

"Well, I'd like to try it and judge that later."

Late in the night while Greg slept, Maureen got up and walked naked out on the balcony. She held the new penny she'd found in her hand. Already it had brought her luck; it was her talisman, her charm. She wasn't superstitious, but it certainly didn't seem to hurt. She looked out at the lights of the city. She beckoned to the lights and they seemed to brighten. A feeling of power surged through her. She had only to stretch out her hands and she could catch the lights and bring them to her, holding them inescapably in her grasp.

FIVE

What had started between them continued because he took her to nice places, helped teach her the business, and was wise enough to avoid further discussion of love. Her first paycheck was a delightful surprise and she went on a credit shopping spree, buying a new wardrobe and, with Greg's help, selecting a car, a used BMW in excellent condition. She was indeed an a.e., handling both H. Leslie Williams, who aspired to television evangelism, and Martin Bradford, a Senate hopeful. Her job was to get them noticed, primarily by "ink" or "time," print media or radio-television. With Greg's coaching and by using his name with TV producers, Maureen did very well, especially with Williams since there always seemed to be controversy about evangelists. She changed him from a dour country puritan to a Personality. In fact he believed in himself so strongly that once after a TV training session he made a pass at her. She slapped his hands away.

"Don't try that again," she said. "Not ever."

He hung his head like a spanked puppy. "I'm sorry. I really am sorry."

"I should think so. You ought to be sorry."

She also had problems with Martin Bradford. He was two personalities—alert when sober, helpless when drunk. She rationed his liquor, wrote his speeches, and took him to appointments in the BMW. When it was time to go on, he didn't bump into the furniture and he always knew his lines.

"It's fun," she told Greg. "I feel guilty about taking pay for having a ball."

"Guilt feelings are a bore. Let me carry the guilt feelings."

"Why you?"

"I've never told you. I was brought up holy, altar boy and all. I wanted to be a priest."

She laughed, but then saw he was serious. "What happened?"

"Nam, I guess. Other things. Parents died young."

"You have a way of turning a conversation to the serious."

"Well, have your ball. You may not be having one a few months down the road."

"I think I will. I love it at CU."

"CU? There is no CU. There are only clients, because they pay for it. Your salary, mine, our rent and electricity. Mention a client name at a meeting, it's an hour's billing. We have the sweetest racket since Mr. Ponzi set up shop."

"You're in a bad mood. Maybe I'd better go home."

"Aren't you home?"

"No, I am not home."

"Miss Des Moines, my earth woman."

"I said I don't like it when you call me that. And I'm not anybody's earth woman."

They handled it well at the office, keeping apart and acting businesslike at meetings, but it probably was no secret they were a happening item. It didn't seem to matter; doubtless several affairs were going on, some perhaps man-man or woman-woman. Besides, there wasn't time for office romance. Her clients kept her busy, and Masterson demanded Greg's attention. He was a prestige client like the Academy Awards or the Emmys who also led in billings—a rare combination.

Maureen had the smallest office in the suite—in back, no outside windows, no secretary—but she didn't mind. At least it was private. Next to it was a large office that appeared unused, guarded by a gray-haired secretary named Mrs. Olsen.

"That space belongs to A. Elroy Anderson, New Yorker, opera buff, gourmet, and president of CU," said Timothy Harte, who, as office gadabout and gossip, often dropped in to see Maureen. "To El of New York, we are aliens. The Coast is Martian to him, a backward territory of queers and steers, one of strange and evil cults. Speaking of cults, how do you and the evangelist get along?"

"We get along just fine. And he has a flock, not a cult."

"That's good. I mean, believing in what you do."

"And I do have things to do. Right now."

He winked. "Got class, kid. Style. Will go far."

"Thanks."

"Quick. A flick of 1947. Clark Gable, Deborah Kerr, Sydney Greenstreet."

"I have no idea, Timothy."

"Tim. Call me Tim. Keenan Wynn was in it, and Edward Arnold. Hint: it was about advertising."

"I give up."

"The Hucksters!"

"Good for you, Timothy. I never heard of it."

"Tim. Second chance. Jennifer Jones and Joseph Cotten, 1945."

"Dammit, Timothy—"

"Love Letters!" he exploded.

"Fuck love letters."

"Hey, now you're talking like an a.e. Listen, about when you came in here. You knew I thought you had a lot on the ball, didn't you? You knew I was just testing you, didn't you? It was a *tease*, man!"

56

"Oh, sure. That's why you showed me the door."

He looked hurt. "You got about as much a sense of humor as Bela Lugosi. All I want is to be friends."

"All right already! We're friends! Now go to your office, please, and look at your pictures or sit on your john."

Mrs. Olsen stood in the corridor glaring at them, a chamois cloth in her hand. Maureen's raised voice undoubtedly had attracted her, as well as some of the words, for Mrs. Olsen was a hall monitor and a keeper of morals. She tossed her head and walked away.

"She's cleaning his office since he's due here for the bank presentation." Harte grinned and hitched up his pants. He tried his best to pull in his enormous belly. "El usually attends client presentations. We present, he closes. He's not called El Closer for nothing." Harte smiled proudly. "We're pitching a *bank*!"

"How very nice for you," Maureen said in as nasty a tone as she could generate.

"You be a good girl and I won't tell him how you got in here."

"How did I get in here?"

"On back, legs spread."

"Well, at least it wasn't through the back door."

Harte's lip curled. "You have a smutty mouth."

"You don't?"

57

"It all goes into the book, sister."

She had baited him and it bothered her, since it appeared Harte indeed was close to A. Elroy Anderson, the phantom boss for whom the posh off-limits office was immaculately maintained. She half-considered an apology. But what the hell, he'd baited her, too, and he probably couldn't do much damage. He wasn't nicknamed the Lightweight because he was slim.

"No, I don't think he can hurt you," Greg said. "But don't go out of your way to spite him."

"I hate office politics."

"Yet I'll bet the ranch you'd be good at it."

"He talks like he owns Mr. Anderson."

"Maybe he has some dirt on Closer."

"Well, when Anderson arrives, I'll just ask him."

"Oh, sure you will."

"I'm wicked, I know, but I always seem to be fighting off a temptation to goose Mrs. Olsen."

"Oh, she's not so bad. It's just that she suffers a misapprehension that our work is serious."

"Well, so do I."

"Then keep a straight face when the bank pitch comes."

It was a touchy matter. There were two large empty offices in the suite, situated at opposite ends of the corridor and identical in accouterments. The second, also guarded and dusted by Mrs. Olsen, belonged to Theodore Piper, chairman of the agency. It was said he knew of and tacitly approved his nickname, Great White Father, but the spin-off undoubtedly would have horrified him. It was Great White Shark. He'd also promised to appear for the bank pitch, the cause of the crisis. Closer and Great White Father never were on the Coast at the same time, obviating the necessity for two Mrs. Olsens. The bank pitch crisis precipitated a rare event, a staff meeting to discuss strategy that didn't result in hourly charges to a client. Nothing was decided; chips would fall where they may. The delicacy was because Anderson and Piper hadn't spoken to each other for two decades, although they were partners, nor had they seen each other for that length of time.

"It makes for a good marriage," Maureen said. They were lolling in bed after an exhausting gymnastic of sex. It was fun to tease him, since he was quite straightlaced deep down.

The alarm she always set jangled abusively. "Time," she said.

He held her arm. "Wait."

"You want a quickie for the road? Any particular flavor?"

"You can be smart-mouthed. And like steel."

"Oh? Well, you keep me in line then. You be Christ Jesus and I'll be Mary Magdalene."

"I wonder what makes you go."

"I wonder what made you stop."

"What do you mean, stop?"

"Ten years ago, you were like me. All on fire. But you stopped. You bad-mouth the job, spout your damn poetry, act like you're above common commercial things."

"You don't know what I was like ten years ago."

"Oh? I think so. You lived like I'm living now. You might have forgotten something. You only go around once in this life. That thing turns, and turns fast. Ask Mona Tyson about that. This isn't a rehearsal. It's happening, and after it happens there is nothing else."

She jumped up naked, fixed her makeup in the mirror, dressed, and shouted a good-bye at him. He didn't answer. Halfway down the hill she stopped the BMW and sat with the engine idling, her fingers lightly tapping the steering wheel. *Damn him, damn him to hell,* she thought. She had told him she didn't want a romance. She didn't have time for it. And love was a frightening concept to her. Yet he had just looked at her quietly with those brown calf's eyes, and now without realizing it she had fallen for him. Away from him she felt alone. It was how she had felt before, she knew, but it had been all right to be alone then because she hadn't known it could be any different. Cursing him, she returned to him, entering the house in darkness. She knew he was aware of her as she undressed, but he said nothing. She went to the bed and

60

moved next to him under the sheet. He held her.

"You are a bastard, damn you," she said.

"Yes."

"But a sweet one."

"Yes."

"You know I want you. You know I don't want to lose you."

"Then say it."

"I want you."

"No. That other thing. I love you."

"It's hard for me to say."

"Why?"

"I wasn't taught about that. I was taught to look out for myself." She held him tightly, feeling his body and smelling his musky man's smell. "Oh, I do! I do, damn you! I do love you!"

"That's all right. You don't have to wake up the neighbors."

"I'm afraid of it. I'm afraid it will end bad."

"Why?"

"Because strong things die. I don't want you hurt."

"How about you?"

"I can't be hurt. You said steel. I'm asbestos."

"You need to be, hot number like you."

"Don't joke. I don't like jokes. Just hold me."

"I will."

"Don't let go."

"I'm not going to, don't worry."

"Ah, I'm happy now. I don't think I've been happy ten minutes since I grew up, and not that much as a child."

"You deserve more than that."

"I'm vulnerable tonight. I may be bitchy tomorrow."

"Move in with me. I'll keep you from going away."

"I can't do that. I'm not ready for that scene."

"All right. One day at a time. Play it as it lays."

"I know we'll be a good team together. We'll kill them."

"You bet."

"Say it. We'll kill them."

"We'll kill them."

"Kill them," she gasped, breathing hard, her mouth and hands all over him.

SIX

Greg felt like a kid again. He whistled while driving to the office, and often in the mornings he paused before the big mirror at the Camden Drive hair salon where he'd first seen her, straightening his tie and brushing his lapels, and then walking away with a skip and a little kick, as if he knew something the others didn't. He did. He had new love, and new love was like first love. It was true he didn't know her. Although she seemed friendly and outgoing, she was a loner with no apparent friends. At least he'd not met any. Nor had he met any relative of hers, although she spoke of parents "back East," nor had he seen what she vaguely called "her place." But it didn't matter. Time would take care of it. Also, they did have different interests. She liked rock, he liked Beethoven; he read a lot, she only when necessary. But they both liked to go out, make the scene, dance and gossip at the right parties.

Their sex continued at fever pitch, she the aggressor and experimenter, and often seeming insatiable. When Greg pleaded exhaustion, she puckered her sensual red lips, smiled, called him silly, and proceeded to demonstrate by expert movements of her mouth and hands that concern about his virility was unfounded. She threw herself into sex as she did into work, with preparation (reading the manuals), dedication, leadership, and lust. Finally drained and relaxed, she lay back cooing and purring, warm and loving, and then circumspectly analyzed a problem at the office.

"Office, office, office," he mumbled.

"Well, it's something we have in common, isn't it? We don't have everything in common, you know."

"Certainly not Debussy or Kafka."

"Who? Kafka?"

"He was a Czechoslovakian psychologist."

"Oh, I know who Kafka was. I'll just let those superior little remarks of yours pass."

"It's just that I have enough of PR during the day."

"What's wrong with public relations?"

"For starters, the idea that a sow's ear can be made into a silk purse, overnight."

"For a legend in his own time, you like your clichés."

He took her arm. "I'll tell you something. My speech. When I got out of Nam and got clean, all I wanted was to settle down on a couple acres and be a cracker barrel philosopher. Maybe write a poem about fish. That quickly got hollow. I told you this before. I wanted to be a vice president of something pretty big before I turned an ancient thirty. I did it, on my thirtieth birthday. But I stepped on heads for it. Maybe I've lost my appetite for trampling. I never exactly relished it."

"Your speech is bullshit, especially the last part of it."

She knew how to cut to the truth. Maureen had fit in exactly, hardening almost overnight, and he had been slipping away, softening. The change in her seemed extraordinary. She was more sophisticated and mature, dressed better, and cursed creatively in mixed company. She was a natural, just as he'd once been. He remembered it, the swift pace under bright lights, the dance of it, limos and bowing waiters and champagne corks and the touch of a dance band at midnight. And of course the young women, loose between the legs, yearning for recognition, willing to sacrifice love and family, home and hope of happiness or even heaven.

In the morning at the office, Maureen intercepted Greg in the hall and stood with her hands on her hips, all business. "I have a client problem. You weren't kidding about the reverend's past milieu."

"Do I ever kid?"

"It's going to surface, I'm afraid, and the timing couldn't be worse. Reverend Jack opens his Theater of the Bible very soon now."

"Did I hear you say Reverend Jack?"

"Well, I had to come up with something. H. Leslie Williams doesn't sound very pious or virtuous. John is his favorite Bible character."

"Why not Reverend John, then?"

"Too universal. Like, all the johns out there. Can we talk about the problem at lunch?"

He looked at his watch. "I have client problems of my own. And Mona is due any second now."

"Oh, her. Well, I'll wait in line."

"I'll meet you at Richard's. Soon as I can."

Mona fluttered by, dressed ostentatiously, in fact outrageously, trailed by cigarette smoke. She was all purple—pumps, dress, hat, elbow-length gloves—frilly and wispy. When she moved, the rustling was like music.

"This insanity on my noggin I call a trilby hat, so as to date myself," she said. "If I'm to make pictures again, you see, it will be in dated person roles."

"Stuff and nonsense," Greg said.

"I'm anxious. I'm practicing my impulsive

and stupid remarks, expected of flutterheads who act. I needn't tell you that an actor is a child. It craves praise and flattery, it likes to show off, it has tantrums, it can be a bully, it is insecure and lonely and often is afraid. I'm claiming my old immunity from censure for asininity. Will you help? I literally roll in ill-gotten dough."

"I won't have you as a client, since we're highway bandits. But I'll handle you personally. No charge, despite my materialistic soul."

"Materialistic? You have the poet's soul."

"I talk of dreams, the children of an idle brain."

"When do we start, Mercutio?"

"We have started, old love."

"You have a date with her. Keep it."

"It's not like you to dislike someone you don't know, love."

"I'm speaking out of school, but I'll say it. She sent a note to Mark after she met him at my place. In fact, she delivered it to his place in Holmby Hills, gave it to the guard."

"So? What's wrong with a nice note saying it was nice to meet you?"

Mona shrugged. "You two are an item, I say good luck."

"What did the note say?"

"He didn't tell me. Look, I know I'm a long-nosed snoop, but I don't want any trauma in your life."

"It's not trauma. You have Maureen all wrong. And I've whomped Hyde, no matter what happens. I stomp on Hyde's grave. I'll never touch the stuff again no more than you ever would again. Period, end of speech."

"Maybe I'm not as strong as you think."

"Nonsense."

"It's not easy to be den mother."

"I know that, love. But don't ever say you're not strong. You're Wonder Woman."

Mona Tyson still attracted attention, exorbitantly costumed or not, and those over forty often recognized her. At her peak, she was the love interest who got the man; before her fadeout, she played sidekicks to the female lead, a sympathetic friend who shrugged carelessly and told jokes. When she'd entered the office, several people had recognized her, including Timothy Harte, Mrs. Olsen, and Theodore Piper, the Great White Father, who'd come to the wilderness of the Coast for the bank pitch and general morale building. The crisis had apparently been avoided, for A. Elroy Anderson, citing duodenum pains, had called to cancel his appearance. When Greg came into the corridor with Mona Tyson, a group lurked like fans seeking autographs at a matinee. Piper and Mrs. Olsen stood dumbly, admiring the extravagant figure in purple. Harte was pale and breathless. Often a show of strength was mustered for a client or potential one, but this was spontaneous.

Tim Harte took the initiative. "Miss Tyson, I saw you on *Hollywood Trivia*. You were *fabulous!*"

"Why, thank you."

"Want to try a quiz?"

She looked askance, gushed smoke, and shrugged, deciding to be a good sport. "All right, go ahead."

"Line from a movie," Harte gasped. "Name the movie, the star who said it, the director, the date, female lead, and two supporting actors. You will have thirty seconds. Ready?"

"Ready."

" 'In the world of advertising there is no such thing as a lie. There's only expedient exaggeration.' "

"Well, let's see," Mona said, stroking her chin with a gloved hand.

"Twenty seconds," Harte said.

"Hmm."

"Ten seconds!"

Rocking back on her heels, Mona Tyson delivered her lines. "Cary Grant in *North by Northwest*. The director, of course, was Alfred Hitchcock. Female lead: Eva Marie Saint. Supporting actors: James Mason, Leo G. Carroll."

"Year, year!" Harte chanted, eyes on his watch.

"It was 1959. Back in the days when pictures were made."

"All *right*!" Harte giggled and started an applause that everyone enthusiastically supported. "Like, super!"

Piper bowed gracefully and invited Mona Tyson to lunch. When she accepted, declaring she was ravenous, Harte commented that he certainly agreed, a joke or a faux pas, and Piper glared him away. Then he began to show his charm, appropriate in the presence of a renowned ladyship. It was an actor on stage with an actress. Greg knew that Piper didn't see star but ex-star, now an eccentric who might have a large enough bank account to become a client. A. Elroy Anderson was the Closer, but the Great White Father's selling talents weren't rusty. Piper and Anderson were equal partners in a successful and conservative Madison Avenue advertising agency, where their offices also were said to be poles apart. Tim Harte supposedly knew why they detested each other so completely, some nefarious event from long ago, and it was assumed that the knowledge was his badge of authority and job security. Lately he'd become exceedingly bold. To a sincere adman, the Cary Grant line surpassed ridicule. It was hideous blasphemy. Either Harte was a complete simpleton or the secret was beyond dreadful. Piper hadn't flinched. He escorted the quaint and garish Babylonian apparition down the hallway and out the door.

Greg went into his office, closed the door, and slumped down in his chair behind his desk. A fax of a Phoenix newspaper article about Masterson had arrived that morning— potential dynamite—and the press was hounding him for comment. It was a wonder Masterson hadn't called. Not even his lawyer,

Albert Norwine, had called. The name made Greg wince; O. Albert Norwine, he signed it, when it should be S. for sniveler. One of the calls was from Mike Thompson, Associated Press-Los Angeles. Mike had been a classmate of Greg's at Cal, a cellmate and soul buddy.

"Hey, mild-mannered reporter," Greg said, returning the call.

"Hey, earth communicator," Mike said.

"What trouble have you for me today, old buddy?"

"I think you know. The Phoenix story by Clay Dodson."

"I know you consider Dodson a great reporter, old buddy. I submit he's not. He went with this without checking with me."

"I asked him about that."

"Oh, you talked to him?"

"Yes. He said he didn't call you because you never comment."

"Oh, bullshit I don't."

"Greg, we're fencing here. Just tell me what Masterson has to say about it."

"I've been trying to reach him. He's not in town." A lie. Two lies. *Sure, lie to your old buddies and to yourself and to God, too, but only if you must. Yet always you must.* He saw Maureen before him, wantonly unashamed in her nakedness, eyes and hair and lips, breast and belly and thighs; he felt her and heard her in full passion as she held him with her legs and arms wrapped around him, speaking of love in her careless, offhand way. He loved her so deeply the thought of it caused him to tremble, frightening him, making him cold and then warm and cold again. He said: "Mike, I'll keep trying to track Masterson down."

"Well, I may get to him first."

"Fat chance."

"Yeah," Mike said. "Fat chance, I know."

"When do you need a response?"

"An hour ago."

"Will you hold off on picking up the story until I can get back to you?"

"I don't know, Greg. I don't own the place, you know. I have bosses."

"How is Pam?"

"Pam is just fine."

"And the twins?"

"Terrible. Yet flawless."

"I envy you."

"Come see us for a change. You've been in hiding."

"Well, I met this girl."

"What else is new? Bring her."

"I will."

Richard's was a rarity—a watering hole in Beverly Hills for people who weren't rich or on an expense account. It also had a waitress who didn't gossip, little Sally the Sphinx. The agency staff usually had lunch at Richard's, as did a.e.'s when they had to pick up their tabs. Clients were taken elsewhere, places that featured a better ambience and a gracious obsequiousness, plus much higher prices. Of course the clients paid, no matter whose plastic was used. Greg listened carefully to Maureen's tale of woe about Reverend Jack. Then he snapped his fingers.

"Not to worry," he said.

"That's easy for you to say."

"Go to the bank and get Larry the manager to give you five thousand cash in old bills. Use my agency card."

Ten minutes after leaving the bank in a squeal of tires, he parked the Mercedes in a municipal lot in Santa Monica. He whistled as they crossed the street to a theater, but Maureen scowled worriedly. *Maisie Does Moline* was paired with *Sex, Death, Taxes*; both were rated XXXXX. A fat bald man sold them tickets, took the tickets, and then appeared behind the confection counter. He eyed his well-dressed customers and then with a what-the-hell shrug waddled away. Greg took her arm. They went past a dirty green door marked MANAGER, up dingy brown stairs lighted by a naked small-watt bulb, and entered the projection room. It had a rank, musty smell like old theater seats. The projectionist sat with his feet up on a chair, watching the color movie, several naked girls who breathed heavily as they wrestled on a circular water bed.

"Shoofly pie!" said the projectionist, a pimply young redhead who wore sunglasses despite the semidarkness of his cage. "You never get enough of that wonderful stuff. Come on in, sit down. I heard you coming up. Can I get you anythin'?"

"Let's get to the point," Greg said.

"Ah, yes. The holy man. I saw him on this talk show and I thought he looked familiar. So I taped it. Then I ran some of my old tapes. I got quite a library at home. What you see here is *mild*, man, compared to some of the stuff I got."

"Get on with it."

"Sure you don't want to sit down? Lady, you want to sit here?"

Maureen turned away in disgust. The young man laughed, more of a sneer or giggle than a laugh, and turned his attention back to the screen. He said:

"Well, there he was, the holy man, on one of my tapes, performing. That boy is *hung*, folks. When I looked into it, I find he's not just the star of this flick and others like it, but he's the producer, the writer, and the director! His holiness is a man of many talents, a regular Orson Welles. In the trade we'd say, 'A film by . . .'"

"What do you want?"

"What do I want? To do right, that's all."

"Is that why you wrote a letter to Reverend Jack, so you could do right? It was blackmail, wasn't it?"

"Blackmail? No, it wasn't blackmail. It was a fan letter."

"Oh. I see."

The projectionist kept his feet up on the chair and his eyes on the screen. "I show these movies day and night. People *like* them. Notice how quiet the audience is? But you got some narrow-minded people that think it's a dirty business. Sometimes they still picket us, would you believe it? Now I find a holy man who's been in our business. I figure, now here's a real endorsement. That's why I wrote to him and said I'd send his flicks over to his TV station here."

"Well, that puts a new light on it," Greg said. "Here we thought it was blackmail. We even brought along some money for you."

"Some money? You went to *that* trouble?"

"If I were to make an offer for those tapes, just because there are these narrow-minded people, I wonder how much they might be worth."

"Well, they're very rare, those tapes."

"Do you think they're worth, say, a thousand?"

"A thousand? Maybe a few years ago. Cost of living keeps going up."

"Two thousand?"

"Two thousand? Well, I really don't know."

"Two thousand five hundred. Cash, here and now."

"Cash, here and now?"

"Read my lips. Cash. Here. Now."

"I hate to part with those classic tapes."

"I know. My gums bleed for you."

75

Outside the theater, the tapes in her purse, Maureen said: "I think I need a drink. Or a bath. Or both."

"Welcome to PR."

"Stop smirking."

"Well, I pulled your reverend's chestnuts out of the fire, didn't I?"

"Maybe not. If that creep knows, maybe others do."

"I don't think so. The creep knew because he's a dirty-movie aficionado."

He called Marge, his secretary, from the Mercedes and got some information he'd requested earlier from one of Masterson's male secretaries. Masterson worked out of his home in San Marino but maintained an office in Century City with an around-the-clock switchboard. The number was unlisted, there was no name on the door, only a number, Suite 2005. One of the secretaries, Michael, kept a log of Masterson's travels, made in a private Jetstar, and Greg had asked for the March report. He dialed AP.

"Bad news for you, newshound," he told Mike Thompson.

"Let's have it."

"First I want to review it. The Phoenix story, byline Clay Dodson, a free-lancer with mob sources, said Cyrus Masterson met one Carl Medondi, a Mr. Big in narcotics trafficking, in Miami on March 9. Right so far?"

"Right."

"We deny it. Masterson was in Cleveland on

March 9. You can check it with FAA flight logs."

"No need. I hear you."

"So what are you going to do?"

"Obviously we can't pick up the story. We were ready to run with it, Greg. You took your time getting back to me."

"You weren't going to run with it."

When he put down the phone, he heard Maureen's laughter.

"Welcome to PR is right," she said, her voice tinkling, her head back. "I work for a drunk who wants to be a senator and a former porno star who masquerades as an evangelist, and you work for a drug dealer who calls himself a financier."

"You just heard me deny that Masterson is in drugs."

"Oh, yes. Sorry. Apologies galore."

"Don't try and be funny."

"Welcome to PR, lover."

"All right. Laugh it up. Let's go see your reverend and give him the good news."

The Ministry of Light was headquartered in an eggshell blue, fairy-tale-quaint house on Melrose. Maureen said it had been willed to Reverend Jack's evangelical cause by an old lady who had recently died. Women worked silently in the living room, stuffing envelopes and answering telephones. H. Leslie Williams led them to his office in back. He was a sprightly, pink-cheeked figure in a black suit with tails, gliding on spidery legs and talking with precise enunciation. Greg marveled at the change from the gaunt, skeletal old man who'd come to the agency some months ago to inquire about representation. He'd seemed hopeless, but he'd had a bank account, somehow acquired from a pastor's position in a Maine town. Now his teeth had been capped, his cheeks sunlamped, his thick eyebrows plucked, his hands manicured, his bald pate fitted with a black toupee. Maureen had reconstructed him.

"How much did it cost?" Williams asked.

Greg told him. The reverend looked at Maureen.

"Yes, two thousand five hundred," she said.

"How can I be sure the sum was paid?"

"Whores and blackmailers do not give receipts," Greg said.

"That was an unnecessary and impertinent remark. You are an insolent and vulgar man."

"And you, reverend, are a fraud."

Maureen took in a quick breath, but the reverend neither moved nor blinked. "A man is not responsible for what he does before the spirit moves him and he is born again."

"A man is always responsible for himself," Greg said.

"Greg—" Maureen said.

But it was the reverend's house, and he took command. He moved on his spider's legs and stood beside a large framed picture of Christ praying in a garden before the crucifixion. His eyes widened and his fists tightened. He was getting worked up, like an actor preparing to go on stage. He spoke in a single breath, staring at Greg.

"I will speak in a practical, worldly way, because I am sure you understand no other way. You called me a fraud. I am no more of a fraud than any other man. Look upon me as a businessman, if you wish. But I am also an entertainer, an artist, and a psychologist. I do good. Most men do not do good. I save the lost. I give hope to the poor and to the old. I offer something beyond that offered by any other of your clients, whether it be a product or a service. I offer immortality. One who accepts my service does not die. So you see I am someone to look up to, to admire, to revere—now for only a few thousand, but someday soon for millions."

The reverend's face was a grotesque mask in the dark and the light, frozen in chiaroscuro, at once frightening and fascinating, now a pale mime with a falsetto voice, then flushed and animated, mechanical like a cartoon character. He was Svengali and Rasputin and Mephistopheles and Christ in one. Greg's head reeled and he felt a retching in his stomach. The reverend drew a Bible from his coat pocket and tapped its leather cover.

"I know my book. It is food for the soul. It is every book ever written." With a quick movement he threw the Bible at Greg, who managed to catch it. "Take it. Open it."

"What?"

"Open it."

Greg did so. He looked up into the flushed face burning above him.

"Book and chapter," the reverend said.

Greg looked, now feeling slightly amused. "Isaiah. Chapter 32."

The reverend rubbed his hands, smiled complacently, and rolled his eyes at the ceiling.

" 'Behold, a king shall reign in righteousness, and princes shall rule in judgment.

" 'And a man shall be as an hiding place from the wind, and a covert from the tempest; as rivers of water in a dry place, as the shadow of a great rock in a weary land.

" 'And the eyes of them that see shall not be dim, and the ears of them that hear shall harken.' "

Greg held up his palm, a sign to stop. "You've convinced me. You know the Good Book."

"I wish you to leave now."

"I'd be delighted to leave."

"Take your superior airs elsewhere. You profane this place. You yourself come as a blackmailer, thinking now you have a hold on me. Do you come with clean hands and a clean heart? Do you cast stones because you have never sinned?"

"You're right, reverend. This place is profane. Maureen, let's go."

"I have matters to discuss with her," the reverend said.

Maureen glared darkly at Greg. "You go. I'll get back."

"Go back with me. We don't need business like his."

"Greg, shall I *carry* you out?" Scowling, she led him by the arm outside to the Mercedes. "You shouldn't have called him a fraud. That was just plain stupid."

"I suppose it was. I couldn't help it. When I saw those women—"

"I think you want us to lose this account."

"Maybe I do."

"You *do*, don't you? In your crazy way, you're jealous of him, my time with him. Or anybody, for that matter."

"He is a charlatan, a Bible-thumping flim-flammer."

"Greg, do you know how much we *bill* that man?"

"Not enough."

She stood with her hands on her hips, legs spread. "All right. Go. Go and think about it. Then come back or phone and tell him you're sorry. Until you do that, I'm not coming over to your place."

She stomped back into the fairy-tale house. Greg drove away, the Mercedes shrieking and roaring. It was a hot day with a streaming sun and a smog alert, and the only thing that had not really worked right on the Mercedes was the air-conditioning. He cut in and out of traffic, sweating and cursing, honking the horn, hating the cars, the street, the city. The cure was simple—a drink, two drinks, a line or two or three of coke. He felt on the verge of wigout, fighting it all the way back to the office. The work cure, as always, was the answer.

Marge was in a twit. O. Albert Norwine had called twice. And Cyrus Masterson had called! Theodore Piper was pacing the halls, waiting for Greg to return. And then, last but most certainly not least, there was a looming crisis. Word had just been received that A. Elroy Anderson, the Closer, had checked into the Beverly Hilton and was on his way to the office. It appeared that Anderson and Piper were on a certain collision path, either by someone's diabolical design or egregious error.

Greg's depression dissolved in the absurdity of it all. He laughed. Then he asked Marge: "Does Piper know Anderson's on the way in?"

"I don't think so. Mrs. Olsen is off sick, so I handled her phones."

"Did you tell anyone?"

"I told Tim Harte."

"Where is he?"

"He went down to Richard's for a drink."

The absurdity wasn't lost on Marge; she was canny and resilient, as well as enduring. Now she snickered behind her steno book. Greg went into his office, his mind on Cyrus Masterson more than anything else. He picked up the receiver to call, mentally rehearsing what he'd say, when Piper strolled in, his face obscured by cigar smoke.

"I had a talk with Mona Tyson," he said. "A long talk. We got her all signed up, sealed, and delivered."

Greg scowled. "But Mona doesn't need full-time representation. I don't think she can afford it."

"Oh, she can afford it. She wants it. She thinks it's springtime again. That's how I sold her, telling her it was springtime. We'll keep her thinking that. One day in town, I land a new client."

Piper blew smoke rings and searched for an ashtray. He'd adjusted to L.A., to showtown, as he called it. His tie was loose and his suit coat was draped over his shoulders, the empty sleeves dangling. Greg sat down, feeling a wave of queasiness.

"You okay?" Piper asked.

"Fine, just fine. What did you tell Mona Tyson we'd do for her? Who's going to handle the account?"

"What we do for her is up to you geniuses here on the Coast. I mean people like you, not people like Tim Harte. We're going to have to start weeding out weak sisters."

"If we're such geniuses, let us cut our own deals."

Piper was getting peeved. "We're not in business to give away the store. I sold Tyson, you handle it. I just sell, I don't write warranties." He winked. "I know. I'm a son of a bitch. Put the new girl on the Tyson account. The girl you called me about? She seems pretty sharp to me." Again he winked. "Ballsy broad. Forgot her name."

Greg couldn't prevent a wince. "Maureen Crawford," he said. "I'm afraid she has no time. She's got enough to do on the Reverend Williams account."

"By the way, about Reverend Williams."

"Yes?"

"First I want to assure you that we in New York think very highly of you. You are our Tiffany of the Coast." Piper looked at his watch, spilling cigar ashes. "The reverend called just now, just before you returned. He had a very serious complaint to register about you, Greg."

"I don't doubt it. The truth is hard to take."

"I know you like to speak your mind. That's healthy. We don't like yes-men. But, Greg, we *want* this man's business." He paused, his eyes fastened on Greg's. "You apologize."

"No."

Piper frowned. Ashes showered. "No? I say you will." He was now more than peeved, yet still in control. "You apologize or by Christ I'll screw you up, believe me, no matter how big you think you are around this shop."

"I'd like to discuss it with Anderson."

"Anderson, shit! *I'm* telling you."

"I don't suppose you'd like to hear the circumstances."

Piper's flare-up cooled as rapidly as it had risen; his voice dropped from shriek to coo. "The circumstances don't concern me. It's your business, and you will do the right thing by the agency. Keep the account, that's all."

"I called him a fraud. He is a fraud. He—"

"Use your bullshit line on him. We all have a little bullshit in us." He smiled, now a father. "We know you're here, Greg. When we think of the Coast, we think of you. We're going to get bigger here now, and diversify accounts, starting with that bank. You're going to grow with us."

Piper flashed a white-toothed smile and left. Greg sat down and dialed Masterson, who answered the private number on the first ring.

"What have you done about the Phoenix matter?" Masterson asked.

Greg told him in as few words as possible.

"I will want to meet with you. We will let you know when."

That was all. Masterson seldom said thank you, hello, or good-bye. He asked questions, listened, gave instructions he never repeated. Conversations could not be recorded, and nothing was written down.

Marge buzzed. Her voice was almost a whisper. "Mr. Anderson is here."

"Where is Piper?"

"Gone."

"Near hit, eh?" Greg said. He laughed. "Or is it called near miss?"

He tapped his fingers, stalling. He might as

well get it over with. Looking up a number, he punched it out on the phone.

"Reverend Jack's Ministry of Light," a woman said.

Greg asked to speak with the reverend. He felt his teeth chatter as he waited. There was a faint taste of blood in his dry mouth.

SEVEN

It was generally conceded at the agency that the real power in New York was A. Elroy Anderson, not Theodore Piper. Piper, the Great White Father, cut a fine figure in a three-piece suit, but he had a chameleon personality, serious one moment and carefree the next. It was said he wasn't a stranger to Las Vegas or Atlantic City. He lived in a penthouse on Fifth Avenue with his third wife. All had been models named Anne who loved mink stoles and feared pregnancy. Anderson, the Closer, also wore suits well, but his personality was one-dimensional. He was vain and priggishly serious. The English would have called him a snob. He'd lived in Rye for twenty years and had been married to the same woman for thirty. She was a mystery to West Coasters, even her name; those who dared to joke about it, such as Harte, called her Woman of Rye. Anderson had two sons— one a lawyer with GM in New York, the other a CPA with Paine Webber. Both were graduates of Harvard B School. Anderson and Piper also were Harvard men, Class of '52. They'd been members of the crew and, Harte would say after a martini or two, inseparable buddies through college. He'd say little else about them, even after a shaker of martinis. Harte didn't appear to be gifted, but he could keep a secret. Clearly he admired Anderson more than Piper. If anyone dared suggest that the bland Anderson contributed less than the flamboyant Piper to the success of the parent ad agency, Harte was there to defend him, saying the Closer was the *real* go-getter who'd launched it, drawing on Harvard contacts for the initial financing. He kept the clients, too, by judicious hand-holding and getting them out of trouble when they needed a discreet, anonymous friend. Piper did little more than drink with clients, although that too was important, since Anderson was a teetotaler and *some*body had to drink with clients.

The public relations outlet, established as a natural adjunct, grew faster and was more profitable than the ad agency, especially after opening in Los Angeles. West Coast operations—due to less restraint in sales pressure, Anderson implied—soon outpaced the East Coast in billings. The PR operation dissolved to the Los Angeles headquarters due to fear of client conflicts with the ad agency. Its branches were really only correspondents, impressive for sales pitches.

Originally the agency was called either Anderson & Piper or Piper & Anderson, the names changing in accordance with the policy of swapping the title of chief executive every year. When the title reversed, it was scraped away and repainted on the doors. Stationery bearing the new name was brought from storage, replacing the old, which was put into storage.

The PR agency became so show business oriented that Anderson decided it was an embarrassment and indeed a danger to his reputation. Piper went along with it; the name became the ostentatious Communications Unlimited. Its partners became absentee and silent. Anderson let it be known in Madison Avenue clubs that he'd sold out, even having an announcement planted in the advertising column of the *New York Times*. The "show biz flackhouse," as *Variety* once had called it, was lucrative enough for Anderson to risk censure by his colleagues and competitors if its true ownership were discovered; besides, those who could and would use it against him weren't intrepid enough to risk a trip West to confirm it.

Anderson and Piper did communicate

when absolutely necessary, despite the fact they didn't see or speak to each other. On those rare, nervous occasions when they both were in Los Angeles, Mrs. Olsen could be seen scurrying back and forth in the corridor like a telegram messenger, bearing their notes to each other. If that wasn't ludicrous enough, on this trip they communicated by fax over the forty yards of carpet that separated their offices. Both had sending and receiving machines. Mrs. Olsen would send from one, rush down the corridor and take it from the machine and place it on the recipient's desk, wait for an answer, dial and send again to the other end. Then she would travel there for another reception. It wasn't mere absurd game-playing. It was a form of one-upmanship. When Piper discovered that Anderson had installed a private fax machine in his Los Angeles office, he demanded equal treatment. Now, finding out that Anderson had after all come in for the bank pitch, Piper had initiated the mischief by sending him a message from his fax, and Anderson had retaliated by replying from *his* fax. It was like a tennis match— serve, volley, lob, backhand. For Piper the repartee was good fun; for Anderson it was excruciating madness. Yet he kept it up. It was foolishness, but this was the Coast where all men were buffoons, a landscape so garish and a culture so sterile it was sufferable only because its profit margin was extraordinarily high, like the risk factor in a 20 percent junk bond.

Greg's summons from Anderson arrived. Anderson greeted him by waving the latest fax message from Piper. "Who is Mona Tyson?" he asked.

"She used to be a movie star," Greg said.

"Oh, *that* Mona Tyson."

"She's a friend of mine."

"And of Theodore Piper's, according to this. A dear and personal close friend. And a client whom he has signed up and who will save us from imminent bankruptcy."

"Hardly. In fact, I agreed to handle her as a favor."

"We are not an eleemosynary organization," Anderson said.

Greg sat down and tried to look as attentive as possible, steeling himself for The Anderson Lecture.

"Business is business of course, and most certainly I do not mind another client in the fold, but this entertainment concentration does disturb me, as you know. Diversification is the key to success in any business endeavor, especially a modern business. I should like to see us better positioned for the future— representing electronics, genetic engineering, telecommunications, financial services."

Anderson wasn't a habitual office pacer, but here on the Coast he took some liberties, a priest out of his parish, so now he began

91

pacing, even picking up one of the pipes he kept only in Los Angeles. He stuffed it with tobacco but didn't light it. The fax machine spewed out a message. Anderson, beating Mrs. Olsen by a stride, crumpled up the paper without looking at it. He nodded her out. The pacing resumed. He was a gray man of sixty— gray suit, hair, face—in top physical shape, a contrast to Piper's red-faced flab. No doubt he could man an oar as well today as he had at Harvard more than three decades ago.

"I need hardly tell you L.A. holds little appeal for me. One tends to nest most comfortably where one was raised. I haven't the slightest desire to meet or associate with actors, with dentists who advertise and maintain branch offices, and much less with automobile salesmen who ride buffalo." He said it without smile or smirk; it was a philosophy of life. He glanced at Greg, his steel-gray eyes fixed and penetrating. "I could continue— thruway shootings, AIDS, drugs, juvenile murders—but I won't. I think you understand. You are a very unusual man."

"Thank you," Greg said.

Anderson sat down, maintaining the pipe as a prop. "We'll get this bank, of that I'm certain. Timothy's presentation is excellent. Frankly, I didn't think he had it in him. Excellent!"

"Good." Greg didn't know what else to say. "I'm happy to hear that."

"Oh, I know what you're thinking. You're

thinking I might be praising another man at
your expense." He rose. Again he paced.
"Timothy is here, yes, but you are our anchor
on the West Coast. I want you to understand
that. New business is his responsibility, however, and he has done his work. Of course he
had the help of our graphics department in
New York, and when we get the business we
will send out our own account executive. I
plan to spend more time here personally
when we have that bank as a client. You
understand that is a personal sacrifice to me."

"Yes."

"But it illustrates the importance of the
West Coast, also. As for you, I have an expanded role in mind as we diversify and grow.
In a sense, you are just starting your career
with us. You have a brilliant road ahead."

"All I can say is that I'm pleased. Thank
you."

He almost clicked his heels.

That night in bed, Greg said to Maureen:
"Both of them promised me the world. No
doubt I'll get a bottle of Nuit d'Amour from
them."

"Another of your literary allusions? I'm not
going to pretend I understand it. You say you
studied humanities and philosophy in college.
I think you studied a lot of air. Most professors
aren't grown up. They teach antimaterialism
because they'll never have anything themselves."

"Why are you always more candid with me in bed?"

"It's just that I think it's time you grew up. I can't stand that childish, careless way you throw things away." She lay back. "If they had talked to me like that, I'd be floating on cloud nine."

"You need some kid in you. You're too serious."

"I am about work."

"There are other things."

"Not for me. Not right now."

She hadn't mentioned his apology to the reverend.

All personnel were conscripted for the bank pitch. Everyone assembled in a large room equipped for the event, including secretaries, who took notes and handled coffee-and-Danish chores. A wag who wasn't invited—the firm had a second office on the floor, a small one housing two outcasts, including the wag—named it Operation Overlord, code name for the Allied invasion of Europe, a term which of course wasn't mentioned in the presence of the potential client, arriving in the form of three young bankers in double-breasted suits. They carried thin leather briefcases. Anderson, who had designated himself the greeter, firmly shook their hands and ushered them to chairs in front of the oval presentation table. The office staff sat behind the bankers on rented chairs five rows deep, five chairs to a row. Several of the men wore new suits, and the women wore new outfits; all had got hairstyles over the weekend.

As Greg entered the room just before the 10 a.m. deadline, he had a presentiment of tragedy. It had been an unusually hot early summer weekend, continuing into Monday, and air-conditioning systems had been on overload. The one in the building, usually efficient, had been operating sporadically that morning and selected just now to expire absolutely. At first it wasn't noticed, or was ignored, but Greg saw that Anderson was hurrying the proceedings into motion. Tim Harte, in a dark suit like the bankers, gave a short introduction. He looked and acted like a different man, serious and articulate, his vest decorated with the chain of what appeared to be a Phi Beta Kappa key. Was that rented, too, like the chairs? Greg discarded the cynical thought; yet Tim Harte, he knew, was no Phi Beta Kappa. The next step was self-introductions— name and title, account responsibilities if appropriate—by all staff members, a routine familiar enough to bankers required to attend Rotary Club and Chamber of Commerce meetings. Discomfort from the faulty air-conditioning was beginning to manifest itself; perfume and shaving lotion scents were accented and hairstyles began to wilt. Yet the bankers sat stoically rigid.

The ostracized wag who had named it Operation Overlord was a cynical fellow—sinister, too, some thought—and he'd intended to be facetious, yet his description wasn't far off the mark. A sort of military precision was necessary to coordinate the exits and entrances so that their paths would never cross. Anderson left. Piper entered. Piper left. Anderson re-entered. Just for the bank pitch their names and titles had been painted in gold on the door, and they considered it appropriate, agreeing by fax memo, that both of them appear. Mrs. Olsen handled the logistics admirably, ushering like a professional. The presentation also was professional—short addresses, slides, elaborate flip charts with copious numbers. Anderson demonstrated a knowledge of banking that impressed both his guests and subordinates. He even told a story about Paul Volcker's cigar, modernizing it with a brief anecdote about Greenspan.

Timothy Harte sat smirking, and the griddled staff members tried not to squirm as the flip charts were shown to the impassive bankers, who studied the data with a fascination that approached hypnotism. The door flew open, but the bankers weren't distracted; the numbers held them riveted. A tall figure in an Uncle Sam suit pushed in, staggering and reeking of liquor. The bankers merely stared at the numbers. Everyone else sat very still. It was an apparition, perhaps born of heat fever, or maybe an intrusion to be expected in an office peripheral to movieland, like Batman plummeting through a skylight or the Frankenstein monster lurching from behind a grand piano. Yet it was real, a man very starry, in red, white and blue, top-hatted, white-bearded, grinning widely, arms outstretched, a vision of love and understanding. Greg managed a glance at Maureen, who sat coolly in the back of the room wearing a summer dress of blue silk. The dress had whispered when she'd entered, and faint perfume scents had followed her. Was Uncle Sam a Fourth-of-July entertainment for the dour bankers? Hardly, if he were drunk, which this one obviously was. He made it to the podium, brushed Anderson aside, belched and hiccuped, frowned importantly, and spoke into the microphone.

"Ladies and gentlemen, if I am elected—"

With a sharp, sudden tick, the air-conditioning came on. There was a stirring. Greg smelled Maureen's perfume. She moved to the front, smiling, her silks swirling without sound. Uncle Sam beamed at her and walked out on her arm. At the door he hesitated, bowed, and was gone.

The bankers stared at the numbers.

"They were the wrong ones," Anderson told Greg. He sat back in his chair, amazingly calm but ashen-faced. "Even if they could have forgiven that outrageous intrusion, which was unlikely, they could never have forgiven our using wrong numbers. The numbers were for another bank."

"Do you know what bank?"

"I believe they were for the bank the agency uses in New York. It was deliberate. It was sabotage."

"But . . . *why*?"

Anderson's fingers touched his forehead. "Who was that absurd man—?" He couldn't finish it.

"Martin Bradford," Greg said. "He's a client, a former actor. He's going to enter the primaries for U.S. senator."

"Oh, Lord."

"Obviously he . . . well, came to the wrong door."

Anderson groaned. Then, his eyes flashing, he said, "That young woman who came to the front. She is to be commended."

"Her name is Maureen Crawford."

"Give her my compliments."

"I will."

"I'm leaving immediately for New York. I will never again return to Los Angeles." He looked at Greg. His features relaxed. It was over for him. He would escape, go home a wiser man; no greater embarrassment could ever befall him, and somehow he'd survived. "I believe you know who sabotaged that bank client."

"I have no idea."

"It was Theodore Piper."

"Piper? You're sure?"

Anderson lowered his voice to a conspiratorial tone. "I want your word that you will not repeat what I am going to tell you."

"Of course you have my word."

"I would sell the public relations part of the agency, but it takes both of us to sell. He won't hear of it. To him, it's a plaything. He enjoys it. You see, the way our financial arrangement is, the one who outlives the other gets everything —after providing for relatives, of course. It could be called tontine, and it used to be more common than you might think. I suppose it appealed to our romantic instincts when we were younger. Of course I regret it now. I can hear him chuckling now. The bank client was Timothy Harte's responsibility, and he was opposed to my sending Timothy here. I did it to defy him." Anderson paused, sighed, sniffed, rubbed his chin, and closed his eyes. "You see, Timothy is my stepson. Did you know that?"

"No."

Anderson's eyes remained closed. "My wife had a son by a previous marriage when she and I married. Frankly, Timothy is an embarrassment to both of us. I sent him here because, quite frankly, well, because he had certain—*tendencies*, shall we say?—that seemed more appropriate or acceptable in this area than in others, such as New York." His eyes opened. He got to his feet and began to speak rapidly. "I want you to take over this office, Greg. May I call you Greg, as the others

99

do? You will be in charge of new business and existing accounts. It is a handsome promotion in terms of remuneration and prestige. Your title will be president."

"I—I don't know quite what to say."

"It may seem rash, precipitate. But I've thought about it for a long time."

"I'm kept very busy on the Masterson account alone."

"You will continue to handle it. No one else could do so."

"I must ask you what Ted Piper thinks of the move."

"I guarantee you his full support." Anderson grimaced. "I need not even discuss it with him, but I nevertheless will."

He used "discuss" as a blind person might use "see." Before today, Anderson had gone to great lengths to make others think that he and Piper conducted business like two normal partners. It was said he even bought four tickets to the theater to convey an impression of harmony. But now the pretense was gone. Anderson had openly discussed the rift. There were sides to take, and Greg knew that with his decision he was aligning himself.

He said: "All right. I accept."

Anderson rushed over and shook Greg's hand. He seemed pleased and relieved. "I'll be sure to leave a memo to the staff about it. We'll put out a press release. Do you think we're capable of that, putting out a press release? I'll want you to move into my office here, of course. Mrs. Olsen—"

"Yes, what about Mrs. Olsen? I have Marge."

"These matters are up to you now, Greg. I said that you are in charge, I mean that you are in charge. You have an opportunity to demonstrate your authority immediately."

"What do you mean?"

"Timothy," Anderson said, shaking his head sadly.

Greg got the first hint of what his new power was like when he walked Anderson to the elevator. Secretaries, their desks in the corridor, looked up at him as he passed. Doors opened along the expanse and heads of account executives popped out, only to duck quickly back when Greg looked at them. It was a strange feeling, one he didn't want. But it was silly to knock the feeling, he thought. Maureen was right. He'd studied too much air in college, taught by ivory tower academicians who had no concept of the world as it was. Once before, lusting for success, he had cast off their spell and the doubts they had engendered in him. Then the doubts had returned. Now he would again free himself of them. He would grow up. In fact, he had. He'd grown quite a bit in a single day.

A momentous event occurred as Greg pushed the elevator button for Anderson. The-

odore Piper walked from the office into the
hallway, an unlighted cigar in his hand, and
stopped still, gazing at Anderson. Anderson
met the gaze. Neither look conveyed much,
not surprise nor anger nor hatred. They were
blank looks. For Greg, everything froze. Time
stopped. There was no sound. Movement was
extended and exaggerated. Everything wavered surrealistically, as if in a dream. Anderson and Piper. Piper and Anderson. They
continued to gaze at one another like animals
in an alien jungle, sizing up, inspecting, as
casual as strangers in a subway station listening for the first faint sounds of the oncoming
train. Greg saw the cigar fall from Piper's
hand. He watched its progress down. It
seemed to flutter, and soundlessly hit the
floor, bouncing and rolling so, so slowly, like a
motion picture shown frame by frame.

The elevator light came on, its bell sounding. Greg shook the spell away. He got on with
Anderson. The door closed and the car began
its express descent to the ground floor. They
were the only passengers. They waited,
obediently facing the front because that was
elevator law or etiquette, neither speaking nor
looking at each other. When they reached the
main floor and the doors opened, Anderson
turned to Greg and held out his hand. Greg
shook it. Anderson's eyes showed nothing.

"You'd like to know what I think, wouldn't
you?" he asked.

"Frankly, yes."

"You know, I didn't recognize him right away. The man looks positively decadent. He has swollen up like a balloon."

He was gone, walking briskly with his head high, his shoes tapping on the glossy marble floor.

Greg fled to his office—his old one, his comfortable one—to hide. Marge came in.

"Congratulations."

"Thank you. It's out already?"

"All over the city, no doubt."

"You're sore because I didn't tell you first."

"I put some messages in your in basket," she said.

"Wait. Listen, I want you to stay with me, all right? Everybody moves up one."

She smiled, obviously pleased, and then retreated before the onrush of Theodore Piper, trailed by blue cigar smoke.

"Well, I'm off to Fun City. Congratulations. What did he have to say about me?"

"Terrible things. It would burn my tongue to tell you."

"I see you're loose. Good. Well, I'm sure I wouldn't want to hear it at that." He dragged on the cigar and blew out a perfect smoke ring. "Look, I know this is a silly farm funhouse without we New York types making it worse for you. You simply will have to excuse us old farts. You have my unqualified backing, and I'm not going to let you get caught in between us."

"I appreciate your saying that."

Piper winked. "Did he reveal the big secret to you?"

"What big secret?"

"Ho, ho. He stands there and asks, 'What big secret?' You know jolly well what I mean. The reason for the years and years of the long knives between us."

"No, he didn't."

"Well, you won't hear it from me. In fact, I'm not too sure I remember what it was all about. Yet let me tell you something. When you fire Tim Harte, he's going to say something about it to you. But it's not going to be the truth of the matter. I guarantee you that. Or have you already canned him?"

"No."

"I'll do it for you, if you like."

"No, I'll handle him."

"Don't let it bother you. He knows it's coming. You start to make progress in management when you learn how to fire."

"I suppose you're right."

Piper stuck out his stomach and grinned. "Did our Uncle Sam get tucked into bed all right?"

"I assume so. I haven't heard from Maureen."

"Wait till I tell that one around the club."

"Frankly, I'd rather you wouldn't. After all, he's a client."

"And you're going to *keep* him?"

"Sure. We're going to make a senator out of him."

"Well, I hope you're planning to keep that new girl. I like the way she handled it."

Greg looked at Piper, his eyes steady. "I'd like to ask you something."

"Ask away."

"The figures for the bank on the flip charts and computer graphics were altered. Did you do that?"

"Is that what Anderson said?"

"Yes."

"He's a liar. Would I fuck up new business?"

"I'm sorry I asked you."

"I'm glad you did. He's trying to drive a wedge between us. The bastard." Again Piper drew on his cigar. He studied the smoke rings. "Anderson looked old. I don't think I would have recognized him if I hadn't known he was here."

After Piper left, leaving his cigar smell behind, Greg did little things. He went through his messages. There was an invitation to dinner at Masterson's house on July 4th, next Tuesday—7 p.m., formal, R.S.V.P. It was an order, issued to him alone, not to him and guest. Maureen buzzed him. She was breathless.

"I just got back. I just heard about your promotion! What can I say? Oh, wow. That's all. Oh, *wow*!"

"I'm afraid our date for the Fourth is off. Duty calls."

"I've had the Fourth already. Since you're boss, I'd better be honest. Martin's Uncle Sam getup was my idea, for his part in the Brentwood parade. Far out, but—"

"Not far out. This is L.A., not Des Moines."

"I didn't know he'd get drunk rehearsing and pay us a visit today. It killed the bank client, didn't it?"

"The bank client was killed, but somebody else did it."

"Oh? Who?"

"Dunno. You get your boy into a cure."

"I will. Right now he's sleeping it off at the Beverly Hills Hotel."

"Sorry about the Fourth."

"Oh, I would have had to break that date anyway. Duty calls, you know."

He hung up. He should find Harte, get it over. But he didn't. He stalled. Staffers were on the phone and at his door. Congratulations. Would he still be a.e. for Masterson? Was it true about the fuck-up on the bank pitch? What about the rumor that Closer and Great White actually saw each other? Greg found his new power to be pleasant, a stimulating rush. Those who had regarded him with indifference or even disdain now were flattering and deferential. Needing some straight talk, he crossed the hall to see the outcasts. The small office there—called the sanctuary; the main office was the cathedral—housed the only two employees essential to the agency's continued existence.

One was a tall, white-haired man of sixty who wore baggy pants and wide suspenders —Willard Sterne, the Planter. He planted handouts with editors. Invariably they were published, often without change or editing. Supposedly he had a list of whores of all ages and sexes. He could get almost anything. If you needed Dodger or Laker tickets, you went to Willy. He'd covered cops for the *News* way back when the beat room had been at city hall and a tough guy named Davis had been chief. The young a.e.'s considered him a silly old fart, yet they asked him for tickets and always used him if they had a tough plant.

"Congrats," he told Greg. "It'll be in the papers, your crowning. Nice to know a man whose future is all ahead of him. Mine, it's behind."

"Nonsense. Obviously you're ancient, but there's some dance in you yet."

"Saint Vitus' dance," the Planter said. He regarded Greg with narrow morose eyes, his brow wrinkled. "My dentist says I have pyorrhea, my dermatologist tells me I have the heartbreak of psoriasis, my urologist says it's gout, my internist says it's a peptic ulcer."

"Well, ashes to ashes."

"Yeah, mine'd have scrofula."

"Then we'd get a machine to replace you."

"Yeah, just like the sowing machine replaced the planter. I'm the last of something,

Mohicans and Victorians, so respect me. Want to be interviewed on Channel 5?"

"Thanks but no thanks."

"Guy said he'd put you on for a ticket to the Dead. That's a rock group, the Dead." The Planter turned his sepulchral eyes to his cellmate, a humped, dwarfish man with an unkempt black beard. "Say hail to our new king, you cur."

"Hail," said the hunched man, not looking up.

His name was Henry Frost and it was hard to tell his age; he was anywhere between thirty-five and fifty-five. Frost was the only authentic genius in public relations. His I.Q. was 184 and he had an M.A. in nuclear physics. These facts had been discovered after his hiring; confronted with his past, he'd admitted it and had almost been fired. He'd fled physics in morbid fear of the atom. Now he was an idea man. If you wanted creative ways to publicize your movie or star, you came to Frost and he thought about it. Usually his ideas worked, the reason he was called the Heavyweight.

Willy the Planter put on his hat, a distinction other men spurned. "Going to NBC," he told Greg. "Want anybody booked on Carson? He owes me a favor. I was the one that put him on to Sonny Tufts."

"Not right now, thanks."

"I moonlight for Antarctica, the continent.

I'm going to pitch Carson on Antarctica. Last frontier.''

"You might get a cold reception on that."

"Hell, no. Antarctica is the hot continent. It's in. Used to be Australia, but it's out, trashed, done every which way."

"It's extraordinary how you utilize the exquisite vernacular of our profession. It rolls trippingly from your tongue."

"Well, I invented it to see how the muppets'd take to it."

Willy left, exaggerating his gouty limp. Frost crouched behind his L. C. Smith. He seemed hidden by it. Only his great shock of dark hair appeared.

"Have you canned Harte yet?" he asked.

"Nope."

"When?"

"Soon."

"I got him and now I feel sorry for him."

"Say again? *You* got him?"

"I changed those numbers."

Greg struck himself on the side of the head. "Oh, good Christ. We live in a cuckoo's nest."

"I disagree. This is normal. It was a cuckoo's nest where I used to live."

"You'll tell me about the numbers when you're good and ready, I suppose."

"Something else. Uncle Sam was my idea."

"Figures."

"It was a good idea, but it got out of control. Once you get an idea, you have to control it, and execute it properly. I could give Shakespeare the idea for *Othello*, but I couldn't tell him how to execute it."

"I detect you are happy in your work."

"Why not? I don't hurt anybody. I perpetrate victimless crimes, at least as accessory. We have great power. We create people, like Dr. Frankenstein did. It was ever so. 'We live in a world of shadows . . . we are not what we are, but what is said of us and what we read in each others' eyes.' *Mary of Scotland*. By Maxwell Anderson. Queen Elizabeth said it. Nothing ever is new."

"You know too much. Maybe I should can you."

The Heavyweight shrugged. "Go ahead. It wouldn't matter one quark. I'm not a hill of beans. In the cathedral across the hall they're unimportant, too, but they don't know it."

"What is important?"

"Nothing and everything. What we think is silly is gospel elsewhere, and what is gospel here is silly elsewhere. Ergo, nothing is gospel, nothing is silly."

Greg sat down on the couch. Dust rose. "Hank, is it true you sleep here?"

"Of course. I make it with the night maids."

"You are not to be believed."

"Quasimodo, phantom of the opera, Heavyweight. Oddballs."

"Tell me about the numbers."

"I got them from the annual report of the New York bank, called up the graphics on the

HOLLYWOOD GRAFFITI

computer, and put them in for the L.A. bank. I
changed them for the good of everybody, your
honor. We had to get rid of Harte. Even the
New York numb nuts knew that. He asked me
for help on the bank pitch, despite the fact he
knows I don't exactly worship him. To him
I'm not just an oddball. To him I'm a monkey."

Frost jumped from behind his desk and
pranced around on his haunches, scratching
his ribs and belly and making sounds like a
chimpanzee.

"Cut it out," Greg said, rising. "Hank, cut it
out!"

"Sure," Frost said. He crawled behind his
typewriter and furiously banged the keys. He
stopped. It was silent. Then Frost said: "What
would we do with a bank for a client? We can't
handle a bank. We'd have the business three
months, fuck up the bank, and they'd go
around the University Club and the Jonathan
Club and talk it up about what we really are, a
Hollywood flackery that fucks everything up."

"I suppose that's one way to look at it."

"It's the only way. It's realistic. We deal in
fantasy so much we can't see what we are. If
we got known for what we are, we'd be up shit
creek without a paddle. We have to pretend,
just like our clients pretend."

"You have a way of deflating things to their
basics." Greg gave him a careless shrug of the
shoulders and a wave of the hand. "I know. It
doesn't mean anything. It's only on earth."

111

Frost stood up. He was two inches above his typewriter. "Hear me! I am Golbasto Momaren Evlame Gurdilo Shefin Mully Ully Gue, Most Mighty Emperor of *Lilliput*, Delight and Terror of the Universe, Monarch of all Monarchs, taller than the Sons of Men, whose Feet press down to the Center, and whose Head strikes against the Sun, at whose Nod the Princes of the Earth shake their knees—"

"Stop, stop," Greg pleaded. "You have the part."

"I am pleasant as the Spring, comfortable as the Summer, fruitful as Autumn, dreadful as Winter—"

"Enough!"

"Harte is the big man, got the only private john on the floor. But he's as airy as the hydrogen atom, one electron per coliseum."

"Assassination isn't like you, Hank."

"It wasn't assassination. With his brains, he will go far in show biz. He will have a house with seventeen johns, one each per brain cell."

"You detest him."

"Well, I don't, not actually," Frost said, resuming his post behind his L. C. Smith. "It's just that I'm as petty and vindictive as anybody else. This Harte thing is partly personal, as I said. The first day he was here he called me to his office and pointed at me and screamed, 'The geek! You remind me of the geek in *Nightmare Alley*, 1947, Tyrone Power, Joan Blondell. The geek that bites off chicken heads.' I knew then he had to go." Frost leapt from his chair, whooping and beating his chest. "The hairy homopterous homunculus strikes!"

"And I carry out the sentence."

"You do him a favor. While you're at it, fire yourself. Do yourself a favor."

Greg said: "Somebody has to keep this funny farm together."

"For that you need a zoo keeper, not a philosophy major."

"I wasn't a philosophy major. Besides, all that is air."

"Sure it is."

"Anderson says he's never coming back to Los Angeles."

"Anderson is an advertising executive. How can you believe anyone who lies for a living?"

"Then why should I believe you?"

"Touché, said the dwarf," Frost said. His ugly, misshapen head popped up, his big eyes alert. "Except I play the clown, the fool, and the fool is a wise man, as everyone knows."

"Then tell me, wise man, how do you figure Anderson and Piper?"

"They're alike, yet very different. William James said there is very little difference between men, but what there is is very important."

"I guess I gave you an opening to get that in."

"They are both dirty little cowards, like that dirty Ron Howard, who shot Jesse James in the back. But you know that. What you really want to ask, but do not dare, is what do I think of the new girl."

"What do you think of the new girl?"

"I think you're riding for a fall."

"That isn't what I meant."

"What do I think of her here? She belongs. She will do very well."

Greg entered the cathedral, thinking, *So will I; I'm going to do very well here*. He walked resolutely to Tim Harte's office. Again the heads emerged along the corridor. Harte's door was locked from the inside. His secretary, Miss Layne, who had the title of assistant, stood indecisively, trembling and pale. She bit her lip.

"Do you have a key?" Greg asked.

"No."

"Buzz him."

She did, several times. No answer. Greg knocked on the door and rattled its handle, feeling foolish and helpless. Turning abruptly, he glared away the prying heads.

"Tim? It's Greg. Open up, Tim."

After a long while, he heard Harte's voice from within. It was muffled, as if it came from far away. "It's open."

Greg tried the door again. It opened with a grating sound like a low moan. He stepped in. The lights were off and the drapes were drawn. He saw the desk, the guest chairs, the couch, the pictures covering the walls. The windows were open and puffs of air rustled the drapes. He heard Harte's voice.

"Keep it dark. Don't open the drapes or turn on the lights. Close the door behind you and lock it."

Greg did so. "Where are you?"

"Here. In the john. On the shitter. With a gun."

Greg went to the door. "Tim?"

"After you fire me, take this office. Not even Anderson or Piper have a can. Do you believe I have a gun?"

"Yes, I do, Tim."

"Police .38 special. It was my father's. Did you know he killed himself?"

"I didn't. I'm very sorry, Tim."

"He killed himself because my mother left him to marry Anderson. I was just five then. I got two shitface step-brothers out of it. Harvard, they went to. Hah-vard, they'd say. Anderson treated my mother like a dog."

Greg slumped down in a chair and drew up his legs. It probably would be a long wait. Behind the door was a stranger, an alien, someone he saw every day yet didn't know. An office of strangers. Greg had joined in on the ridicule of Harte, laughed at jokes about Harte; he'd cursed the man's bungling inanity and also cursed the idiots in New York for sending the company dolt to manage L.A. Now he no longer felt that way. He felt sorry for the fat little man behind the door.

Harte said: "The only way I could get away from it was to sneak off to the movies. They saved me. Nobody is more of an expert on movies in the world than I am."

"I believe that for certain. It is no contest."

"Test me."

"I said I believe you."

"Name any movie. I'll tell you who starred."

"All right. *Casablanca.*"

"Oh, come *on*! That's too easy."

"How about *Casanova*?"

"I'm on! There was a *Casanova & Co.* with Tony Curtis and Britt Ekland, a *Casanova '70* with Marcello Mastroianni and Michele Mercier, a *Casanova Brown* in 1944 with Gary Cooper and Teresa Wright, and a *Casanova in Burlesque* with Joe E. Brown and June Havoc, also 1944. Wait. *Casanova's Big Night*. With Bob Hope. That was in 1954."

He paused for praise. Greg applauded.

"What word starts most movie titles?" Harte asked.

"I have no idea."

"Love. What's next?"

"Tell me."

"Murder! So you see, love and murder are what interest people the most. What's third?" He let out a yell. "Tarzan!"

Good. Harte was screaming it away. *Say, you're one helluva shrink, Gregory. For a Hollywood flack, you give good head.* That amused

Greg and he started to laugh; it became contagious and he heard Harte's laughter in return. Good. Soon Harte would come out, grin foolishly, and walk away as if nothing had happened. But then the laughter stopped. Greg listened, not moving, holding his breath. He heard sobbing.

"Tim?"

He waited. The sobbing sounds were gone. Then he heard Harte's voice, weak and low, like a child's.

"Is everybody outside the door, just waiting?"

"Don't tell me you're afraid of those airheads."

"They are airheads, aren't they?"

"Damn right they are."

"Send them away."

"All right. I will. Away they go." Greg got up, went to Harte's desk, and buzzed Marge. "Here is my first order as the new king. Everybody takes the afternoon off. That means they're all to leave the building."

"Across the hall, too?"

"Especially across the hall."

Soon he heard excited voices in the corridor. He was accustomed to the semidarkness now and could see well in it, aided by a large golden bar of sunlight on the carpet, beaming in through a crack in the drapes. A glass paperweight had been placed on top of a single sheet of paper on the desk; thinking it possibly could be a suicide note, Greg reached over and picked it up. Typed on it were the words:

THE FILMS OF JOAN CRAWFORD
A Critical Analysis
By Timothy S. Harte

The films of Joan Crawford.

There was no more. Greg replaced the sheet exactly where he had found it and put the paperweight over it, feeling as if he'd pried. He still heard the voices and shufflings of the departing staff. He glanced around. The framed photographs and drawings of stars filled almost all the wall space available. He went to one wall. All were signed. "To Tim, The Darling Boy, Ava." "Timmy, The Unforgettable, Lana." And so on. Most of them were female stars—Loretta and Kim and Marilyn and "Kathy." It was a galaxy of stars as impressive as that along Hollywood Boulevard. Greg studied them, fascinated. No one from the staff came often to Harte's office, since he usually went to theirs, so Greg had never really looked at the pictures before. Now he detected something. The handwriting on many was similar. It wasn't absolutely the same, but the loops and crosses and other characteristics were. Also, many were signed in red ink from what appeared to be the same pen. Greg realized with a chill that Harte had signed most of them himself. They were cheap

publicity photos, the kind sent to fans, undoubtedly bought in Hollywood shops. Greg
sighed. Harte couldn't even show off his auto-
graph collection, except at a distance, fearful
that scrutiny would betray his fraud. Anger
stabbed at Greg.

"Listen," he said. "Screw you in there.
You're not man enough to come out, pack up
these autographed pictures, and escape from
this shit hole, I say to hell with you."

It worked. Harte came out. His pants were
wet. "Peed my pants," he said. "Here I'm in a
can and I pee my pants."

Greg laughed. "I shit my pants once. In
Nam."

They both laughed, relieved and letting it
out.

"Anderson is afraid of flying," Harte said.

"Is that his big secret?"

"He's never pissed in the air. Scared
pissless."

Again they laughed. Harte showed Greg the
pistol. He did a Clint Eastwood with it,
crouching and pointing. "Make my day," he
said.

"Give it to me."

Instead Harte put it on the floor and kicked
it away. "I'll tell you what the big secret is
between Anderson and Piper," he said, a
childlike whisper.

Greg did a Gable. "Frankly, my dear, I don't
give a damn."

But Harte insisted. He whispered into

119

Greg's ear and stepped back, looking triumphant.

"I'll be go to hell," Greg said.

Harte winked. "Let Anderson know you know. You got a job forever. Well, until shit happens, anyway. You wait long enough, shit happens."

"What do you mean?"

"Shit happens, conditions change. Same, same. It's how you explain things. Your wife or girlfriend runs off, she says, 'Well, shit happens.' You can explain anything that way. Father dies. Shit happens. Murder and love. Shit happens. Wars, earthquakes, floods, hurricanes. Shit happens. Shit happens, conditions change. Sameo, sameo."

Greg shrugged. He didn't know what to say. Harte glanced around the office, looking at his pictures on the wall. He looked lost and forlorn, on the edge of tears, like the overweight kid on a playground who'd just had the stuffings kicked out of him by the bully.

"Jesus H on a crutch, I hope it has a Walt Disney ending," he said.

EIGHT

Maureen kept Martin Bradford sober until July 4th. She also kept his hands off her. Both were significant accomplishments of tact and intelligence.

"You might as well understand," she said. "I do not sleep with clients."

"Company policy?"

"My policy."

"You are Captain Bligh and Simon Legree rolled up into one pretty package. I wake up with a hard-on, and there's no girl. I wake up trembling, and there's no whiskey. What am I to do?"

"You can call in any girl you like and do anything you like with her, as long as I'm not here. As for whiskey, it's a no-no. Whiskey, and I'm out."

"You're worse than a wife."

"I have some matters to attend to. If you don't behave yourself, I'll know it."

"I'm sure you will," he said.

"I'll be back soon."

"Promise?"

"Promise."

"Good. I'm not such a bad guy, you know."

And he wasn't, not when sober. When he was drunk, however, he was impossible. He'd do anything—jump into the swimming pool fully clothed, interrupt a church service, make a speech in Pershing Square, sit on a barrel in the middle of a busy intersection. Maureen had seen only the pool jump, but she'd heard about the other stunts and believed every story.

It was extraordinary that Martin Bradford looked so good, considering his long devotion to dissipation. He stood just over six feet tall and weighed 160; he was sixty-five if he was a day, but his face was unwrinkled and babyish, dominated by clear blue eyes and a great shock of white hair. His voice was excellent and he spoke well extemporaneously. He wasn't middle-of-the-road; he was aware of issues and took positions. He'd backed Ronald Reagan and now had Reagan's best wishes. But the party balked, skittish about drinkers. Martin Bradford wasn't a closet drinker; like his buddy W. C. Fields, he thought it added to his charm. Yet he was always sober at public functions and had never been in trouble with the law. He was malleable, but it was going to be difficult, even if he stayed sober.

For Maureen it was a big day. She was moving, escaping the top-floor single off La Brea for a one-bedroom off Wilshire near the Miracle Mile. No more midnight serenading from beer-logged Teamsters in the halls and indigent blacks on the streets, no more dirty-faced Mexican brats making obscene gestures from neighboring windows, no more moth-eaten furniture and smelly closets. She had new furniture, bought on time, and her apartment was airy and light and clean. The neighbors dressed well and drove good cars. Kids weren't allowed. There was a private patio where she could sunbathe and grow flowers. When she opened her living room drapes, she didn't see a fly-infested sidewalk fruit market and Chevys on lawns. She saw a garden and beyond that a small park with palm trees.

It was an older apartment house, but substantial and safe. One panel in the bathroom window was pink and yellow, an old Spanish design, and the morning sun coming through it cast a faint flush on her cheeks and lips, warming them and giving her a good and sensual feeling, even before makeup. In the living room was a large wall mirror; now, preparing to pick up Martin Bradford for the Brentwood parade, she stood before it, knowing the full force of her intellectual and sexual powers. Yellow sunhat, pink-rimmed sunglasses, white shorts and halter blouse with yellow trim, white tennis shoes. She was ready. Car, furniture, clothing, apartment, job—all new, all just fine. Her progress had been extraordinary, and she was just starting. She kept glancing into the rear-view and side mirrors of the BMW, checking herself, all the way to the Beverly Hills Hotel. When she saw who answered the doorbell of Martin's suite, she almost dropped her sunglasses.

"You're the PR?" asked Mark Ashley, displaying his smile.

He examined her, his dark eyes steady, as she stood stunned and weak-kneed. He wasn't beautifully handsome, tall and slicked down, suave; he was ruggedly handsome, everything right, mustache and hair, eyes and mouth.

"We've met," he said.

"Yes. At Mona Tyson's place."

"You came there to observe the freaks."

"Well, no. I—"

"I never forget eyes. I do forget names."

"Maureen Crawford."

"You're the Crawford who sent me the note."

"I admit it. It was impetuous and childish."

"Not at all. All attention is appreciated."

She didn't know what to say, yet felt compelled to continue. "You must be sick of attention."

"Then why did you send me a note?"

"Quite frankly, because I wanted to get

acquainted with you. Me and the million others."

"Hello, I'm Mark Ashley. Wind me up and I charm."

"Hello, I'm Maureen Crawford."

"Wind you up and what?"

"I don't get wound up," she said.

It was a hot day with a yellow sun and big white clouds, so clear the ocean was visible from the higher points of Brentwood. She remembered Fourths like this as a child—pressing crowds, noisy bands, smells of mustard and popcorn. Maureen felt totally aware of herself. She belonged; in fact, she stood out. She'd come a long and hard way since the July 4ths of her girlhood, when bashful farm boys in clean overalls had asked her to dance, shuffling awkwardly in waltz or lindy, their harvest faces sunburned scarlet, their downcast eyes sneaking glances at her developing breasts and hips.

Mark Ashley, tossing up peanuts and catching them in his mouth, almost escaped recognition. The exception was his cornering by a group of giggling teen-aged girls. He graciously signed autographs, thrilling them with his dimpled smile, and posed for cameras. Then he and Maureen blended with the others. The parade was short—horses and high school bands and vintage Thunderbird cars, convertibles painted shocking pinks and reds and greens. Martin Bradford, a Brentwood resident, was grand marshal. He stood in the back of the lead car in his Uncle Sam suit, waving and smiling. Six girls in flimsy Western attire preceded him on foot, flaunting a huge red, white and blue political sign. His wife, a handy accouterment for a political aspirant, unfortunately was absent. The last Thunderbird passed by and the crowd began to disperse. Maureen congratulated herself. She'd spent an afternoon with the nation's leading movie star and most eligible bachelor and she'd handled it well, casually. He was as handsome dressed informally—in blue corduroy pants, V-necked shirt, floppy hat—as he was in a tuxedo on screen; people glanced at him, giving him a second look, wondering who he might be, perhaps thinking about halfway home: *Mark Ashley, that was who*! He was with the girl in yellow shorts. Who was she?

Martin Bradford was being interviewed by a television reporter. Yes, he supported Tower's appointment; no, he didn't think the budget and trade deficits were leading to recession or depression; yes, Ronald Reagan's greatest accomplishment well might have been detente with the Russians; no, Japanese investment in California was not a bad thing, instead it was an economic stimulus and therefore welcomed. He smiled as he talked. When they left, he had his arms around two of the cowgirls who'd carried his sign. Everybody was laughing. Nothing had been planned, but somehow everybody knew a good time was ahead, no matter where it was held and who was there.

It turned out to be at Martin's residence, which was actually in Pacific Palisades, not Brentwood. As amazing as it was for a Southern Californian, he didn't know how to drive a car and had no desire to learn—a fact that had saved him God knows how many 502s and perhaps even his life—and although he wasn't broke he couldn't afford a chauffeur. So he took taxis or cadged rides from friends when his wife was gone, which was often; she liked Hong Kong, Paris, and the Riviera and could afford them, having money of her own. She also was a bitch and a good Catholic, which precluded divorce—the Catholic part, not necessarily the bitch part, Martin had said to Maureen. He was garrulous as well as lecherous when drunk. Providing his ride today was Mark Ashley, who *could* afford a chauffeur, a young black man in full uniform despite the heat. It was a stretched Cadillac limo with frosted windows and a bar. With the help of the cowgirls, Martin stripped down to his socks and purple boxer shorts. The girls mixed martinis; Martin drank from the pitcher.

"Ah, ambrosia," he said. Giggling, the cowgirls rubbed his back and legs. "Home, James. Party time."

It was a huge house, three levels, with an

ocean view, doubtless a mortgage paid by the wife. The party was well under way by the time they arrived. A hot four-o'clock sun was high and bright over the Pacific, but already firecrackers banged and partygoers in hats more like New Year's Eve than the Fourth were carelessly waving live sparklers. Somebody had paid out something for the event; again, perhaps the wife. There was a long buffet sagging with food and three bars attended by uniformed men. The pool was crowded. Some of the girls there were topless; a few were naked. A huge black man in bikini trunks drew loud applause and cheers as he executed various dives from the high board. He did swans and half-gainers and even belly flops. He seemed flawless, like an Olympian; even his comedic flops had grace. His performance over, he bowed to a burst of heavy-handed clapping and whistles and mingled with whites.

"Who is he?" Maureen asked Martin, who had put on red trunks and lay in a lounge chair beside the pool, his martini pitcher and cowgirls by his side.

"How should I know?"

"Oh, come on!"

"All right, it's T. D. Desmond, as if you didn't know."

"I didn't know."

"Football? Making movies now? T.D.? Touchdown? Only *that* T.D. stands for Tax

Deduction, his real name. Blacks give names like that. I don't know who brought him. I certainly didn't invite him."

"I'd like to meet him."

"Go ahead. He needs PR. Like the surgeon general says, be sure to use a condom."

The cowgirls giggled. They had opened their blouses and the nipples of their breasts showed. Martin started to say something else but instead drained his martini glass and flipped the olive into the pool. His voice was starting to slur. When he got like this, preliminary to a binge, he became snobbish and sometimes belligerent. The fact he didn't like blacks was one of his political drawbacks. He called it a flaw and considered all his flaws Maureen's problem, since she was his a.e. He said the initials stood for "almost enything," and charged her with curing his drunkenness, lasciviousness, and racial prejudice. Maureen said now was as good a time as any to start.

"No, tomorrow," he said.

The cowgirls giggled. Maureen stalked away. She felt slightly dizzy. The fleshy revelers around the pool shifted together in a sexual dance. It all seemed to sway before her, white-lighted in the stream of sun; the grass was spongy and insubstantial, sinking, and the sky was a giant descending sheet that blended with the ocean. She found herself inside a marble-floored room with a fireplace and a high ceiling from which a giant chandelier dangled. A narrow circular staircase led to a hallway above, where she could see closed doors to several rooms. She went to an adjacent hall and opened what seemed to be a bathroom door. A couple inside were in the throes of upright sex, she leaning against the mirror, he with his pants down over his ankles. Maureen closed the door. Firecrackers exploded outside. One of Martin's cowgirls came up, her eyes big as quarters. She wore red tights.

"Party needs more kick," she said, kicking. "Ha-ha, ha-ha."

"You seem happy enough."

"Oh, I'm so happy! Ha-ha, ha-ha. I can float. I can fly to the moon."

"So I see."

The cowgirl shuffled away, her behind wriggling. Maureen turned to see Mark Ashley rise from a deep chair in the marble-floored room. He walked up to her.

"You look a little pale," he said.

"I think it's the sun. I can't take sun."

He took her arm and led her to a chair near the fireplace. In another chair nearby sat the black man who had done the diving. He wore his swim trunks and a blue silk shirt with tails that went below his knees. Ashley didn't introduce them. The black man didn't look up. He was cutting cocaine into rows on the coffee-table glass. Maureen found that she wasn't shocked; it was as if she'd expected it. The black man folded up the knife blade, put the knife in his shirt pocket, and drew out a plastic straw. It could be bent, like a hospital straw. Slowly he inhaled a row of the white powder. He breathed deeply, his wide nostrils dilating. Then he sniffed up another row. He handed the straw to Ashley, who consumed the two remaining rows. Both men leaned back in the tall-backed chairs and relaxed, breathing deeply and holding it, letting the air out through their mouths.

"Ain't like the first time," said the black man.

Ashley said to Maureen: "That's T. D. Desmond. When he goes up, he always says that. It ain't like the first time. Mr. Desmond, have you met Miss Crawford?"

"Pleased," Desmond said, not moving.

"I forgot what you do, Miss Crawford."

"Public relations."

"Oh, yes. T.D., are you interested in public relations?"

"What interests me in relations is sexual relations."

"Well, here's your woman, for public relations."

"You want to go upstairs to talk about it?" Desmond asked, not looking at Maureen.

"I beg your pardon?" she said.

"I beg your pardon?" Desmond said, aping her.

He had huge shoulders and a crest of Afro

131

hair. Anger sparked in his eyes, but he smiled. His teeth were very white. His body was hard, like carved black marble.

"Do you have a boyfriend?" Ashley asked Maureen.

"Why, actually, yes," Maureen said, thinking about Greg for the first time today.

"Why, actually, yes," Desmond aped.

"Tell him to stop that."

"T.D., you stop that now."

"Yas, suh!"

"You know him," Maureen said to Ashley. "Arthur Gregory. He was there at Mona Tyson's party."

"I guess I know him. Is he on coke?"

"No."

"No?" Ashley said. "Well, he's one of us. Never grew out of rompers. Still on the slide. Do you know about the slide, the Hollywood slide?"

"I don't think so."

"You go up it, your Mama helping you, fighting off other kids. Then you come down, fast, and land in mud. And—guess what?— even Mama's not there to help you up."

"I used to run through stone walls playin' football," Desmond said. "Feel no pain, feel no pain."

The cowgirl in red tights kneeled beside Desmond. "I can fly, just like you," she said.

"You jus' a baby, Mickey Mouse around. Go on, crash." Desmond mumbled on, talking to himself. "What I liked with football was the rules. You play dirty, the rules catch up with you. Out of football, there's no rules. It's who plays dirtiest who wins. Only ones who play it clean, those born with money. Never dirt on them."

"Maureen the PR lady is going to put Marty Bradford into the White House, U.S.A.," Ashley said.

"Well, first the Senate," Maureen said.

"Ronnie was president," Desmond said. "He can, anybody can. Well, not a nigger. White House is for the white man." He looked at Maureen. "Could I become president?"

"I think so," Maureen said.

"She thinks so," Desmond said, pointing at her.

"Sure," Ashley said. "Piece of cake."

"No it ain't," Desmond said. "Marty can run for senator and make it to president even though he's a nothing, broken-down, never-was actor who couldn't be a good dogcatcher but I could be Honest Abe Lincoln and George Washington but I couldn't be president because I'm nigger blood. Nigger blood."

There was a silence. They were high, Maureen thought, so they were saying things they normally wouldn't say. Yet she felt a little nervous. Ashley broke the tension.

"How about a game? Two out of three?"

"You're on," Desmond said.

They sat like small boys, snapping their fingers in an odd-even game. Ashley failed to

133

match and lost the first two games. He drew a roll of bills from his pocket and peeled off twenty hundreds, handing them to Desmond, who stuffed them into his swim trunks.

Ashley looked at Maureen. "What could you make me into? A senator?"

"Frankly, I don't know. You just might be too good-looking."

"I want to be something different. Make me into something different, somebody who's at least slightly happy."

"That sounds strange, coming from you."

"T.D., do you think I'm too good-looking to be a senator?"

"If you was a nigger, boss, you'd be *ugly!*"

"Game for a little game?" Ashley asked Maureen.

"At a thousand dollars? Too rich for me."

"No bets. Just repeat after me. 'What's the matter with you, anyway?'"

"'What's the matter with you, anyway?'"

"'I got hurt in the war.'"

She smiled. "I don't understand."

"It's from *The Sun Also Rises*. The prostitute asks Jake Barnes, when he doesn't want to go, 'What's the matter with you, anyway?' He replies, 'I got hurt in the war.' Then she says, 'Oh, that dirty war.' Want to try it again?"

"I'd rather not."

"I thought you were game."

"I don't like the part of prostitute."

"What happened to this guy in the war?" Desmond asked.

"He got his dong shot off," Ashley said. "Something like that. He couldn't get it up, not that he didn't want to."

"Oh, I get it. All the time, saltpetered."

"I've seen Ty Power in that role ten times. I'd love to play it. Mark Ashley makes love to Brett Ashley. Dongless love. If we didn't worry about our dongs, maybe we'd be happier and stay out of trouble. Run for president, like old Marty Bradford."

"Marty Bradford couldn't be dogcatcher," Desmond said.

From outside came the loud banging of firecrackers. Ashley stood up and began to emote, scratching his face so hard he bled. "Hollywood has the guts of a moth. It flutters and swishes with queer power. Why doesn't it do *Lear* or *Hamlet*?"

"Is that a part for me?" Desmond asked.

"You could play Othello."

"Do he die in the end?"

Ashley gestured. "Out, out, brief candle. Turn up the lights, dear mother, for I do not wish to go home in the dark." He gestured wildly now, blood running down his face. "He is mad who trusts in the tameness of a wolf, a horse's health, a boy's love, or a whore's oath."

Everybody laughed and clapped, stomping the hard marble floor. Ashley was high and foolish but he was a star and he deserved applause. Maureen felt uneasy. She despised drugs; her greatest fear was addiction to any-

135

thing, liquor or candy or even love. Addiction was like a captivity and slavery. Her father had been weak, liking his whiskey. She would never be weak.

"Tee-hee, tee-hee!" cried a girlish voice from above. "Look at me!"

Eyes turned up. Gasps sounded. A glass shattered on the floor. The cowgirl in red tights stood on the railing of the upstairs hallway, balanced on her toetips, hands over her head, elbows bent. Crying, "I can fly!" she launched herself into the air, springing upward and then falling, her arms spreading in a swan dive as she plunged toward the marble floor.

NINE

Dinner at the Mastersons' in San Marino was sedate, formal, old-fashioned. Greg felt thrust into the Victorian era, complete with the efficient and humorless butler, surname address, and towering house with gables and roundtowers. It was on an acre of ground and hidden behind cypress and pine trees, almost a forestlike thickness of them. Ornate iron fences with spear-point tops and a gate guarded by a thick-browed man in uniform surrounded the house.

There were six at dinner—Masterson and Norwine and their wives, Greg, and a young woman of subtle and imposing beauty. She was in her mid-twenties, dark-haired and slender, with finely chiseled bone structure and soft black eyes that seemed sad and distant. She had been introduced to Greg as Denise Stevens. She spoke only in response. Her voice had a slight accent, Spanish or perhaps Italian. Her manner was diffident but not self-conscious. She seemed a toy in a blue gown, yet a part of the gathering; she knew how to sit and how to move. The ambience was old European, but the food was decidedly American—vegetable soup, green salad, baked potatoes, rare prime ribs. The butler in black tails gave silent directions to two elderly serving maids in crisp aproned uniforms who moved about with the deftness of a ghostly pantomime.

Masterson was a small dark man of perhaps seventy with a smooth gray face. He seemed almost vaporous, phantasmagorical, moving stealthily, his hands pale and ghostly in the light and his face obscured, occasionally almost fading away against his dark background. Greg did not know him and he wondered who really did. He'd worked on the account, in fact, for several weeks before he'd met Masterson. Albert Norwine had solicited the business, and the retainer and expenses were paid through his office. Greg knew only that Masterson had been born on Corsica, educated in France, and, after the fall of Paris, had gone to England and proved valuable to the Allies. It was said Masterson also served in Yugoslavia during the war. His first commer-

cial venture in America had been the importa-
tion of Corsican wines. He'd diversified into
several areas, most of them trade-related, including merchant banking. Only recently had
he become interested in a motion picture
studio, a reason why he'd sought a public
relations agency that specialized in entertainment clients.

The wives, seated next to each other, looked
remarkably similar. They wore silk formals
with yellow orchids. When they moved, the
silk seemed to hiss. They were elderly, fluffy
women, both overweight and not given to
laughter or even smiles, scented like powder
puffs and painted like queens. Like Denise
Stevens, they spoke only when spoken to. And
they listened and nodded when men talked.
They were in jeweled regalia, big diamonds
that sparkled, gold that glittered, jade that
seemed to emit green sparks. Denise Stevens
wore a single-strand mother-of-pearl neck-
lace.

"I am by now enough of an American to
observe Independence Day," Masterson said.
His voice was deep and clear, with no trace of
accent. "Men are like nations. Both should
have freedom if it is freedom they desire."

Norwine and his wife nodded. They drew
bloody knives over their red prime ribs.

"Corsica had a hero of independence,"
Masterson continued. "One might call him a
founding father of Corsican freedom from the
Genoese. Who was he?"

"It wasn't Napoleon, I am sure," Norwine said.

Masterson's cheeks took on spots of color as he warmed to his game. "Was Napoleon a hero?"

"Certainly to the French," Norwine said.

"What do you think, Mr. Gregory?" Masterson asked.

Greg's head snapped up. "PR men prefer to avoid questions," he said, a pale joke but at least a response.

"Please say what is on your mind."

"I think Napoleon was an egomaniac. European unity was his charade, nothing more."

"Bravo, Mr. Gregory," Masterson said. "But who was our hero of Corsica?"

"It was Pasquale Paoli," said Denise Stevens.

Masterson smiled. "Brava," he said.

Norwine directed a dour look at Greg. He was a pale, ferretlike man with a red skull edged by white hair. He often communicated with his eyes, which now conveyed disgust. Masterson, who missed very little, seemed to detect that and moved to conciliate by changing the subject.

"You have a young son," he said to Greg.

"Yes."

"You should be with your son on holidays. It was my oversight not to invite both of you. How old is he?"

"Rob is ten."

If Norwine communicated with eye movements, Masterson did likewise with gestures. Now he moved his hand, a signal that the conversation about the son was over. It had served its purpose, whatever that really was. Dessert was brought in, continuing the American tradition with apple pie a la mode. After the meal the women went to the sitting room and the men to a paneled den. There were books with titles obscured by their bindings behind glass cases, paintings of hunting scenes and huge dark portraits on the wall, and a mounted elk's head as a centerpiece. Vivaldi's "The Seasons" danced gaily from speakers in the wall, alternating with Respighi's "Pines of Rome." Cigars were offered by the butler, but not accepted. Norwine took a small brandy in a big snifter. The butler exited silently. Masterson sat back in a soft high-backed chair by the cold fireplace and motioned Greg and Norwine to smaller chairs facing him. There was a view of a swimming pool through the windows behind Masterson. The sun was bright and the water of the pool glistened. Beside it stood a tall blond man with cropped hair, wearing a gray suit and tie. Black iron bars protected the windows. Masterson gestured, and Norwine rose to close the drapes. Respighi's music played softly. Masterson closed his eyes and nestled back in his chair like a dark, hunched bird, his gray face fading, blending with the fabric. There was light from a nearby pole lamp, faint but enough to cast a pale shadow of him on the floor, enlarged and somehow ominous, the uncertain and distorted reflection of a chimerical king in a rude room of his barred palace.

"I find it best that men talk among men and women also do that," he said quietly, his eyes remaining closed, his hands clapsed over his chest. "That way, both can talk without inhibition. I am old-fashioned enough to believe there is the business of women and the business of men, a twain that should never cross."

Norwine sniffed the edge of his brandy glass.

Masterson's eyes snapped open. He sat up straight. "It is a day to relax, but business unfortunately must intrude. Business will not wait. At my age I measure time not in days and weeks but in hours and indeed even in minutes." He fumbled in his jacket pocket and brought out glasses. They were thick and horn-rimmed, and when he had them on he seemed a different person, alert and businesslike, impatient. "Mr. Norwine, I believe you have a progress report on the studio acquisition."

Norwine glanced at Greg, his eyes shifting. "I'm not sure this is the proper time—"

"What is proper is my judgment," Masterson said. His teeth snapped. Then he smiled. "I am a judge of men, Mr. Gregory, just as some judge horses and others judge women. It was my decision to employ you, my judgment. Now I offer you a choice. As I grow older I realize more and more how little control we have over our lives. We make certain turns, yes, but once we do, there is little for us to do but follow blindly on a path."

He paused, breathing slowly. The quiet was like a palpable force, a weight. Masterson's features were now drawn and austere, hard as iron. Greg became aware that it was very warm in the room. Masterson knew him, he realized, either through investigation or by instinct, and quite suddenly Greg also realized he knew more than before about Masterson. This was a man capable of cutting to another's mind and soul, a man of puissance raw and malignant under his deceptively benign cloak. Greg stirred. He felt perspiration trickle down his arms and back.

"You may leave or you may stay," Masterson said, speaking to Greg but not looking at him, his eyes downcast and his glasses reflecting small beams from the lamp. "It is that certain turn I mentioned. If you leave, you cannot return. If you stay, you cannot leave unless you have my permission, or order, to do so. I'm afraid I must have your decision now."

Greg stood up. His mind was blank. The room went away from him—the gray man in the chair, the little lawyer with the envious eyes, this hot shadowy place with its dank paintings and doleful elk's head—and in a flash so bright it caused pain in his temples he saw himself in the future, his yearnings and his dreams fulfilled beyond expectation. He heard the music, now Vivaldi, rising to the season of summer.

"I'd like to stay," he said.

Masterson's face again was an obscure dark mask. Norwine rose. His face was flushed and sweaty. He slapped the brandy snifter down on the table and crossed the floor, the steel cleats on his shoes echoing on the hardwood floor. Returning with quieter strides, he unzipped a briefcase that smelled of new leather, drew out a sheaf of legal-sized papers, and offered them to Masterson.

"No, please just tell me," Masterson said, waving.

"Videoscope will accept our offer," Norwine said. "The papers are ready for your signature."

"If you will leave the papers, I will sign them this evening," Masterson said. "Now, Mr. Norwine, if you would excuse us and join the ladies, that would please me. I have a few matters to discuss with Mr. Gregory."

Norwine placed the papers on the table next to the snifter, eyed Greg askance, and left. His heels clattered. Greg found himself staring down at the papers. He was familiar with Videoscope, a production facility in the valley that had been a dream of Victor Wise, who'd had a string of successes for major studios before going on his own. Then it had quickly soured. Budgets ran over, pictures flopped, a plague of freak accidents and lawsuits struck. Now Wise was nearly bankrupt, forced to sell. His dream had been reduced to a small sheaf of legal papers. He'd once been the talk of New Hollywood. Soon his name would be forgotten.

As if he read Greg's mind, Masterson said: "A man can want too intensely and overreach. What is it that you want, Mr. Gregory?"

"I don't understand."

"Of course you understand. What is important to you? What would you like to have, to accomplish?"

Greg fidgeted, hot and uncomfortable. "Believe it or not, I'd like a few acres in the country. A garden and some trees. Horses, a couple dogs. Simple stuff."

"Nonsense," Masterson said, waving his hand.

"Well, as you know, I'd like to produce pictures."

"Then you shall."

"Somehow I don't think it's quite that simple."

"What is your impression of Miss Stevens?"

"Beautiful," Greg said without hesitation.

"She wants to become an actress. I tell her, 'Well, then you will become an actress.' She answers like you answer. It is not that simple. Yet it is. Do you believe the newspaper in Phoenix printed the truth about me?"

"I notice you shift subjects very rapidly."

"Please answer."

"No, I don't think it was the truth."

"No one appreciates freedom and independence more than I do. In this country there is freedom. A man cannot be arrested without cause. Everyone of a certain age can vote. One need not carry identification papers to be surrendered on demand. Yet it seems some freedoms go too far."

"The free press, do you mean?"

"I do not understand the press. That is why you are important as my go-between with the press, my alter ego, so to speak. I respect your abilities. I like your attitude. I have said I am an excellent judge of men. I flatter myself by believing that some of my associates joust among each other for my favor and my time. It is a perverse form of jealousy. You have that favor, and that time, as long as I have your trust."

"Thank you."

"You will get what you want. I think you will look back to remember this day as one of the most important in your life."

Greg opened his mouth but no words came out. He found himself speechless. His emotions were contrasting—elation yet anxiety, understanding edged with doubt, relief and distress. Again Masterson seemed to know.

"Sometimes it is not possible to explain, Mr. Gregory. But I believe we understand each other. You also will understand this what I say. That which people believe often is not that which really is or was, but instead that which is perceived. Often we see what we wish to see, even in our mirrors. We do not face ourselves. We pretend. We even fear to face the most basic reality of all, which is death. So we invent a myth of an immortal soul. Truth is not an absolute. There is no single truth. The Phoenix article was true, yet not true."

"How can that be?"

"I am unable to explain it. I do certain things for certain purposes, which I cannot discuss. Perhaps it is my paying back, my noblesse oblige." Slowly Masterson raised his brown-splotched hands and removed his glasses. His eyes were dark and sunken, yet steady and alive. "I ask that you trust me. You must stop this man in Phoenix from writing material of this nature, or he could be stopped in a violent way by forces over which I have no control. He is defying great power. I understand power, and respect it. Sometimes it has no reason. This man is defeating his own purpose. By stopping him, Mr. Gregory, you will be doing a service."

"A service for whom?"

Masterson changed subjects. His voice softened. "You should spend as much time as you can with your son, Mr. Gregory. They grow and are gone with the winking of an eye. Family is above all in importance. A man needs a home, a son, and a good wife."

"Yes, I agree."

"Your son could be taken from you."

Greg jerked upright, shock running through his body. Again he fumbled to speak. He felt suddenly weak. Masterson's steady gray eyes now seemed sad and distant. He rose with some effort, perhaps with pain, and gestured. Greg followed silently, somewhat stunned. They went into a hallway of red Mexican tile, Masterson leading, walking with hunched shoulders like a very old man. He paused to push open an arched mahogany door. They entered an enclosed area like a large closet, and at its end bright bulbs revealed a wide descending staircase with handrails on both sides. Masterson went down slowly, holding the rail, now seeming even more bent, a dark misshapen figure seeming to feel its way like a prowling animal. He began to speak in a dull monotone.

"One must see power to understand it. I have seen it, at its most intense level. Pure power cannot function except in anarchy, even in totalitarian states, and never does it last long. But when in force it is like a hurricane, beyond belief or description. It is not to be equated with sin. Sin does not exist under two circumstances—where one has a great deal of money and where there is the asininity and inanity of war.

"I have a facility with languages and at one time I spoke fluent Serbo-Croatian and some Macedonian. Also, I had spent a summer in

the Balkans. So during the last war I was sent
to Yugoslavia to aid the partisans of Tito in the
resistance against the Germans. This was in
1943, and perhaps I had communist leanings.
My job was to coordinate a supply line.

"The Germans and their collaborators of
course had license to kill—a hundred Yugo-
slavians for every dead German was the order
—but when I say the Croatians, some of the
Ustashi and Chetniks, were more vicious and
bloodthirsty than the Nazis I am not exaggerating. The Germans killed quickly, by hanging or firing squad, but the Croatians killed
their kind with knives and hammers and saws
and quicklime. They would carry salt to sprin-
kle into wounds. You see, they wanted to be
feared, for fear in anarchy is power. Gypsies
and Jews were special targets. I have seen men
buried to their waists and hacked to pieces bit
by bit. Of course it was madness. But those
people were not mad. They were quite sane.
They had families. They prayed on their
knees. I also saw men and women walk
proudly to their deaths by torture to protect
loved ones. One man died for his dog, all that
he had to love. What I learned was respect for
power. I also learned firsthand that man was a
dual creature, capable of extremes from no-
bility to abomination."

Masterson paused. They had come to a
large, dimly lighted basement room with a
cobblestone floor and cement walls. It was

cool and moist. Blue flames from gas jets burned from the upper corners. Masterson turned. His eyes were moist.

Greg glanced around. He felt a rising chill. He wanted to turn and dash away, up the stairs and out of this place, a run to freedom, but he didn't move. He couldn't. The chill consumed him.

TEN

He reached Maureen on the car phone driving home from the Mastersons'. She told him about the girl's death.

"You sound pretty calm," he said.

"You wouldn't say that if you could see me."

"The shakes?"

"Like a leaf."

"Can you drive?"

"Well, I got home all right."

"Come over to my place. Leave now."

He tried Albert Norwine, who had left San Marino before Greg, getting only the answering service. At home Greg kept trying, succeeding just before Maureen arrived.

"Well, what do you expect me to do about

it?" Norwine asked after Greg explained the situation.

"There was drug use at the party. I would rather that not be mentioned in the media accounts."

"You're the genius with the press, not I."

"But you're close to Mr. Masterson."

"I am not the only one, as is becoming apparent."

"But you do have considerable influence with him."

"Why do you think he can help in the matter?"

"I don't know. But he is a man of many resources."

"Drugs are a sensitive issue with Mr. Masterson."

"Of course. It's just that this is very important to me, so I'm asking for his help. Your call to him would be much more persuasive than mine."

"Well, I won't promise anything," Norwine said.

Maureen arrived, looking disheveled. She bit her lips, and her hands were unsteady. It was hitting her. She sat stiffly on the couch, refusing his offer of a drink, and then she nestled back into his arms.

"It was terrible," she said. "Just terrible. Those bastard cops! They were like the Gestapo."

"I'll put you to bed. Tuck you in."

"Why did that ninny spoil things by doing it *there*?"

Her eyes were narrow slits. She began to move against him, placing his hand between her legs and rubbing, kissing him hard and long, her mouth open, her tongue probing. She pulled him on top of her and took him inside without undressing, wrapping her legs around him and moving her hips rapidly, holding him strongly, gasping and sobbing. It was over for her quickly and she pulled away. She lay wetly against him.

"I'm alive," she said. "I'm going to do things tomorrow. I'm alive. The girl's dead, but I'm alive."

He held her. Soon she dropped off to sleep.

Drugs were not mentioned in the reports about the girl's death. He didn't tell Maureen about his call to Norwine until a week later, when they were in the Mercedes heading to the valley for dinner at Pam and Mike Thompsons'.

"Why Albert Norwine?" she asked. "I thought you hated him. Why not call Cyrus Masterson directly?"

"I can't afford to hate Norwine. He's got too much clout. So it was a buttering-up job. His nose is out of joint because of Masterson and me."

"Jealous?"

"You might say that."

"So Masterson is Mr. Fixit with the cops. That makes him handy to know."

"Favors call for return favors."

"Do you think you can stretch it enough to squeeze a few shekels from him for the Bradford campaign? Now that you've saved Marty from a drug-nest scandal, you're stuck with him."

"Oh, no. You are."

"The way you talk, you could squeeze anything out of that old man."

"You don't squeeze Cyrus Masterson. And he's not an old man. He was in WW Two."

"Isn't that old?"

"It's one of the reasons why I think he has high connections, perhaps CIA. He was in OSS in WW Two. Office of Strategic Services."

"I know what the OSS was."

"It was a forerunner of the CIA."

"Masterson *is* mob, isn't he?"

"No. He is not mob."

"What about the Phoenix story?"

"Talk. Talk I have to stop."

"But is it true?"

"No," Greg said. "Masterson might even be a federal narc, at least indirectly. He seems protected and he's certainly got influence."

"A good man to know."

"Know? I don't think his sainted mother knew that man."

He was slightly apprehensive about bringing Maureen to the Thompsons', but it worked out all right, although Maureen avoided the twins and caused the dog, Pepper, to be banished to the backyard. She was allergic to animals. After the rib roast dinner, they played some poker—five card stud, nothing wild. Maureen won most of the chips.

"Greg, take the girl to Vegas," Mike said.

"I'm chicken when it comes to real money," Maureen said.

"What d'you mean, real money? You raised a whole *dime* back then. Do you realize what a dime is to a wire service galley slave?"

Maureen had assumed a low-glamour pose for the evening, wearing slacks and just a dab of makeup. "I don't know how you do it, Pam. I mean, family and house and job, all that."

"The whole catastrophe," Mike said.

"A nice catastrophe," Maureen said, trying her best.

Greg drew Mike into his "poltergeist room," where he was working on a novel. There was an ancient L. C. Smith. Scrawled notes were tacked to and pasted on the walls. They crossed the carpet, sending up tiny flurries of dust, and sat on the floor facing each other.

"To old times," Mike said, extending his brandy glass.

"But not better ones, at least not for you. You have it made in the shade."

"Who's talking? I see your name in the papers, *president* no less."

"Emperor of ice cream."

"Don't knock it."

"Question. Honest answer?"

"Honest answer."

155

"What do you think of Maureen?"

"She's a good poker player."

"That's not an answer."

"You're serious about her."

"I'm in love, old buddy."

"Better to settle down and marry than be in love."

"Who's the cynic, you or me?"

Mike sipped brandy. "My opinion of Maureen is on hold. I don't know her. It's easy to see she's a beauty, though. And intelligent."

"I'm hooked on her. Gone. Helpless."

"An old party named W. Somerset Maugham once wrote a novel, *Theatre,* about a married actress in love with a much younger—and far inferior—man. But finally she falls out of love, and, after a triumphant performance, gorges herself with a rare good meal and beer. 'What is love compared with steak and onions?' she asks."

"I see. It doesn't mean a diddle. And Maureen is inferior to me."

"Now did I say that?"

"I think we ought to talk about something else, old buddy."

"Does your becoming president and office manager mean you'll be doing less for Cyrus Masterson?"

"I guess we're talking about something else."

"No comment? Do you know what you're called at AP and over at UPI, too?"

"Not the Legend."

"No Comment Gregory. That's what we newshawks call you."

"Good. Tell Masterson. I'll get a raise."

Mike put down his glass, crossed his legs, and regarded Greg with a wrinkled brow. "I'm not blaming you, because you do what you have to do, but I still think there's something to what Clay Dodson has been writing about your client. I talked with Dodson again, and—"

"Put in a good word for me, will you? I'm going to Phoenix to see him."

"When?"

"Dunno, not for sure. Soon."

"I'll set it up for you, if you like."

"Thanks, but I'd rather go in cold."

Mike shrugged. "You won't like what he's going to tell you."

"I don't pretend it's easy to work for Masterson. It's easier to walk a razor's edge. I'll tell you a couple things if you promise you won't use them, at least until I say you can."

"Well, I don't know, Greg. I hate off-the-record shit."

"Of course you do. But it's the only way I can give it to you."

"All right. Shoot."

"Cyrus Masterson is not into drugs."

"Sure. And he wasn't in Miami with Mr. Big. Clay Dodson, best-connected mob reporter in the country, runs with a story without checking things out. He's all wet."

"I can't say any more and I can't give you

157

reasons—not now—to back it up. But he's not into drugs. I'm going to tell you something else, old buddy mine. Now this is *really* off the record."

"Maybe I should have another brandy first."

"Maybe you should. Make it a double."

"Your story's that good?"

"Dunno. Maybe."

Mike left the room and returned in a few minutes with the bottle. "Pam and Maureen are doing okay," he said, pouring brandy over ice.

"You thought they wouldn't?"

"Well, no. I—"

"I did," Greg said. "Thought they wouldn't, I mean."

"You were saying."

"About Masterson, I was saying. I had dinner with him and his wife on the Fourth, at their place in San Marino. After dinner, he took me aside. Are you ready for this? We went down to the basement, and—"

A creaking door interrupted him and he looked over to see Jill and Ralph enter, sneaking. They were wearing nightgowns but didn't look at all sleepy. Greg usually brought them small presents when he came, like a sea captain uncle, but, better yet, he often played with them, something he enjoyed as much as they did. Both had been nagging him all evening. He decided on a small performance. He got down on his hands and knees and sniffed and snorted like a bear, absurdly comic, sending the twins on their backs in cherry-cheeked paroxysms of glee. They began to climb on his back, attacking the funny bear, choked with laughter. After five minutes of permitting it, Mike came over and hauled them off to bed, protesting and stomping. Then he came back, picked up his brandy glass, closed the door, and stood with his arms outstretched.

"Your story," he said. "You left me off in a basement."

"A crypt," Greg said.

"Did you say a crypt?"

"Masterson said those old houses typically had crypts or mausoleums built in to deposit their dead. I didn't buy that, but it hardly mattered. There was one before us, complete with a stone coffin with a carved name and date and an eternal flame."

"Ah!" Mike said, drinking. "*in pace Requiescat*!"

"I am kidding you not."

"Was there a cask of amontillado, too? Or a black cat?"

"No," Greg said. "He had his son there."

"Oh, Christ."

"The son died at sixteen. Overdose."

After a long pause, Mike said: "Are you sure he wasn't sort of putting you on? I mean, just to make a point?" His tone of voice was measured and very serious.

"I thought about that. But I believe Masterson."

"Did he say anything?"

Greg shook his head. "It was all show, no tell."

"Well, what is it you want me to say?" Mike said, pacing briefly. "That his implication to you was how could he possibly be in drugs, that terrible thing which caused the death of his son?"

"There was some more."

"What more?"

"I can't tell you, not even off the record. I've already talked out of school way too much."

"Have you? I wonder. Suppose Masterson wants you to spread the crypt tale around to the press, off the record. It implies he's clean."

"In other words, he's lying to me and using me."

"Greg, it has to be a thought."

"I don't think he is."

"Maybe because you want to think that way."

"Maybe."

"I see you're getting pissed at me now."

"Well, I *am* pissed, yes. I tell you things that could put my tit in a wringer and you react by telling me that I'm a naive jerk. A jerk and an asshole who flacks for a drug king."

Mike held up his arms, a stop signal. "I apologize."

"Forget it," Greg said, flashing his smile. "Just know I don't have to work for a drug lord."

"Again, my most humble apologies, sir."

"Apologize, pull out his eyes. Apologize, pull out his eyes. Behead the Dormouse! Suppress him! Off with his whiskers!"

"Fella, you're mad as the March Hare."

"So what did you boys talk about?" Maureen asked on the way home.

"Masterson."

"Oh? Your Masterson."

"I have to go to Phoenix."

"There was a song with that name, wasn't there?"

"It was a line in a song. 'When I get to Phoenix' or something like that, I think."

"Well, ten solid days ahead for me. Would you like to hear Reverend Jack at the Shrine? No, I didn't think so. How about a political speech? By the way, I'm talking to a potential client next week."

"Who?"

"Mark Ashley."

"He's with CAA, isn't he?"

"Not for publicity. He has nobody full-time for publicity. Just picture by picture from the unit publicist. Imagine, a star like him with no full-time representation."

"I don't want to talk about stars. I don't want to talk about business."

"What else?"

"Do you like your new apartment?"

"Love it."

"When am I going to see it?"

"Soon."

"What did you think of the Thompsons?"

"Square. But nice square."

"Twins and a dog and a mortgage. Would you want twins and a dog and a mortgage?"

"I don't have to answer that, do I?"

"How about going to Phoenix with me?"

"No chance. You know that."

"Okay. Maybe I'll take Denise Stevens."

"Who?"

"Denise Stevens. You see, Masterson is offering her to me. She was at our big dinner on the Fourth. Raving beauty. He investigates everything and he had his operatives look into you and found you wanting, so he offered me Denise Stevens in compensation."

"I don't think that's very funny, Greg."

"Don't tell me I've gotten a rise out of you."

"Is that what you're trying to do, get a rise out of me?"

"No. I just like to think I'd be missed a little if I go out of town, that's all."

"I'm not the tidy little wife like Pam with the station wagon and all. You know who I am."

"Let's stop this before it gets going."

She paused. Then she said: "Does he really investigate things? Masterson, I mean?"

"I'm sure he does."

"I'd hate that. I hate the thought of it."

"He's a careful man."

"This Denise Stevens you mentioned. Obviously she's his mistress."

"With his wife there at the same table?"

"Sure. He's Italian, isn't he?"

"I don't think so, as a matter of fact. I think he's French."

"Well, he's European. European mistresses sit at the same dinner table as the wife."

"I doubt that."

"What do you think she is?"

"His protégée."

"My ass. To use the euphemism, she's his mistress."

"What is it without euphemism?"

"Whore," Maureen said.

Mike and Pam stayed up almost until dawn, talking, which they used to do a lot before the twins were born.

"We're becoming nighthawks," Pam said.

"Greg was the nighthawk. He'd stay up all weekend and hit classes Monday morning bright-eyed and bushy-tailed."

"What did he do at night?"

"Oh, talk, philosophize, play poker."

"Maureen is the poker player."

"She cheats," Mike said.

"She does?"

"I saw her dealing from the bottom of the deck."

"In a penny ante game? Why?"

"I suppose she wants to win."

"If she cheats at cards she'll cheat elsewhere."

"You didn't like her at all, did you?"

"I tried. I don't dislike her. But I do like Greg. And I think there's troubled water ahead."

"Do you think she's using him?"

"He's not an easy mark to use."

"Well, when somebody like Greg falls, he falls hard."

"I see he loves her, all right. Worships her."

"Does she love him?"

"I don't think she has any concept of love."

"Well, anyone who uses those who offer faith or friendship or love has to pay for it in the end."

"Poetic justice?" Pam sniffed. "I wonder."

"I see it all as something potentially dangerous."

"How do you mean that, dangerous?"

"Greg meets this woman, Maureen, when he's been questioning himself about the job. She's him a decade or so ago, filled with ambition. So he tries to get back on his old road, fire up his ambition. Trouble is, his success depends solely on a man named Cyrus Masterson."

"Well, Greg is a big boy."

"I'm not so sure."

"He has a mind of his own, willpower. Didn't he beat cocaine?"

"I suppose he does have willpower. By the way, do you know what he told me about that chemical dependency clinic he was in? He said they made him wear diapers."

"Diapers? Heavens. Why?"

"A psychological reversion back to birth, or almost, to try and find out what made him vulnerable."

"Silly," Pam said.

"Well, it was government."

"Those psychologists," Pam said.

"I think Masterson is Greg's Mr. Hyde right now. Masterson may be mob."

"Don't say it. I get shivers."

"So do I," Mike said.

ELEVEN

Maureen stayed with him over the weekend but went back to her apartment on Sunday afternoon. She had brought work with her and wanted to finish it alone. Greg drew the line on bringing work home, although he often stayed late at the office and sometimes went in on Saturday. Now he lazed about, playing Brahms and rereading parts from one of his favorite books, Malory's *Morte d'Arthur*. But he couldn't concentrate. An idea came to him. He put it into motion quickly. Once he'd made the first phone call, in fact, the idea took on a life of its own.

The call was to a limousine service he used often. He ordered a white Cadillac, requested

James as driver, and told them to stock it well. Then he checked flight schedules and called Maureen, telling her something important had come up and asking her to meet him at ten. When the big Caddy rolled up to her at a bus stop and James, an imposing black man in uniform, got out and opened the door, Maureen hesitated and backed away. Greg pulled her in by the arm, kissed her, and put a glass of champagne into her hand, pinned an orchid corsage on her dress, and offered her a choice between strawberries with sugar and cream or caviar hors d'oeuvres, or both. She was overwhelmed, flabbergasted.

"Airport, James," Greg said.

"Where are we going?" Maureen asked.

"Vegas."

"Vegas? We have to work tomorrow!"

"That's tomorrow," he said.

At the terminal he asked James to wait, took her hand, and they raced for a plane. She sat silently in the plane, still in shock, all the way to McCarran Airport. They caught a taxi there for Caesars Palace and Greg led her directly to the roulette table. He got a thousand dollars in black chips—ten of them—and made a place for Maureen to sit, ordering champagne for her. He placed a chip on eight, and ten came up. He put two chips on eight, and two came up. Next he played three blacks, again on eight, and sixteen came up. Already a small crowd had gathered; you didn't often see a fool playing black chips on the sucker wheel.

Greg's next bet was four hundred, once again on eight. The spin seemed extraordinarily slow. Eight hit. The dealer paid out more than $12,000 to him while his audience cheered. Greg cashed it in, took Maureen's hand, rushed outside, hailed a cab back to McCarran, and slept on the flight back to LAX. James was waiting. It was 1:55 a.m.; the entire adventure had taken just under four hours.

"We'll split the loot," Greg said, eating strawberries in the limousine. "Thou for the limo, six bills for taxi, air fares, tips. Net, four thou each." He counted it out. "Buy yourself a hoop, kid."

"Well, don't think I won't take it. My daddy said never look a gift horse in the mouth."

"Good rule."

"Why did you play number eight?"

"It's the number of sections in *Morte d'Arthur*."

"You're crazy."

"Absolutely. And I always feel sexually inclined after strawberries."

"Oh, no. Wrong time of the month."

"Well, we'll stop at Thrifty's. Or make a baby."

"Oh, no again. I know all about diapers. Then it gets even worse. The babies grow into brats and potheads."

He seldom agreed with her views, yet he'd do almost anything to surprise or please her. Once when she said she liked yellow roses he filled the house with them for weeks. He stored his furniture after she made a remark about the bed and dragged her to Robinson's to pick out an entire new houseful. He also bought her gifts, mostly jewelry, which she accepted, if reluctantly, saying she preferred to earn her own luxuries and pamperings.

"You overdo," she said.

"Why not? Live fast, leave a handsome cadaver."

"Don't talk like that," she said, meaning it.

Greg moved into Tim Harte's old office and ordered a new sign painted in gold on the glass door of the suite:

ARTHUR GREGORY
President

He was in by eight on Monday, and about ten Maureen burst into his office, brushing past Marge and closing the door. "I want to say I'm sorry about something. I was bitchy when we were driving home from the Thompsons', and I'm sorry."

"You took a while to admit it."

"I am sorry."

"You made up for it later, especially after we stopped at the drugstore."

"Male chauvinist," she said, smiling. She stood before him, looking refreshed despite the late hours, tall and sensual and lissome, reminding Greg of a cat or a sunning panther. Her look was serious. "I envied the Thomp-

sons, I guess, in a funny way. I don't want
what they have, but still it's sometimes difficult for me because I know I could never have
those things."

"Why not?"

"Talk about it later. Got to run."

"Look, when you come in here next time,
knock. Okay?"

She gave him a mock salute. "Yes, sir.
Weekday slave."

"Well, we have to play it cool."

"Why? Even the termites here know we see
one another."

"Nevertheless, we play it cool."

"Yes, sir."

He buzzed Marge, apologized for Maureen's
brusqueness, and explained his door was
open, but not without an appointment or an
announcement.

Greg sat behind his desk, tapping a pencil.
The office was chilly, its white walls bleak and
empty. There were tiny nail holes where Tim
Harte's counterfeit memorabilia had hung.

Greg wasn't idle; if anything, he was over-
worked. He'd discovered a law of business: the
competent always are busy. Before, knowing
that Harte could only compound problems,
everyone had merely done their jobs. If they
made a mistake, they covered it up or suffered
for it. Now, knowing that Greg was competent, they brought everything to him for discussion or approval. As a result he was often
behind, and if mistakes occurred he could

blame only himself. The Heavyweight and the Planter crossed the hall with an abandon they'd never exhibited before. On the theory you assigned a job to a busy man if you wanted it done, Greg placed Sterne, who'd been a newspaper investigator, in charge of checking out employment forms.

"Why?" Sterne asked.

"Because I, your boss, say so."

"Her," Sterne said, scowling.

The Planter, as usual, was right. Greg had a fearful premonition that something would be discovered about Maureen, something he wouldn't like. He didn't know what, but was driven to find out. He *had* to know. He told himself to call Planter off the job, but he didn't.

He had hardly a minute to spare during the day. Account executives consulted him on minor problems. They wanted to go to lunch or dinner with him; they lingered to gossip, to flatter, to impress. Greg had budgets, office politics, new business, hiring to worry about. Meanwhile, he had his own client. Fortunately, Cyrus Masterson hadn't called.

Anderson and Piper phoned him almost daily. It wasn't uncommon for one to call and the other to follow minutes later. They never dialed directly, but contacted Mrs. Olsen, who buzzed Greg, a process that didn't enrapture Marge. She wanted an exclusive on him. Greg didn't blame her. She had enough to do without interference from Mrs. Olsen, whose calls had authority and priority. Marge and Mrs. Olsen no longer spoke to each other, crossing paths with icy eyes.

"Fire one of them," Maureen said.

"Mrs. Olsen I can't fire, Marge I don't want to."

"Then fire both."

"I said I can't do that."

"They're trouble-making kindergarten toddlers."

"Off with their heads?"

"Off with their heads!"

"You're in a sour mood. Worried, aren't you?"

She was. She had a premiere tonight at the Shrine Auditorium, a full production starring Reverend Jack. Looking into the red sun from their window table at the skyroom restaurant in the Transamerica Building, he saw the oval towers of the Shrine and the test flashes of searchlights. It was Reverend Jack's national debut, a show to be taped for television distribution. Tickets were eight dollars. A sellout would defray costs of production and advertising and cover initial fees for syndication, important because the ministry's main source of revenue was to be donations from television viewers.

Greg touched Maureen's hand. "Apropos of nothing, would you like to know why Anderson and Piper do not speak?"

"You're trying to relax me. Good. I can use some comic relief."

She smiled. It was still a nice smile. She had toughened with responsibility and work, becoming an efficient performer who seemed as infallible and dehumanized as a computer, in the process seeming to lose some of her femininity. But now she looked young and fresh, dressed in a tan suit, her eyes radiant blue, a dark curl over her forehead. He loved her to distraction.

"Yoo-hoo," she said. "Hello. Are you home?"

"Oh. Sorry. Well, Anderson started it. Then it grew and grew and here it is today, years later, still a total and foolish impasse."

"Tell me one thing first. Was a woman involved?"

"No."

"I didn't think so. Go on."

"When Anderson and Piper were in college they were on the crew at Harvard. Being Western barbarians, we have no concept of the importance of rowing as an Ivy League competition. Harvard's archrival, of course, is Yale."

He glanced at his watch, called the waiter and paid the check, and continued the story during the elevator's descent.

"Harvard had lost three years in a row to Yale, but had grown closer and closer, with almost the same crew, year after year. The

senior year was their last chance to beat Yale.
Anderson was in fit shape. But Piper got very
ill before the event and couldn't participate.
He was Harvard's best oarsman. And Harvard
lost the match by a half a length."

"That's it?" Maureen asked.

"Not quite."

They were waiting for his Mercedes in the
valet parking area. When it came, he drove
out on Grand before continuing.

"It seems that Piper had not really been ill.
He'd faked it. And then he'd bet on Yale."

"Oh, golly gee!" She giggled.

"Anderson didn't hear about it for a decade
or so, and by the time he got Piper to confess,
their business together was firmly established.
They never spoke again. Until this last trip to
Los Angeles, they hadn't seen each other for
twenty years."

"What is your source of information on
that?"

"I'd rather not say."

"Well, I know, of course. Harte."

"Could be."

"Well, who else?"

"It's true. It's so silly it has to be true. Yet
Piper once warned me not to believe Tim
Harte."

"True or not, you used the right word.
Silly."

"Maybe. But wouldn't it be rather a crush-
ing blow for an establishment stuffed shirt like

175

Anderson to find out his partner cheated and lied and was disloyal? It's rather like your wife had done those things."

"Maybe Anderson didn't have to do them and Piper had to in order to make the grade."

"Does that pardon him?"

"I think so," Maureen said.

She turned away, no longer interested in the matter. Her features were taut. Searchlights sprang into life in the street ahead. Maureen's concentration was total; she had a client with a show to put on.

It was a hit. Covering were newspapers, *Variety*, KFWB, KMPC, and Channels 2 and 7. The house was filled, in copious response to advertising and local TV appearances by the reverend. They cheered, gasped, applauded, stomped, wept, and trembled. Several women and two men fainted. Greg had to leave early, drawn away by an unexpected development, but later he would see footage taken by a crew Maureen had placed outside the auditorium to interview survivors after it was all over. Several declared it to be the best show in town, worth twice the price of admission. Some, pale and weak-kneed, confessed they were so frightened they could stand it no longer and so had fled the auditorium. Maureen had somehow arranged for a police horse patrol, which added to the color and lent an atmosphere of riotous intensity to the event. Several private ambulances began to appear at dark. They parked in a significant row, their attendants standing alertly by, and as the evening progressed they began to come and go, sirens blaring whether they had a patient or not.

Reverend Jack took Genesis 18 and 19 as his text. The topic was Abraham and his nephew, the good merchant Lot, and the destruction of the evil cities of Sodom and Gomorrah by the wrath of God. It was much more than a sermon. It was a spectacle. Reverend Jack, after the orchestra introduced him with a stirring rendition of "The Battle Hymn of the Republic," began slowly, a hushed audience in front, a mute angelic choir in back of him. He told how the Lord visited an elderly Abraham and his wife Sarah in the plains of Mamre and said Sarah would have a son, and that son would mark the beginning of a mighty tribe for Abraham. Now the choir dispersed unnoticed and a stage opened behind the reverend, and there was the figure of Abraham and in red light was the Lord. Other men appeared and in the far distance there were lights and noises of revelry from the city of Sodom. Four television cameras recorded the event as Reverend Jack continued his narration.

"And the Lord said, 'I will destroy Sodom and Gomorrah because there sin is very grievous.' But Abraham, knowing that Lot and his family lived in Sodom and knowing also that Lot was a good man, said, 'Wilt thou also destroy the righteous with the wicked? Peradventure there be fifty righteous within the city. Wilt thou also destroy and not spare the place for the fifty righteous that are therein?' And the Lord said, 'If I find in Sodom fifty righteous within the city, then I will spare all the place for their sakes.' And so Abraham then said, 'Peradventure there shall lack five of the fifty righteous. Wilt thou destroy all the city for lack of five?' And the Lord answered: 'If I find there forty and five, I will not destroy it.' "

The spotlight on Reverend Jack showed only his face and his hands, and when his face or hands moved, the spotlight moved with them so those parts of his body, and none other, were seen by the audience. On the stage behind him the colors shifted and twisted kinetoscopically; silent figures, etched in brilliant light, came and left, acting out the scene in pantomime, on occasion with the accompanying strains of the orchestra.

And the reverend continued: "And still Abraham spoke, although he feared the anger of the Lord: 'Peradventure there shall thirty be found there.' And the Lord said, 'I will not do it, if I find thirty there.' And then Abraham asked his Lord if Sodom would be spared if only twenty of the righteous were found there and again the Lord replied: 'I will not destroy it for twenty's sake.' And Abraham then said:

" 'Oh, let not the Lord be angry, and I will speak yet but this once. Peradventure ten shall be found there.' And the Lord replied: 'I will not destroy it for ten's sake.' "

The reverend's face was a chalky mask and his eyes blazed hotly, seeming to send out rays that found the eyes of everyone in the audience. He did not speak to all; he spoke to each. Mothers reached out for their children, men nervously tapped their shoes on the floor, old women fell to their knees, young dating couples clung to each other. The stage dissolved in a dazzling display of lights to a scene in Sodom—drinking and robbery and rape and murder, lawless anarchy. Reverend Jack continued his dramatic narration. Hearing that Lot was befriending strangers— actually, they were angels disguised as men who had come to warn Lot of the city's impending destruction—a mob advanced on his house, ordering him to give up his visitors to capture and torture. But Lot, of course, wouldn't surrender his guests. The mob howled for blood. Then an eerie silence fell among them, followed by a frightened murmur. On stage the mob dispersed with shrieks of terror, leaving only its leaders, three men who writhed on the ground in agony, hands over their eyes. Blood oozed between their fingers. They took away their hands. Their palms were red and their eyes were hollow sockets. They had been blinded.

The audience gasped. They felt a part of it.

Again the scene shifted. Lot and his wife and two daughters were seen preparing to flee

Sodom to Zoar, where they had been promised sanctuary. Lot did not want to leave Sodom, his home for many years, and he could save the city if he found ten righteous people. He dashed about, searching. But no one, even his sons-in-law, would listen to him; they mocked him and sneered. Morning—and doom—was not far off. Lot returned to his family, disconsolate and defeated; he had failed to find ten righteous persons in Sodom, which meant the end.

Said Reverend Jack to his spellbound listeners: " 'And when the morning arose, then the angels hastened Lot, saying, Arise, take thy wife, and thy two daughters, which are here, lest thou be consumed in the iniquity of the city.' "

On the stage, Lot moved slowly, hesistant to leave.

"While he lingered, still unsure, the angels who came in the form of men took his hand and the hand of his wife and the hands of his daughters and led them, with the mercy of the Lord, from the city. And when the family had been brought forth, in the red of the morning sun, one of the angels said to Lot:

" 'Look not behind thee, lest thou be consumed.' "

The stage was red, the beginning of the end for the doomed cities along the Salt Sea, the twin evil cities of Sodom and Gomorrah. The audience felt the impending doom, and each member squirmed nervously with remem-

bered sins; their city, like many others, with
its drugs and painted women and dark-alley
crimes and lust and adultery was another
Sodom, another Gomorrah, and retribution
no doubt was to come.

Then the pyrotechnics exploded.

It was earthquake and hurricane, tidal wave
and fire; the sky and the ground opened,
swallowing up and splitting asunder. Flames
and blue-smoked sulfur and brimstone
poured from the heavens. The lake boiled and
overflowed, a great steaming mass that
scalded the screaming people with walls of
water.

The auditorium trembled, as if an actual
earthquake had struck. On stage steam
gushed from hot waterfalls and geysers. Explosions boomed from the walls and floors
and ceilings. There were gasps and screams. A
woman left, running down the aisle, weeping
in fear, followed by several others. But only a
few were frightened away. The rest remained
entranced, caught in a form of mass hypnotism. On stage Lot's wife, fleeing behind her
husband and daughters, paused fatally to
glance back, defying the angel's warning.
Lightning sizzled down. Before the eyes of the
gasping onlookers, she was transformed into a
pillar of salt. Suddenly the auditorium was
quiet. It was dark. The beam of a spotlight
flickered and Reverend Jack's face appeared,
pale and disembodied. He held up his hands,
hushing the murmuring crowd, and when the

silence was absolute he spoke, faintly yet clearly:

"The Lord can forgive, and cleanse, just as He can destroy the wicked. Are there here in this place tonight ten who would be cleansed? If there are, please now raise your hands—" The lights came back on, faintly. "—so we might know who you are, ye lambs that are lost but would be found this evening, found and saved."

Ten hands went up. Twenty.

The faint light held. The choir had returned and it was singing softly, ever so softly. "Home, come home, ye who are weary, come home, come home."

Reverend Jack said gently, "And would then you who have raised your hands come forward and kneel before the altar and be saved by the blood of the lamb and for the glory of the Lord who forgives and saves?"

Twenty came forward. Thirty and forty, fifty and a hundred. They formed rows around the curved altar three and four and then five deep—men and women, young and old, some infirm on crutches, some with children, many of them weeping, sobbing openly, a few wailing in fear and joy.

The sweet choir voices murmured: "Jesus is waiting and tenderly watching, ye who are weary come home, come home . . . tenderly watching, saying O sinner come home, come home."

Greg, in the fifth row from the front, aisle

seat in the middle section, watched and listened with fascination. Someone tapped his shoulder and he glanced back, hesitating as he thought of the deadly pause that had reduced Lot's wife to a pillar of salt. Behind him stood Willard Sterne, the Planter, twitching anxiously. He wore a raincoat despite the fact it was dry outside, and he hadn't removed his hat in deference to the reverend's temple. The show was over and the crowd was beginning to leave except the few hundred at the front who had been saved. They were receiving personal handshakes of congratulations on their new lives by Reverend Jack, accompanied by the tearful support of others, the faint strains of the orchestra, and the hum of the choir.

The Planter bent down to rub his gouty foot, straightened up and winced, groaned and scowled. "The Heavyweight's got himself pinched," he said, sniffing at the triumphant reverend.

"What?"

"Hank's in the slammer."

"On what charge?"

He shrugged. "Dunno. Not 502. He doesn't drive."

"I have to take Maureen back to her car."

"Oh, I'll take her, old chap," said a voice. Mark Ashley stood smiling. He wore a black leather jacket and a red beret, a disguise so casual and perfect that he wasn't recognized. "She sent me a ticket. Good stuff, this God business. That preacher nearly had me walking the plank to salvation." He winked. "Go on, old chap. I'll get her home. I always get the girl, y'know."

He was obviously high, yet Greg decided to leave. To hell with Maureen. She was a big girl, as she often reminded him. He drove out of the parking lot, Sterne beside him, feeling a little giddy. The show had an aftershock. Greg checked his service for calls. Albert Norwine was trying to reach him. The Mercedes broke free of traffic and rolled at sixty through the Third Street tunnel.

"Planter, what do you think about women?" he asked.

"Women? I think they're the opposite sex."

"You are brilliantly and originally creative."

"A woman," said Planter, "is a riddle wrapped in a mystery inside an enigma. If a nation is to prosper, it must keep its women pregnant and downtrodden. Look what that has done for Japan."

"What do you think about love?"

"Love? Well, a woman doesn't do that. A woman is too smart for that. They have to be on the watch or they get crushed, and if you're in love you can't be on the watch."

"What d'you think about God?"

"God? There might have been a god at one time, way back, but not now. They say God is dead, and I believe that. God died when he shit out the world. It was just too big a shit for anybody to take."

Greg laughed, but Sterne sat seriously, Buster Keaton straightface on his features. At the Rampart police station they unhooked their seat belts and got silently out, walking up the steps in the warm air of the night. Greg asked the desk sergeant if they were holding a Henry Frost. The sergeant was fat and red-faced, bald with tufts of white hair, and he took his time looking up the matter.

"Yeah, little guy, Henry Frost," he said.

"What's the charge?"

"We're holding him on indecent exposure."

"On what?"

"Indecent exposure, like I just said."

"What did he do?"

"It don't say here. I ain't got in his report yet."

Greg asked to see the Heavyweight and was taken into a white, windowless room with a table and two chairs while the Planter waited by the desk outside. Soon Henry Frost was ushered in by a big cop in uniform. He sat down. The cop stayed.

"Well, what's it all about?" Greg asked, seating himself opposite Frost.

"How'd the big show go?" Frost asked.

"Just fine. How much of that was your responsibility?"

"I help out, that's all."

"Do you want to tell me why you got yourself pinched?"

"I don't mind explaining it to you. I couldn't explain it to the cops. Did you ever meet a cop who's read a book? I like to read, so I go into bookstores a lot. So I went into this store tonight on my way down to the Shrine to take in the big show. I looked around. The more I looked, the more pissed I got. It was a bookstore full of junk. Crap. Fancy covers, nothing inside. I got to thinking. This is people today. Fancy covers, nothing inside. I got so mad I whipped out my dick and pissed all over the so-called books."

"Oh, God."

"It was worth it."

"Oh, God!"

The Planter, being a former reporter with connections, knew an ex-fighter, a Mexican named Romano, who was a bail bondsman and who, like the Heavyweight, slept in his office. They went and woke him up.

"What's the bail for pissing on books?" Greg asked.

"Ain't no bail for that I know about," Romano said seriously, yawning and scratching his head. He had a flat nose and red knobs for ears. "It sounds pretty serious to me, though. What kind of books was they?"

They got the Heavyweight out on five thousand bail and took him home, which was the office. The cops said they'd let him know when he had to appear for arraignment. They advised him to get a good lawyer, one who could read. Ha-ha. The Planter said he'd keep it out of the papers.

"Tell me, O Planter," said Greg, suddenly in a good mood, "how do you keep things out of the papers?"

"It's my secrets that keep my job for me."

"Oh, you can tell me."

"I give 'em tickets to the opera," Planter said.

"How do you get things *into* the papers?"

"Well, I pay by the inch."

The Heavyweight said: "Wiseass cops. A lawyer that reads! I don't need a lawyer. I'm sure the judge will see it my way if I explain. Pissing on the books they got out today isn't a crime."

Both he and the Planter spoke deadpan, but Greg laughed so hard he almost drove the Mercedes off the road. After they left the Heavyweight off, the Planter decided to take advantage of the boss's mood and handed him a typed report about his employee investigations. He forecast that Greg would not find it light reading.

"Just tell me," Greg said.

"Naw, I'd rather not."

"C'mon, Willy! Tell me."

"You don't want to hear it."

Greg stopped the Mercedes and glared at Sterne. "What don't I want to hear?"

"Well, it's about Maureen Crawford."

"What about her?"

"You take it home, read it."

"Tell me."

Sterne paused. "Awright, but you asked for it."

"Go ahead. I asked."

"Well, she said she finished Stanford and UCLA, master's at UCLA. She didn't finish either one. She attended classes at both, that's all. She never did graduate. And—"

"And what? C'mon."

"She got booted out at Stanford."

"Why?"

"Read it."

"Goddammit, Willy, *tell* me, for Christ's sake!"

"Well, she got booted out because . . . eh, er . . . well, because she was caught selling herself, a sideline to make her tuition money."

Greg saw black. He fought for control. Then he lost it. He reached out and grabbed the lapels of Sterne's coat and pinned him against the car door.

"You're lying, you bastard. You're *lying!*"

"It's God's truth, Greg."

"Who did you tell?"

"Nobody. You know that."

"You did this because you wanted to blackmail me into a job. You're a scared, old guy. You'd do it to keep your job."

"No."

"Oh, shit."

He let Sterne go. He sat with his fingertips absently running over his forehead, wanting to cry, wanting to scream.

"Well, shit," he said.

"I didn't tell nobody," Sterne said. "You know that."

"Sure."

"I'm sorry. We forget about it."

"Sure," Greg said.

TWELVE

He felt a yearning to see his son, so he phoned Marie, his former wife, and asked her if he could pick up Rob.

"Of course," she said. "When?"

"Now."

"Now? It's almost midnight. He's asleep."

"I want to take him with me to Arizona. The airplane is warming up on the runway."

"Greg, you're not—?"

"No. I'm clean and sober. You know that. I know it's crazy, but will you wake him up and have him ready in a half hour?"

There was a pause and he knew she was consulting with her new husband, a doctor. She came back on the line.

"Well, I suppose it's all right. I know he'd be anxious to go. How long will you be gone?"

"Not very long."

"He shouldn't miss much school."

"School's out, isn't it?"

"He's going to summer school."

"How did he do in the tests?"

"They were a breeze for him."

"I thought as much. Everything is a breeze for him."

"That's what worries me," Marie said.

He picked up Rob and they headed through Santa Monica and Marina del Rey toward the airport. Rob had brought a large suitcase, undoubtedly packed by Marie.

"You won't need anything you brought," Greg said. "We're going to buy new stuff. Expense account, man."

"Well, I'll wear what I brought. Donate the expense money to the Indian cause."

"Is that your latest cause? Indians?"

"It's just that I don't need clothes."

"What you need is to have some fun. We'll find a park with a merry-go-round in Phoenix. Just like we used to."

"Aw, that's kid stuff, Dad."

"Maybe you need some kid stuff. Maybe I do. Remember when we'd watch the kid shows on TV? The guy would sing, 'Anybody here got an aardvark, anybody here got an aardvark?' You'd bundle up into a little ball of laughter, all red-cheeked and shrieking." Greg was just warming up. He spoke so rapidly he had to gasp for breath. "Remember when we were at the Dodgers game and Yogi Berra was there and he shook your hand and said to you, 'Make the majors, kid'?"

"Yeah, me in the majors, that's a joke all right."

"We could go back from Phoenix through Vegas and take a drive down the Strip at night and then rent a car and come back through Death Valley. Eat a rattlesnake at Scotty's. We could stop at the Bonnie and Clyde death car and at the Calico Ghost Town."

"Aw, Dad," Rob said.

"What I need is to get a farm and get you on it. We'd have horses and dogs. We'd have a spotted pinto horse. Everything would be okay then."

He was a good-looking boy, freckled and brown-haired like his mother, and had her pleasantness and forbearance. Greg felt a longing for Marie, for their times of happiness together, laughing and crying, he finishing school then, she working nights at the hospital. They'd had a small apartment with hot water often tepid at best and a leaky roof. Marie caught rainwater in pots and washed her hair in it. It had been a love marriage, a hopeful one.

A husky black chauffeur was waiting for them when the Jetstar landed at Sky Harbor Airport in Phoenix, taking them to their hotel in a Cadillac limousine. The city smelled of desert, hot and dry, and had a spaciousness

193

that suggested freedom. Rob went right to bed in his room while Greg in his lay back and tried not to think. Masterson had ordered him here, through Norwine. His marching orders were unspecified, but he knew what they were. Stop Dodson. He wouldn't think about it, not now. He dialed Maureen and counted the rings; at ten, he hung up. Hell with it. Hell with her.

Early in the morning, after a fitful rest, he called the office, the switchboard number, and Maureen answered.

"Well, you're in early," he said.

"Tell me. That's my yawn you hear."

"I'm in Phoenix. I was summoned last night. Sorry I couldn't wait for you after the performance."

"We call it the ministry."

"I tried to call you last night. Well, this morning, I mean. Early."

"Well, we were out most the night. I got about two hours, that's all." Her voice rose excitedly. "It was a smash hit, beyond all our expectations. It's almost unbelievable. We're going on the *road* with it. You ought to see the clippings. I mean, it's like *movie* reviews."

"No backlash?"

"What d'you mean, blacklash?"

"Well, it is a religious subject."

"I know it's a religious subject. That's how it's being treated, a new way to reach people at revival meetings. Reverend Jack, almost overnight, is a new sensation as a religious leader. I came in early on purpose, in case there were any calls from the East. You see, AP picked it up. It's all over the country. And there *were* calls. I think I could book him on twenty talk shows, right today."

She paused, out of breath.

He said: "I love you."

"Oh! Something else! This is even more exciting. I can hardly believe it. Are you ready?"

"I guess I am."

"Mark Ashley is considering signing with us!"

"Oh."

"You don't sound very excited."

"How close is he?"

"He's pretty close. And, I might add, so is T. D. Desmond. I had a long talk with both of them last night. We closed the Polo Lounge up and then went to his place."

"Whose? Desmond's?"

"We all went to Mark's place. I couldn't *imagine!* He has not five, not seven, but *eight* bathrooms!"

"Was he high?"

"No. Not at all."

"He was when I saw him at the Shrine."

"He was cold sober. He was serious. Greg, he's really a sad man, down deep. At one point he even cried. Honestly."

"Maybe I'd better bring the Closer in on this one."

"Don't you dare. This one is mine."

195

"Have Marge call me when she comes in," he said.

He had work to do, and he vowed to himself that he would not think about Maureen until his job had been completed. Thinking about her produced only anger, frustration, and longing. He looked up Dodson's number.

"So you got here," Dodson said, answering on the first ring.

"You've been expecting me?"

"Sooner or later you had to come by. You represent my top target."

"Mike Thompson says hello."

"Hello to him. Come out to see me." Dodson gave instructions. "Can't miss it."

"My son is with me. May I bring him?"

"Course. I got a packet of kids."

A chauffeured limousine wouldn't impress Dodson, so Greg rented a Ford Bronco. The heat slapped at them as they left the hotel; it seemed to attack, curling and snapping. Waves rose in visible, undulating layers and the sand whirled with miniature brown geysers. The sun was a caldron, white-hot and merciless, but the natives relished it. They walked briskly, ignoring patches of shade; they played enthusiastic tennis and golf. Greg headed the Bronco north. A mile out of town, surrounded by a desert of brown sand and saguaro cactus reaching up like dry old men, he turned by a red mailbox.

Rob, who'd been listless, had revived. "Phoenix, from the Greek *phoinix*, or crimson; also, French *phoinos*, blood red; or, Greek, *phonous*, murder. The phoenix is the mythological bird of the ancient Egyptians burned up in a fire only to rise from its ashes, youthful and reborn.''

Clay Dodson lived with his family on five acres of sand dotted with cactus plants, tall and erect like guards. The wind stirred the sand into a gray fog that obscured the buildings, clearing as the Bronco neared them. A cactus garden and green lawn fronted the house, with a patio and swimming pool to one side. The other buildings were scattered—a red barn, unpainted shacks, pumphouse. Chickens and goats roamed loose. Dogs swarmed around the Pinto, barking symphonically and nipping its tires. A tall man in a Dodger baseball cap strolled over.

''Hiya,'' he said to Rob, peeking in. He handed him his cap. ''Go out back of the house there. I got a whole team playing.''

Rob did as ordered. Kids began to peep furtively around the corner of the house, mostly boys, red-haired and freckled, like the man. He looked like a scarecrow or a clown, with a perpetual grin and red cheeks. He wore dirty shorts, ragged tennis shoes, and a T-shirt with the lettering S.F. SUCKS. He reminded Greg of the terrain—sandy yet rugged, hard to wear down, like the boulders.

''What do I call you?'' he said, petting a dog.
''Greg.''
''Well, Greg, I know you're going to have to

197

lie to me, so we can get that out of the way now. You're too intelligent to tell the truth."

"I don't know whether to be flattered or insulted."

"I'll show you what I have on your boss. But let's chow down first. What d'you think of the place?"

"I'm reminded of Ma and Pa Kettle's farm."

"My Pa built the house. I added on when the kids came. Pa was part Indian and he'd keep scalps in the basement."

"You're putting me on."

"We got swamp coolers. N.g., but you get used to the heat. I work in that shack over there with nothing but a fan. How's Mike Thompson?"

"Mike is fine. You shift conversation like someone else I know."

"Masterson? Speaking of, who is that Norwine?"

"A lawyer."

Dodson's grin widened. "That much I know. I had an uncle who was a lawyer, but he's recovering now, going straight."

"Ah, ah, you're generalizing."

"Guilty," Dodson said, raising his hand. "And because your man Masterson is mob doesn't mean Hollywood is mob. Where does Masterson the mouthpiece get his slime from?"

"I guess it's hereditary."

"We'll get along, you and I."

Lunch was tacos and beans, laced with a hot sauce that cleaned sinus passages, watered eyes, and could steam up ears. The Dodson kids pranced and laughed uproariously, a couple of them even rolling on the floor like drunken chimpanzees as Greg gasped and snorted, trying to swallow. Apparently it was a family tradition to asphyxiate strangers with the red acid for the amusement of the kids. Greg played it to the hilt, hamming it up, waving and wheezing. It doubled the convulsions of his torturers. But Rob ate four hot tacos without reaction, puzzling the fun-loving imps, and then contrived to take his father aside.

"Dad, I can't play baseball like they do. They call me a city kid."

"They don't mean it. Why don't you try?"

Rob was taking it all very seriously. He was almost in tears. "Gee, Dad, why can't I be like other kids?"

"I guess it's my fault. I should have played baseball with you."

Rob set his chin. "Maybe I'll show 'em."

"Sure, you bet," Greg said, making a fist and tapping the boy's chin.

Clay Dodson's wife was as friendly and easy to know as Dodson himself, or his kids. She was half Indian, half Mexican. He called her Mother, a name she responded to no matter who used it. She was thin and flat-faced, with Mongolian cheeks and eyes and slim strong hands, beautifully tapered. Her hair was raven black, thick and straight, very long. Her hands and hair attracted, but it was her eyes that held. They were benign and pleasant eyes, almost as dark as her hair, but they also seemed sad and distant, as if she looked not at but beyond. She was open and cheerful, yet there was something stoic in her demeanor, foreboding or fatalistic, an opacity like the distant gathering of storm clouds. It was difficult to tell her age. Greg guessed she was in her mid-forties. The youngest child was about four, the eldest fourteen or so.

"How many kids do you have?" Greg asked Dodson as they walked to the work shack.

"Dunno. The tax collector might know."

"You like to put on strangers, don't you?"

Dodson counted on his fingers. "Well, there's Tom, Hank, Missy, Glory, Maryanne, Howie, Lettie, Timmy. Two that died, two boys. That makes ten. It's probably enough. Here's my office." He jerked his thumb, the perpetual smile widening. "Over there is Mother's studio. She paints when she has time. She's good."

His office-shack was partly garage, housing two black Ford pickup trucks and a red Farmall tractor. A whining fan drove away the heat. The equipment was modern—word processor, printer, copier, fax, phone with message box. But the couch and chair looked diseased with age, spilling their cotton insides through gaping holes. Coiled springs stuck out. Dodson sat down in the chair, motioned Greg to the couch, and took two Coor's from an ice bucket. Greg shook his head no. Three dogs wandered in, their tongues hanging out, and found shade near the desk. Dodson opened a can of beer, drank, and sighed deeply.

"Cyrus Masterson is mob and he's big in drugs, maybe Mr. Big in the West," he said, smiling. "Everything else is cover-up. It's laundry. The bank, the movie interest. Money washers."

"The trouble with you mob watchers is that you see mob under every rock."

Again the smile. "As a matter of fact, I look for the best in people. You look for the best in a man and usually you'll find good men. You look for the worst and you'll find bad ones. I looked for the best in Masterson but I didn't find much that's good."

"He might do certain things that make him appear suspicious, but he has his reasons."

"You're referring to the dodge that he's undercover CIA, counterspyish."

Greg didn't flinch. "CIA? That's a new one."

"Oh? Well, I said you'd have to lie to me."

"Behind that smile, you're pretty tough and blunt."

The phone sounded and Dodson chattered on it for a few minutes. "My lawyer," he said, hanging up. "Finally I'm having a will made.

White man's law no understand by Injun. I came to the conclusion, after long study, that nobody lives forever."

"Myself, I'm going to beat the rap. Or die trying."

"Best of luck. As for me, I shall go to the happy hunting grounds at age one-ought-five, like my Pa before me. You want to know if I get death threats."

"Did I ask that?"

Dodson bent the Coor's can and flipped it into a container by the tractor. "Two points," he said. His eyes narrowed to blue slits and he sat pensively. "No, I never had a death threat. They only kill each other, as you no doubt have heard. And I have an insurance policy. I'm sure they know about it. Do you?"

"No, I'm afraid I don't."

"I have a series of articles all set to go if something happens to me. The lead is 'I wanted to live, embrace the love of life, but they would not allow me to live. Now I name my murderers.' Corny, eh?"

"No, not corny. Not at all."

The fan whirred and from outside came the shrieks of the kids. Dodson said: "You want to know if Masterson is among my murderers."

"I know he's not," Greg said, standing up. "Frankly, this is a little bizarre and grotesque for me."

"Masterson isn't his real name, you know."

"Many people change their names."

"True. So it means nothing that his real

name is Alberto Cervi, and although born in Corsica he's Italian, roots in Sicily. Has he ever told you his war stories?"

"I've heard him allude to the war."

"Then you may know that in the Second World War he was sent by Mussolini fascists to the Balkans to recruit Albanian and Yugoslavian saboteurs for the campaign against Greece." Dodson laughed, slapping his knee. "Once he recruited a few hundred Albanians, paid them, and they cut out. He never forgot that."

"What else?"

"Not much I'll talk about. After the Italians gave it up, our OSS recruited him as a sort of counterspy. At this point, he becomes a shadow. But I've filled in some of the blanks. It's all in my insurance policy. I have two files, one in my head and the other on my floppy disk."

"What do you propose to do?"

"Well, how about an interview with Masterson? With Howard Huges dead, I can't think of anyone I'd rather interview than Cyrus Masterson."

"I'll put you on the list."

"That's what you tell all the girls." Dodson flashed his grin. One of the dogs came over, an old one too exhausted by the heat to scratch for fleas. Dodson scratched for him; the dog lay down and whimpered with pleasure. "Since you came to me, obviously you have a message from Masterson. What?"

"He's not mob. He's not into drugs."

"Is that for the record? I can quote?"

"Yes."

"Anything else?"

"Well, did you know he had a son?"

"Yes, I did know that."

"And that his son died of a drug overdose?"

"I'd heard that."

"Would a man whose only son died of a drug overdose engage in the drug trade?"

"It's a hard world, Mr. Gregory."

"Greg."

"Your Mr. Masterson is a man of contrasts. He was responsible for thousands of deaths in the war yet he's a pacifist, he goes to High Mass every Sunday and tithes and gives millions to charity each year yet he's a member of a criminal element, his son o.d.'d on H and died yet the old man is one of the leading drug dealers on the West Coast." Dodson stood up. He crammed his hands deep in his pockets and grinned broadly, again assuming a boyish, clownish appearance. "But let's forget it. We're wasting each other's time. Stay for supper. Maybe we can become friends, anyway."

"I wish I could convince you."

"Greg, you're not convinced yourself."

"Oh, yes I am."

"No. Ask Mother. She can read people. The Indian eye. I have it, too. It tells me you're a good man in a lousy job. You'd be happier free of it."

"So I've been told before. But I can't walk away."

"I know," Dodson said. "That's the hell of it, right?"

Greg turned away. "No comment."

"I know Masterson won't give a personal interview and I can't say I blame him. Suppose I write down some questions and you show them to him? If he wants to answer, fine; if he doesn't, okay then too. Is that fair enough?"

"All right. Fair enough."

They went outside. The sun had softened, now showing the gold-red of afternoon. Dogs raced down the driveway, barking in a swirl of sand, their target the unperturbed mailman who had stopped at the red box. Dodson would say very little more about himself or his work. He'd ventured as far east as Missouri, graduating from the university's journalism school, and had been a staff writer on papers in Tucson and Flagstaff before coming to Phoenix, where he'd been promoted from the police beat to investigative reporting and eventually become a specialist in organized crime. Now he was a free-lancer with a national reputation. "Heap big success for Injun," he'd say, making fun of it. But he was proud of his heritage. "Shoshonean," he said. "Mother's part Yuman. You can find remnants of dozens of clans in Arizona and New Mexico—Tanoan, Keresan, Zunian, Piman, Athapascan. That's a few. You can find fifty

205

languages, different as Greek is to Japanese. And don't think we can't evil eye."

"I'm sure of it."

He showed Greg his wife's paintings, canvases of varying sizes strewn about her "studio," a shack like Dodson's office. Most were desert and Indian scenes; all of them, Greg thought, were remarkable. He particularly liked one of an Indian girl kneeling in prayer under a blazing sun. The sand looked hot, as if it would burn if touched.

"Homo sapiens prays, God laughs," Dodson said.

"It's magnificent."

"Well, then it's yours."

"Oh, I couldn't do that."

"Sure you can. It's family tradition here to give away what our guests like. Why do you think I keep my tractor hidden? I'll have Mother touch it up a little for you. She can frame it for you, too."

"I insist on paying for it."

"You talk to her about that."

Mother came out of the house and motioned to them. She led them to an area in back of the pool where a half-dozen of the kids, Rob among them, lay groaning in agony. At first Greg thought they were faking, that it was a game, but soon it became clear they weren't. Their faces were pale, almost greenish; clearly they were sick kids. He knelt down beside Rob.

"What is it?"

"Dad, I'm going to die." Rob gasped for breath. His face was almost white. "I did it . . . my fault—"

"Did what?"

Dodson let out a loud laugh, his head back. He examined his kids—half of them were down, the other half had scattered—by rolling them over with his foot. Dogs came by, snooping curiously. Again Dodson laughed. His wife joined in the laughter.

Finally Dodson said: "They'll be okay. They'll be sick awhile, but they'll be okay."

"But what's wrong with them?" Greg asked.

"They've been smoking loco grass. It's the way an Indian gets high. Only, the first couple times you try it, you get sicker'n a dog."

"Should they have a doctor?"

"Naw. They'll be fine, come morning. Mother here knows how to fix 'em up. You leave Rob here overnight, she'll fix 'im up."

"No, I don't think I'd better do that."

"Why? I'll be working half the night on those questions. You can come out here and get them in the morning and pick Rob up then."

"Well, I don't know."

"For the uninitiated, that stuff doesn't wear off right away."

"What is it?"

"Poison," Dodson said. "A hellebore. Eat enough of it outright, you die a thousand deaths. Iguanas love it for dessert. So do Gila monsters. How they get their poison, eating it."

"Oh, Clay!" Mother said.

Dodson grinned. His casualness minimized the seriousness of the sickness, but Rob continued to plea for a merciful execution. Mother forced the afflicted kids to vomit and gag down some foul-smelling white liquid she heated in a pan on the stove. Then she settled them down to sleep.

"You have ways," Greg said.

"Yes."

"I've always wanted something like this. Kids and animals, a place to roam."

"Then you will have it," Mother said, her dark eyes steady.

"Just like that?"

"If you want it badly enough, you'll have it. Good men find contentment."

"Will I?"

"No one should know their future."

One of the Dodson clan, the boy named Howie, who was unaffected by the loco weed, stuck his head between his father's legs and peered at Greg. "Baxbakualanuchsiwae," he said, ducking away and giggling uncontrollably.

Dodson captured the boy and hoisted him high on his shoulders. Howie's cheeks turned bright red and he laughed so hard his body curled into a little ball.

"Scat," Dodson said, lowering him and slapping his rump. "Go play with the other Gila monsters." He looked at Greg, his face split in a grin. "Baxbakualanuchsiwae," he said, and began to giggle himself. "You spell it b-a-x-b-a-k-u-a-l-a-n-u-c-h-s-i-w-a-e. Take the middle part, l-a-n-u-c-h, and take out the 'a' in there and transpose a bit and what do you have? L-u-n-c-h."

Howie returned, scooting, and rolled on the floor in glee. Mother shooed him away once again.

Dodson said: "It means something like 'Man who eat human flesh at the beginning of the river.' It's the Kwakiutl name for cannibal spirit. You see we redskins got our mobs, too. Secret societies. Call it the Red Hand." Dodson paused to laugh. "One of the mobs was the cannibal mob. They used to eat people, too, the brains and livers and everything."

"They didn't!" Mother said. "Ugh!"

"What's for supper?" Dodson asked.

Rob slept next to his fellow miscreants for almost two hours and awoke wobbly legged. The sun fell, painting the desert with its fat red fingers. The alive sand shifted and crawled. Greg was reluctant to leave, as if held under a spell. Supper was tacos again, free of hot sauce, a clan gathering to eat and laugh and joke. Rob turned from green to pink. Then Mother told her story, an eagerly anticipated event at tribe Dodson. She spoke from a chair, her eyes unmoving, her voice soft and hypnotizing.

"The spirit Olelbis, creator of man, took such pride in his creation he didn't want it to die. So he had the eagle Hus build two fountains at Olelpanti in the sky. One was for bathing, external life, the other for drinking, internal life. Men and women from earth journeyed to that place, Olelpanti, to drink and become young. But the journey was long, taking a lifetime, and people who left Olelpanti young were aged when they returned to earth. So, desiring youth, they were obliged to go back immediately to Olelpanti.

"Now on earth was a powerful lawmaker, Sedit the Coyote. A thinker, he reasoned this was not good. Life was only strife, an endless journey. So he ordered Hus to destroy the fountains, declaring: 'Joy at birth and grief at death are better, for this means love.' Hus responded: 'But then you, too, Sedit, will die and lie forever in the ground, never to wear your headband of beaver skin or carry your quiver of arrows with its designs of great beauty.' Sedit the thinker saw that. But his order had been given. There was no changing it. Lawmakers sometimes forget their rules are for all. The path to Olelpanti was closed, guarded by hawks. Sedit then made himself wings of the feathers of the bluejay, red feathers of the woodpecker, and of sunflower blossoms. He tried to fly to Olelpanti. But the blossoms withered and the feathers fell and he plummeted to his death. 'He is killed by his

own law, his words,' said Hus. That was the
beginning of death."

"A real laugher, your story," Dodson said.
"Give that to Ingmar Bergman to film. Eh,
Greg?"

"I thought it was a beautiful story," Greg
said.

"Children, remember only the flesh died,"
Mother said. "The spirit of man remains. It is
immortal."

She looked very serious.

When Greg and Rob finally did leave, late in
the night, the clan accompanied them to the
Bronco, including the dogs, who wanted parting nips at the tires. Mother said she'd framed
the painting and wrapped it. One of the boys
had put it in the back of the Bronco.

"Will you bill me?" Greg asked.

"No. It's a gift. When you give to a charity
or help someone in some manner, then think
of that as payment."

"All right. I will."

"Use it well."

"I don't understand."

"What knowledge you gain, use it well."

"Don't let her kid you," Dodson said. "Free,
nothing. The potlatch only seems to be a
giveaway. You have to give back everything,
with interest. The giver, you see, stays wealthy
because all those I.O.U.'s are out."

In the Bronco heading back, Rob said:
"Dad, it was my fault. The kids told me about

that stuff, but it was me who made them try it.
I dared them, they dared me."

"Well, I hope you learned your lesson."

"I learned, Dad. I died a slow death."

"Do any of the kids at school try stuff like
that?"

"You mean dope, huh?"

"Yes."

"Some of 'em smoke pot. I saw a guy
shooting up in the john."

"Did you report it?"

"Are you kidding? I'm no tattler."

"Well, don't you try it. Never."

"Don't worry, Dad. I'd rather die."

They heard sirens screaming just after leaving the hotel in the morning, heading out to
the Dodson place to pick up his questions for
Masterson. Greg pulled over. A stream of
vehicles roared past—police cars, ambulances, fire trucks. Other sirens screamed
ahead.

"Can we go see what it is?" Rob asked.

"We'd better not. We might get in the way."

They were at the edge of the city,
surrounded by desert. A dense plume of black
smoke rose against the purple hills in the
distance. The fire engines and police cars
screamed in that direction. Greg drove on
slowly. Then he stopped. The smoke was
heavier and blacker and he could smell it,
thick and choking. He closed the window and
looked at Rob.

"I think it's the Dodson place," he said.

"But . . . what *hap*pened?"

"I don't know."

"We have to go see."

"Wait. Wait just a minute. I want to think."

His hands were cold and heavy. He gripped the steering wheel tightly so Rob could not see that he'd begun to tremble. A tap sounded on the door. Greg whirled. The tall black chauffeur who'd met them at the airport stood outside. Greg rolled down the window.

The chauffeur said: "Mr. Masterson has been trying to reach you, sir. He would like you to call. Right away, sir, if you could. There is a telephone in the limousine, sir."

THIRTEEN

But he didn't call Masterson. He drove. He passed shopping centers, golf courses, new resort hotels and homes under construction, cutting in and out of traffic, moving fast, on a highway now into the desert, wanting to get away, to blank out, knowing but not knowing. He felt nothing. He was numb. He wanted to feel anger and sorrow and shame, but he couldn't. Finally he stopped on a gravel shoulder of the highway. Gray sand stretched on both sides, out to where the hills met the sky. It whisked across the road in thin patterns like dirty drifts of snow.

"Dad?" Rob said.

Greg didn't answer. He reached out and held the boy.

On the way back to the hotel, Rob asked: "Do you want me to turn on the radio?"

"No."

Rob sat back. His face remained pale.

The black chauffeur was in the lobby and he stood up when Greg and Rob entered. Two men in suits were beside him. They came up to Greg and identified themselves. Phoenix police. They wanted to ask questions.

"I can't answer any of your questions," Greg said. "I have the boy here."

"The driver here'll watch 'im," one of the men said.

"No. I'm sorry. He's been sick. I—"

"You're going to have to answer some questions," the detective said. Only the older one spoke. His face was craggy and red. "This is a murder investigation, and Mrs. Dodson told us you were the last person outside the family to see him."

"Then it was Dodson? He's dead?"

"Of course it was Dodson."

Greg sat down. He felt faint. Everything was blurred and pulsating. He closed his eyes. He saw Dodson with his inevitable smile and red hair and silly clown's face; he saw his wife, Mother, with her flat face and fatalistic eyes; he saw the kids, a stairstep bunch given to fun, the discovery of life. Dammit, *dammit*! It was important to stay calm. He must think it out. He opened his eyes.

"How did Dodson die?" he asked.

"They got him with a bomb."

"Who?"

"Mr. Gregory, I'm the one asks the questions."

"You can ask, but I won't answer." He looked at the chauffeur, who helped him to his feet. "My boy and I are going to our rooms. I have nothing to say to you, at least not right now. I will say only that I know nothing about this matter. I'm appalled and sickened by it. Now my son and I are going to our room now and you can try your best to stop us if you wish, but—"

They didn't. The chauffeur escorted Greg and Rob, a beefy guard who ran interference. It was apparent the detectives knew and respected him; in fact, everyone seemed to know him and give him space. The message light was on in the room. Greg punched the number. Everybody had called—Masterson, Norwine, Maureen, Marge, Piper, Anderson, Mike Thompson. He went down to a public phone booth in the lobby and called Masterson.

"It is best now that you return to Los Angeles," Masterson said.

"I'm not sure they'll let me return."

"They will. It's already been arranged."

"Before I do anything, I want to *know*!"

"We'll talk when you're calmer."

"Oh, I'm calm, all right. My head is clear as a bell. I want to talk right now."

"Not right now," Masterson said, a dry quiet monotone. "I ask you to trust me, as I have asked of you before today. When we talk next, soon, it will be face to face."

He tried to reach Masterson almost immediately after returning to Los Angeles, but discovered that the private line had been disconnected. That was not uncommon. Masterson had several private lines and was constantly changing the numbers. Before, however, Greg had always been immediately informed of a change. This time he wasn't. Albert Norwine, however, was eminently reachable, and gave Greg instructions with legal precision. Norwine was going to use his power while he had it; he was in his element, cavalier and pompous, almost insufferable. Mr. Masterson would see Mr. Gregory when it was deemed appropriate. In the meantime, his instructions were as follows: Mr. Gregory is not to discuss the matter at hand with the news media, the police, or any other investigatory organization; if Mr. Gregory is subpoened or otherwise summoned for deposition or any kind or form of testimony, he is to notify Mr. Norwine immediately.

Greg returned to Phoenix for Dodson's funeral, but he didn't attend it. The event was covered by live television. When the cameras panned to Mother and the kids, Greg turned off the set. Mother's face reminded him of the praying Indian girl in the painting.

He wanted to feel anger, but could not. There was only numbness. His head reeled in confusion. When Mike Thompson called,

Greg invoked Norwine's ban. Anderson and Piper followed their pattern of twice-weekly calls, but neither mentioned Dodson, as if the news had been of insufficient import to reach New York. It did recede quickly on a national level, but ballooned into a cause célèbre in the West. Several newspapers and television stations combined their funds and reportorial talents to approach it on a pooled investigative basis. An editor was appointed to coordinate the effort; he declared they would find the truth if it took years, and in the process would deal a blow to organized crime. The group had the cooperation of state and local authorities, as well as the federal government's Organized Crime Strike Force.

Meanwhile, local police got nowhere in their investigation. Even the facts were scanty. Clay Dodson had entered his work area at precisely 7 a.m. as was his habit, and the building had exploded in flames at 7:14, dynamite apparently fused by an electric charge when he switched on his word processor. The supposition was that Dodson had been killed instantaneously. His body had been burned beyond recognition in the ensuing fire that had consumed the building. Identification had to be made from dental plates. The bombing obviously had been professional, done by someone who knew or had studied Dodson's habit patterns, which were very regular. On weekdays he always rose at 6 a.m., usually made his own breakfast, and, carrying a pot of coffee, went to his "office" with his two favorite dogs, Brownie and Blackie, also killed by the explosion or fire. A curious aspect of it was that no one could get close to the Dodson property without a warning sent up by the dogs. Yet someone had wired in a bomb there within the past week or so, a process experts said would take at least an hour to rig. Dodson worked by telephone and fax; he seldom left his home, and since there were small children, his wife was always there in the rare times when he was gone. There hadn't been an unguarded hour on the premises in the past two months, much less a week. No maintenance crew—phone, electricity, plumbing —had been there all year. The investigators scratched their heads and continued in their slow, plodding way; at first they were angry, for Dodson had been one of them and what they knew of him they liked, but soon the anger cooled and matters lagged. Even the state's papers and wire services, which had kept it hot by following up every little lead, slackened their coverage.

Greg thought: *The dogs were killed. It could have been one or more of his kids. It could have been Rob.*

He waited in mounting anxiety, and spates of fury, for Masterson's summons, which of course would come. But the fury abated. He calmed. He thought of questions he'd ask and how he would handle himself when the confrontation came. Obviously Masterson was stalling. Norwine said he was in Europe to arrange funding to acquire the studio, but Greg didn't believe it. Masterson was merely giving him time to think it over. Time changed one's perspective. He'd not discussed the Dodson matter in any detail with Maureen; to her, it was his affair, his client, and she had enough to do with hers. She came into his office one evening after everyone had left and plunked a file folder down on his desk.

"New-client time," she said. "I closed Mark Ashley. I also inked T. D. Desmond. There they are—signed, sealed, delivered."

"Crawford, you are a miracle worker. I talked to Piper today and he agrees."

"Yes, I talked with him, too."

"Oh?" Greg opened the file and glanced at the contracts. "How do you do it, Wonder Woman?"

"By talking man-to-man with them. The way they gamble, I figure we might as well get some of it."

"Give me an honest answer. What do you think of Ashley?"

"I think he's a fool. He's on top of the world and he's letting his life drip away. What do *you* think of him?"

"I think he's a prick."

"So am I," Maureen said.

"Oh? What brought that on?"

"If I were a man, people would call me a prick. Who cares? A wiseass said to me yesterday, 'Yes, sir.'" She shrugged. She was wearing a green silk dress with wide shoulder pads and she looked good, very good. "If they think of me as a man, let them. I operate like a man. I think like a man."

"Let me guess. The wiseass who yes-sirred you was Willy Sterne."

"Yes. He dislikes me with a purple passion and he's been feeling his oats since you were promoted. He *loves* you."

"I think you've found out something. I had Sterne look into the personal files."

She didn't flinch. "No, I didn't know that. I thought his specialty was buying off newspaper drunks, not snooping."

"You never graduated from Stanford."

"No."

"But your form says you did. And UCLA."

"I went two years to Stanford, a semester to UCLA extension. I ran out of money, that's all."

"Is that why you bad-mouth college? Call it air?"

Her jaw snapped. "Well, it didn't take a college degree to sign up Mark Ashley and T. D. Desmond."

"What did it take?"

"Not a gang bang, and damn you if you think that." She stomped her foot and glared at him, now taking the offensive. "You're stupidly jealous. What's another piece of ass to men like Ashley and Desmond? They can get much more than they could handle by snapping their fingers."

"I think the lady doth protest too much."

"Oh, screw you. Damn you to hell."

He wasn't getting to her. She was a mask. She sat still, a lovely, polished stone. Greg got up and strolled. He'd had the painting of the Indian girl by Clay Dodson's wife put up. Now he paused to look at it.

Without turning, he said: "The skinny is that Stanford kicked you out. You had a business going on the side. Word-of-mouth prostitution, you might call it."

She spoke quietly. "So that's what it's been! You've been a bear, you know. I thought it was the Dodson thing."

"No. It was this whore thing."

He crammed his hands into his pockets, feeling foolish. He should have let it go. Was he so perfect he could preach to her? Was he a judge who condemned without a hearing? Yet it had gnawed at him. He sighed deeply. All of it overwhelmed him—his work, Masterson, Dodson's murder, Maureen, Anderson and Piper. He should get out. Escape. Get Rob. Get that farm. Yet he wouldn't. He wanted it here. He had to have it, just as he wanted and had to have Maureen. He turned to see that she was crying. She seemed smaller, her head down, trembling, her shoulders hunched. Greg went soft inside.

"Look, it's all right," he said. "I hit you hard. I didn't mean it. I'm sorry. I'm truly sorry, honey."

Her head snapped up. Her words sprang

out in a shower of angry tears. "I didn't have money like the others had. My parents were poor dirt farmers. What could they give me? Oh, how I hated those people at school! I could have waited tables, something like that, but it wasn't enough money. What was wrong with what I did? Other girls took other things in return for spreading their legs. Oh, don't you think the professors weren't my customers! I scored more than one dean. Maybe that's why I got caught. Who's guilty? The whore or those who pay the whore? Men are so stupid and priggish about sex. They'll fuck a dozen women and brag about it, but heaven help the woman who's unfaithful once!"

Greg went to her and held her tightly, feeling her warmth against him, his throat thick. It would be all right. They would find a way.

"I love you," he said.

She broke away, taking a handkerchief from her purse and dabbing her eyes. She looked at herself in her compact.

"I'm going to try," she said. "I'm going to try hard to be better for you. I don't know things like love and giving. I was taught to go for the jugular. But I'll try."

He caught her arm. "Move in with me."

"No. I can't. Not yet. Maybe never. I need space. I was raised with a family of seven in a little house. I want you to understand that you're important to me and that I care for you, but I can't do everything you want. Not now. Do you understand any of this I'm trying to say?"

"I guess I'll have to understand."

"When do you see Masterson?"

"Oh, back to business, is it?"

"When do you?"

"When he summons."

"What will you say?"

"I haven't the slightest idea."

"You don't have much choice, do you?"

"What do you mean?"

"Well, he's your golden goose, you know."

"If I close my eyes. See no evil, hear no evil?"

"Something like that, I suppose."

"Let's have dinner."

"Thought you'd never ask. I'm starving."

"We'll celebrate the new accounts. Tomorrow Planter announces them to the world."

"Tomorrow the world."

"We're on a roll," he said.

"We're on a roll," she said.

"Rolling, rolling, rolling, rolling, gently down the stream."

"Rolling, rolling, rolling, rolling, gently down the stream."

"Merrily, merrily, merrily, merrily . . ."

"Merrily, merrily, merrily, merrily . . ."

"Life is but a dream."

"Life is but a dream."

"But a dreammmm!"

"But a dreammm!"

* * *

225

Arelo Sederberg

His summons from Masterson finally came, via Norwine. It was a pleasant day in late summer, sunny but smogless, so he took the long route—the San Bernardino Freeway to Baldwin and then Huntington Drive to San Marino. The mountains were clearly etched against the sky. It was a sedate area of wide streets and palm trees, old houses and old money, the wealthy who had refused to move after undesirable elements encroached on adjacent areas, such as Pasadena and Altadena. Instead, they had installed higher fences and sturdier gates.

Masterson took the initiative. "You may ask what you wish, but allow me to anticipate. You want to know if I played any part in Mr. Dodson's death. I did not. Of course I did not. Why would I have arranged to have my representative in the area—you, of course—at the time he was killed, sent in my airplane?"

"Then what did happen?"

"I don't know what happened." It was a very informal meeting, at the swimming pool. Masterson lay back on a chaise longue under a large umbrella, a red towel over his swimming trunks. He looked small and insubstantial, his scrawny body dotted with white hairs barely visible on his pale skin. Sunglasses hid his eyes. Greg sat in a wicker chair beside him. A butler in black had served coffee and vanished. From speakers beside the pool came strains from *Pagliacci*, a favorite opera of Greg's. Birds shrilled intermittently and also

226

sounded on the recording, preceding Nedda's aria "Stridono lassù." The sounds seemed to blend, becoming one. Greg strained to hear Masterson's voice. "It now appears that my sending you to Phoenix was an error in judgment. Mr. Dodson had recently attacked me in print, at least by innuendo, and then you went to Phoenix to talk to him. Perhaps his enemies precipitated the matter to cast suspicion on me. You realize that Mr. Dodson did have dangerous enemies."

"Will you explain why you know that?"

"You are an inquisitor, Mr. Gregory. For reasons I cannot discuss, there are some questions I cannot answer."

"But I think I deserve to know the answers."

Masterson removed his sunglasses. His eyes were hard. "You have a simple choice. You can leave here and our association is ended. Or you can stay with me for an indefinite period of time, at considerable comfort and remuneration. I offered this to you in the past and now I offer it once again."

"You could have sent me to Phoenix knowing what was going to happen so my presence would divert suspicion from you. No one would think you'd have the audacity to send—"

"You are the one who exhibits audacity, Mr. Gregory." Masterson glared, replacing the sunglasses with a little snap. He seldom raised his voice, but now he seemed quite angry. "I told you I had nothing to do with Mr. Dodson's death. Now, in effect, you accuse me of lying. That is not wise." He raised his hand to stop Greg's response, listening to a Nedda-Silvio duet. It seemed to soothe him. He said calmly: "Your suggestion is that I merely used you to my advantage, as an object. Why would I act in this manner when it could only bring public wrath and suspicion upon my house?"

"Dodson was going to write down some questions for you. I didn't see them, but I can imagine what they were."

"You may ask," Masterson said, gesturing.

"He wanted to know your ethnic background."

"I am part French, part Italian, born in Corsica."

"Is Cyrus Masterson an assumed name?"

"I changed my name, yes. Many immigrants do."

"Is your actual name Alberto Cervi?"

"No."

"Did you serve with Italian forces at any time during the Second World War?"

"No."

"How did you make your money?"

"Real estate investments."

"Do you know a man named Carl Medondi?"

"Stop, stop," Masterson said, holding up both hands. "I shall have to telephone Mr. Norwine. Shall I refuse to answer on the grounds it might incriminate me?"

"You are making a joke of it."

"It is somewhat of a joke, Mr. Gregory, these absurd insinuations."

"I'm sorry. It's unnerved me. I liked Dodson and his family."

"Of course. I understand." Masterson's tone was gentle; the snap of anger was gone. "But you're all right now, aren't you?"

"Yes."

He was. It was over and he had lost. He'd known he would lose all along. He would close his mind to it, accept it, forget it, continue to live, ask no more questions. It was best that way. And, as Maureen had said, he had very little choice.

"'*Vesti la giubba*,'" Masterson said. "The clown of *Pagliacci* has a personal life, a personal tragedy perhaps, but still he must put on the costume and play the clown to amuse the public. I have personal tragedy, for life is tragedy, but for public posturing, I am a businessman and an investor, a successful one. I dislike the limelight and for personal reasons I live a retiring life. I am not a well-educated man, formally educated, and therefore unsure of myself in public. I seek opportunities. I pay taxes. I regard this country, now my home, as greater than any other. This is what I am and wish you to inform the public."

"I have."

"And will."

"Yes."

"I am not a fatalist. I believe we may have our fondest dream or suffer our nightmares as we choose. We must not hesitate to speak our minds to one another, Mr. Gregory. I want there to be trust between us." Again he removed the sunglasses. He lay back listening to the music, his eyes closed. After a while he said: "When we grow older, we are grateful for that we take for granted when we are young, such as hearing or eyesight or taste. We cherish a painting more when we fear its beauty may be removed from us shortly. We also think about what we have missed, what we will never have or see again. Old men should never reminisce or regret. There are always matters to regret, and they are best forgotten. Is your son well, Mr. Gregory?"

"Why, yes."

"Good."

"You said we should speak our minds. Quite frankly, it bothers me that you seem to say one thing and mean another."

He wished immediately that he hadn't said it. It had just come out. Masterson didn't move. He rested as if he hadn't heard or as if considering his response, his eyes remaining closed. The music swelled, surrounding them, holding everything suspended for a high moment. Then it collapsed, and again came strident bird sounds above and behind them, echoing or seeming to invoke far-off responses.

Masterson said: "When I was a boy I listened to opera as avidly as the young of today listen to the gibberish modern philistines call music. Opera is one of my few arrogances. This one, *Pagliacci*, is opera beyond opera. It is life itself. Are we to believe what we see and hear? Are the clowns real? Is the drama real or is it staged? Here is a play within a play, entertainers and their audience onstage, watched by another audience, the real one. You and I, Mr. Gregory, watching and listening. Then the play becomes not a play but an actual drama, one of jealous murder, and that is apparent to the onstage audience. Or is it? Does the acting of fools fool the watchers? And what of the other audience, the real one? Does it see a play within a play or does it witness murder? The real audience shrugs. It does not care. It wants nothing to do with the real because it is there to see the unreal, and besides the real is involvement. So it is in the world. We avoid the real. The make-believe, even if real to the players, is our preference. We flee from the actual because it is unbearable. Some merely excuse themselves from it. And now I must apologize and excuse myself, Mr. Gregory. I have guests coming and I must dress for them, make my exit, so to speak. *La commedia è finita!*"

"Wait. Please."

Masterson smiled gently. "I will anticipate you. To repeat, I had no part in Mr. Dodson's death, although I may have knowledge concerning him that others do not have."

231

Arelo Sederberg

"What knowledge?"

"He had prepared some particularly damaging articles, spurious and in fact nonsensical, as a form of vengeance upon his assassins. He was obsessed, like many journalists and others who are convinced that right is on their side. Knowing this, as you see I do, I most certainly would not have had a hand in his death. It would cause the articles to be published, despite their obvious libel, out of sympathy for an American martyr." The butler brought out a cordless telephone and Masterson spoke cordially for a few minutes. Hanging up, he said: "People often are too chatty on telephones, and I'm afraid I have a reputation of being too brusque when I speak on them. Only my closest friends dare phone me. You will hear from me soon, Mr. Gregory."

As Greg left he glanced back at the house and saw a figure in the upstairs window, peering down at him. It was a woman, no doubt Mrs. Masterson, and although her standing there was innocuous enough, he felt a chill. Before, when he'd accompanied Masterson to the crypt room below, they had emerged via a different stairway from the one they'd used to enter, coming out near the pool. Now Greg saw the doorway of that exit, camouflaged in ivy by the fence. He glanced up again. The woman in the window was gone. Abruptly the music stopped, having started over with the prologue, at the baritone's high G. "Incominciamo!" All was silent. The birds no longer shrilled. Greg shuddered. He left hurriedly. As he went through the gate, a limousine with frosted windows entered. He drove slowly through the impassive, tree-shaded neighborhood with its palatial houses, iron-barred and secure from violence within and without. He knew that he had made a pact. He also knew that he did not know the man with whom he'd made the pact and he probably never would know him. But there would be no turning back now, and no escape.

FOURTEEN

They were indeed on a roll. CU became known as the PR agency with the magic touch, the place to be if you were hot or a has-been, a beginner or veteran, had talent or thought you did. The offices were expanded. Potential clients called, asking to be represented.

"I hardly have words," Anderson told Greg on the phone. "Success breeds success."

CU's roll had enabled Anderson to become more particular and snobbish on Madison Avenue. He accepted only prestige accounts, *New Yorker* or *Connoisseur* or *G.Q.* advertisers, allowing him to criticize the agency business as juvenile panderers to common taste. He moved the advertising agency's office from

Madison to Park. Piper, who also loved rolls, merely went along with it, although he refused to support Anderson's pristine bite-the-hand-that-feeds-you pomposity.

Maureen had done an outstanding job, and Greg made sure that El Eastern Overlords—Planter's description, which stuck—knew about it. Not only had she sobered up Martin Bradford but also she had reconciled him with his wife, a miracle performed with the apparent ease of a sorceress. Wifely, Mrs. Bradford attended his speeches, visions of First Lady queenliness dancing in her head, and Bradford moved steadily up in the polls. Reverend Jack's tour was an outstanding success, filling his and CU's coffers. In a miracle he attributed to Maureen and God, his smiling, pious face glowed divinely from the cover of *Time*. He wasn't told that that achievement often represented a peak and subsequent downfall. Mark Ashley again was crowned the nation's leading male box office star, although critics continued to lambaste both his films and his acting. T. D. Desmond signed a four-picture, multimillion-dollar contract with Videoscope Productions, recently acquired and resuscitated by Cyrus Masterson. It made T.D. a "megabucks star," according to *Variety*, and *People* confirmed his fame with a picture layout.

Greg astounded himself by securing a financial backing over the telephone from Masterson for a picture with the shooting title of *Let Old Times Roll*, starring Mona Tyson. Masterson committed the studio to half if Greg, as executive producer, could raise the rest. Such backing made him bankable. The script was warm, funny, sad, nostalgic, a picture based not on connections but on solid demographics, the graying of America. Ashley had a cameo role in it, and Martin Bradford made a short speech as President Wilson. The picture had long been Greg's dream. He had Mona round up the old-timers, which caused her to squeal with delight. It made him feel good; it was an element of the streak.

"Well, I guess I knew you when," said Henry Frost, the Heavyweight. "By the way, you're looking at a fool."

"How so?"

"The old line. Who represents himself in court has a fool for a client. I did. But I was a fool that fooled them. I beat the rap."

"Tell Planter. It'll be on KMPC."

"It was," Heavyweight said. "You're not interested."

"I am."

The Heavyweight looked very serious. "I told the judge in chambers I wanted a jury trial and we'd take the jury to the scene of the crime for reenactment. If they didn't agree, twelve good and intelligent persons of my peer, that pissing on modern books was not commendable, I'd be willing to be sent over to a dungeon at Sing Sing or anywhere. The judge gave me a suspended sentence and wiped it off the record. He had criminals to judge, not crusaders."

"You are not to be believed."

"Well, that judge knew he'd have to read a bunch of modern novels if the case went on and he knew what that entailed. Talk about indecent exposure."

Greg laughed. It was a part of the absurdity of it all, the fun house aspect. Sometimes he imagined he stood at the entrance to a long chamber of mirrors and beside him stood the others—Maureen, Anderson and Piper, the Heavyweight and Planter, Ashley and Desmond and Bradford, Cyrus Masterson and Albert Norwine, Mona Tyson in purple, Reverend Jack in black, Tim Harte with his bubble-gum neck—and their reflections glinted endlessly, shining in a great succession of mirror upon mirror, one image causing another and another, onward to infinity.

"Nice painting, Indian girl," Heavyweight said.

It brought Greg back. The fun house dissolved, the mirrors blackened. An edge was off his roll. He'd tried to forget but he couldn't, not completely. Clay Dodson's grin and Mother's eyes and the laughing clan had tenacity, visiting him like a recurrent dream. Yet he had diversions, escape paths. He buried himself in the motion picture project. He spent as much time as possible with Maureen. Their relationship was good, almost too good, as she sometimes reminded him.

"Have you ever been lost? Mentally, I mean?" she asked him one night in bed at his place.

"I suppose so. Although I don't know really what you mean, lost."

"Maybe that's not the right word for it. It's just that I don't know where my home is."

"It's here."

"Not really."

"You have the Hollywood syndrome. It's the waiting-by-the-phone thing."

"I don't wait by the phone. It's not that, anyway. It's a scary thing, love. But I think I love you."

"You came to that roundabout. But I'll hold you to it."

"Don't. Not yet."

"When do I meet the parents and the rest of the family? Let's fly them out here and show them how successful you are."

"Oh, they know that. I send them money. I'm the original skinflint, the original inse-cure, but I send them what I can."

"Well, when I am the big producer, you will be the rich kept woman."

"Never. Not kept."

"When do I see your new apartment?"

"It's not really worth seeing, although bet-ter than the one before."

"And it's yours."

"That, too. There are times when I have to be alone."

"Are you still too much of a loner to meet Rob?"

"I'm afraid so. I'm just not ready yet for the little stepmother scene." She reached out and held him tightly, her arms and legs entwined about him. "Oh, I *do* love you! And the picture will make it. We'll be in Beverly Hills, maybe in Holmby Hills."

"I thought you liked our house."

"I do, but it's not exactly a producer's house, is it? If you're going to be a somebody, you have to live like a somebody. Hold me hard. Harder. Will you remember I love you? No matter what happens?"

He kissed her, touching her all over, the scent of her in his nostrils, the taste of her like heady wine. A foreboding jarred him, a premonition that it would go wrong, but he shook it away. It would work. They would continue on the hot streak, the roll in the big casino, holding the brass ring, rolling on and over faster and faster until they were at the top, on a mountain above the rest.

"Ah, do that," she said, moaning. "Do it, *do* it!"

On Monday morning Marge informed him that Tim Harte was pacing outside the office. Greg agreed to see him. Harte wore a green plaid double-breasted suit and a silk tie. He'd lost weight and was tanned almost bronze. His sunglasses had mirror lenses that reflected as he bobbed his head.

"Hear you're *producing*, Greg."

"Executive producer. Mortgage the house, pass the hat."

"That's what I'm going to be doing, produce."

"Oh?"

"Sure. Watch my smoke. See this suit? Fifty-dollar tie, no less. I even got a shrink. He does house calls. On his card it says, 'Have couch, will travel.' Ha-ha, ha-ha. Hardy, ha-ha. I hear your flick's about senior citizens."

"It could be described that way."

"A rip-off on *Cocoon*? Well, I hope it makes it. I hope you get way up. Remember if you go up, though, you can come down. It always happens. Sooner or later they stop buying your lunch. Hear you need a unit publicist."

"Actually, I'm using Willard Sterne on a moonlighting basis."

"Old guy like that?"

"The movie is about old guys, remember?"

"The way you guys are adding clients around here, you got to be needing an a.e. or two here."

"We're full up, Tim."

"I'd call El, but I thought I'd ask you, knowing you're on the line here."

"Tim, you know good and well Anderson isn't going to help you."

"Oh? Is that what he tells you, that he wouldn't lift a finger for me?"

Greg turned away and shuffled papers. "You'll have to talk with him about it. It's out of my hands."

Harte grinned. He wasn't going to let it get him down. "How's the old gang?"

"Just fine."

"How's Frost? I hear he got in Dutch with John Law. Was he diddling a little girl or something?"

"No."

"What, then?"

"Go across the hall and ask him."

"How's Maureen?"

"Maureen is just fine."

"I don't blame you for what happened to me here, Greg. You're a regular guy. I always thought that. It's her I blame. Everything was all right around here until she came. I could tell she was bad news the minute I laid eyes on her."

"I really am busy, Tim."

"She's bad news, Greg. I'm telling you because I like you and I'm your friend, okay?"

"You'd better go now."

Tim stood up. He jerked his head back and forth, sending out glistening rays. "Sure, I'm off, no sweat, my man. You watch your p's and q's, hear?"

He waddled away. Maureen was waiting in the hall. Harte brushed by as if he didn't recognize her. She came in, hurrying, her face pale and contorted.

"We have a problem," she said.

"If you have a problem, solve it."

"Don't be nasty with me just because you might be pissed off at that fat airhead. I said we, I meant we. Desmond has run down a woman in a crosswalk. Hit and run, and he was bombed out of his skull."

"Bombed at 10 *a*.m.?"

"What does it matter, day or night? He was pissed to the gills. He was coming home from an orgy his friends had bought for him to celebrate his contract with Videoscope."

"Is that the new thing for a man who has everything? An orgy?"

"Greg, please! This is serious. In case you've forgotten, we're in the middle of a campaign for T.D., making him the all-American boy."

"Where is he now?"

"At home. He had enough sense to phone the studio head and tell him, and the studio head phoned me."

"Is the woman he hit dead?"

"I—I don't know."

"How about witnesses?"

Maureen spoke rapidly. "It happened in Westwood in broad daylight, so I assume there were witnesses. He has a red Porsche with vanity plates—MR. T.D.?—so if somebody saw that, it's not going to be hard for the police to trace him."

Marge appeared, wringing her hands, to inform him that Masterson was on the phone. Whenever he called, she assumed a catastrophe was imminent and her announcements had the somber tone of a funeral dirge. He picked up the phone. As usual, Masterson was soft-spoken and brief. He knew about Desmond. Joseph Corwin, the Videoscope studio boss he'd hired to replace the founder, Victor Wise, had told him. Would Greg meet Corwin, now, at Desmond's house in Brentwood? Masterson added: "I'm sure you will handle the matter efficiently." That was all. He was gone.

They took Greg's Mercedes. Maureen sat silently, letting him think. He'd been sent to save a property, a human property of Masterson's named T. D. Desmond, and it was a test of sorts. He felt a wave of disgust and also of helplessness. He, too, was a property. He was in a trap of his own doing, a quicksand that would drag him down deeper and deeper with each successive act until it smothered him. Yet it was fascinating and enticing, this Masterson quicksand. In its midst moved only the invited, learning its tribal laws and mores and language. It was grotesque, but mesmerizing. Could he stop now? No. It was far too late. He looked at Maureen, her head high, her face perfect in profile. He sped up.

Joe Corwin was pacing outside Desmond's brick-facade house off San Vincente. Greg recalled there had been some trouble when Desmond had moved in, difficult to imagine in a neighborhood so quiet and impersonal. It was a senior citizen's Oz, bright and perfect, a sanctuary with manicured lawns, parks, no kids, neighborhood watch, dogs on leashes.

In this fairyland Corwin played the ogre. "What the hell took you?" he growled at Greg. He scowled in Maureen's direction. "Who's this?"

"She's Desmond's a.e. at the agency," Greg said.

"Well, the fewer in on this, the better."

"In on what?"

Corwin's cheeks flashed color. "In on what? Christ on a crutch, gimme a break. This big spade nearly *killed* a woman, driving stoned out of his mind. She might pull through, no fault of his. He's my boy, under contract, so we got to save his black ass. I got something going down on it." Again he glowered at Maureen.

"Whatever it is, she's part of it," Greg said.

"Okay, here's the deal then." Corwin talked as he waddled ahead of them, leading the way into the house. His chin and lower jaw extended the length of his neck, and his stomach fell nearly to the middle of his thighs, so he moved with a forward-slanting step, penguinlike. Greg had a name for him, the Frog. He wasn't an ally, dead set against *Let Old Times Roll* from the outset. He hadn't read

245

the script, but judged by the title. Now he pushed into the living room, lined with football trophies, and went on: "Cops got 'im dead to rights. How many red Porsches there around with T.D. plates driven by a spook in a yellow shirt? So I beat 'em to it. I called the cops. We got a stand-in for Desmond."

Corwin snapped his fingers. A tall black man in a yellow shirt and Levi's emerged from a dark corner. He stood still, his shoulders back. Corwin went over to him. He turned back to Greg and Maureen.

"His name's Ryder," he explained, reaching up and patting the man's shoulder. Corwin seemed like a midget beside the big man. "He's Sack Ryder, or that's what he's called. He was a stuntman for us and was going to do T.D.'s stunts in the movies for him, but he got busted up. Stuntmen do that, get busted up and that's it. Now he does a *stint* for our T.D. See, he borrowed the Porsche and was returning it when the old dame stepped in his way. He was cold sober—he don't drink—but he lost his head and came over here to Desmond's place." The Frog reached up and patted the black man's arm. The man flinched and drew back, scowling. The Frog's high-pitched voice prated on. "Sack's got a mammy in Alabamy and six kids he'll admit to. We take care of them. He gets a good lawyer and character witnesses. He's out in a year, maybe less. Then he's got a job for life and a hundred grand in a CD in Bank of America. A hundred grand buys a lot of watermelons. Tell the folks you're willing, Sack."

"Get it on," Sack said, a deep-voiced growl.

Corwin stood back proudly, a machinator who had pulled off a clever coup.

"Where is Desmond?" Greg asked.

Corwin pointed. "Sleeping it off."

Greg darted into the hallway. He looked into several rooms before he found Desmond. A huge photograph of him carrying a football covered one wall.

"Huh, huh?" Desmond mumbled as Greg shook him.

Greg glanced behind him and saw that Maureen had followed. He asked Desmond: "Do you know what's happening?"

"Jus' wanna sleep. Lemme sleep, man."

"You ran over a woman. Do you remember that?" Greg reached down and shook Desmond again, hard. "Do you know about this fellow, Sack Ryder?"

"Sack? Yeah, know Sack. Was on the Steelers." Snorting, he fell back, his eyes closed. "I'll stand the rap. Jus' lemme sleep, man."

He'd probably been free-basing, perhaps most of the weekend, and also drinking heavily. God knew what else. He was still down, but coming up; he knew what was happening, all right. Greg could tell. He'd been there.

"Do you want to get clean?" he asked.

Desmond mumbled: "Wanna get clean, yeah."

247

There was spittle on his lips, and he'd vomited on his blankets. Greg heard tires screeching outside. The doorbell rang, followed by a heavy knocking on the door.

"All right," he said. "You're going to get clean."

Maureen walked beside him into the hall. "Greg, what are you going to do?"

"I don't like it. I'm going to turn him in."

"You can't do that! It's too late for that!"

"It's not too late. It's almost too late, but not quite."

Her eyes hardened. "You're making a mistake, Greg."

He shrugged. "It's a far, far better thing that I do—"

"Oh, for the good sake of Christ!" she said, stomping her heel.

He went into the living room. Corwin looked at him and immediately read the situation. He flushed scarlet.

"You bastard son of a bitch." The words were like a hiss. Corwin pointed, trembling. "I'll have your balls."

"I know. I'll never work in this town again."

The Frog scowled, stomped, snorted. He was almost speechless with rage. He shook his fist, found his voice, and said: "Listen up, sonny boy. I been in this racket since when there wasn't talkies. It's based on one thing. Illusion. Deception and illusion. One deception is that there are good guys and bad guys.

The stars are good guys. You protect them. Lose 'em, you're out of business. Now—''

Desmond appeared and stood swaying, his eyes red. Sack skipped to the Frog, reached out, and tapped his jaw. The Frog sagged into Sack's arms, out cold. Sack pulled him into the next room. Greg, thinking of the opening of a horror flick where the monster dragged away a victim, began to laugh. Desmond laughed with him, and together they went to open the door for the noisy cops. Maureen continued to regard them with hard eyes, tapping her heel.

It would cost him, yet he felt elated about it. It was like it had been long ago—before Nam, before Hyde—when he had walked out to embrace the city, free and innocent like a kid on a carousel, happy, knowing full well who he was and what his values were. He didn't know why he'd opposed the Frog's scheme. Perhaps it had been a flash of instinct, a warning. He continued to feel good about it, however; if he could sustain that feeling, he'd be all right.

It wasn't easy. The Desmond publicity was gruesome, reflecting badly on Videoscope. The Frog sent a barrage of clippings to Greg, salient paragraphs marked in yellow. Desmond was out on bail and taking the cure, but his star value as a clean-cut hero clearly was diminished. The Frog repeatedly told

Greg that T.D. blamed him for the ruined career and warned that he'd better watch his back.

"Mark Ashley agrees with that," Maureen said.

"Well, if T.D. gets clean, he'll thank me."

"Maybe not."

"I did the right thing."

"Did you?"

"Don't you believe I did?"

"No," she said. "Quite frankly, no."

Greg turned his back to it. It was another tinsel storm that would pass. Masterson, his biggest concern, remained ominously silent. The Frog called with daily taunts, and one morning his voice rang triumphantly.

"Sonny boy, your geriatrics flick is canceled, finished, kaput, out! You want this verified, I give you Mr. Masterson's private number to call."

"I have his numbers," Greg said, a lifeless reaction.

Mona Tyson called a minute later. "Did you hear?"

"Yes. A little frog just told me."

"I won't pretend it doesn't hurt."

"Keep your head up though. Promise?"

"They're giving you the gears because of Desmond."

"It was more like they were laying back and waiting for an opening. Call it the Napoleonic ambush."

"Well, Desmond was the opening."

"You know nothing about the Desmond thing."

"No. I'm the middle monkey who hears no evil. Since the picture is off and I won't be needing PR, how about getting a bill sent?"

"No bill for you, love."

"I hope Desmond is grateful."

"Grateful? I'm the stoolie who sent him over."

"You might have saved his life," Mona said. "As for mine, well, I'm not so sure. The air's out of the balloon."

So he'd failed Mona as well. Her comeback was squelched and she'd lose money, since she had a point in the project. Greg would lose, too; he hadn't been kidding when he'd said his house had been mortgaged. He considered calling Masterson to see if he could get the project back on. But he did nothing. Despair settled over him like a dark cloud.

Desmond was sentenced to six months. He was lucky, since a hanging judge he was scheduled to face died of a stroke a week earlier. The new judge issued the sentence after a scathing lecture on athletes who set bad examples for youth—more grist for the media mills. Maureen said Mark Ashley had been there, unnoticed in the back.

"Maybe we should ask Mark to lunch," Greg said. "I could try to explain to him."

She shook her head. "Forget it. It's not

251

smart to remind him. He could have been the one standing before that judge just as well as T.D."

"They expect too much. A time comes when you have to draw the line. We'll lie for them to the press, but not to the cops."

"I have something to say."

"Your tone tells me I'm not going to like it."

"I'm going to a party at Mark's home Saturday night. It's an everybody-who's-anybody affair to celebrate his box office ranking. I'm going to go by myself."

"Why? Because Ashley is pissed off at me?"

"Partly. I'll be perfectly honest. I'm going there to look for business, and I don't think I'd do well if I was restricted by a man."

"I'm a restriction?"

"Of course."

"Okay," he said.

"Just okay? No arguments?"

"No arguments."

She smiled. "You're beginning to understand me."

"Oh, I'm a quick study."

On Saturday he tried to relax but found himself pacing at midnight. He'd advertised the house for sale in *Variety*, primarily to please Maureen, and real estate agents had been calling all day, wanting to list it. He felt irritated, lonely, and angry. Finally, unable to bear it, he went out. He drove. He went up Laurel Canyon to the top of Mulholland Drive, where he stopped to look out over the city, a panorama of lights he'd first viewed years ago, just out of Nam and triumphant over Hyde, shaking his fist and vowing a secret pledge of conquest. He was down now, but he'd never expected it to be all up. He wasn't finished. Yet now he didn't feel like a conqueror, or very big at all, alone under a limitless roof of brilliant stars. Hank Frost the Heavyweight had been right. It wasn't important, it was only earth. Yet Greg couldn't shake it off. He drove rapidly, heading down Coldwater Canyon toward Beverly Hills and Mark Ashley's house. He wasn't invited to the party, but had no trouble getting in. The gate was open and unguarded. Valet parking was by sexy young blondes in yellow tights who looked, walked, drove, and laughed alike. Greg went to the door, stopped and listened to music from within, and entered.

He walked down a marble-floored hall into a huge open room. Velvet drapes edged in red covered the windows. The chandelier lights were dim. Greg paused, feeling alien. Ashley had played a doomed bullfighter in his latest film, *Grace*, a critical flop but a commercial success based on *Blood and Sand*, so his party had a Spanish theme. Clearly it had seen better moments. It was past 3 a.m. and the guests who remained were survivors of a wreck. They sat and stood or danced in bleary-eyed somnolence; some slept in chairs or on the floor, snoring in loud spurts. To Greg, sober, it seemed grotesque and writh-

ing, a phantasmagoric procession at the end
of revel, balloons having burst and the maria-
chi band reduced to tired, tortured strains,
everything and everybody spent and monoto-
nous. Waiters in flamenco suits and hats still
served drinks, and all the bars remained open.
Several maids, dressed in red and wearing
bangles, tried their best to clean up. They
moved as inconspicuously as possible, drifting silently and smiling blankly. Some of the
women guests were dressed in Carmen costumes, and a number of men wore the dress of
matadors. Huge still photographs of scenes
from the movie hung from the ceiling, magi-
cally suspended on invisible wires. The main
attraction, by now drawing but scant attention, was a large black bull in a cage in the
center of the room. It lay lazily on straw, its
eyes closed, looking utterly bored.

"Cutesy-poo, cutesy-poo," said a woman in
red.

The bull regally ignored her.

"Look'it the *balls* on that sucker!" said a
man dressed as Friar Tuck. "That sucker's
hung!"

"Toro, toro," said the woman, dancing on
her toes.

Others were in costume—the inevitable
Snow White and Marie Antoinette, a Lafayette
and Morgan the Pirate, an obese Lone Ranger
who held hands with a gracile Tonto. They
looked and acted like tired circus performers
left at a train station. Yet they weren't going

home. It was as if they were waiting for something.

A Batman singled out Greg. "The mask is a great equalizer," he explained. "I might be famous. I might not be. As it is, I am not. I am a lawyer. A mouthpiece. Of that I am not ashamed. After all, the immortal Shakespeare was a mouthpiece for the Elizabethan court, was he not?"

"For sure," Greg said.

He looked around. The room quivered before him—the listless bull, the worn dancers, the bizarrely adorned guests engaged in tired, drunken conversations. It was the dregs of another Hollywood party, thick with pot and booze odors.

"S'Greg!"

It was Martin Bradford, dressed like a picador. His fly was open. He was schnockered to the gills, seeing bats. Greg was surprised that Bradford had recognized him, considering how absolutely he was tanked.

"Marty, I thought you took the cure," Greg said.

"S'tomorrow," Bradford said. He waved his hand. "S'take bull through cows, bull'll snort."

"I suppose so."

"You kill my wife, I'll sober up," Bradford said plainly, enunciating the words with his trained voice so carefully that it appeared as if he'd miraculously sobered up then and there. But he patted Greg's shoulder and continued in his sloshed tones. "Women, s'different. Prude bee, you must be. See? Poet, doan knowit. Proud boy. There. Said it. Proud boy."

"Why must I be a proud boy?"

"Prude bee," Bradford said, drinking. He bowed and nearly fell over. "S'Maureen. S-s-she won door prize."

The man who had made the observation about the bull's testicles said to Greg: "The door prize was a real lollipop for the girls. It was Mark Ashley himself." The man drew pictures in the air with exaggerated movements of his hands. "Comes with a certificate in a gold frame that says, 'I fucked the brains out of Mark Ashley.' Now what girl wouldn't give her left tit for something like that?"

Greg felt himself going cold. Again it had begun to waver before him—something unreal, a dream, a moonscape of the mind. He blinked. The mariachis struck up with the wedding march, and on a stairway that seemed to drop behind them like scenery in a play appeared a man and a woman—a Carmen in black with her bullfighter in gold, complete with his sword. The matador was Mark Ashley. The Carmen was Maureen.

Greg felt faint. He needed a drink. He needed to cut and snort a line.

Get it together. Cool it.

Maureen came by on Ashley's arm, passing Greg as if he weren't there. "Poor baby," she said to Bradford, patting his cheek. She winked and said, "Fly check, senator." Then she whirled on Greg, her eyes cold. "Why are you here?"

"Oh, I thought I'd just drop by."

"To check up on me."

"Apparently with good reason."

"You ust me prude bee," mumbled Bradford.

Ashley drew the sword and passed his fingers over the blade. "The *estoque*," he said. "Ah! Deep penetration, the *estocada*." He passed the sword over Greg's shoulder with a quick thrust.

"Olé, olé!" chanted the onlookers, applauding.

Ashley grinned and made another pass, with obvious sexual connotations.

Again the audience chanted: "Olé, olé!"

Greg reached out, pushing the blade away and cutting his hand. He saw blood but felt nothing. Maureen stuck out her lower lip, her eyes icy blue slits. Greg drew back his hand and slapped her, not hard but enough to make her draw back and flinch. Blood spattered from his hand. From the corner of his eye, Greg saw that the bull had risen in its pen and stood pawing, eyeing them. The guests drew silently back. They were like dancers in a musical, moving in choreographed rhythm, their arms and shoulders jerking mechanically. Greg looked at Maureen. She touched her cheek and smiled. The blood was from his hand but it appeared to be coming out her mouth.

Greg fled. He didn't know where. The Mercedes moved in circles, ever widening and then narrowing until by dawn he was within a mile of the place he had started from. He stopped at a booth and phoned Marie.

"Hawaii?" she said. "It's rather short notice."

"You know how compulsive I am. I guarantee it's on the up-and-up, and safe and sound."

"I'll have Rob ready," she said.

He slept soundly on the plane and didn't wake up until they were ready to land at Honolulu. He felt rested and calm.

"What will we see in Hawaii, Dad?" Rob asked.

"Hula girls."

"Girls?"

"Yep."

"Dad, you're sure a surprising Dad. Is this a dream?"

"Yep," he said.

They lazed on the beach. They floated in the ocean. They went out on a glass-bottomed boat at noon and on a catamaran at midnight. They played shuffleboard, tennis, and golf. The sound and the smell of the ocean lulled him into deep sleep at night. On the third day Maureen called.

"How did you find out?" he asked.

"Marge."

"Marge is a telltale."

"I'd like to say Masterson is looking for you,

or Anderson or Piper. But they're not. I'm the one who's looking for you. I miss you."

"Oh?"

"I love you," she said.

"I see."

"Greg, don't be like that."

"How should I be? I'm not the one who claims door prizes before a hundred people at a party."

"Greg, maybe it's time you entered the current century."

"I might not like the current century."

"Will you come home?"

He was overjoyed. He'd outwaited her and felt he'd won a point. Greg made reservations to return to Los Angeles. Rob was disappointed, hiding his sunburned face, but he put on a brave front. He stuck out his chin. Greg gave it a fake punch. He felt good again, whistling and skipping. On the plane, Rob leaned over to him and said:

"Sometimes I'm scared for you."

"Why?"

"Nothing. But will you be careful?"

Greg reached out and hugged him. This time it was he who hid his sunburned face.

FIFTEEN

The roll ended. Anderson had a heart attack just before Thanksgiving, and the doctors ordered him to stay away from the office, putting a strain on Piper. Greg was used to Anderson, not Piper. It didn't matter as long as CU was doing well, but the new year began bleakly. The agency turned as cold as it once had been hot.

Desmond, out of jail, resumed his contract with Videoscope, but not CU. Mark Ashley also canceled CU, giving no reason. One day in February Reverend Jack's past gibbered at him in headlines, killing his television ratings and bookings for his Theater of the Bible. He telegraphed from Anderson, Indiana, firing CU. Martin Bradford also faded. He was arrested for breaking a martini pitcher over his wife's head. Greg went to his hearing. The case was dismissed without arguments.

"He understood, that judge," Bradford said. "A married man. I promised him in chambers I'd stay sober."

"Will you?"

"When I'm a thousand miles away from her I will. I never wanted to be a senator. It was she, pushing me. She thought she could become first lady. She pushed me just like my mother used to. It was her money, you know. Well, curtain call. Good night, sweet prince. Alaska for me."

Bowing, he strolled north.

The hardest blow came when Masterson, in San Marino, said a review of his operations by a management consultant had determined that the agency no longer was needed. Greg had been expecting a cutback, not firing, yet he took the news without flinching. "Is there anything I can say to make you reconsider?" he asked.

"I'm afraid not, Mr. Gregory."

"Perhaps we can discuss the matter in a few months."

Masterson smiled. He shook his head. "I assure you, however, that I am aware of your abilities. If you think I can assist you personally in the future, please do not hesitate to call me."

They were in the library, the room with untouched books presided over by the imposing elk's head. The drapes were drawn, and Masterson's face was obscured by shadow. That described him, a nebulous shadow man. Now that it was over, Greg had mixed emotions of dismay and relief. Yet it gnawed at him. He felt betrayed, used, and angry. Many questions remained, particularly about Clay Dodson, and it seemed incredible that Masterson would dismiss him without answering them. Perhaps he thought he had. Or maybe the old man was protecting him. Greg sat still, searching for answers in the indistinct face across a big desk from him, not quite knowing what to say or do. He turned his head to see that Albert Norwine had slipped silently into the room. Norwine had the smug look of a pampered cat. He unsnapped his briefcase with a flourish, withdrew an envelope, and handed it to Greg, his shifting eyes triumphant.

"Your final billing," he said. "Now may I show you out?"

"I know my way out," Greg said. "I know how to leave and I know how to enter."

Masterson was gone; somehow, he'd vanished. Greg took his time. He examined the check and the letter canceling CU's contract. Norwine brushed his coat lapels, his pale little hands vibrating, his eyes averted. Greg strolled away. He turned wrong in the hallway and came out by the pool. He stopped abruptly. Denise Stevens sat naked by the diving board, her feet in the water. Her body was like a panther's, dark and pliant. She eyed him vacantly, letting him look, and then slipped noiselessly into the pool. Greg left, hurrying, feeling sweat gather under his arms.

A telegram from the Frog awaited him at the office. It read: CONGRATULATIONS, GENIUS. HONESTY IS ALWAYS THE BEST POLICY. Greg called in Maureen, who read the telegram and then stood with her hands on her hips.

"Well," she said.

"In some ways, I'm glad it's over."

"It may not be over. Didn't they leave the door open?"

"A crack," Greg said.

Piper took it hard. "Christ," he said on the phone. "You'd better come in to New York for a conference. The problem is—" Twenty-four hours later, seated before Greg at the Harvard Club in Manhattan, a martini straight up before him, it seemed as if Piper continued the sentence where he'd left off. "—that we're having some problems with clients here, too. By the way, Greg, I've been meaning to ask you. What ever happened to that dame in purple I sold on the Coast a while back?"

"Mona Tyson?"

"That was her name, sure."

"She had a picture scheduled but it was canceled."

"Did she ever pay her bill?"

"No. I didn't bill her."

"I see. Well, we're not a charitable organization, you know, Greg. Who else didn't you bill?"

He was beginning to feel uncomfortable. "I haven't caught up yet. It was one helluva mess after Harte left."

"I can understand that," Piper said, sipping his martini. He removed the olive, examined it, and ate it. "I get good reports on Maureen Crawford."

"Yes, she's very good."

"We were thinking of bringing her back here to work with some of the ad agency clients, but it never really got out of the talk stage. Then Anderson got sick and everything went on hold. Now don't misunderstand. I am running things."

"When do you think he'll be back?"

Piper shrugged. He wore a tailored three-piece suit, small gold cuff links, sincere narrow tie, and a new pepper-gray hairpiece. His watch was a gold Baume & Mercier, Genève.

"Maureen Crawford is in New York," he said.

"Oh?"

"Yes, at the Americana. I'm bringing in some key members of the team on the Coast to look at the operation here. I've wanted to do it, but, quite frankly, Anderson always pocket vetoed the idea. He became positively neurotic about the Coast, calling it a fen and a bog. I suppose because it's fashionable to use drugs there. Myself, I rather enjoyed it out

there." He began to speak rapidly, his voice
rising in pitch and volume, his hand fumbling
for a cigar in his vest pocket. "I haven't been
all that decisive, frankly, letting Anderson
make moves like hiring and promoting, firing,
but now that he's incapacitated, I have to do
things even if I don't enjoy all of them. I'm
making several moves while I can, frankly."

"Moves at CU?"

"Well, frankly, yes."

"I was told I was in charge at CU."

"Well, actually, Greg, the fact is, I'm afraid,
that we're letting you go. What's left there
doesn't need a man of your experience. We're
putting Maureen in charge."

Greg offered no defense. He merely left.
Piper saluted with his cigar. Greg found himself outside. The city seemed silent. He was
numb, under water and then coming to the
surface, ears plugged, lungs hurting. He
shook his head and it broke. Horns bleated
painfully. Pedestrians shoved aggressively. He
felt a terrible, pervasive depression.

"Americana," he told a taxi driver.

He called her on the house phone. "All
right, come up then," she said, her voice flat
and unsurprised. She wore a robe and her
hair was swept up. She sat cross-legged on the
bed and began to explain. "Piper called me
late last night, after you had left. He told me
to come to New York. That's all I know."

"Oh, sure."

"Greg, I don't think I like that tone. I also don't think I have to explain myself to you."

"Have you seen Piper?"

"No. He called. He's taking me to dinner."

"And you have no idea what it's all about?"

"None."

"I'll spoil his surprise. He's going to put you in charge of L.A. He canned me."

"Oh, Greg," she said. Her face was impassive. She sat still for a long time and then said, "I *did* know. He made me swear not to tell you. I hated it, sneaking around, knowing like I did."

"Yes, I'm sure."

"Don't use that tone of voice with me, damn you! For a while I was sick. I was physically sick."

"Of course you were, poor baby."

"Greg, don't *do* that!"

"When Piper says, 'When we think of the Coast, we think of you,' you'd better start watching your back."

It was a good imitation of Piper, and she smiled. She said, "I always watch my back. Piper I can handle."

"I'm sure. In the prone position."

"If I must," she said without flinching. Her eyes were hard and cold. "I'll use what I got while I got it. After all, I was a pretty good whore. Greg, it's been nice at times."

"Just like that?"

"Well, things go down in a hurry."

"Shit happens. Is that it?"

"Put it any way it pleases you." She stood with her arms folded and her chin raised, a beautiful dark animal sensual and alert, poised to spring if necessary. "But it wasn't just out of the blue. You're far too possessive and demanding. You won't have me halfway."

"What is halfway? Sharing you?"

"Just letting me go when I need to function by myself."

He bounded to her side and seized her arm, grasping it tightly. "I think Piper made a proposition to you. He said you can have the Coast if you throw me out of your bed. No tangling alliances. After all, the office head shouldn't date a disgruntled ex-employee, especially one she replaced. What he really wanted was my ass, since I'd never yes-man him and I had Anderson's ear. What will you do, by the way, when Anderson wakes up?"

"If he does, he'll have to go along with it."

"I'll bet Piper makes his first move on you tonight."

"Will it make you feel any better if I tell you he hasn't a chance? I'll work for him, but I detest the old fart."

"Though you wished me dead, you hate my murderer."

She let it pass. She tried to break away from his grasp but he squeezed harder, hurting her, forcing her to look at him. He couldn't read her eyes. Perhaps it was hate or perhaps love; maybe nothing, just nothing.

"I know you inside," he said. "Something there hurts for me and it's not going away. You can be tough as a tomcat, but it won't go away. You and I are the same. We came up from the back alley the other side of the tracks and we both know what it is to suffer and to hurt." He touched her breasts, feeling her heart. "It's in there. You can't cut it out. I'll be back. You'll be waiting."

"Don't bet the farm on it," she said coldly.

"Kill 'em for me, will you? For old times' sake."

"Oh, I'll kill them, all right."

"Go for the jugular."

"Well, you know me, pal."

After paying off the mortgages, he cleared about a hundred thousand on the sale of his house. He got two cashier's checks for fifty thousand each, one to Marie to hold for Rob, the other to himself. Then he hit Vegas, and four days later he had exactly a hundred and one dollars. He put the dollar, four quarters, into a slot and assigned it to a little old lady, who hit three bars, cackled, winked, collected her loot in a cup, and headed for the blackjack tables. Greg smiled, enjoying it. He called an auto dealer he knew in Santa Monica and told him to pick up the Mercedes at LAX.

"Nine thou," the dealer said, calling back.

"Okay. Wire it to Caesars Palace."

"Sure?"

"Sure."

269

"Some guys," said the dealer.

At first the dice at the craps table were hot but they soon turned cold and he was broke by 4 a.m. He pawned his watch and ring downtown to pay his bill at the Palace. Then he called his tailor in Beverly Hills, Weinstein.

"I'm not running out on you, but I can't pay for the suits," Greg said.

"It's all right already," Weinstein said. "When you can."

"No, you go pick them up. They're at the Highland Motel. Take the cuff links there. Anything you find."

"I'll hold it for you. I suppose you not pay the motel bill, either."

"I'm afraid you're right."

"I pay it. I hold the suits, the cuff links. Anytime you're ready."

At LAX Greg got into a taxi and said, "I got a C-note left. Where to for a C-note?" The cabbie shrugged, turned sad eyes to Greg, and said he was Russian. "C?" he said. After he got the old cab rolling up to eighty on the 405, he began to sing and then talk in broken English about his mother and the revolution. Soon, incredibly, he was crying. Greg directed him to Maureen's apartment. He said, "Wait, Ivan. I shall return." It was just talk. His heart was as heavy as the Russian's. He didn't have a key, but he knew her habits and quickly found one under the drainpipe. He went in, turning on the lights. He looked around, feeling leaden. He touched her clothing and jewelry and mirrors. Then he left. He replaced the key. The taxi took him to Beverly Hills. Greg gave the Russian the C-note and watched as the cab roared away, its faulty exhaust pipe snorting. He looked around. It was close to dawn. Fog clung to the streetlights like yellow smoke. He was penniless and alone. He felt like yowling, so he crammed his hands into his pockets and yowled. There was no response, not even an echo. Greg went to his office, turned on the lights, went to the john, and returned to the hallway holding the painting of the Indian girl. He heard a noise.

"Hear you been canned," said Henry Frost, the Heavyweight. "Hear she moves in."

"That's the skinny."

"Well, I guess it lets out Willy and me."

"I don't think so. She doesn't like you two—who could?—but she needs you. She may add room service."

"You're lucky, out of here. They mashed your bones. Now you can heal."

"Any departing words of wisdom? A blessing, perhaps?"

"No tears, for sure. You're sprung." The Heavyweight drew himself up to his full five feet and sniffed disdainfully. He was unshaven and bleary-eyed, his clothes wrinkled and his hair mussed, but he'd be ready for the day after a while in the john. He said, "I rank as one of your biggest fans. I admire you. You did a tough thing after you left Nam. You looked at yourself, didn't like what you saw, and went

271

out and whipped it. You said 'Thanks but no thanks' whenever temptation reared, which was often in this racket. Now you're down and you're not letting it get you again. So you got control. You know who you are."

"Words of wisdom," Greg said. "And a blessing."

"See ya around."

"Sure. See ya around."

He called Mike, who was working graveyard, and in twenty minutes they were having breakfast at Richard's.

"Come over and stay with Pam and me for a while," Mike said.

"I want something bigger than that. A thou cash."

"Jesus, I don't know, Greg."

"All suburbia husbands have a mad-money fund of a thou."

"I have a few bucks in the credit union."

"Let's go get them."

"Tell me what you're going to do."

"Start again from square one, buddy mine. I'm going to get Maureen back."

"You are a stupid ass, Greg."

Greg glanced at his painting on the seat beside him. Besides the clothing he wore, it was one of three items he'd kept. The other two were his Visa card and driver's license. He'd given his Gucci wallet to a bag lady in Santa Monica and dropped a pair of diamond cuff links into the poor box at St. Joan of Arc in West Los Angeles. It was important that he go all the way down. Only then could he begin again, just as wisdom was possible only with a confession that one was abysmally ignorant. Now he smiled and looked into Mike's eyes.

"I want her. I can't explain it and I won't try. I must have her and I will. I've never been stronger or more clear-headed and sure of myself. I can come back. I tested myself and I won. I had to go down to test. The Heavyweight understands that. I'm down on the mat and I'm not back on the stuff. I have all kinds of excuses but I'm not back. Look. What is accomplishment in this silly life of ours? Money? Fame? No. It's getting control of yourself once you've been out of control. That is what's difficult. Everything else is little next to it. I've been sicker than a skunk a hundred times, both physically and in the heart, wanting the stuff. It comes on you years after you've quit. You see, it always has you because it's always there. There is no cure, because the only cure is *it*. Do you see that? But I haven't gone back. I won't go back. That makes me pretty damn good. It makes me better than a lot of people. It makes me better than Mark Ashley, who's been through God knows how many cures and still is on it. I'm still beating it and I feel like a lark, buddy mine, no matter what else happens. Do you see?"

"Yes."

"A long speech. Too long. The director would cut it."

"I suppose so."

Arelo Sederberg

"Let's go get the thou."

"Will you keep in touch?"

"That is guaranteed. That and the thou. You can bet your bippy on both."

"Shake on it," Mike said.

"Shake," Greg said.

SIXTEEN

April 2 was a date of double importance for Pam and Mike: her birthday and their wedding anniversary. Making it close to triple, the twins had been born on April 5. This April 2 had particular significance, for Mike's novel had just been accepted. A letter from the publisher praised the book's merit but expressed concern about its sales potential. No combination could be better. Mike framed the letter, squared his chin, and began his second novel. He was on his tenth start when the doorbell rang. Pam smiled and the twins giggled as a red-haired telegram boy sang a strained rendition of happy birthday. The boy handed Pam an envelope, extracted a signature, and scampered away.

"Mike!" she cried. "Look!"

It contained twelve hundred-dollar bills and a note: "Principal and interest for a year, at 20 percent loan shark mob rate. Thanks and happy day, Greg."

There was a blush of early summer in the air that April 2, a day of early sun and a cloudless sky. Maureen paused before the Camden Drive hair salon and scrutinized herself in the mirror. She wore a tan suit that emphasized the straightness of her back and shoulders; the tailored look was in for business dress, and she had always liked it on her. A breeze kept blowing a dark curl down over her forehead. She pouted and pushed it back. Then she found herself looking down. Here she had found the new penny that day now so long, long ago, the beginning of her good-luck streak. She remembered it well. The penny itself was lost, discarded or thrown out; superstition, after all, was foolish, and only those who didn't believe in themselves trusted the spiritual. Again Maureen peered into the mirror. The image of a man in a blue pin-stripe suit visualized there.

"Look dressed to kill, Des Moines," Arthur Gregory said.

Maureen squealed in delight. "Greg! I don't believe it!" She dashed into his arms. "Oh, shit, it's good to see you!"

"Will you show me Hollywood? Lunch at the Derby?"

She looked at him. How long had it been? A year? Two? She wasn't sure. She'd kept busy, driving him from her thoughts, but he'd refused to disappear, returning sometimes at night in lonely hotel rooms or in a photograph or at a place they had shared in the past. It had been necessary to drive him out of her mind. She'd felt no remorse or loss, only the occasional loneliness, sometimes so acute she had tightened her fists to stop her hands from trembling. But then she plunged herself back into work, a sure cure that allowed her to forget. In fact, she didn't want to believe there was anything to forget. There had been some good times that had become good memories. She had learned from him and would always be grateful because he'd given her that first break. There was no more. Yet in the deep of night, coming awake, she found herself jarred from a dream and remembering, and there were times when her eyes misted with tears before she drifted back to sleep. It continued to disturb her, the period of her life when she had felt something that others called love. She still didn't understand it and knew she never really would. But she knew it was an enemy to resist or outwait until it faded.

She had dated during the year, primarily Hollywood-related dates, such as previews, the Academy Awards, the Bowl, the Greek Theater. She was seen at Chasen's some evenings and the Bistro Gardens at lunch. Her new apartment was a Sunset highrise, and on

weekends she often brunched at the Bel Air
Hotel and biked on Rexford or Alpine Drive.
There had been a few times in bed with
attractive men to satisfy basic needs, but
nothing that threatened to last. Once in New
York she had met a man in a hotel bar and
they had spent the weekend in his suite. He
said he was a stage actor; she said she was in
real estate. She didn't care what he was, or
even want to know his real name. She got
what she had sought, an extended period of
uninhibited sex with a handsome stranger,
well-endowed and virile, and then freedom,
no regrets or questions. The only difference
between her and any other young woman was
that she had gone ahead and done it while
they only thought about it. Nor had she any
worries about it. The experience in college
had taught her a lot about health care. She'd
also learned how to handle men, to be wary of
many and to hate most.

Maureen had a client meeting, so she took
Greg to her office—his old one—and asked
him to wait.

"Nice office," Greg commented, glancing
around.

"Only one with a john," she said.

"Where is everybody?"

"Everybody you know? Oh, out. Out or
gone." She slipped to her desk and turned
over a plaque she'd had encased in plastic, the
one attesting to conquest of Mark Ashley.
Greg looked with-it, up-to-date in his Mr. Guy

suit and Gucci shoes and tie, but under it he probably was the same old-fashioned, adorable prude. "Listen, here's an idea. Why don't you attend our client meeting? Pretend you're a new a.e. It will scare my a.e.'s shitless and might help them. Will you?"

"You're on," he said.

She placed him at the head of the table like a chairman of the board. His presence was not explained to the a.e.'s, a delicious trick. The meeting was with the producers of a new movie, a very funny and frequently poignant one about a homosexual volleyball team, beach boys from Venice who try for the Olympics. They prove to be so good they're forced to take steroid tests. It probably would play well in San Francisco and certain artsy communities, but there were concerns about the hinterlands. The producers were straight, and they worried about being accused of exploitation. They had a couple of million dollars invested in a project that had looked pretty good in story-idea conferences but that now, edited and in the can for release, might be outdated by AIDS. Nobody around the table had a suggestion on what to do.

"Shelve it," Greg said.

The producers turned in unison and glared at him.

Greg went on, looking beyond and through everyone: "There are peaks and valleys for everything. Right now, homosexual rights is down. But it will flare up again, because it always does. Shelve your picture for, say, a year. Meanwhile, we'll go to work on it. We'll hint around that it's too frank and daring to release. The mothers of America are against it. The American Legion threatens to slash the screen of any theater bold enough to exhibit it. The John Birch Society is outraged; this takes free enterprise too far. Catholics and Protestants alike, and Islam and Judaism, are vehemently against it. After all that, the public will be howling for it. You will be forced to release it to very receptive audiences."

A long and profound silence followed. Then one of the producers, the youngest one (whose father, Maureen knew, had staked him to the picture but hadn't read the script), began to clap his hands. Soon the others joined. Greg was given such applause he was forced to stand and bow.

"That was very shrewd," the young producer told Maureen as they left. "Audacious. Striking. Modern. It was *very* 1990 of him. Who is he?"

"Oh, he's new here," she said, adding with a straight face: "He studied at Stanford under Dr. Saxe-Commings."

"He *did*?"

At lunch Maureen told Greg: "You're not going to believe me, but I was going to suggest something like that. Putting it on the shelf, I mean."

"Oh?"

"Didn't you teach me that when you don't

know what to do, you come out of left field?
And didn't you say it was a mistake to let a
client think they know anything? If they did,
why would they hire you to tell them?"

They were at Richard's. Sally the Sphinx
brought tea for Maureen and a pastrami on
rye for Greg. She merely nodded at Greg, as if
he'd been there yesterday instead of more
than a year ago. A strange feeling came over
Maureen. She felt that he'd not been gone,
that he'd been by her side at the office, omni-
present and giving advice. Yet this man was a
different Arthur Gregory, she sensed, one who
was confident of himself and had no lingering
doubts. That was part of the strangeness. He
was different, yet she felt she had known him
for many years. She, too, was no doubt different. A part of him had become some of her,
just as a part of her had fused within him.

"Where did you get those new a.e.'s?" he
asked. "Hollywood High?"

"Well, we can't afford legends like Arthur
Gregory." She added quickly: "Although
we're doing all right."

"So I hear."

"What do you hear?"

"Oh, I hear around. I hear, for example,
that your handle is Legend II."

She smiled. "In deference to the Great
One."

"I didn't see Heavyweight."

"Oh, he's still there."

"Still sleeping over?"

"I suppose so. Just as long as he doesn't use my office as a bedroom, I don't care."

"And Planter?"

"Planter is out planting. He still hates women, thinks I'm a horrible cunt, but of course I keep him on. Without Heavyweight and Planter, we're gone. You know that. You told me that, more than once."

"How are Closer and Great White?"

"Closer recovered and is running things again. Great White is sorry Closer didn't die, of course, but he's confident there'll be a second heart attack soon."

"Mrs. Olsen?"

"Back to New York with her. And one day Marge just upped and walked out."

"I know," Greg said. "I hired her."

He retained the exasperating characteristic of dropping hints without telling her, preferring to show. He paid the bill, leaving Sally a five-dollar tip. Taking Maureen's arm, he led her to a parking lot on Dayton Way. It was a lot that catered to special customers who paid extra for service, care, and safety. The attendant knew Greg. He promptly brought up a red Porsche and held open the passenger's door for Maureen. Greg drove silently, letting the Porsche out on the Ventura Freeway, weaving in and out of traffic. He was showing her the new Greg, a freeway flyer in a Porsche, maybe telling her the prudish side of him was gone. He turned off just past Calabassas, clashed the Porsche's gears up a circular drive into the hills, and braked before a gold-painted twenty-foot gate that seemed suddenly to appear at the peak of a sharp upgrade. It opened like magic before the red Porsche and a guard in blue waved them on, standing straight, almost a military posture. Large letters in a half circle spelled out V I D E O S C O P E. Maureen had never been there. It was considered a sort of inner sanctum studio, especially since its acquisition by Cyrus Masterson; it released pictures, all right, on a four-a-year schedule, with major directors and stars, but its policy was never to discuss a project until just before it was to be premiered. Maureen had tried, with absolutely no success, to interest Videoscope in using CU as the publicity agency for some of its releases. It was a closed door. But now she had effortlessly been transported through the guarded gate into the secluded tabernacle. It appeared quite ordinary; in fact, rather unfinished. There was a large brick building, four stories, with rows of windows that had a prison look except for the series of large television discs on the roof. A dozen olive-drab Quonset huts were scattered about, fronted by tall, crooked palm trees. The lawns were artificial turf. Everything looked temporary, like a hurriedly erected fair grounds that could be quickly disassembled and moved. Even the brick look of the main building was a facade. Maureen had been to the major studios—Fox, Universal, Warners—and found them bustling with activity. This one

283

seemed dead. Greg parked in a space where his name was stenciled in red. A young black man in a uniform lounged beside a limousine, smoking a cigarette. Maureen recognized him as Mark Ashley's chauffeur. She drew in a quick breath of air. Greg took her arm. They went into the building, passed by a male guard, and took the elevator to the top floor. He guided her through double doors at the end of a carpeted corridor. Inside it was like a busy doctor's waiting room, crammed with people, some of them children. A few stood up as they entered, but Greg brushed smilingly past and opened a second door for Maureen. She saw Marge seated behind a desk strewn with papers, a phone in her hand.

"Crisis time," Marge said to Greg.

"When isn't it?" he responded, smiling.

Marge ignored Maureen. They had never liked each other; in fact, Maureen had kept her on at the agency in deference to Greg, a foolish sentimentality that had resulted in some knife thrusts to the back. But she couldn't blame Marge for disliking her. It was useless to explain that she'd had nothing to do with Greg's firing. You couldn't change a small mind when it was set, particularly a woman's.

Greg took her through a third door into his office. It was paneled and well furnished—a hand-carved desk, a credenza with a large-screen television, wet bar, a view of the hills through the windows. The carpet was spongy.

That horrid painting of the kneeling Indian woman that Greg had brought back from Arizona was on one wall, the only obvious disfigurement in the office.

"I'm impressed," she said.

"It has its own john," Greg said.

"Oh. I see. It's show and tell. You brought me out here for an object lesson."

"Wrong. I have a deeper motive."

"Who are those people in the outer office?"

"Job-seekers. Actors, stage mothers, writers. Marge is a softy. She gives them studio passes."

"Will you see them?"

"As many as I can. I can't just stomp on their dreams."

"I think you're the softy. If I may play your shrink, I'd say you have a need to be loved."

"Exactly, doctor."

She gestured at the room. "I suppose you'll tell me what this is all about when you're good and ready."

"Simple. You knew me in my other life as the best-loved flack in Hollywood. Now I rank among the most-hated producers in Hollywood."

"Most hated? I can't believe that."

"Of course you can. I learned how to go for the jugular."

"You're going to say I taught you."

He brushed it off. He sat down behind his desk and put his feet up, showing off $300 Gucci alligator shoes. "I also learned, as a producer, that for every star there are sixty nonstars who are just as irritating and tantrum-prone." He ticked them off, tapping his finger on the desk for each. "Sound editor, dialogue coach, script clerk, film loader, clapper boy, grip, music composer and arranger, dubbing editor, art director, prop man, painter and plasterer and plumber, publicist, still photog, hairdresser and makeup artist and wardrobe girl, gaffer, best boy, stuntman—"

"Stop, stop. Enough, enough."

"To name a few," he said, smiling.

She sat before him, her legs crossed and fingers linked, meeting his brown-eyed gaze. This much she knew: They would end up in bed today—somewhere, anywhere. She could tell it by his eyes and body language, and she could feel it in herself. She'd admit it to no one, but she had been lonely almost always in the past year, lonely by herself and lonely with others. She realized how much she'd missed him and also felt old fears. For the first time in her life, after he'd left she had felt hurt and actual physical pain, a sense of loss, over a man. She never wanted to feel that pain again. It had cost her sleep and affected her work. And it proved that love was a weakness.

The door flew open and a flustered Marge stood there, unable to restrain a man who pushed past her. He was bald except for dark fringes of hair along the back and sides of his head and he walked with a limp—no, not a limp, more of a drunken lurch. Greg removed his feet from the desk and rose to greet the intruder. It wasn't until then that Maureen recognized Mark Ashley. She'd known that he wore a toupee but she hadn't realized how different he looked without it. He looked over sixty, a generation older than his screen image. Ashley didn't recognize Maureen, or maybe he didn't even see her. He went right to Greg, his eyes blazing, waving his hands wildly.

"I want that woman removed from the picture and I want her removed today!" he shouted. "Now! Do you hear? Now! If she is here tomorrow, I walk. Do you hear?"

"I hear," Greg said quietly.

Ashley's hands pawed the air. His lips tightened and his eyes bulged. He looked on the verge of tears. "She has the nerve to make suggestions to me on how I'll play the scene. She's just beginning and she acts like queen of the set. She thinks she owns the fucking place. I want her *out*!"

"All right," Greg said.

"What?"

"I said all right. She's out."

"You don't mean that."

"But I do. I'll take up your request with the boss this afternoon. I'll tell him you want her out."

Ashley responded with a vigorous shaking of his head. "No. You say *you* want her out. You're the producer, and you say it won't work with her there."

"But I don't want her out. You want her out. One thing I have learned is that you do not lie to this man."

"You're a cocksucker," Ashley said.

He looked at Maureen, his eyes blank, stomped, and then turned and lurched out. The door slammed. Greg stood gazing after Ashley and then glanced at Maureen. He smiled.

"See? I'm one of the most-hated, as I said."

"What was that all about?"

"First things first. Would you like to see the studio? Believe it or not, it's all here—sound stages, prop rooms, even a stable with four white horses."

"No, I don't want to see the studio. Not today, at least."

"All right. What, then?"

"I want to go someplace else."

"Where?"

"Oh, you'll know where. Just take me— well, anywhere."

Outside they saw Ashley in a heated conversation with his chauffeur, who took a verbal lashing without cringing; in fact, as Greg backed up the Porsche, she noticed that the man was lashing back at Ashley. Greg drove silently. He didn't speak until they were off the freeway, passing UCLA on Sunset. He turned North on Beverly Glen.

"What that with Ashley was all about was a form of psychological reversal," he said.

"We're making a picture called *Life to Live Over*, sort of a remake of *A Star Is Born*, yet different. It doesn't pay to be too original. Ashley plays the aging star."

"He looked much older."

"He looked like he's supposed to look for the role. The up-and-coming bright light in the script is a girl played by Denise Stevens. She's the one Ashley was raising hell about."

"Denise Stevens? The name is familiar."

"Denise Stevens is Cyrus Masterson's protégée."

"Oh, yes! His mistress. So he's put her in the movies, and you're the producer."

"I'm the producer. But your implication is dead wrong. Denise Stevens has talent."

"She has talent. Yes, sir."

"She does! Masterson put her through workshops, and she's appeared off Broadway. She can act. And she's never late and always knows her lines. It's Ashley who's always late. We have to shoot around him. He's as bad as M.M."

"Who?"

"Marilyn Monroe. She was always late."

"Oh."

"He's the one who tries to give acting lessons on the set. He blames her for his own failings."

"How did you connect with him?"

"I went to him and said I had a script with something different for him. He'd been

289

screaming in the press for a challenge. He asked for some concessions, and I gave him the concessions."

"What concessions?"

"Oh, like pay in cash every day. Like having his personal shrink on the set."

She laughed, a little snorting laugh. "Why doesn't he take his gripes to the shrink?"

"Because the shrink has walked off. No pay, no play. Truth is, Ashley's broke and couldn't get a part until I came along."

"Now that I find hard to believe."

"Oh? In this trade we are known as fast up, but much faster down."

"Then his complaint to you was a charade. With Masterson behind her, who could get her off the picture?"

"Nobody but him wants her off. And he doesn't really, because he knows, down deep, she's teaching him."

"Maybe his shrink said so."

"Yes, and then ran."

He took the curves at high speed, gearing a lot and using both sides of the road. Maureen hung on. He went up a narrow bypath, careened left, and pushed an opener on the sun visor. A gate parted in front of them. Greg went up a driveway and stopped beside the white porch columns of a giant colonial house.

"What do you call it?" Maureen said. "Tara?"

"I'm afraid it has only six bathrooms."

"How many bedrooms?"

"Nine. I think."

"Let's get going if we're going to try them all."

A wide, red-carpeted stairway led from the sun room in front. Maureen dashed up to the first landing and took off her shoes, dropping them below one at a time. Then she took off her jacket and stood with her hip angled toward him, her legs spread, looking as sultry and sexy as she could. He held her and kissed her, hard.

"Are we alone?" she asked, breaking away.

"Yes."

"No maids? No butler?"

"They're taking the day off. I said I had something very hot coming in here."

"You've become crafty."

"Very."

"And sure of yourself."

"Very."

Maureen laughed and ran up the remaining steps to the top. She entered a wide hallway with numerous doors on both sides. The first one led to a bathroom. The second opened to a large bedroom with sheeted furniture. She crossed the room, moving noiselessly on the carpet, and opened the drapes, letting in a crack of light. The bed was a huge four-poster with a canopy. She crawled in and lay down, spreading her legs and stretching out her ankles. She felt the throb of her heart and she breathed through her mouth, her head back on the big pillow, her hair strewn. She was ready. She wanted him, an aching she'd felt for him all day. He was seated on the bed, his back to her, hurriedly undressing.

"Come on, come on," she said, moving her legs.

He was just as ready, something she'd sensed on the drive. He was rougher and even more passionate than she'd known him in the past, kissing her so hard it hurt, taking her breath away, pushing up her bra and cupping her breasts, kissing the hard nipples. He pushed her skirt up and entered her deeply without removing her panties. She held him, thrusting up and down, moving rapidly, and it came to her quickly, an explosion she felt throughout her body. She was gasping and pounding him with her fists and screaming deep in her throat. Never had it happened to her like this, never even close to it.

"God, oh, God," she said, falling back, holding him inside of her. "Oh, God, God."

They took a long shower together and then lay close beside each other, naked, the sun now a warm afternoon gold. She wasn't afraid. She had overcome the fear. Whatever was to happen would happen. To hell with it. To hell with everything. She was here, tasting him and smelling him, and here was where she wanted to be.

"Fuck the future," she said.

"Eh?" he responded sleepily.

"I said fuck the future."

"Sure. Fuck it, the future."

"Tell me what you've been up to now."

"We haven't tried the other bedrooms yet."

"We will. Tell me first."

He propped himself up, chin in hand. "You're gorgeous."

"So are you."

"I love you."

"You, too. You bastard."

"I'm a bastard because I make you admit it."

"Exactly."

"Well, where shall I start? I'll start when I was broke. I borrowed a thou from my pal Mike. You remember Mike and Pam. The valley squares?"

"You said that for my benefit. You don't think they're a bit square."

"At any rate, to continue the narrative, I borrowed a thou from Mike. I spent it the first day. A suit, shoes, a shirt, a tie. It was gone, more than gone. Then I rented a Ferrari on a credit card and went to see Cyrus Masterson."

"Just like that?"

"Well, I made an appointment, through proper channels at that. Albert Norwine."

"Why a Ferrari?"

"I thought it would be a nice touch. After all, Masterson is Italian. At least I think he is. Anyway, he did see me and he listened. I reminded him that on the day he sacked the agency he told me I would be welcomed if I called. I said what I really wanted to do in this life was to produce movies. It was almost too easy. It was almost, in fact, as if he'd been expecting me. He said I should drive out to Videoscope and see Joseph Corwin, whom he would telephone. That's the Frog, Joe Corwin.''

"Yes. You hated him.''

"Oh? Don't remember.''

"You remember, all right.''

"Well, it's true that the Frog and I have had differences in the past. But now we're the best of friends. Of course. Masterson signed my passport.''

"That's all?''

"Just about.''

"You're not beholden to Masterson?''

"Only to do a good job. And, of course, put Denise Stevens into a picture.''

"It sounds too easy. You said that first, too easy.''

"Why? What's so complicated about it? I knew Masterson and had done a good job for him before. He's in the picture business now. In the picture business you need producers. To be a producer you have to have money or know how to raise it. I don't have it and I don't know how to raise it, but I have Masterson. He knows I have a good sense of promotion and that I know what sells.''

"What are you doing in this house if you don't have any money?''

"Leased, little love. The pots and pans are leased. I bill a maid to Videoscope. I haven't had a party here, but if I did, again it would be billed to Videoscope. It's not true that I have a gentleman's gentleman to dress me."

"Or Denise Stevens to undress you?"

"Denise Stevens? Surely you joke. Do I want my balls cut out?"

"Don't you worry about working for Masterson?"

"Why should I?"

"Well, you know."

"I don't worry about working for him any more than I would about any other boss. Neither will you."

"What d'you mean, neither will I?"

"We're almost finished with the shooting on *Life to Live Over*. It goes to editing and then into release. We need a good flack. I want to hire CU—if you do the work—on a one-shot basis for the picture."

"Well, I'll have to think it over."

"Think it over, hell. CU never ever thought over a prospective client or job."

"I don't want to talk business right now. Let's try another bedroom."

"You are a wanton woman."

"Of course I am."

"We can't fail. Legend the First teams with Legend the Second. We can't fail."

"No. We can't."

"We'll kill them," he said.

"We'll kill them."

"Gregory's back and Crawford's got him. You missed me."

"I did miss you, you bastard. I'll admit it."

"I missed you," he said.

"Why didn't you at least call?"

"I had nothing to tell you."

"I'm glad you're back."

"I'm glad I'm back myself."

"We'll make it a big picture. You'll be a big man in Hollywood. Produced by Arthur Gregory. I like the sound of that."

"Yes, it does have a rather nice ring."

"Yes."

"Come here," he said.

"I'm here," she said.

SEVENTEEN

Greg took Maureen to the Academy Awards at the Shrine Auditorium and afterward they made some of the parties. They stopped at Vertigo, Helena's, and pc; then, well after midnight, lingered at Colin Webster's traditional all-night post-awards bash at Spago. Webster used to be known as the Dealer, an abandoned handle because it suggested drugs, not movie dealmaking. He had been around the studios forever doing everything —including, he joked, some of the lowly jobs, such as grip, stuntman, location scrounger, script girl, assistant director, publicist. He'd been chewed out by Mayer, given the practical-joke electric-chair shock by Goldwyn, actually seen Howard Hughes, and set up gag sequences for Keaton and Chaplin. He remembered the silents, the first color, the first talkie. Now he headed a new talent agency—AoA, Artists of America—formed by mergers between small shops and proselytism from biggies such as Morris, CAA, ICM. The crowd every year said nobody would attend his party next time—he was too old school, the era of Bogart and Tracy, Crawford and Davis—yet everybody always showed up, perhaps to see if others had downplayed Colin Webster's party so they themselves could have more time with the ancient fox. He had started out as an actor a long time ago, playing Polonius on the stage. Several new waves in Hollywood had written him off, but he wouldn't die. The joke was Dealer, Part XIII. The truth was that he still counted, or a great number of Hollywood lords and princes thought he did. He was a master at keeping people off guard. You never knew when he was joking and when he was serious, especially about himself. He said he was out of gas, an old party who yearned for the peace of Forest Lawn; at the same time, behind your back, he made a deal for your star with your enemy. He also said he was old enough to tell the truth, having told enough lies when he'd been a publicist. His personal favorite among his publicity stunts was to premiere an oater at a Texas drive-in theater with only horses in the audience. It got a lot of ink. But studios had too much dignity for that nonsense nowadays.

Maybe that was why so many were doing belly flops into bankruptcy. There weren't filmmakers in Hollywood anymore, only used-car dealers and other mountebanks. You laughed at that, even if you were one of them. As soon as you stopped taking the old fart seriously, you might get hit. Either he was a man of deceptive power or of no power at all, but you couldn't take a chance.

One thing for sure. His parties had class. There were young and old, beautiful people and faded has-beens nobody knew, winners and losers, crashers, press, public officials, and always working clowns, comics, and musicians on midnight-to-dawn gigs. There was Mumm's champagne, caviar from Vladivostok, crab from Chesapeake Bay, shrimp from Alaska, macadamia nut tarts from Hawaii, lobster from Maine, red snapper from Massachusetts. Webster held a key spot all night long; people came to him. He was a short, bald man with sagging jowls and bright blue eyes above deep, puffy circles. His detractors were reminded of a penguin, starlets thought of sugar daddy, acquaintances who knew him or believed they did had images of an imposing Buddhalike mogul. None was correct. When stirred to action, he moved more like a gazelle than a penguin, he'd been a faithful husband for five decades, and he realized the day of the mogul was over. But Webster could still strike a deal, create a headline, launch a project, or cripple an opponent's production.

"I hear good things about your picture, dear boy," he said to Greg. "I hear it has a surprise or two in it."

"Could be."

"I hear it's Mark Ashley's first job of acting."

"That's funny. I'll tell him that."

"I already have. What's next on your horizon?"

"If this flick goes, I'm on my own, free and clear."

"Well, say hello to Cyrus for me, dear boy."

Greg got no more time with the old Dealer; others pressed in, groveling and smiling. Using proper protocol, he ushered Maureen out about 3 a.m., not saying good-bye to Webster or his sleepy-eyed, rouged little wife. It was an all-night party, but only cronies took advantage of that hospitality, which included breakfast. Others also had observed the protocol, causing attendants to race for the Corvettes, Rolls-Royces, Mercedeses, Ferraris, BMWs, Jaguars, and Porsches. The famous didn't get precedence, despite waving hefty tips, because they had to compete with each other.

"I didn't know the old goat knew Masterson," Greg said as the Porsche moved through the fog-shrouded Beverly Hills streets. "I wonder how well they know each other."

"I didn't know the old goat knew you," Maureen said, a hint of respect for both in her voice. "You surprise me more every day. The

new Arthur Gregory. And, speaking of surprises, what are the surprises in your picture
he was talking about?"

"Let's go see," Greg said.

He stopped on the way to the studio and
woke up a projectionist who lived in the
valley. By the time Greg and Maureen got to
the projection room at Videoscope, the film
was ready to roll. The audio hadn't been
mixed yet, so the projectionist had to string
the sound track separately, which meant a
half-dozen starts and stops before he got it
right. Maureen drew on glasses and leaned
back. Just as he was a new Arthur Gregory,
she was a new Maureen Crawford. She
seemed more mature, more dependent, more
loving. Celebrities no longer impressed her.
She was used to them, their crankiness and
pettiness, their childish demands and tantrums, their fears and despair, their grim
ordinariness without makeup, hairpieces,
massaging, or even plastic surgery. No longer
did she flirt at parties, instead giving the
impression she belonged to the man who
brought her. Yet an element of elusiveness
remained in her, and he wanted her absolutely. To have her absolutely was not possible
without having success absolutely. He would.
He must. There had been qualms before,
conflicts and needlings of conscience, but no
longer. He knew what he wanted and he knew
how to get it. Masterson offered success;
therefore he also offered Maureen. Greg had

sickened with wanting and loneliness when he had been away from her. Now she was here, breathing next to him, warm to his touch. He would never let her go.

After the picture, he parked in Santa Monica by the ocean. The air was heavy with salt spray from the cracking surf. Dawn broke pink in the sky, slits that reddened like fire as they expanded and dissolved into billowy ash.

"I figure I'm bankable to go on my own if we do fifty mill box office with this," he said. "What did you think of the picture?"

"Like your Webster person said, it has surprises."

"I have ten points, the studio has the rest. I brought it in for just under fifteen mill."

"Business, business, business," Maureen chanted. She put her hand on his leg. "Let's find a bed."

"Your place is nearer than mine."

"Actually, I had my eye on that grungy-looking motel we passed."

"Be serious."

"I am serious." Her fingers explored, soft and sensual. "Would you get a hurry on, please?"

The premiere of *Life to Live Over* exploded in the night. It was an event terrible and splendid, horrible and magnificent, garish and refined, disorderly and controlled. It splashed with color, resounded with noise, scented of cherry blossoms, tasted of auto exhaust and threatening rain. Maureen, who

coordinated it, decided on an old-fashioned
ostentation for the update of an old-fashioned
picture. The movie was about love and ambition and seeking and decay, the stuff of life
and particularly of Hollywood. So all that—
the lust for and love of life, the rage and
obsession of living, of wanting and getting, of
spending and wasting—was rolled into a giant tinsel ball and unrolled at dusk on the
streets of Hollywood. Cherry blossoms were a
theme of the picture, symbolic of peace and
serenity, of love. They littered the sidewalks in
pink profusion, scattering from boxed trees.
Despite their number, they were obscured by
the sheer scope of the event. It was like a
small fair, or a zoo. There were searchlights,
blimps in the sky, grandstands, bands, floats,
tumblers, jugglers, clowns, giveaway vendors,
horses, camels, giraffes, dolphins in a tank. A
thousand luminous balloons ascended. A can-
non cracked from a roof. There were politi-
cians, astronauts, sports celebrities, and of
course movie stars, old and new, arriving in
new cars and ancient ones, but all of them
long and large. The rain did come, a stinging
shower, but it had no adverse effect on the
performance. The cheering was just as loud,
the stars just as bright and smiling. When it
was over and quiet, spent confetti and banners
littered the sidewalks and street and gathered
in the gutters, soaked and vanquished.

One incident at the premiere was misinter-
preted by the crowd, but not by Maureen, who

understood it completely. A black Buick, vintage about 1930, dispensed a man in a long-tailed tuxedo. He blinked in the lights, tall and thin and gaunt, looking around as if blinded.

"It's John Carradine!" said one of the fans behind red ropes, an older man.

"Aw, he's dead, John Carradine," said a woman.

The crowd squinted at the gaunt figure and the gaunt figure squinted at the crowd. The man strutted, arms outstretched, but the fans did not respond, turning their attention to the next-arriving limousine. The television crews also ignored the gaunt man. He stood forlornly. Then two tall men in suits and hats pushed forward and positioned themselves on either side of the shunned figure. One spoke. The other took out handcuffs. The man offered his wrists to captivity without resistance. Now the crowd had noticed. It was a small pantomine act to add to the gaiety of the event, a diversion, perhaps a reenactment of a scene from the film. They applauded. The man bowed deeply to the crowd before he was led away.

"All right, tell me," Maureen said to Greg at the post-premiere party, upstairs at Bistro Gardens. "Why was Reverend Jack arrested, and did you entice him out here so he would be pinched?"

"Why would I do a thing like that?"

"You didn't exactly love him."

The place was so packed and interruptions

were so many that it was almost impossible to carry on a conversation. They did, although sometimes ten minutes ensued between the asking and answering of a question. It was the time of champagne and music and roses, a great sendoff for a film that everybody agreed would be a hit, even some important critics in private snatches of conversation with Greg. Sometimes you had to bellow to be heard. The band wasn't loud, but the people were. They laughed, shouted, yelped, wept, danced, drank, all a part of it even if they were no part of it.

The film had three major surprises. One was the appearance, slightly more than a cameo role, of H. Leslie Williams, the Reverend Jack who had flared to brief fame with his Theater of the Bible. He played an evangelical preacher who gave such an impassioned sermon at a tent meeting that children had convulsions and the aroused townsfolk, instead of kneeling in worship, almost lynched him at a subsequent barn dance. Reverend Jack, after his troubles, had skipped from Anderson, Indiana, right to Canada and had not been heard of up to this point.

"What did they get him for?" Maureen asked.

"I assume it was tax avoidance," Greg said.

"You invited him to the premiere, didn't you?"

"Guilty as charged."

"Go on."

He was taking her home in the Porsche, well after 3 a.m. All was quiet and the rain was a pleasant, sleepy tap, tap, tap on the roof. The windshield wipers squeaked.

"You showed admirable restraint in not mentioning Reverend Jack when you saw the movie at the studio," Greg said.

"I am a woman of admirable restraint. Go on."

"Well, I'll admit I suggested the part to the screenwriter, and I was thinking about the reverend when I did. When we were filming a sequence in Canada, who shows up on the set but Reverend Jack himself? I'd taken the part out, but I couldn't resist putting it back in."

"I wonder why he risked arrest by showing up."

"Easy answer. He's a ham. He couldn't resist it. It was killing him, out of the spotlight in Canada."

"It's all grotesque."

"Only in Hollywood. Don't forget you created him."

"A million years ago."

"Two million."

"In another life," she said.

Mark Ashley's performance was the second surprise in the picture. He settled down and acted. It was a new role for him, and critical praise also was something new. At the same time it ruined him. He played an aging star, one about to be forgotten. The carefree adventurer who frustrated redneck law with a dimpled wink and the lover with the devastating little smile was seen close to what he really was—bald, his face drawn, unsure and unsteady, a has-been. A star had become an actor, said the critics, high praise that destroyed Ashley. He went to Vegas and worked at reclaiming his old image by losing a quarter-million dollars at baccarat. He got drunk, took a swing at the casino manager, was decked, and made the gossip columns for the last time.

The third surprise was Denise Stevens, playing a faithful lover of the aging star. She almost stole the show, stirring talk of an Oscar nomination. *Life to Live Over* was a hit, grossing seventy million domestic. Audiences paid to see the newcomer Stevens and Mark Ashley in an unusual role. They left disillusioned about him but raving about her. Greg was hot. Backers called him. So did the media. Overnight, he'd become wealthy. *Variety* proclaimed:

Ex-Flack
Sets Flit
to Own Flix

After the picture proved to have legs, Masterson held a poolside party nominally to acknowledge its success. As usual, Greg was invited alone. It was a scalding July day, its discomfort intensified by humidity and smog. A band in maroon costumes braved the sun while the guests competed for shade. Norwine huddled beside his dour wife. A chubby, dimpled blonde clung to the Frog's arm, cooing like a sated pigeon. He said she was his granddaughter. Once umbrella lounges were occupied they weren't often surrendered. A row of unattached women of varying vintages, looking forlorn yet queenly in silks and satins, their cheeks glowing and their lips savagely red, lay wilting and quivering in the uncertain shade. Most of the guests were middle-aged or older, the music was restrained, the conversations subdued. Perhaps the heat tempered the pace, a high-noon blaze that slowed movement and sound and seemed to descend and encapsulate everyone in a moist, blistery bubble.

But early in the afternoon the party took on a different aspect, a younger and livelier one. Squealing children were released from the house and dived into the pool, splashing and shouting. The band increased its tempo and the adults became a little more animated, perhaps loosened up by the strong red wine served in big glasses by waiters in black. Before the children, the character of the party had seemed somewhat ominous to Greg, something beyond mere sedateness, an order maintained by some form of invisible enforcement. Now it had become more spontaneous, a family party, and its guests seemed younger, happier, and fuller with life.

Yet Greg remained uncomfortable, cautious, and slightly nervous. He felt out of place, alone. The sun slashed down in heavy white sheets, undisturbed by the slightest breeze. Masterson, in a green shirt and black pants, wearing a red bow tie, circulated gregariously, greeting and chatting, seeming impervious to the heat. Never had Greg seen him as friendly and animated.

A few young men in light suits and loose ties moved about inconspicuously, looking impatient and bored. One, ahead of Greg in the buffet line, said he was in real estate. He was squat and broad-shouldered, with dark bushy eyebrows that ran together. He and another man of similar build and dress had arrived about the same time as Denise Stevens, who'd apparently learned enough about Hollywood to come fashionably late. She was the only celebrity there, an overnight sensation, and attracted some attention, especially from the younger guests. She wore a light blue pantsuit and a wide-brimmed hat to match. One of the lounging ladies offered her a seat in the shade, but she smiled a polite refusal and instead removed her shoes and sat at the edge of the pool, her feet immersed. She looked small and unhappy.

Greg kneeled beside her. "Brava, lonely contessa."

They liked and respected each other, genuine feelings, and he wasn't afraid to talk to her. "You look as if you'd prefer to be elsewhere."

"Oh, heat never bothered me."

"How about a drink?"

"Some lemonade, if he has it."

He found the lemonade, but didn't make it back to her. Norwine intercepted him, and again he found himself in the den, under the dead eyes of the elk. A butler in tails entered and closed the drapes. As the room grew darker it also grew quieter, and in the stillness the temperature seemed to rise. Masterson entered. He poured three brandies in snifters, taking one for himself and handing the second to Norwine. A man entered and picked up the third snifter.

"I believe you know Mr. Webster," Masterson said. He raised his glass. "A toast to our producer. To Mr. Gregory."

"Dear boy," Webster said. "Hear, hear."

Masterson said, "If I am to believe news reports, Mr. Gregory, you are about to become an independent producer. Isn't that in violation of the contract between us?"

"I'm not aware we had a contract."

Masterson placed his snifter down on a table, the brandy untouched. "The best contracts, Mr. Gregory, are unwritten, like the best constitutions. Mr. Norwine, is there a legal contract between Mr. Gregory and myself?"

"Absolutely," Norwine said.

Masterson's thin dry hand touched Greg's shoulder. His eyes were blank, expressionless. "The time has not yet come for your independence. Continue as you have started. Mr. Norwine will provide your legal advice. And please work with Mr. Webster, whom I have financed."

"I deserve a chance on my own," Greg said. "I made money for the studio."

"You must be patient," Masterson said.

"But I've already begun an independent production."

Masterson had no more to say. He turned and left.

Norwine sniffed. "You've upset him."

"Well, he's to understand I'm not his puppet."

"None of us is his puppet."

"What then, if not puppets? You dance on his string. You don't take a crap without his permission."

"I beg your pardon?"

"I'm getting out. I'm cutting the strings. I have no contract with him and I do not owe him. I'm paid in full."

Greg hurried away, almost running. He heard Webster's throaty chuckle. Outside, he skirted the guests by the pool and then stopped. He must not rush. He glanced up. In the high window again stood the figure of the old woman, motionless and gray, shrouded obscurely, gazing down like a prisoner in a tower. Greg's heart rammed and his breathing quickened. He moved slowly, almost furtively. Then he was outside. Air burned in his nostrils. The Porsche was brought up, and he accelerated down the driveway. Through the gate, away, he slowed and gulped for air. The sun was so bright it dazzled, obscuring his vision, hurling yellowish rays that danced like tiny explosions on the hood. A blue flash visualized in front of him, and as he braked, blinking, he saw it was a woman. Sweat stung his eyes. Denise Stevens stood holding up her hands. She walked around and got in beside him, seated silently and motionlessly as the Porsche moved ahead, again slowly, tentatively. On the set she'd been like that, quiet and patient, willing to rehearse time and time again, friendly with technicians but aloof to her costars. Perhaps that was her screen appeal, a calmness and assuredness, also an innocence that wasn't pretense. At first she was resented, but she earned respect. She arrived at six each morning in a chauffeured limousine and sometimes left after midnight.

"Take me to a taxi, please," she said.

"Where are you going?"

"Home," she said. "It is a good chance now. He would expect me to pack and stall, like another woman would. I am not like another woman."

"Then I'll drive you home."

"Actually, where I'm going is the airport."

"All right then, the airport."

"There is a place where he cannot reach me." She spoke with an accent, a contrast to her usual flat American Midwest English; she had learned quickly and now apparently was reverting quickly. "People there are stronger than he is."

"You sound as if you're escaping."

"Escaping? Yes, exactly. I escape him."

"But you have a career to consider. Fame—"

She said rapidly, "As I have seen it, nothing is as destructive or as agonizing as fame. When it dies, as it always does, the agony is even worse. I would prefer even a jungle to a zoo." Noticing that he kept glancing into the rear-view mirror, she added, "You are escaping, too?"

"I'm not positive yet what I'm doing."

"Perhaps you had better let me out here."

"Why?"

"He is an unpredictable man, a sick one. Or perhaps he is healthy and we others are sick."

"I think you exaggerate."

"Do I? He has no feelings. People mean nothing to him."

"Has he treated you badly?"

"He treats me like any other object or possession."

"Tell me about his wife. Is she ill?"

"He never speaks of his wife."

"I saw her in the window."

"It is difficult to escape him. Perhaps you cannot."

Greg felt a cold shudder. "Why do you say that?"

"At any rate, I don't think he would harm you. He regards you as a son."

"A son? You just said he was a man without feelings."

"For his son he had feelings. Only men in his society are important. In most of the world, women are play dolls. If he'd had a daughter who had died, it would not have mattered. But it was a son. A son is a father in his society, so when the son died the father also died."

"Did you know his son?"

"I was to marry him. Mario. It was a political match, but became a love match. When Mario died I wanted to die. But I discovered that love is one of the easier emotions to forget."

"He has shown me the—" Greg's voice trailed off.

"Yes, and that is sickness enough, a crypt, but he has made it worse. He keeps a pistol, an old Italian pistol from the war, under it. He used to sit by it for hours, the pistol to his head. I have been made to witness this, so I know."

He urged her to say more, but she leaned back in silence. When she left him at the airport, she held back her long hair in the wind and glanced at him and then was gone, a mirage that had appeared and faded. Greg edged the Porsche into traffic. A blue Mercedes seemed to be following, but when he reached the freeway he saw it was not. He was alone and free.

EIGHTEEN

His new movie, a comedy called *Crazy Mice*, was a disaster. Like *Let Old Times Roll*, it never got off the ground. He rented a sound stage at Videoscope to shoot interiors, and on the eighth day there was a fire. It wasn't disastrous, but it stopped production and destroyed the rushes. A week after the set had been repaired, Hollywood technicians went on strike, using Videoscope as the test studio. The first day of production after the strike was stalled until late afternoon by a succession of small mishaps. Then the picture's star, a former striptease comic named Teddy Leslie who'd charmed the nation for five years as the loving and understanding Dad on a top-rated television sitcom, flattened Greg's director with a fat knee to the groin.

"You are a fucking stupid son of a bitch," said Teddy Leslie. "I quit this fucking mess."

He waddled away. Greg called Colin Webster, Teddy Leslie's agent, and could almost hear Webster shrug his shoulders on the other end of the line.

"Look at Teddy's contract, dear boy," Webster said. "It might be there, the right-to-tantrum clause."

The bank called Greg's note. He yearned for the days when they were shooting *Life to Live Over*; then, in a budget squeeze, he'd had only to call Norwine and the money appeared soon, usually in cash. Now, penniless and starless, he had to fold *Crazy Mice*. A year ago he had been a millionaire. Now he was broke, in debt, and his backers had lost everything they'd ventured.

"What the hell, movie angels are used to losing," said Mona Tyson, hired as a script girl and overall morale booster on the set. "Just another tax write-off for them, that's all."

"That's me," Greg said. "A write-off."

"Oh, you'll come back again."

"I don't think so, Mona. Not this time. My name is written in red on a black list. Believe it or not, I'm more sorry for the backers than I am for myself."

"You carry the world, that's why."

They were in the commissary at Videoscope, his last day there. You could judge the health of a studio by the activity in the lunch-room, and this one was filled and abuzz. And warm. It had been an unusually hot summer, and since the fire the air-conditioning had been malfunctioning. Yet the lunchers seemed in good humor. A fat man dressed as a yellow chicken shrieked a hardy cock-a-doodle-doo as the buxom girls at his table tickled his ribs and tried to find his private parts under the costume. Whenever a plate dropped, which seemed to be more than usual today, heavy applause followed. Some swarthy and scowling Indians, half-naked and occasionally letting out yelps, played five card stud, two musketeers in purple and gold shouted and cursed as they staged a mock duel with swords, and in a far corner Cinder-ella lectured her ugly sisters. No one paid much attention to Greg and Mona, old-timers on their way out, but the Frog, who seldom lunched in the commissary, crossed to their table. He hadn't exactly welcomed Greg back to Videoscope with open arms, disliking inde-pendence, but since Masterson obviously had approved it had to be all right, so what the hell. The Frog was a realist; realists didn't harbor grudges.

"If you're interested, I got this Jimmy Stew-art part for you where the guy fights City Hall," he said. "Guy ends up ashcanned, but he's got his pride."

319

Arelo Sederberg

"You're all heart. It was my lesson to know you."

"Gimme a break. I only wanted to say no hard feelings. You're a good guy, finish last. We're bad guys."

The Frog waddled away, winking at his subjects.

"What did he mean, bad people?" Mona asked.

"Eat your lunch."

"Maybe you are lucky to be out. Besides, people don't want things when they get them. They want only the dream. 'Men prize the thing ungained.'"

"Now she's the philosopher."

"Besides, you don't want it for yourself. You wanted it to impress some skirt."

"Why not complete the assassination? A skirt who clings to me when I'm up, runs off when I'm down."

"Oh, who's faithful these days? Well, I read that geese are monogamous. And the raven, gibbon, and painted shrimp."

"You shouldn't read so much, Mona."

"Can you go back to Sugar Daddy Masterson?"

"Not hardly. I expected to hear from him after I chauffeured Denise Stevens to the airport, but I didn't."

"Speaking of, *there* went an actress."

"Agreed."

"And I was a good one, too. Am."

320

"Again, old love, agreed."

"At least I fooled you. A Hyde is supposed to know a Hyde. But you don't know me. I fooled you flat."

He looked at her. Mona's face seemed to crack and open before him, and he saw that she was an old lady.

"Oh, Mona," he said, taking her hand.

She pulled away from him, jammed a cigarette into her holder, and tried to light it. She was trembling like a dry leaf. Greg helped her with the light.

"I started back after our picture folded," she said. "I guess I couldn't take it, the buildup and letdown. Worse than bad reviews, because you didn't get a chance. My ego was built up, too. Even old women have egos if they've once been under the lights."

"Mona, you were the one we *lean*ed on!"

"I know. It shows you how you have to look out."

He gritted his teeth. He pounded the table. "I hate this business. I hate this world. Mona, you were our *saint*!"

"Well, you be the saint. I think you're better suited to the part than me anyway."

"What will you do?"

"I sold the house. I'm going up to Frisco to live off a sister. She never used, so she might help. Dunno."

"Mona—"

"Christ, will you turn off those calf eyes? I

feel like I'm doing a *scene* or something! I hate those crybaby hospital endings. Well, s'long, love."

She snuffed out the cigarette and went away, walking the way she had in movies, the exit that had been so much copied, her head high, ostentatious in her floppy purple hat and spike heels. She got attention only as a zany mimicking a well-known movie walk. Greg wanted to go after her, but he didn't. It wouldn't help. You kicked it alone. Friends were important later, but you beat it in the suffering of a terrible loneliness. He'd known the loneliness and now he felt its touch again, a touch for Mona.

He kept the folding of *Crazy Mice* out of the trades, so Maureen didn't find out. They were seen at Chasen's and bc; the Visa card held out. He took drives and long walks in the day, sometimes stopping at banks to fill out loan applications. One day Colin Webster called him for lunch.

"Imagine playing golf in this weather," Webster said over his bowl of bouillabaisse at the Bel Air Country Club. "Or—my Lord, even worse—tennis?"

"May I know why you called this meeting?"

Webster peered lecherously at his bouillabaisse, his jowls undulating like jelly, his eyes glazing. "I bear an olive branch from Mr. Masterson. All you need do is call him—

actually, his sycophant, Mr. Norwine—and you will be in business."

"What business?"

"Why, a stable business, dear boy. Do you wish to call?"

"No, thanks."

"You claim sovereignty, dear boy, and I admire that. Do you think our Dodgers have a chance this year? What do you think of the size of the contracts the boys are getting nowadays?"

"How about your boy? Jolly Teddy Leslie, His Royal Fatness?"

"Yes, he said he had left your picture."

"I'm sure you had nothing to do with it."

Webster broke a lobster claw with a sharp crack. "I'd let you have some money myself except I'm temporarily short. I've repurchased a share in my company I had earlier sold to Mr. Masterson. I'll tell you what, though. There is a loan company I know that would help you out. I'll give you their card. You say I sent you."

"You're no longer associated with Masterson?"

"I didn't quite say that, dear boy."

"Do you know Masterson is mob?"

"My dear boy, I know of no such thing. I fear you've been reading too many movie scripts."

"Why would you want to arrange a loan for me?"

"Because I like your style. You're like I used to be. You swing from the heels. You go for broke. You're a throwback to the old producers I used to know. When you told Masterson and his shadow, Norwine, to shove it up their asses, I chuckled up my sleeve, dear boy. I knew you had something people couldn't buy. Pardon my French, dear boy, but that's about the only way I can describe it. I hear that weather like this precedes earthquakes. I guess we're going to get a big one, like it or not. Do you believe in earthquake insurance?"

Greg went to the Acme Loan office on Melrose near Beverly two weeks later, using Webster's name as reference. He walked away with a certified check for a hundred thousand. A month later it was gone and he hadn't reduced his debt on the movie by a penny. He paid the arrearage lease fees on the house and the car and took Maureen to New York. That was a special occasion; of all things, they went to a funeral in Scarsdale, a cemetery where Mrs. Theodore Piper had bought a lot for her husband. Piper had keeled over dead on Park Avenue, walking home after a party at which he'd been the life. Heart attack; there had been no warning. At the funeral Mrs. Piper glared at Mrs. Anderson, and Greg realized that they, too, like their husbands, didn't speak to each other and probably hadn't seen one another for decades. A. Elroy Anderson, the Closer, did not attend the funeral of the

Great White Father. He had recovered completely from his own heart attack, was more fit than ever, and had business to attend to at the office, which he no doubt conducted with a smug smile on his lips. Greg heard later he had worn a red carnation in his lapel that day and had lunched at the Harvard Club. Cheaters got what they deserved, and the just and hard-working were rewarded, no matter how long they had to wait. When Greg got back to his big house in the hills above the city lights, there were three messages from his service to call Rod, his account executive at Acme Loan. Rod's third message was: "Need full interest payment by Sunday." It was Friday night.

NINETEEN

Tim Harte called Maureen at the office the day she got back from New York. "Hey, I was there," he said. "You didn't see me, did you?"

"Where?"

"When they put old Piper down. I didn't go to the grave—I hate graves—but I was at the church, way in back. Isn't that a scream, old Piper croaking first?"

"A real scream," she said.

"I want to see you. I have a bit of business for you. I got some info, too. How about lunch?"

"Only if you pay," Maureen said.

He insisted on meeting her at the Los Angeles Tennis Club. It was another hot day and he was wearing shorts and tennis shoes and a T-shirt that said in large black letters: HITLER'S VAMPIRES. Also, Harte had made an entrance—a chauffeured Cadillac. The chauffeur was a black man who wore a dark suit and boots. He stayed outside, but Harte made Maureen aware of him by calling for him after they were seated in the dining room.

"Otto, would you kindly bring my racket?" he asked when the man appeared.

"Yes, sir," Otto said. He clicked his heels.

"I taught him that, clicking his heels," Harte said. "It's what the Nazis did in all the pictures. I wonder if they really did that? In real life, I mean?"

"I'm sure I wouldn't know."

She was sounding as bored as possible, but it didn't phase Tim Harte. "Y'know? Even fifty years after, our industry doesn't like to use the name Hitler or Nazi in a flick. Did you know Ava Gardner had a bit part in *Hitler's Madman* in 1943? There's been *Hitler's Gang*, Ward Bond in *Hitler—Dead or Alive*, and you'll never remember this, there was Tony Randall and José Ferrer in *Hitler's S.S.* There's been only a couple Nazi flicks—*Nazi Agent* was one and there was *Nazi Hunter* in 1986. Farrah Fawcett, no less. Of course there's been a million flicks about Nazis, but for some reason they don't like it in the title, Nazi or Hitler."

"Tim, I'm impressed. All right? Now would

you kindly spare me any more extraordinary displays of your knowledge? It's too hot for idle chatter."

"Take off your clothes. Ha-ha."

"I seem to remember you had a similar innuendo the first time we met. You don't fool people, Timmy. Why don't you stop pretending?"

"Speaking of, what did you think of the chauffeur?"

"Tall and handsome and black."

"Adores me," Harte said. "But expensive." He displayed the T-shirt by puffing his chest. "My flick. *Hitler's Vampires*. It has nothing to do with Hitler. It's a fright flick with sex and drugs and things. About vampires, so there's lots of blood. For the teens. T-X, teen exploitation. To them, it's a trip, see?"

"Tim, I always knew you'd make a contribution."

"It was my lucky day when CU sacked me. I got the short leg there from the word go."

"Short leg? Is that anything like short arm?"

"Y' don't know what short leg is? It's when they hire you and give you a chair, all right, but one that's got one short leg. No matter what you do or what you say, you're never going to sit straight."

"What do you have to do with the vampire picture?"

"Producer, love bug, producer. I got

329

Anderson—d'you believe it?—and some of his cronies to angel it. We release it next month. I want you to flack it."

"How much?"

"I always knew you'd make a contribution, Maureen."

"Touché," she said.

"We want to make it an overnight cult classic, like *Night of the Living Dead*. There's a gimmick. The vampires are women ghouls. They give good eat."

"That's funny," she said.

"What's funny? Do we have a deal, you and me?"

"I'd better sleep on it."

"How's Greg?"

"Fine."

"Sure, and my uncle is Bing Crosby."

"What do you mean by that?"

He wouldn't say. He ordered two double cheeseburgers and triple fries and ate with maddening slowness, smearing the burgers with circling layers of mayonnaise, mustard, relish and ketchup. He was fatter than ever, a bona fide pig, and she felt revulsion and disgust. But, what the hell? Business was business. They might get fifty, sixty thousand out of it. Harte squirted ketchup on his fries and picked them up with his fingers, sucking them into his mouth. The ketchup ran down his chin.

"Bloody, bloody, bloody," he said. "Don't think people don't like violence."

"I don't. I had enough violence when I was a kid."

"Well, most people love it. It gets their jollies off. Violence is something we as a people can relate to. You may not like it, but it's all around us always. Pictures are a mirror of life. You're getting a lesson here. You ought to take notes."

"I have a good memory."

"Well, I knew you were a sharp one when I first saw you. I can tell things like that. In fact, you were just too smart. You can't be too smart and be successful in this business. You got to like things like comic books and games like Old Maid and TV reruns. Know what I mean?"

"Know what you mean," she said.

She turned away, unable to watch him eat. What had he meant about Greg? Greg had been acting nervous and brooding, but she had attributed it to the strain over *Crazy Mice*, which he said finally was going well. A waiter brought a phone and Harte jabbered nonsense, loud and profane. He was playing the stereotype of the bastard producer, loving it.

"They want to cut this part," he said, trashing the phone with a producer's verve. "Scene where she gives him head? She, this vampire, bites his peter right off. What I mean is, she *really* eats him."

"Tim, is this an X-rated picture?"

"Oh, heavens, no," he said, his eyes wide and innocent. "It's P-G, Parental Guidance.

331

The sex is simulated. You know. You see Ms. Vampire after she eats the peter, you don't see her do it. It's the *expression* on her face. Priceless. That's the scene they'll pay to see. You know how many people go to a flick just for one scene?" Harte's eyes glistened. He drooled. "You got your asshole producer in *The Godfather* waking up to the bloody horse's head in his bed. You got that ugly thing jumping out of the guy's chest in *Alien*. Christ, how I love that scene! I get a hard-on every time I see it. Lemme tell you, sister, Cecil B. DeMille knew about that, the scene. He never made a good picture, Cecil B. DeMille didn't, no more than Otto Preminger ever made a good picture or Susan Hayworth ever acted in a good one—ha-ha, ha-ha—but he did understand the scene, Cecil B. DeMille did. I might do a book, *Great Movie Scenes*."

"Your vampire flick sounds pretty X'y to me."

"Well, I don't pretend it's Walt Disney or anything, but it's really just good fun for the kids."

"Just the same, Daddy Warbucks in New York might not see it that way."

"What's he know about it? He goes to the opera, not the movies. All he wants is return. Then we make *Vampire II, Vampire III*, and so on. If you're queasy, you don't have to watch it. Why does a publicist have to see the flick?"

"Well, I do not like horror films."

"Or violence. I know. If I can be psychological, I'd say you got pawed when you were a kid. Well, I had a lousy childhood, too, sister. We're not that far apart."

"Don't ever call me that again. Sister."

"Sure. No harm, no foul."

"Tim, what about Greg?"

He shrugged. "Nothing about Greg, really. Except I'm sorry his flick *Crazy Mice* folded."

"Folded? *Crazy Mice* hasn't folded."

"Sure, and Elvis Presley lives. It's kaput, *Crazy Mice*. It's all over the place like a madwoman's shit. It's a voodoo project, bad luck."

"Tim, you're wrong."

"Wrong? About pictures, Tim is never wrong. Never. When I came here from Gotham I found a home in the army. About pictures, Tim always knows. It's a rule you can set your clock by. Ask Tim, he knows. I might do a book with that title, about the flicks. Now, about my picture—"

Talking about vampires, Tim Harte attacked his second heap of fries.

It was Friday night and Greg took her to Chasen's, where they often had dinner on weekends. Usually somebody came to their table, a producer or director and sometimes a star, to have a drink or dessert. If you came early you usually got second-raters, but you could get the top ones if you came late, despite the fact that competition for table-hoppers was greater then. It was a way to measure your influence, how the big ones came to you, and it was an unwritten creed that if somebody had a drink at your table it was on your tab. This evening they arrived early and stayed late, but no one came to them. Greg was unusually quiet; the dinner passed with hardly a word between them. Always, they left without paying—the tab was settled, including tips, with a monthly statement—but tonight the waiter brought a check. Greg asked for Michael, the captain, who fumbled about, embarrassed, but indicated there was nothing he could do. Nor would they take a credit card. They wanted cash. If Greg was upset, he didn't show it. Maureen, however, felt like hiding under the table. She didn't mind a scene at a place like the L.A. Tennis Club or Richard's, but this was Chasen's. And it was a scene because they wanted cash and people at nearby tables knew it. To make it worse, Greg was short on cash, even though the check wasn't much over a hundred dollars. She had to slip him some twenties.

They went outside. The heat wave was still on, lingering into the night, making people a little more snappish and impatient. Yet Greg kept his calm when the parking attendant, looking abashed, explained he couldn't find the Porsche, even though he'd taken the keys. He'd had a busy night, two men short, the summer flu, how it hangs on, you know, and maybe he hadn't been able to watch the cars like he usually did. But they had insurance, of course, and would stand a taxi ride home for them, as well as handle the matter with the police. Greg calmly asked him to call a cab. He remained silent all the way up to his house, where Maureen had joined him, leaving her BMW. They got out and she paid the cabbie. The heat pressed around them and the stars were bright and close, a big sweep of the dippers and Orion. Below lay the city in her radiant glow, jeweled mile upon mile. The house sat dark on its lawns and gardens except for a light Greg always left on that peered like silver eyes from twin windows of a cupola. It was what they had wanted, a castle above the city. Now they had it. But, quite suddenly, she felt a terrible and inexplicable fear.

"Greg," she said.

He had her arm. She was trembling.

"What is it?" he asked.

She couldn't speak. Her mouth had gone dry. Slowly they moved up the driveway, toward the house. Then lights caught them, coming on ahead, near the garage—a car, no, two cars, four headlights, blinding her momentarily. She reached for Greg, but he wasn't there, as if something had grabbed him and shoved him away into the darkness. There were men around her, several men, and she could not make out their faces in the dazzle of light and its darkness beyond. It was as if they were hooded. A scream was frozen in her throat. Two of the men were holding her back. Then Greg appeared vividly in the beam of headlights. Other men were with him, pinning him against the hood of one of the cars and raising their fists to strike. She could hear no sounds. It was as if her ears had been plugged, coming out from under water. She shook her head. The men held her. She saw Greg falling to the ground. One of the men picked him up and pushed him roughly forward. He staggered, moved a few steps, and fell heavily.

"It's from Rod, Rod of the Acme company," one of the men said.

The men—four of them, she saw—got into the two cars. Engines started. They drove away, their lights shining on Greg where he lay, shuddering and trying to rise. The cars drove past him about two feet away and one of the men threw out a lighted cigarette, which landed and glowed by Greg's outstretched arm. Then the cars were gone, their taillights twinkling redly and disappearing. She went to Greg and tried to help him up. But she couldn't. He was heavy and he didn't seem to want to move. Maureen looked at her hands and saw in the starlight that they were sticky with his blood. Only then did she find her voice. She shrieked, once and then twice, and then sat on her knees, sobbing with her head in her hands.

She stayed the night, seated in the living room, the lights off except for the television, which she kept on with the sound way down.

Fear stiffened her. She hadn't even been able to look at Greg. She hadn't really, in fact, been very good at all. She berated herself for cowardice, but she couldn't help it. She was deathly afraid, too weak to drive, too nervous to sleep, drained to the point where she could hardly move. She couldn't even ask him what had happened, nor did he volunteer to say. He cleaned himself up, took a handful of aspirin, and lay down on the alcove couch by the front door. Tomorrow was Saturday—no, today of course; it was past midnight—and the maids were due, but somehow she knew they would not be coming. Something terrible was happening, *had* happened, and Greg hadn't told her. He had left her out, perhaps fearful that she would go away. And now in crisis she knew she couldn't help him. She wanted to. She told herself that she loved him. Yet she couldn't help. She was afraid. She wanted to go, to run. But she stayed the night, listening to his groans; twice, just as she was drifting off to sleep, he cried out in pain, jarring her awake. She could not even go to him. She could see only the sudden blinding headlights of the cars and the big men who looked like hooded men coming toward them, seizing them, taking Greg aside and pushing him against the hood of a car, beating him with their fists rising and descending.

When there was enough light of dawn so that she could see clearly, she rose and turned off the television. Her back ached and her legs were sore. She had a murderous headache. The light, pale as it was, hurt her eyes. She looked up and saw Greg standing by the big double doorway to the room, his hands behind his back. She glanced at him only once, and then turned away. His eyes looked like deep red sockets, surrounded by dark, puffed skin. His face was crimson, as if the skin had been torn off. He was wearing a robe and obviously had been bleeding in the night, for it was stained with large brown splotches.

"Do you want me to call a doctor?" she managed to ask.

"No."

"Will you tell me what it was all about?"

"Oh, I owe a fellow a few dollars, that's all." His hand went up and he held his jaw, as if it hurt to talk. "He has no sense of humor. Or his collection agency hasn't."

"You don't have any money, do you?"

"Not right now."

"That was no normal collection agency, Greg."

"I told you he has no sense of humor."

"I'm going to leave now. I'm sorry, but it's something I just have to do."

He took a step toward her. "No, don't go. It'll be all right. I have some irons in the fire. I—"

Maureen moved cautiously, actually afraid of him now. He reached out for her, but she dodged away. He was very weak and no doubt dizzy, so his small movement propelled him to

the floor. He rose painfully, a little at a time.
She wanted to help him. Oh, she wanted to!
But she couldn't. Her fear and instincts for
self-preservation took over. She ran. She was
out the door, into the driveway, pausing to
search around, the key to the BMW in her
hand. It was by the garage. She heard her
name being called and turned to see Greg
lurching from the front door, his hand in the
air, signaling her to stop. She didn't. She got
into the BMW, turned the key, and heard the
engine grinding. It always started right off,
but now, dammit, the thing was sputtering
and catching and dying. She pumped the
accelerator. Careful. Don't flood it. Greg was
coming toward her, blood running down his
cheeks and forehead, his hands grasping the
air like claws. The BMW's engine caught. She
shoved the transmission into drive and moved
ahead slowly. Greg had caught up, one hand
on the doorknob outside and the other clutch-
ing the radio antenna. Maureen stepped on
the gas and turned the steering wheel sharply.
The antenna snapped off in Greg's hand and
she saw his face for a fraction of a second—
bloody and desperate, wanting and pleading
and pitiful, his puffed and blood-red eyes
streaked with tears. It frightened her even
more. She turned away. He fell to the ground,
and in the rear-view mirror she saw him lying
there, trying to raise his head, his hands
pawing, a small figure suddenly swept over by
the sun breaking through the clouds.

TWENTY

It was one of the worst weekends of his life, but he had suffered before, so he endured it stoically. The heat wave continued, in fact intensified, and since his electricity went out Saturday morning he had no air-conditioning. He was too sick and weak to use the pool. He had a telephone, a few tins of food, water, and a small amount of expensive liquor. Maybe he should get drunk. You can handle anything when you're drunk, except getting sober. But he knew he couldn't drink. He'd get sick. He was nauseous, shaking, and sore all over. When he'd lie down and close his eyes, everything began to go around in circles and his stomach turned; when he rose and tried to

Arelo Sederberg

walk, his knees buckled and he had to clutch
the furniture for balance. His face looked like
something out of a horror movie, covered
with purple welts and criss-crossed with cuts
that wouldn't close. One eye was swollen shut
and two of his front teeth were loose. His
lower lip had swelled so severely that it was
difficult to talk. Everything hurt, especially his
head, and aspirin did no good. The heat held
him in a wet embrace, clinging to branches of
the dry and spiritless shrubs and trees outside
and attacking inside from closets and drawers
and the pantry. He was in a big house on the
top of a hill, but he was penniless and alone
and he was also afraid.

He was afraid principally for one reason. It
was the knowledge that he had a way out.
There was a solution. And he wanted it,
thirsted for it, yearned for it. It was balm and
power and the answer to everything. He
needed a drug, any drug, but preferably a few
sweet white lines of good cocaine. It was bliss.
It gave him strength and vitality; he could
speak well with it in him, persuasively and
cogently, and his head was clear and his eyes
wide to new visions. You could go on coke for
weeks, a month, without hardly anything else.
You grew thin and wiry, supple and vigorous.
And, oh, how you could go in bed! His mouth,
bone dry in the heat, moistened for it, and he
licked his lips in anticipation. He could get it.
He could get it without any money. He knew
where. Pick up the goddamn phone, call.

342

Make your day, buddy boy. Why suffer? You've suffered long enough, trying to make a living, make it big, wanting that bitch in your bed, loving it when she took off her dress and pantyhose and panties for you and you only when she could have done it for almost any guy on the block, like the Mark Ashleys of the world. Where the hell was Mark Ashley, anyway? He'd be good for a line or two, that was for sure. But he'd just disappeared, slipped away in the night; the trades said he was taking a long rest, exhausted as he was, between pictures. But why think about him? Think about yourself. He reached for the telephone. The doorbell chimes went off, echoing around him, cutting into his ears, loud and then again even louder, forcing him to stand and hold his hands over his ears to blot out the terror of it. Mentally, he knew, he was back on the stuff, frightened in the delusions of it. Then they said:

What are we going to do about Greg?

And he said:

Leave me alone. Why don't you leave me alone?

The door pushed open. "Jesus H. Christ on a fucking crutch, who ran over you?" asked Henry Frost, the Heavyweight.

He'd come with Willy Sterne the Planter and they had brought about thirty cartons of Chinese food, a huge pot of coffee Planter said he'd brewed, and a half-dozen fifty-pound blocks of ice. The ice looked delicious. Planter and Heavyweight took charge, moving silently and wordlessly. Planter held Greg's head in ice water for a while and then pinned him down on the carpet while the Heavyweight applied first aid, salves that soothed, iodine that stung, bandages that closed the cuts. Then they all sat cross-legged like Indians on the floor, a motorized fan blowing across the ice in a tub, eating the Chinese food. Greg could only take the Wonton soup, but it was very good and he could hold it down. He felt stronger and his black mood lifted somewhat.

"What brings you boys to this neck of the woods?" he asked.

It came out like baby talk between his bruised lips, and they all had a laugh over it. Greg joined in, although it hurt his stomach and made his head ache again.

"It's our basic love of mankind, why we came," Planter said.

Heavyweight strolled. His beard had grown and he looked absurd, like one of Snow White's dwarfs, Grumpy maybe. "You dumb bastard," he said, looking at Greg.

"I'm a dumb bastard, then why are you here?" Greg said. "Maureen told you to come, didn't she?"

"She wept like Xanthippe," said Planter.

"She said you'd had some trouble, that's all," Heavyweight said. "She didn't say a Mack truck squished you. Who you been doing business with? Hulk Hogan?"

"This is good soup," Greg said.

344

"You still got a chance," Planter said. "Get into a car and drive. Go pick up your kid—Rob's his name?—and get in a car and drive."

"No car," Greg said. His mouth hurt.

"Here," Planter said, throwing him some keys. "Take mine. There's five hundred cash in the glove compartment that's yours if you get outta town. No questions asked."

"What about the car?"

"Who cares about the car? Shit, send it back Federal Express."

The Heavyweight stopped pacing and stood beside Greg. Since Greg was seated, the little man was the taller, and he looked down as he spoke, his eyes squinting. He was very serious.

"I know you're into something deep and I don't think you're going to get out of it," he said, his tone a lecture. "If you are going to get out of it, you have to make up your mind and move right now. If you wait, you're finished. I think you know that."

Greg said nothing.

"It's a '78 Impala, but it's got new rings on it," said the Planter. His ugly face was almost pleading. "It's got air."

"Thanks, but I'm okay," Greg said.

"He thinks he's okay," the Heavyweight said, hands on hips, looking up at the Planter. "He can hardly say it, but he thinks he's okay."

"Well, he's a grown man," Planter said, shrugging. "You can fight most things in a man, but you can't fight pussy power. I seen it time and time again."

345

Greg looked at Planter. "That mouth of yours is going to be the death of you yet."

"It's been said," the Planter responded, sighing.

"I do appreciate what both of you are doing."

"Then it's thanks all the same?" the Heavyweight said.

"I guess that's it," Greg said.

"I don't say please but now I say please," Planter said.

"It's my life," Greg said.

"You're in deep shit," Heavyweight said. He left.

"Offer of the car still goes," Planter said.

"It wouldn't help. Hyde is all over. Thanks again for the offer."

"Yeah."

"Take care," Greg said.

"Take care," Planter said.

He was gone, limping. The door opened and the Heavyweight returned. He stared at Greg. The eyes said, *Get out. Escape now.* They didn't know. Non-Hydes knew very, very little. That was the world, non-Hydes and Hydes.

"We're both flakes," Heavyweight said. "Both runaways."

"Let's have your lecture, professor."

"For years I worked on remote-control devices to separate isotopes for radiological warfare and develop a process to make the dust, the death dust. I even worked on how to stockpile it. But when I nearly had it, after the obsession of working on it, I quit. What I figured, you see, was nobody but me could do it. Dead wrong. But I ran away. I keep on running."

The Heavyweight left, this time for good. Greg felt like crying, but that wouldn't help. He loved those screwballs and they loved him. But it wasn't enough. He sat amid the cartons of Chinese food and the tubs. The fan was dead. Now he'd do what he would do. Planter and the Heavyweight, both intelligent men, had tried their best, but apparently they were under the impression it was easy to elude Hyde. They didn't understand that there was no escape. He wanted to call Mike Thompson. He didn't. He wanted to call Rob. He didn't. He called O. Albert Norwine, the Sniveler.

"Yes, you," Norwine said.

"I would like to see Mr. Masterson."

"That is not necessary."

"What do you want me to do?"

"That will soon become apparent to you."

"If I've been out of line, I'd like to apologize."

"Your apology is accepted."

"I *am* sorry."

"You need not be profuse about it," Norwine said.

He went outside by the pool and waited in the sun, listening to birds chirping. It would be all right now. He had suffered terribly, an almost unbearable solitude and disappointment so absolute that it left him weak and limp, and he deserved a break. He *needed* a break, needed it to save his life. He had suffered, and it wasn't necessary to suffer this life. He had a drink, chipping ice off a block and pouring Jack Daniel's over it in a glass. It tasted good. He kept a small supply of booze for guests and was down to the heels of two bottles. He had another Daniel's-rocks. Great. Old John Barleycorn, how I missed you. Booze was a road back to coke, to Mr. Hyde, he knew, the way back to the grinning skull and a way out, too, drinking to get off the other stuff, the white stuff of the pipe or the straw, the stuff he wanted now, wanted in the worst way. But he stayed with the alcohol. He had little bites of the cold Chinese food to go with it. It didn't seem so hot now, and his face no longer hurt. He could hold down the booze. He was all right again. In fact, he was feeling very good. Perhaps he should call Maureen, tell her to come over. But he didn't. Something prevented him. He wasn't quite ready. He had to get ready first.

The lights came on just as the sun was going down. Miracle of miracles, one call to the right person, to Mr. Big's mouthpiece, and his troubles were being solved. Soon brother Rod at Acme Loan would call, asking forgiveness, and he would forgive, of course. Sure. He was a nice guy. So what if a few thugs pounded on him when he was bringing his girl home to his mansion above the lights? Just a misunderstanding, that was all. He went through the house, every room, turning on the lights, testing, and he left most of them on. He would be a shining beam above the world. Foolish Planter, foolish Heavyweight. They had wanted him to run. Greg shrugged his shoulders. Well, they had felt it was best. They didn't know what he knew, of course. They didn't have his connections.

He heard a noise. It was a truck, a small bread truck, coming up the driveway and stopping by the front door. A man got out and looked around. He had a pencil behind his ear and wore a delivery man's hat. Greg opened the door and peeked out.

"Sign here," the man said.

Greg signed and took the package, two loaves of bread wrapped in tinfoil.

"Sure's a hot mother," the man said, smiling. He had broken teeth, and the smile was like a smirk or a sneer. "Think it'll cool now?"

Greg slammed the door shut and tested the lock. Then he slipped down, his back to the door. He sat looking at the loaves for a long time. Sweat ran down his back and sides, tickling along his ribs. But the air-conditioning was working again and the lights were on, so everything would be fine. Just fine. He giggled. He opened the package. There were two large plastic tubes inside, two beautiful tubes filled with the lovely white stuff.

It was much later. He was waiting. If you waited, it was better. He gloated. He felt his

eyes getting big and his heart thump. His
tongue hurt and his throat was dry with
anticipation. He sprinkled the crystals onto a
mirror and cut them into powdery talcum
with a razor. He looked at it for a long time.
He could still run. He could still escape. But
when he looked at the powder, it seemed to
beckon to him like the creamy soft arms of a
beautiful seductive woman, white breasts
swollen and upright, alive with libidinous
promise.

Come to me, come to me. I am the life as it
can be and will be. It is so easy.

Take me. A way to Jones, lovely Jones.

Smash it.

Take me. Take me. Jones, Jones. Heaven,
heaven.

Smash it. Smash it.

You are no fool, take me.

You are no fool, smash it.

*Mr. Hyde, Mr. Hyde, Hyde, Hyde, come to me,
come to me, serenely arriving, serenely arriving.
Come, I need you.*

*But I detest you and I repudiate you. You do
not have me. I have sent you away. Long ago I
sent you away. I sent you packing, you bastard,
and you do not have me. You had me but you no
longer do.*

With sudden resolve, he brought his fist
down on the mirror. It shattered and the
white powder puffed into the air and seemed
to disappear. Greg got the plastic tubes and,

holding one in each fist, grasping them tightly, ran into the bathroom. He opened the tubes over the toilet bowl.

Throw it away.

Don't be a fool.

Throw it.

Don't. Go to heaven. Get off earth, mundane earth; go to God, go like Superman. A bird, a plane, faster than—

Throw!

Don't!

Throw!

He did. Quickly he flushed the toilet and fled.

About midnight he came awake on the couch. The lights were still on. He sat up. A terrible need went through him, one he had never felt before, much more intense than ever; it was more than a need, it was a hurt, a deep physical pain that seemed to rise and throb in every part of his body. He'd been an absolute fool. He cursed himself. He'd flushed his life down the toilet. Even the liquor was gone. He glanced at his watch. Then he looked up a number in the phone book and called.

"Hello. You do deliver? Good. Send a supply. Party here. All-out. Desperate. Yes, bourbon. And Scotch, gin, vodka, brandy, beer. Case of each. You take the Visa plastic, right?"

When the liquor came he signed for it, giving the boy a large tip, and drank deep slugs of Jack Daniel's from the bottle. But it wasn't enough. Mr. Hyde crawled on his skin like an ugly red bug, trying to get in, begging and pleading, weeping, cursing, demanding. Greg ran upstairs, threw off his clothes, and got under a hot shower. Then he switched to cold. It didn't help. He drew on a robe, tearing the cloth in his awkwardness, and went downstairs, leaving the shower running. The red bugs crawled all over his skin. He was swelling, he was shrinking, he was rapidly growing taller, he was shedding weight by the pound. He crawled on his hands and knees in the area where he had broken the mirror, searching for traces of the powder on the floor. But he couldn't find it. He could find nothing. He sat cross-legged, cursing loudly. He ran up and down the stairs. He screamed. He beat his chest and head. He tipped over lamps, upset the furniture, shattered bottles, threw books about.

There was Mr. Hyde, an elflike man with a red beard, seated on the floor across the room, smiling and beckoning to him. He had a red mouth and white face and a spider's eyes. It was Hyde who called Norwine.

"What, already?" Norwine said, his voice annoyed and sleepy.

"Yes, I'm sorry," Greg said.

"What happened?"

"I can't explain it. I lost it."

"You'll be responsible for it."

"I understand that."

Norwine chuckled. "Such a smart one, you," he said.

The bread truck returned just as dawn was breaking. Greg was waiting outside. He had put on shorts and tennis shoes. When he saw the truck, he didn't hurry. It had been hell waiting, but now that it was here he could wait a little longer. All that counted, really, was the knowledge it was here. He had it. This time he would not throw it away. He felt the bugs, but outwardly he was calm.

"Think it'll be another hot mother t'day?" said the driver, tipping back his cap.

It wasn't as good as the first time, but almost.

A new world opened up for him. He was brilliant. He felt the expansion and stretching of his mind. No problem seemed very difficult. He strutted with full confidence in silk shirts and ties, new suits, Gucci shoes and cuff links. Before, he had succumbed to Mr. Hyde, detesting the foul putrescence of him; now, he embraced and welcomed him as a friend, a partner whom he could trust and without whom he probably would fail. Hyde was essential. It was amazing what Greg had missed when he'd been sober. Sunsets now had a new dazzling beauty. He made extraordinary discoveries in Brahms and Liszt and Mahler. Hume and Locke no longer were puzzles; the lyrics of Wordsworth, Coleridge, Shelley and Keats and Blake sometimes brought tears to his eyes. He had fantastic energy. He could stay up most of the night and be fresh in the morning. He was back in business, looking for a property to produce. Scripts were sent to him by messenger from the Frog, he had his Porsche and table at Chasen's back, and Rod of Acme Loan *had* called with profuse apologies, saying there had been a terrible mistake. His debt was forgiven. Rod even helped him explain the mistake to Maureen.

He had no worries. He was doing about five thousand a week as a dealer within two months, and it had been not much of a struggle to build up the business. In fact, many of his customers came to him. It was if he wore a flag to them, saying, "I deal. Best prices." Those who knew just knew, that was all. Most of it was cash money, and under unwritten terms, suggested by Norwine, he kept 20 percent. Punctually at 2 p.m. each Sunday the bread truck came and he gave the driver his receipts minus commissions and a requisition slip estimating how much of a supply he would need for the following week. There were no signatures, just an understanding. It was the cleanest of businesses; no one tried to cheat. Everyone involved knew that cheating could result in a visit from the boys at Acme Loan. If all businesses were regulated like that, Greg said to himself, we all might be better off. He had become an accomplished rationalizer. He was doing nothing wrong. After all, the only crime in drugs was that perpetrated by the unfortunate ones who were hooked and couldn't afford the cost of their habit. Certainly his customers could afford it. Most weren't hooked, and neither was he. Unlike before, he could quit. But he didn't want to quit, not yet. He was enjoying it. Life whirled around him in a rosy spiral, a dancing and musical whirligig of laughter and good times. He was losing weight, he felt good, his judgment was excellent, his mind clear. He and Maureen were seen at theatrical openings, outrageously expensive restaurants, and the best parties. They mingled with Hydes and non-Hydes, moving among beautiful people, themselves beautiful—witty and graceful, fabulously successful, and just slightly mysterious. He was the producer looking for material, she was the publicist to the stars. They were modern, in, hep, young, wealthy; they were praised, envied, sought after.

He was a wet nose, often leaking fluids, but he was very clever, and Maureen, who knew him best and also was the smartest one of their crowd, did not suspect. If she did, she wouldn't have stayed with him. Their relationship had changed, matured, but in some ways was better than ever. She slept over on weekends, and he saw her for lunch or dinner regularly on weekdays. Their sex was less intense, but at times hit the highs of before. Maureen didn't pretend they had a good deal in common—books or music or art—but that was all right because pretense could go only so far. Except for his drug use, it was an honest relationship. He assumed she was faithful.

Maureen didn't discourage his seeing Rob, although she was indifferent about it. As a result he saw Rob less and less. He was too busy, he had to go out of town, there was an important preview to see. On the phone Rob seemed distant. They were growing apart, a fact Greg faced with sadness. But it happened as children matured and developed their own friends and interests. Sometimes Greg yearned for the past, a circus act or amusement park ride or the crack and gunsmoke odor of fireworks on the 4th of July. Rob had been with him, and that probably wouldn't happen again. When he thought of Rob he also thought of Phoenix, of Clay Dodson, Mother, the freckled kids. The painting of the Indian girl hung in his den, but he didn't often look at it. It was past. It was foolish to think of the past. He had a bright present and a brilliant future. He would think of them.

One Sunday the bread truck failed to arrive.

TWENTY-ONE

There were hallucinations, but he was quite sure he could tell the difference between reality and mirage, no matter how authentic and palpable the illusions seemed. Yet there were times when he didn't know that he was himself. He wasn't positive the entity he touched and pinched wasn't false and his real self watched from above or around, invisible and disembodied, not subject to the sensations and limitations of flesh. But he was in control, careful to be consistent, not to show change. He felt fine. He had the edge back. No one who need not know was aware he dealt. His customers were strangers. They never came to his home. He dealt at restaurants, nightclubs, sometimes offices and parking

357

lots, usually after dark. He had a compartment under the Porsche's seat and hidden pockets in his clothing. He feigned ignorance to callers he didn't know, even if they had impeccable references. It was impossible to be overly circumspect.

He was calm. He didn't worry. He was wary, and besides he was protected. It meant nothing that the bread truck hadn't come. It would return or he'd be supplied in a different manner. Greg lounged about by day, reading scripts, rereading literature, principally Dostoyevsky, Solzhenitsyn, Poe, Camus, Kafka —writers who suited his soul. His world was Kafkaesque—shadowy, uncertain, frustrating, sometimes jaggedly surrealistic and helplessly fatalistic. That was Greg's inner self. His outer self was quite different. He was erudite, accomplished, intelligent, charming. The white powder made him so and told him so. He was also canny and devious, he realized, plus ruthless and selfish, just like his customers. Often they said their purchases were for someone else—a business associate or customer, friend or wife or husband, even for parents as a comfort in their old-age illnesses. Some were talent agents who bought for celebrities they represented, or for themselves. Others were the celebrities in person. They were seldom recognized unless dressed and made up to be seen. But they couldn't fool Greg. He knew who they were, and he knew when they were buying for their own use. He could spot a user across a crowded room. A Hyde knew a Hyde. At the same time, he fooled them. They didn't know he knew. And because he knew didn't necessarily mean he was addicted; he had quit before and he could quit again.

"Sure you can," said T. D. Desmond. "We know you can cold turkey, man, anytime you want, man. Ain't that right, Mark?"

"Sure he can," said Mark Ashley.

"We garbage-pail addicts ourselves, but we prefer the nice white stuff," T. D. Desmond said. "Me, I do, I know. What nigger didn't prefer white meat? Eh, Mark?"

"Right on, my man," Ashley said.

Ashley had called Greg, saying he had money and asking for delivery of a supply, giving an address; it was against his convictions and an unaccountable warning voice within him, but Greg had gone, driven by curiosity as much as anything else. Ashley had simply dropped out about a year ago. There had been no announcements, no explanation of any kind, and the entertainment press, busy with other matters, had been incurious. A star had disappeared and nobody seemed to care. Greg found him, and T. D. Desmond, on the top floor of a downtown flophouse, not far from the Greyhound depot.

"We got class, a john of our own," Ashley had said when Greg opened the door to Number 18 at the far end of a dark corridor that stank of dust and mildew and rot.

T. D. Desmond was looking out the open window, down at the street where hollow-eyed derelicts roamed. The lights of a bar twinkled off and on and occasionally horns sounded mournfully, like a ship in fog. He was gaunt and gray and spidery, his clothes far too big for him. Ashley too had lost a lot of weight. He was bald, shriveled and pale.

"Saved my life," he said, taking the material. "How much?"

"On the house," Greg said, adding flippantly, "We deliver."

"He delivers," T. D. Desmond said without moving from his vigil.

They all had a line and it felt good. Greg mumbled, "Golden lads and girls all must, like chimney-sweepers, come to dust. Shakespeare."

"Eh?" Ashley mumbled.

"It's not so bad, this place."

"Got a john," Ashley said.

Desmond turned and regarded them with lazy eyes. "I didn't come from no poor black trash, man. I came from *bourgeois* niggers. My old man sold insurance, door to door. He'd collect by the week and deliver the gossip. He was a *story teller*, man."

"Play," Ashley said, snapping his fingers. "Famous forgettable movie lines. Susan Hayward to John Wayne, in *The Conqueror*: 'For me, there will be no peace while you live, mongrel.'"

Desmond squatted and hopped across the

floor. "John Wayne to Susan Hayward: 'You're so beautiful in your wrath.'"

"Fred MacMurray, *The Swarm*, to Olivia de Havilland: "'Maureen, how long have we known each other? About thirty years? All that time, have you ever heard me beg? Maureen, I'm willing to beg now. I want you to marry me. I know people look at me and think that I'm just the man behind the aspirin counter, but inside I love you.'"

"Olivia de Havilland, back to Fred MacMurray: 'How lucky I am.'"

Desmond hopped back to his vigil at the window. Their imitations were really quite good, and Greg laughed. At the same time he felt a shudder of sadness. "I'd better be going," he said.

Desmond stopped him, springing up cat-like. "You watch out here while I go to the can," he said to Greg. He opened a door in a dark far corner and looked back, his eyes bright. "Once I ran through the whole other team, neat as canned peaches. I took the ball ten yards deep in the end zone and cut and faked to the thirty, the fifty, into their territory, the forty, the twenty—gone, man, *gone*!" He danced and motioned with his hips and arms as he described the run. "Knew I was going all the way when I got the ball. Knew where I'd go. Zigzaggin' I go, cuttin' and fakin', man, stiff-armin'. Like runnin' in a dream, where you couldn't hear anythin' and knew you'd go. I knew I'd go. When I got over

361

the goal and spiked the ball, that's when I heard the crowd. You never heard nothin' like it, that crowd."

He opened the door, went inside, and then came back. He bowed. Then he disappeared. There was silence.

Ashley looked at Greg. His face was pale, almost white. "I should talk about bad lines. I had enough bad lines. I used to go look at the people standing in line for my movies and I wanted to go over to them and say, 'Don't pay your money. It stinks. I stink.'" He touched Greg's arm. "As it turned out, you were the one who gave me something that might last. When I settled down and stopped being a bastard, I did a pretty fair job of acting."

"You did a great job of acting."

"Maybe it will end up in celluloid heaven." He grinned his old familiar dimpled grin. "If it does, it'll be the only thing about me that does."

"You have a star on Hollywood Boulevard."

"For people to step on."

"Don't knock it. You were something. You can be something again."

"Gregory, for a producer and a flack you're not a bad guy. Maybe this is the beginning of a beautiful friendship."

"I don't think so. I want you to get another connection, in fact."

Ashley's eyes flashed. "You're sore because you think I screwed that broad of yours. Well, I didn't. I let you think so because I thought you'd sold T.D. down the river. But we never came close. Some broads rack up scores, proud of them, sort of like a résumé. I was a big score. But she didn't score me. Hell, I don't even remember her name."

"Maureen. Like in the MacMurray lines."

"Maureen what's-her-name," Ashley said. "Davis?"

His voice seemed to echo from a distance. Greg felt strange, queasy. He must leave. He'd be all right when he got back to the Porsche. A sharp rap sounded. The doorknob rattled. Greg whirled. When he turned back, he saw that Ashley no longer was there. The door flew open and two men came in. They were about the same age and looked alike, bland men in suits, youngish, with granite faces and hard mouths like cracks in ice. Greg felt a hollowness in his stomach. The men moved silently to his side.

It was a gag. It had to be a gag. Ashley and Desmond had lured him here, an elaborate, perverse gag, done on some whim. Well, he'd go along with it, at least a ways.

"Tenth-rate actors they sent for me," he said. "What theater are you playing at?"

The men led him into the hallway, dimly lighted with a naked low-watt bulb. He heard the shrill crying of a baby. They went down the stairs, stumbling, and outside. The street-lights cast a faint yellow glow, and fog puffed along the curbs like dirty cotton. There was no traffic. They passed the Porsche, walking in stride, linked like one. Greg decided not to acknowledge the Porsche. They paused beside a square under a streetlight. There were flowers growing along the sidewalk, yellow open poppies. The men held him. He had the image in mind of a fly held by flypaper, pulling until its legs came off.

A figure stood in fog in the distance, one about Cyrus Masterson's height. Was it Masterson? Of course not. This was an extended joke. Or was it? Were they going to kill him? He wouldn't give them the satisfaction of showing fear. Perhaps that was a part of the joke, to make him show fear, a sick game no doubt, but he wouldn't put it past people like Ashley or Desmond. He had seen them in their degradation, and now they were forcing that degradation upon him. He was about to shake himself loose and walk away when one of the men began to read him his rights and the man up the block, the one he thought might be Cyrus Masterson, walked slowly toward them and he saw it was a uniformed policeman on foot patrol. The officer approached and passed them, touching his hat with his nightstick to acknowledge Greg's captors. Then the two plain-faced men led Greg away. He kept looking back to see if the patrolman was following, but apparently he was not. The men pushed Greg. He started to run. They ran alongside him. It was not long before they seemed to be away from downtown, in a desolate spot near a stone quarry—

or at least it looked like a stone quarry, black and bottomless it seemed, smelling of limestone. In the far distance he could see the lights of the city.

This was no joke. This was no sick game. This was real.

"We know you're dealing," one of the men said. "Who are you dealing for?"

"I don't know what you're talking about," Greg said. He was out of breath from running and had to gasp between the words. "You have no right—"

"In cases like yours, we have rights," the other man, the one who'd been silent and who really hadn't shown his face, said or rather sneered, sniffing as he talked, his nostrils pinched and white.

"I demand to see my lawyer."

"Is your lawyer named Albert Norwine?" said the first man.

"I don't have to answer that."

"Do you deal for a man named Cyrus Masterson?"

"I tell you I don't have to answer your questions."

"Name him, you go free," said the second man. "Don't, and—"

He opened his coat and drew a long butcher knife from a sheath. He held it up. Its edge sparkled in the moonlight. He handed the knife to the other man, who handed it back. It was being offered then to Greg, so that he might use it on himself. Then he knew that they had been sent here to kill him, but neither one apparently had the stomach for it. They continued to pass the knife, one to the other.

Then Greg heard a noise. A light came on above him and to his left. He saw a brick apartment house, and a figure appeared in a window. Who was it? A friend? A good man? Someone who sympathized? Someone who wanted to help? Was help at hand?

Peering up, feeling sweat gather on the back of his neck and run down his back, he appealed silently to the man in the window. He squinted. He thought he recognized him but he couldn't be sure. What seemed to be a long time passed. He continued to look up at the man. There was more light now, a moon returning from behind a cloud, and he recognized the man. There could be no doubt this time. It *was* Masterson! Panic was rising in Greg—panic he tried to control, but couldn't. His mouth opened and he let it out. He screamed. It was a loud scream, and a long one, so vivid that it echoed and threw itself back at him. The very sidewalk seemed to tremble. The figure in the window held up his hands, which gleamed whitely in the moonlight, and turned down both thumbs. Greg looked at the men in front of him. The one who had the knife at the time of the signal from the figure in the window raised it and, his face remaining expressionless, pale and blank and lifeless as if a cleansing hand had scrubbed out its furrows and identification, plunged it into Greg's chest. He felt the knife twisting inside him.

"Like a dog!" he said as he fell.

The scream dissolved into a dull buzzing sound that seemed at first to come from inside his head, and only after opening his eyes and lying there for a long time, staring at the ceiling, did he realize it was his telephone. He was in bed at home, and a faint light crept in through the curtains. He held the receiver to his ear.

"Mr. Gregory?" said a woman.

It was Albert Norwine's secretary. She was concerned because she hadn't received the R.S.V.P. from Mr. Gregory for the dinner at Mr. Masterson's home in San Marino this Friday at 7 p.m. Formal.

"I'm sorry, but I don't think I received the invitation," he said, wincing because it hurt to talk.

"Oh, but it was sent, Mr. Gregory. In fact, it was messengered, sir."

"Oh. Well, I'll be there. Friday?"

"At 7 p.m., sir, and it's formal."

"Pardon me, but I've been ill. What day is it?"

"Why, it's Wednesday, sir."

His head blazed with pain. His throat was dry. Outside a horn sounded, loud and long, sending renewed hot spear thrusts of pain to his brain. He got up, wavered, and dragged

himself to the windows. He was naked except
for one sock. Parting the curtains, he squinted
out and saw the bread truck parked beside his
Porsche near the garage, its driver leaning on
the door, hat pushed back.

The most frightening aspect of it was that
he didn't know what had been real and what
had been imagined. Perhaps it all had been
fantasy; or, except for the knife thrust, real.
He had no evidence that anything had occurred. His memory was vague. He recalled
driving downtown, talking with Ashley and
Desmond; he remembered the plain-faced
men, the fog along the curb, the yellow street-
lights. It had all the surrealistic aspects of a
dream. Yet it was so real and vivid he was
certain he could find his way back to where it
had occurred, or where he'd imagined or
dreamed it had occurred. But he didn't at-
tempt to do that. Something prevented him.
Perhaps it was fear. Perhaps it was his feeling
that he'd awaken one day and know it had
been a nightmare. He'd been reading Kafka
the night before, the final chapter of *The Trial*
where Joseph K., who'd been arrested and
tried for a crime that had never been speci-
fied, is taken out at night into the quiet street
by two men in hats, a nondescript, unembel-
lished scene in a nondescript city, and executed, "like a dog," by a knife thrust to the
heart. So his reading experience, intensified
by drugs, obviously had extended into a realis-

tic nightmare. There even had been blood on his sheets when he'd awakened, no doubt from a nosebleed. It was very real, and he couldn't explain it. He trembled when he relived it or even thought about it, but he had no choice but to dismiss it as a nightmare. It was over. It would not happen again.

TWENTY-TWO

He awoke under black satin sheets deep in the night, knowing he soon would die. Maureen nestled against him. Greg lay stiffly. A year? A month? He had fooled himself. He was hooked. He fed at Mr. Hyde's trough, a garbage-pail addict. He wore Mr. Guy suits and Gucci shoes, drove a car worth fifty thousand and lived in a million-dollar house; Zsa Zsa called him gorgeous, producers hopped to his table, photographers sought him at parties. But it was deception. He was spiritually destitute. There was no escape.

He rose, drew on a robe and slippers, and went to his bathroom, feeling nauseous. His hands were unsteady, his throat dry, his temples throbbing. He felt the dark terror of depression. But that could be fixed. The cure was hidden in a compartment he'd had built behind the medicine cabinet. It was his personal cache, not for sale. He looked at it gloomily, again feeling a premonition of death, but then gloated, smugly satisfied. He was supplied. Readers had been written for him by croakers the world over, from Paris to Zurich to Boston. There were uppers and downers, beanies, softballs, reds and blues, peaches, blue heaven, ludes. He salivated, ogling his treasure. There was more—beans, speedball, pink chicks, scag, red bird, blue velvet, dinky dows, uptown aplenty. Sport of the gods. Again, he salivated. And there was artillery—gongs, bridges, hook haks, ties. He chuckled. But he was trembling, sick; he detested himself, his weakness and pusilla- nimity and stupidity. He swallowed two up- pers without water and cut a line to sniff and then he washed his face and hands and soon felt a lot better. The robe and slippers were comfortable. The carpet under him was warm. His head was clear. It was fine. No, not death, no; ever living, a bastardly n.g. s.o.b., but alive and breathing, getting a hard-on, a kid again, strawberry fields forever man, shit man shit, red chicken and chase that dragon, man. They called it the military disease, but he couldn't blame the army. Nam was vague to him now, a land wrapped in a bloody sheet. After he'd been hit, and hit hard, gut-shot, they'd filled him with pain-killers—he didn't know what—but he'd been using before, old Double U-O Globe. Stuff that had kept him awake kept him asleep in the hospital, and that was wonderful. Sleep was his greatest pleasure, sleep and meals. All day he'd lie without moving, even when the sun hit his eyes, dazed but aware where he was, alive, hearing the faint rumble of vehicles and murmur of foreign voices outside—days, weeks, months—watching a crack on the ceiling widen to reveal secrets. He got his idea then. Find a farm and scrape in the dirt, plant peas and roses, have a dog. Several dogs. Horses. But that had eluded him. It was lost in the race, busting ass.

He sat in his den and watched through the window as the light broke, silver cracks in a black sky. Maureen seldom came to his room, a converted bedroom with a couch and several chairs, a stereo with good speakers, TV set, a bumper pool table, books he liked, a view of the trees and hills by day and lights by night. He found his attention drawn to a painting he usually sought to ignore—Mother's Indian girl, as he'd named it. He couldn't look at it and not see a vision before him of Mother's dark molded face and knowing eyes, eyes prophetic and haunting, and also he saw the kids, ugly and freckled and puffed with laughter, lizards in their pockets, smoking weeds, peaking out like shy chipmunks. The family had accepted its misfortune with stoic forbearance, as one might accept a natural disaster, flood or drought or sandstorm; it was as if they knew that disasters, too, were a part of life, along with joy and laughter and love and discovery.

The face of the Indian girl mirrored acceptance as she kneeled in prayer to an anonymous god, a cruel and indifferent god, for the prayer would not be answered. Yet there was hope in her eyes—or a wish, a dream. If the dream lived, hope could not end. Those who liked the painting saw it that way, a look of faith and not resignation, not a blind and superstitious appeal to a capricious master. Those who disliked it saw quite a different picture, a depiction of a primitive trapped in ignorance, generation after endless generation, trapped in a hostile, tormenting environment. "Ms. Sisyphus," cracked one discerning wag, an MBA and CPA who'd recently completed a culture rub-on course at Harvard, invaluable for a Hollywood parasite. Greg had responded, "Yes, head bloodied but unbowed."

He stared at the figure, transfixed. His eyes blurred. He blinked and shook his head, driving away the fuzziness. Something was hanging down from the bottom frame of the painting. It was as if it had not fallen but had merely appeared, created by a conjurer's command, and at first he thought it might be a trick of his eyes, an illusion. But it was not. It appeared to be a sheet of white paper, or rather several sheets, a bundle, that had fallen from the backing of the painting. Greg kneeled. He took the papers in his hand. It was a computer printout, yellowed and somewhat faded, perhaps two dozen pages, single-spaced.

An hour later Maureen peeked in. "Well, I'm off to queersville," she said.

"Eh?"

"Frisco. Remember?"

"Oh, yes."

"What are you reading?"

He looked up, jerking off his glasses. "Oh, nothing. Just a script."

"Well, 'bye."

She lingered, looking at him curiously, frowning. Greg reached out and took her hand.

"I want to say I love you. Whatever I may do, I do it with you in mind."

"Greg, is there something wrong?"

"Why should there be something wrong? Can't I say I love you?"

"Well, you too. I do. You get words out of me."

She was gone, leaving a faint scent of perfume. He continued to read, finishing and rereading. Clearly it was Clay Dodson's missing manuscript, the one that supposedly had burned. It was as if it had been intended for posthumous publication, written in blood and tears, a clarity that hurt the eyes. It tied Masterson to organized crime, directly to the

Sicilian Mafia, and to narcotics dealing through connections in South and Central America, as well as Asia. Drug money was laundered by his various enterprises; taxless cash went in, taxed profits came out. Even more startling, Masterson was allowed to continue, almost under the protection of the federal government, because he was an information supplier to narcotics officials concerning the operations of others, his competitors. He was in effect sustained by authorities sworn to obliberate his kind, much in the manner that some Asian opium growers and traffickers were supported in exchange for aid against Communists.

Then who had killed Dodson? The government? Masterson? Perhaps it didn't matter. Perhaps the entire rotten system was responsible.

Dodson's material doubtless was enough to stir grand jury action. Could it convict Masterson? Perhaps, perhaps not. But it would cause a sensation. It was particularly damaging to Masterson because Dodson was dead, slain violently, and the document not only prophesied such an occurrence but also suggested that Masterson was responsible.

Had Mother read it? Of course she had.

He spent the morning on the telephone, trying to reach her in Phoenix, feeling a mounting excitement. Before, he had run, escaped from it in cowardice. Now he felt stronger. He wanted to find out. But he had absolutely no luck, as if Mother and her family had vanished. Finally he reached an assistant city editor at the *Republic*.

"Yeah, sure. You're Masterson's flack. What's up, Doc?"

"Well, I've been trying to reach Clay Dodson's wife."

"Oh, she's gone. Long gone."

"Where?"

"Dunno. Disappeared. Maybe back to the tribe. She was Indian, y'know."

"She was a painter," Greg said. "A pretty good one."

"Well, Indians they got a way with paint."

"So do cave men," Greg said, hanging up.

He pondered. He cut a line and sniffed it. How clearly he thought! Maybe he wasn't hooked. After all, he hadn't graduated to free-basing, a sign he might be just a dibbler. A brown shoe, no, but he could kick it. Thoughts of death were silly. No longer would such thoughts afflict him. He'd think about Maureen, the house, bigger houses, the life they had, about keeping it together, making it even better. Wine and roses. Living well, the best revenge. Owning it. No longer wanting, but having. Clear was his vision, clear as the day was clear, and limitless, like the space out there, the ocean and the sky.

Coldly he considered his options. He could give the Dodson manuscript to a newspaper, perhaps someone like Mike Thompson. He could simply destroy it. Or he could give it to

Masterson. There was another option. He could tell Masterson he had it, hidden away, and see what the reaction would be. That would be a dangerous game, but life was a dangerous game. Masterson had used him. Now he was in a position to use Masterson.

Yet it was unnecessary to threaten Masterson. Couldn't he achieve the same goal merely by turning over the papers to him? It was possible, in fact, that Masterson knew he had them. Perhaps he suspected, wrongly, that Greg had had them all the time. Had the men in the street been Masterson's agents? Had it been a threat, a warning? Or had it been a trick of the mind, a malicious prank by Mr. Hyde? Hyde was, after all, capricious and whimsical.

Questions rang in Greg's mind. Why had Mother given him the papers? Why were they hidden? Had she indeed some mystic faculty, clairvoyance? Or did she merely consider herself so gifted? He saw her dark eyes and heard her soft voice as she told of the interminable trek by mankind in search of youth and therefore of life. But the very struggle of it made life hollow—joyless, griefless, loveless. What did it mean? It meant nothing; it was the stuff of myth, of dreams. He, Arthur Gregory, was alive. He had more life ahead, much more. He'd raged for justice in his youth, only to be hosed down and jailed; he'd served in Nam, getting gut-shot for it. That foolish idealism was over. It had been a phase.

Could Clay Dodson himself have inserted the papers into the frame?

Greg shook his head. He couldn't answer the questions. No doubt he'd never know the answers. He didn't want to know. Sitting bolt upright and still, he thought very clearly, his mind stretching. He hadn't been sent an R.S.V.P. invitation to dinner at the Mastersons' on Friday. He'd been invited by telephone only after passing the old man's sardonic little test. The faceless men who had accosted him had been sent by Masterson. Of that there could be no doubt. It had been unnecessary, even juvenile, but one couldn't judge actions in a society where truth and trust were unknown. Did truth and trust exist anywhere, for that matter? Last night he'd earned Masterson's trust, and this Friday it would be reinforced. Greg would give him the Dodson papers. Why not? Who would care for him otherwise? The fact was he could do nothing else.

He settled back. He didn't look at the painting.

There was nothing wrong with dealing. It was an act of mercy. Greg had heart. He extended too much, if anything, to people who would whore or steal or kill to get it, unfortunates who couldn't take it or leave it. Bad chemistry, call it. Yet they were people, human beings, hooked because they were human. He empathized with them. He loved them. They were forced into it, stressed into it, born into it, bored into it. Nobody was worse than anybody else. Winos and panhandlers and pimps were no worse than the fine ladies powdering their noses in Chasen's lounge or lawmakers or judges or preachers. The drug scene wasn't the dark world depicted in novels and movies. It was the normal world. The guy who sold you insurance might be a user. Maybe the cop or the teacher or even the priest. Sometimes Greg thought everybody used.

In this frame of mind, he sniffed another line.

Then Marie called. It was about Rob.

TWENTY-THREE

He met Marie and her husband in the emergency ward waiting room at St. John's Hospital in Santa Monica. The news had sobered him, but never had he felt a greater need. It was in the Porsche, in his hidden compartment, and as he raced into the small white room he found himself thinking about it, visualizing it, licking his lips for it. He pinched his cheeks, hitting them, and slapped control into his trembling knees and hands. His stomach felt hollow and his throat was thick. He couldn't remember the husband's name, and somehow it seemed important that he should. A doctor. A common first name. John or Joe, something like that. When he saw Marie, white-faced and clinging to the bench like a little humped bird, he thought of what could have been, years that had passed and those that would have been there, except he'd turned and they were gone. He knew something else. Rob was dead. He didn't have to ask. He knew. His premonition had been right. The son was dead and the father was dead and it was all dead, all of the hopes and the dreams, all dead and withering, collapsed under layer upon layer of mold and dust, hardening already. He entered the room and stopped, blinded by pain and dizziness. Marie didn't look up. Greg shook away the dizziness. He took Marie's husband by the arm and led him out into the hall.

"What was it?" he asked.

"Well, I have to put it straight to you. It was an overdose."

"An overdose? But . . . *how*?"

"Will you take your hands off me, please?"

"You're a *doctor*! Marie is a *nurse*! How could it escape you?"

"How could it escape you, Mr. Gregory?"

The man looked at Greg down through his horn-rimmed glasses. His eyes were popping, his face was swelling. His voice came from a deep pit.

Greg let go of his lapels. He turned, staggering, and saw Marie standing behind them. They both went to her.

Later they talked calmly, too calmly it seemed.

He said: "When we got married, I believed

in something, something good. I believed you stood by those you loved. It wasn't like that in real life. I got terribly mixed up, Marie. I lost sight of love. Maybe it's all an illusion, love and life itself. Everything."

She said: "No. It's real. It's too real."

"If we had stayed together, it would have been better."

"I don't know. A person knows very little."

"I'm going to do something about it."

"What do you mean?"

"Even it," he said. "Eye for an eye."

He went away. It really didn't hit him until then. He opened his mouth to scream, to let it out, but there was nothing there, no energy, no wind or voice or even emotion; he was merely a hollow man with rubbery legs and an arid body that shrieked silently, expressing an agony beyond any possible conscious expression.

He ran. It was still early and the streets were well populated on a warm, moist night, but he did not notice. He skirted in and out, pushed his way past gatherings at intersections, into the street against the lights amid screeching brakes and curses from motorists, running with his knees high into what seemed a heavy yellowish fog or sea mist, cool on his forehead and cheeks and enveloping him protectively. He might be screaming; he really didn't know. He could hear nothing after a while, and all movement around him seemed slow and jerky, objects large and small strung on a mechanical chain. He was across Ocean Park, past the sidewalk above the cliffs leading to the highway and the Pacific, and then onto the Santa Monica pier, again weaving, acutely aware of a pain in his chest and that his knees were hurting and his legs were weary. But he didn't stop running. Nor did he slow his pace.

"Hey, buddy!" said a sailor as Greg dashed past him, brushing him. Lights of the arcade game parlors danced at him. Barkers shouted at him. Neon lights of fish restaurants loomed like specters in the mist. He stopped, leaning over a railing and breathing heavily. The ocean dashed darkly below, crashing against the pilings with gunshot cracks. Greg started his motion to spring over. He felt strong hands grasping him, stopping him. He sank to his knees. It came out then, a moan that extended to a long wailing cry and, peaking shrilly, fell back to a moan. He seized his hair with both hands and bashed his head repeatedly against the rail. It hurt. It was good to feel pain. He was coming out of the fog. He was here and alive and he tasted his blood on his mouth and felt the pain in his head. "It better now?" a voice said.

Old gnarled hands held him—the hands that had prevented him from leaping over the rail—and the wrinkled face of a fisherman in a rubber coat came into focus. Greg looked up to see that a small crowd had gathered. Curious eyes swept over him, but the crowd shrank back as if afraid. The fisherman helped him up. Then, with a quick wink, he drew a pint of Old Taylor from his back pocket and handed it to Greg.

"Have a snort," he said. "On the house."

Greg took a long pull. He let out a breath of air. He felt his heart beating. Warmth flooded back to him. He smelled the sea and tasted the brine in the air. A foghorn sounded, far off, and he thought he could hear a ship's bell from the darkness at sea.

"Thank you," he said, handing back the bottle.

The old fisherman grinned toothlessly. Greg felt a surge of love for him. At the same time he was hollow with loss. He reached out and held the man, this stranger who stank of fish and brine. Somehow the man seemed to understand and he made no protest. The crowd dispersed, embarrassed and confused.

There was an indoor merry-go-round with bright lights and loud music on the pier. Something now drew Greg to it. He remembered times in the past when he had left work early and had gone to Rob's school to wait at the playground, looking at the motionless swings and the slide silver in the sun and the softball diamond with its half-buried wooden slat for home plate and well-trampled indentations in the sand for bases. He'd wanted to try the slide and swings. And then the bell rings and soon the kids come out. There is Rob, looking lonely and sad until he sees me, and then his eyes light up as he starts to run, passing the other kids, his hair streaming wildly, his eyes bright and moist.

He got on the merry-go-round, up on one of the horses. The man who took tickets looked queerly at him.

"There a brass ring here?" Greg asked.

"Naw, not no more there ain't," the ticket-taker said.

He was an old man with rubber bands on his sleeves and he wore a straw hat.

"Maybe there never was," Greg said.

The lights glistened and they were going around, slowly at first and then faster. He held tightly onto his horse, fighting his tears before he let them come in a great rush until he was sobbing bitterly and uncontrollably.

The plan took shape. Maybe it wasn't really a plan, but more of a pattern, something decreed long ago. He was going to do what would happen, not because he started or would control it but because it was something that was in motion and would be done. It was as if he'd been moving toward it, step by resolute step, for months and even years. He didn't know. He didn't think about it.

In the Porsche he sniffed a line and had another later at the house. It was that now, a house, just that; certainly it was not a home. He felt he really no longer needed the stuff, but he took the lines because it was important not to vary from the past. Was that a rationalization? He didn't know. He was moving in a pattern, and it was not him but the pattern itself.

His service had several messages from customers, so, understanding their need, he agreed to meet them. It was close to midnight, Thursday. Greg went out by the pool and looked at the stars and then down at the city lights, gazing sadly. A mist had arisen and there was the scent of rain in the air. The stars were faint and the city looked oblique and blurred. He dressed in one of his old suits, a favorite one, and put a tuxedo, shaving kit, and the Dodson papers and some of his own into the Porsche. By 2 a.m. he'd made his connections and collected about a thousand dollars. He gave most of it to a priest at St. Sebastian's.

"Light three candles, please," he said to the priest.

"I will. God bless you."

"A candle for a boy named Rob and a woman called Marie. And one for an old fisherman."

He returned to the Porsche. The rain had started, sweeping suddenly and furiously. Between rows of news racks outside the Santa Monica post office crouched the dark humped form of the bag lady whose spot it was, day or night, rain or shine. The grocery cart beside her was heaped with collectibles, rags and cans and bottles and other treasures, some done up with ribbons. Who? From what

place? A mother? A wife? It was a bleak lonely
street in a lonely city, wet and dark, a desolate
and alien landscape. Greg stopped, backed
up, got out and took a blanket from the trunk.
He went to the bag lady and draped it over her
shoulders. She kept her face hidden, her body
bent under ragged clothing like a discarded
sack.

On the Ventura Freeway, heading toward
the valley to see Mike Thompson, Greg braked
on a shoulder and got out, leaving the lights
on. Again terrible agony and terrible grief
struck him. He had not given enough, re-
pented enough, suffered enough. He rolled on
the ground, tearing at his clothes, forcing his
face into the mud. Then he stood up in the
rain. Cars whizzed by viciously, their tires
singing. After a while Greg got back into the
Porsche. He edged slowly into traffic. He felt
better. Silly man, silly and absurd mankind.
He opened the window and smelled the rain.
He would try to see Maureen and explain, but
she wouldn't understand. No one would.
Something beyond his control guided him, a
force that could not be explained or understood. He didn't understand it himself. But he
whistled. He felt clean, and ahead of him was
a light.

TWENTY-FOUR

A tapping at the door roused Mike from a deep sleep. For a moment he lay in a gray, uncertain fog. He blinked. The clock read 3:44. Again came the tapping, slightly louder. Rain slapped the roof and windows. Mike touched Pam's shoulder. She mumbled in her sleep and turned away from him. Mike got up, groaning quietly, and stood shivering in his pajama top, hearing the rain. He started a retreat to the bed. But the tapping sounded once more, distinct and measured, unmistakable.

He went to the hall closet and fumbled for a robe. It was the karate robe Pam had bought him last year in Hawaii, a trip to celebrate

Arelo Sederberg

their seventh wedding anniversary. He
glanced in on the twins, who slept quietly,
tangled in their covers. Their stuffed animals
were perched on the dresser like sentinels,
pink eyes glistening. In the living room Mike
paused to listen. For a second it was quiet.
Then: tap, tap, tap.

A twinge of apprehension went through
him. They had a pistol, a Ruger P-85, but it
was in the garage safe, hidden from curious
kids. He peered through a crack in the drapes,
seeing only faint silver sheets of rain. Abruptly
the rap sounded, jarring him.

"Who is it?" Mike asked, his ear against the
door.

A hollow voice came from outside. "I am
thy father's spirit, doomed for a certain term
to talk the night."

"Oh, for the sake of Christ," Mike said,
opening the door.

Greg staggered in, bringing a thick odor of
rain. His suit was torn. His tie was coiled
around his neck like a noose. He stood drip-
ping water. Mike closed the door and folded
his arms over his chest.

"Should see you, old buddy!" Greg said,
pointing and chuckling. "Should see your
body language. I like the robe. Nice outfit. I
like the headband. You get a part in my next
flick."

"Please keep your voice down. Pam—"

"Oh. Sorry." Greg peered at him, his eyes

390

dark and hollow. "Hey, I paid you back, didn't I? You and I are square, aren't we?"

"We're square."

"You're square."

"I'm square."

"How about some grog? Grog for Greg?"

Pam appeared, wearing a robe and slippers. "You need coffee, not grog," she said, smiling tolerantly at Greg.

"Good evening, Pam," Greg said.

"Good morning, Greg."

"Did I ever tell you you ought to be in pictures? The *arts*!"

"Art? Art who?"

Greg laughed. "Quick," he said, pointing at her. "Quick."

Pam gave Mike a significant look—*your* friends—and went into the kitchen. Pepper wandered in sleepily and went to Greg.

"Somebody likes me," Greg said, kneeling to pet the dog. "Somebody likes the wreck."

"What caused the wreck?" Mike asked.

"There is rancor in your voice, old buddy. Rancor is not like you."

"What I see isn't like you."

"I apologize. Forgive the wreck. What caused the wreck? Well, I got tangled up in my lies. But I got naked. Now I see. I know Greg. Greg is an illusionist. Now you see it—" He turned abruptly and waved his hands. "—and now you don't." He laughed shrilly. "Hey! Remember when we came down to L.A. from

Cal for the UCLA game? Remember the broad at the Hilton with the jeweled dog that I bet you guys I couldn't go up to and take her upstairs? And I did. Remember?"

"I remember. Nobody ever said you were without talent."

"Talent or juvenile chicanery? I told her I'd bet my buddies fifty bucks I could take her upstairs. She went along with it. She was a good sport."

"Then why didn't we see you until half time the next day?"

"I said, she was a good sport."

Mike peered at him. "You've been snorting, haven't you?"

"I cannot tell a lie. I have been snorting."

"You were off it."

"A non-soldier cannot judge a soldier."

"I'm not judging you."

"Your eyes judge me."

"I'd like to know what's on your mind."

"I've brought some papers for you. TNT papers. Perhaps you can fashion it all into a novel some day, the TNT papers and the rest of the stuff I brought for you. Included are Greg's memoirs. And—hey, forgot to say!—I *liked* your novel. Much too good for a movie."

"Thank you."

"Now I'd like to say that I want to borrow your Ruger."

Mike felt a chill. "What do you want with a gun?"

"I have noisy neighbors I wish to eliminate."

"I see."

"Do I get the Ruger?"

"No. Of course you do not get the Ruger."

Greg shrugged. "It's just as well. I'll stop at the five and dime and pick up an AK-46, or an Uzi or two."

"Greg, for Christ's sake will you talk straight?"

"You think Maureen caused the wreck, don't you?"

"I have no way of answering that."

"There is nothing so awful as love, old buddy. We must be on the alert always, for it lurks like the plague, striking without warning. No clues, no nothing. No dead rats in the alleys to warn us."

Greg slouched down, crossed his legs and put his chin in his hands. The rain cracked on the roof. The lights jumped. He looked forlorn and small in his corner.

Pam came in, carrying coffee and cups on a tray, walking with feather movements, her blue robe trailing, a petite and pretty redhead. No. Not just pretty. Beautiful. Mike felt a surge of love for her. She was due at a Wilshire ad agency, where she did art layouts, by eight; here she was making coffee for her husband's drop-in buddy at wee hours, not showing it if she was sore.

"Mike, make sure you get his car keys," she said. "He's going to sleep it off."

393

"I will," Mike said. When he'd peeked out he had noticed a red Porsche, one he hadn't seen before. "He won't get away."

"I'm going to try for another hour's sleep," Pam said.

She gave Mike a little kiss, hugged Greg, and left.

"Lucky you," Greg said.

"You just said love is awful."

"Some love is awful. Yours isn't."

"Okay. Then lucky me."

"Who was the most successful of us all?"

"You."

"And I had the fairest of them all." He looked up, his face in shadows. "Now I've got myself up against something maybe I can't do. But I've got to try."

"What is it?"

"Sometimes you have to roll in shit before you earn the right to stand up straight. It's punishment, you see." Greg jumped to his feet and became animated, his arms dangling and his legs loose, jerking mechanically, grinning. Glancing at Mike, he chanted: "And then one bright day, Pinocchio the wooden puppet, having rolled in shit, awakens to find that he's a *real boy*! One of the beautiful people!" He began to move in a ludicrous comic dance. He staggered. His eyes darted. Slowly he drew an envelope from the inside pocket of his suit coat and placed it on the coffee table. "My memoirs. You are not to open it until dawn. I mean that, old buddy."

He was interrupted by the creak of a slowly opening door behind him. The twins emerged, yawning and rubbing their eyes. Jill clutched her favorite rag doll. Ralph crouched behind her. Both seemed confused, more asleep than awake. Then they recognized Greg. They shrieked simultaneously and dashed to him, prancing and hugging. Greg kneeled and hugged them back.

"Play a bear for us," Jill said.

"Yeah, play a bear," Ralph said.

"Well, I'm just not feeling in the mood right now," Greg said.

He got up and turned his face away. Mike wanted to ask about Rob but he didn't, not knowing why. He drew the twins aside.

"I'll put them back to bed," he said. He felt a sudden inexplicable dread. "Then we'll talk. Okay?"

The twins were back asleep almost before he pulled the covers up to their chins. Mike went back to the living room and glanced about, puzzled. Greg was no longer there.

Pam returned, silently gliding. "Did I hear the twins?"

"They were up. I just put them back."

"Up to see Greg, no doubt. Where *is* Greg?"

"I have no idea."

"What's wrong with him? He looked . . . well, *wild*."

"I think you know."

"Oh, good Christ," she said.

They looked at each other. From outside

above the rain came a sound like a moan or deep sigh. Pam gasped. Mike darted outside. The rain was luminescent in the porch light, a pulsating glow, spilling heavily from the downspouts with a hollow whooshing thud. Greg stood on the lawn, his arms outspread, his chin upturned. Mike went to him. Greg didn't move. He stood in the rain, letting it hit him, clean him, hurt him, punish him.

"I'm not petty," he said.

"Of course you're not petty."

"You don't understand. I'm not petty because I'm dead. The dead are above pettiness. They're above revenge or jealousy or acquisitiveness. They're above the littleness of living. It wasn't Maureen's fault."

"I know that."

"I loved her. I no longer do. I'm above loving. Loving runs you over. Ask her about that."

"Come inside."

"No. Got to go."

Mike reached out and held him. He saw Pam in the doorway, her arm shielding her face, looking at them, the man who held the other man, and then she turned away, leaving them to themselves.

Greg slipped away as stealthily as he'd arrived, gone as soon as he was not watched. Mike took the VW out to look for him, squinting through the windshield wipers. The yellowish rain carried a faint odor from the equestrian club on Riverside Drive. It was no use. The Porsche was gone. Mike guided the sputtering VW back, his glasses blurred. Pam, waiting for him by the door, took his raincoat and poured coffee for him. She sat huddled, her shoulders hunched.

"That awful stuff," she said, trembling. "He was so thin it scared me."

"Yes. I sure as hell wish I had kept a closer eye on him."

"What will you do now?"

"I'm going to read the material he left. Then I suppose I'll try to find him. I apologize for crazy friends."

She stood up. "I'm going to take a shower. Now I don't want you running off."

She gave him a puzzled, concerned look. Then, turning abruptly, she was gone. Mike sat on the couch, adjusted his glasses, and opened the envelope Greg had left. He took out the pages and read slowly. He whistled, long and low, and got up to pace, listening to the rain. Then he sat down and read some more. Again he whistled. He jerked off his glasses.

Pam returned, dressed for work. "What?" she said.

"Do we have Maureen Crawford's number?"

"No. Why should we? Are those papers about her?"

"No, not about her." Springing up, he took

Arelo Sederberg

her arm. "Don't go to work today. Call in sick. I don't know where I'll be so I can't watch the twins. You take them, maybe to your mother's."

"Mike, what *is* it?"

"I don't know. I need time to think it out."

"Is there some danger involved?"

"No," he said.

Pam bit her lip. "There's something very wrong with Greg, isn't there?"

"No."

"But there is. I can tell. What was in the envelope?"

"A will, for one thing."

"A *will?*"

"Well, the will is kind of a joke. But the other material isn't."

"I'm going to stay right here, Mike. With you."

"What about the twins?"

Pam stomped her foot. "Damn your Arthur Gregory! Damn that . . . that floozy of his!"

"You will take the twins away, won't you?"

"I suppose so. I don't have to like it, but I'll do it."

When he was alone, Mike got the Ruger from the safe and took down the box of ammunition. He loaded it slowly. It might be foolish, a spear against cannons if it came to that, but somehow he felt better with the little pistol in his hand. Pepper came by, sniffing, no doubt searching for Greg. Pam was right.

Damn him! The kids loved him, the dog loved him, the wife probably loved him. *And me, me too*. Waves of indecision and vacillation went through him. Then he settled down. He went to the phone, taking the Ruger, his gut wrenching.

TWENTY-FIVE

After he left the Thompsons, Greg drove to Malibu and parked by the ocean until dawn broke, thick pink rays that became brighter and brighter until they formed a full yellow sun, hurting his eyes. He wasn't hungry. He wasn't tired. A deadness was inside him like a weight.

He looked at his watch. It was just 6 a.m. Two skin-divers waddled past, goggled and flippered, sleek as seals in their wetsuits, eager to plunge. The sea smells were pleasant and stimulating, almost intoxicating. He reeled drunkenly, under a spell. Never had his senses been keener. A wind tickled the debris along the curb and white caps broke on the ocean. Greg headed back to the city, taking 101. He

left the Porsche with an attendant at the
Beverly Hilton and went to the desk. The prim
clerk looked him over, squinting through
thick-lensed glasses.

"Don't ever let anybody tell you a Porsche
won't break down," Greg said. "Rain gets in
the coil."

The clerk continued to squint suspiciously,
but granted Greg a suite. Greg gave the bell-
man the suit for cleaning and then slept for an
hour, going deeply down, dreaming of an
ocean alive with swells and foam. The operator awakened him. He bathed and shaved,
powdered his bruised face, used hair spray
and deodorant. The suit was back; he dressed
meticulously. An attractive woman in furs
shared the elevator, and he thought of the
time in college when he'd taken the one
upstairs on a bet. Old times, irretrievable
times. A stone, a leaf, an unfound door . . . O
lost, and by the wind grieved, ghost, come
back again. He tipped the parking attendant a
ten. In traffic on Wilshire, he called Maureen.

"Now?" she said. "I have a meeting."

But she would be there. He knew that. He
drove. The air smacked of recent rain, and it
came to him that he loved this city—
Coldwater Canyon and Mulholland Drive, Dis-
neyland, Cal Tech and UCLA, the Rose Bowl,
North of Montana, the Palisades, the Greek
and the Music Center. He whistled, feeling
good. The shirt felt cool and the shoes,
Guccis, pinched a little, the way new shoes

do. He had a red Porsche that purred and sang to him. He was going to meet his girl. He stopped at a car wash on Santa Monica and watched the Porsche go through the suds bath and rinse.

"Hey, some wheels, mister," said the Mexican boy as he dried it, reverently moving his cloth.

Greg tipped him a five. "Here, get yourself a hoop."

"Sí, big hoop!" the boy said.

It would be fun to take the boy for a ride, let him try the Porsche so he could tell his family that night while they watched the ball game on TV and drank beer, his eyes big as saucers, but Greg didn't have the time. There was time for very little now. He had to use it well. He did. The earth swelled to embrace him, its odors filling him. He had an intense feeling of love for life. All life was a split second in the stream of time, and many squandered its gift. It should be cherished and savored, each second. He wanted to share that feeling with everyone. But there wasn't time, and few would understand. Reaching down, he pulled out the plastic bag of cocaine and scattered its contents on the street. Somehow that seemed very funny to him and he began to laugh, attracting some attention but not very much. Drivers were crazy here and much too intent on their missions to pay heed to a laughing madman in a red Porsche.

Maureen was in front of the salon on Camden Drive, looking at herself in the mirror. "This better be good," she said, tapping her heel.

She was beautiful, tall and trim in a cream suit with padded shoulders, her dark eyes liquid and her black hair full and lustrous in the sun. She fit in here, belonged to the place. People hurried by, rushing, impatient when stopped by lights.

"I just want to see you, that's all," he said.

She peered at him. "Greg, I think you've been using."

"No way, José," he said, flashing a grin. "I'm clean and sober, sober as a pilgrim."

Again she tapped her heel. She glanced into the mirror, brushed her hair with her hand, and stood with arms akimbo, eyeing him.

"I didn't get a chance to tell you that I'm having dinner at Masterson's place tonight," he said. "Command performance, came up suddenly. It's an opportunity for me, because I have unfinished business with him."

"What do you mean, unfinished business?"

"I owe God a death."

"Greg, you're not making sense."

"I love you," he said.

"You know how important it is to me that you stay clean. I don't think you have."

He reached out and seized her hand, holding it tightly. "I wanted to say some things before you left the other day, but there wasn't time. Maybe there's not time now. I know I didn't live a perfect life. I've been foolish a lot and I feel sorry because of it. I've bumbled around a lot. But I'm going to make up for it. I'm going to settle it."

"Settle what, Greg?"

He turned her toward the window. "We met here, remember?"

"Of course I remember."

"There we are, in the mirror. Hold it, now. Click, click. There. Mirror took a picture. We'll be in that mirror now, together."

She sighed, breaking away from him. "You're hopelessly unrealistic, Greg. A romantic."

"I suppose that's right."

"I simply must get back now."

"Say you love me."

"I can't, Greg. Not right now, not here. I'm sorry."

"Is there a heaven?"

"A heaven? What kind of question is that?"

"A foolish one, I suppose."

She forced a laugh. "I can't concern myself with things like heaven. I have enough to concern me right here on earth."

"Heaven is a small town. That's from Emily Dickinson. The poet?"

"I know who Emily Dickinson is."

"Of course you do."

"I don't like you like this. You know I don't."

"Like what?"

"High."

"I'm not high."

"Well, you're on something."

"Poetry. I'm on poetry."

"You're bonkers today, just bonkers."

" 'When ships of purple gently toss/On sea of daffodil/Fantastic sailors mingle/And then —the wharf is still.' "

"Very nice," Maureen said.

"You never really liked poetry."

"It's not real, Greg."

"What is real?"

"My job is real."

"It is?"

"Yes, it's real," Maureen said, whirling, her eyes blazing. "This street is real. That shop is. Those cars. The people. They're all real. They're not some old dead lines from an old stuffy poet dead long ago and sealed up in an old dusty room when she did live. *If* she did live."

"You're right," Greg said, snapping out the words. He added slowly, "Of course you're right."

He bowed and backed away. Then he turned, hurrying to cross the street. When he reached the other side, he paused and looked back to see that Maureen was peering at herself in the mirror.

Then for a while he shut everything from his mind, preparing for and concentrating to the absolute upon what he would do. He returned to the Beverly Hilton and got into bed, calling for a wake-up in four hours.

Almost instantly he was asleep, and it seemed only a few seconds later when the operator aroused him, bringing him up from a black pit so deep it seemed like death. Again he showered and shaved. He put on the tuxedo, dressing carefully, tying the tie, buffing the shoes, brushing the coat and trousers. He looked into the mirror and saw a gentleman with savoir faire—successful, purposeful, and confident, with a firm chin and eyes that commanded and held attention. He was ready.

He left his suit and shaving kit behind and paid the bill with the credit card from Videoscope. He had forty dollars left, thirty after again tipping the parking attendant, a redhead in a maroon uniform who knew him by name and served him with respect and alacrity. Darkness had come. The moon was a thin crescent and clouds hid the stars. He drove down Wilshire, moving so slowly other motorists honked shrilly at him and screeched past, some hurling curses. A Porsche, after all, was built to move, not loiter like a Model T with a fuddy-duddy behind the wheel. Greg didn't care. He wasn't in a hurry. He drove with the windows down, missing nothing.

On the Santa Monica Freeway, heading downtown to the interchange, his mind began to wander. He thought about T. D. Desmond, weaving his way down the field and not hearing the crowd's cheering as he danced and pranced in his moment of glory. He thought about Mark Ashley, crumpled in defeat. When this business whipped you, it whipped you absolutely. At least, as Ashley had suggested, he'd had one good role. They all paraded briefly before Greg's vision, so real they seemed alive and here beside him in the car—the Heavyweight and the Planter, the Closer and Great White Father, Reverend Jack and Marty Bradford and Mona Tyson, Tim Harte the Lightweight, Pam and Mike. Dodson and Mother and their kids, laughing as they played. He thought about Maureen, but quickly dismissed her from his mind. Then there was Marie, and he saw her in sadness, and Rob. Rob. He hit the accelerator, jumping the Porsche to eighty, not wanting to think. A cop's light flashed behind him. Why not lead the cop on a chase, end up in the jug, all dressed up and no place to go, no money for bail? It was a way out, a way to go on existing. But that, he knew, would lead back to the white powder. He pulled over.

"It got away from you, eh?" said the cop, looking over the Porsche and its driver in formal dress.

"Well, it'll do that," Greg said.

He drove slowly the rest of the way, tearing up the ticket and sending its bits flying out of his window, one at a time. He took the Pasadena Freeway, enjoying the cornering of the Porsche on the curves, and went up Colorado Boulevard into San Marino. It was just 7 p.m. when he arrived at the gate of Masterson's place. There was a black guard who ran a metal detector over the seat. That was new, and Greg asked about it.

"I'm sorry, sir," the guard said. "It was Mr. Masterson's orders for tonight, sir."

Greg shrugged. At the end of the driveway a man in a black suit took his car. He was a big man with closely cropped blond hair and broad shoulders who looked vaguely familiar. He knew Greg, calling him Mr. Gregory. No doubt he'd been given a list of guests and the model of their cars, so he merely matched the vehicle and name. Either that or Greg was the only guest. Had he been invited to his coronation or assassination? He felt a slight chill; at the same time, he was excited and alert. This mission of his seemed so unreal it was as if he'd entered it with the uncertainty of a dream. Yet he was here. It was real. He would play it out.

He was not the only, although the first guest to arrive. Others came shortly thereafter— the inevitable Norwine with his inevitable weak smile, the Frog with his smirk, and Colin Webster the Dealer, who looked pale and ill. No more arrived. All had come by themselves. So it was to be a stag dinner at Masterson's, for an uncertain purpose. They gathered in the living room for drinks served by an ashen-faced butler Greg had never seen before. The house had a remodeled exterior, built in a modern rambling ranch style, but much of the interior revealed its original Spanish architecture. There were arched doorways, domelike ceilings, and stucco walls. Some of the rooms, such as the den and the dining area, were furnished in a fashionable, very modern way, but the room in which they now met had a decidedly traditional look. Rich velvet drapes billowed over the windows. The furnishings were Louis XVI, huge chairs and tables that despite their size and weight appeared small against the vastness of the area. A massive chandelier dangled on a silver chain from the rounded ceiling, glowing with innumerable small bulbs. Its light was insufficient to reach the far walls, which were shadowy and indistinct. Arabesque rugs were scattered about. The hardwood floor was so highly polished it cast distorted reflections. The paintings were large landscapes with ornate frames. Greg remarked on a Gainsborough to Webster.

"Dear boy, it's a fake," Webster said, punctuating the revelation with an exaggerated wink.

"A fake? How could that be?"

"How could anything be, dear boy? The wagering is that *Batman* will be bigger than *Rocky*. What do you think?"

"We live in high culture. Fakes and Batman."

"Oh, we're the best actors in the world—tragedy, comedy, history, pastoral, pastoral-comical, historical-pastoral, tragical-historical, tragical-comical-historical-pastoral, scene individable, or poem unlimited."

Greg shook his head. He felt as if they were at Alice's tea party. It might have been a scene captured by an artist in a baroque frame on the wall. He found himself studying the strokes of the supposed Gainsborough.

"I got it," said the Frog, hopping silently to Greg's side. "Old man is Bela Lugosi, reincarnated. His bed is in the basement."

The mention of basement startled Greg, but he didn't show it. "At least then we'll be out of here by dawn," he said, continuing the banter.

"You got any idea how much those flicks made for Universal in the thirties?"

Greg smiled. Suddenly he felt very amused, sort of pixieish. Norwine stood across the room, alone and looking sour. Greg went to him, took his sleeve, and tugged him over to the painting.

"Look closely," he said, his voice hushed. "Is it a fake?"

Norwine peered. He took a monocle from his vest pocket and peered again. "Of course not," he said.

"Another question," Greg said in the same tone. "Do you know where the john is?"

Norwine puckered his lips in disgust and turned a cold shoulder. Greg walked slowly to the door and went out into the hallway. He closed the door behind him and stood for a full minute, getting his bearings. The hall was

411

dank and silent. He moved cautiously, almost on tiptoe, hugging the wall. The floor creaked slightly under his step. Suddenly the butler appeared ahead of him, stepping briskly out into the center of the passageway; there he stood, somewhat menacingly, darkly gathering his brows, blocking the path. Then, with an exaggerated gesture, almost a bow, the butler indicated a door to Greg and opened it. He went in. It was a large bathroom, brightly lit and mirrored on one wall. Greg took his time. He puttered around, washing his hands carefully and flushing the toilet twice. Then he returned to the hallway. He expected to see the butler waiting there, ready to guide him back, but the hall was empty and quiet. He'd been here only once before, with Masterson, and he knew there was a door around the next corner that led to a second door which in turn opened to the stairway to the crypt room. He found the door immediately, but discovered it was locked. Greg felt a strange blend of disappointment and relief. Now he need go no farther. His mission had been a failure.

He felt a breeze. Ahead of him were French windows leading to a balcony that was just above the lawn and swimming pool area. He hurried ahead, feeling a surge of excitement, pushed open the windows, and went out on the balcony. He looked around. In the distance a dog barked sharply, echoing in the cool darkness. A brazier burned near the pool. Greg closed the windows behind him and lowered himself to the ground. He passed the pool quickly and searched in the ivy for the gate he knew was there. Again came the barking of the dog, now more of a howl than a bark, and from elsewhere came returning barks and howls. Greg stopped still. His hand brushed the steel circular handle of the gate. He pulled and the gate came open, squeaking shrilly. He knew the passage, for he and Masterson had come up this way, but it was dark before him now and he wasn't sure he could make his way through it. The only light came from the single brazier. He could see the descending steps and the plastered walls. He went in, dragging the gate closed behind him. Now it was pitch black.

He could do nothing except feel his way, which he did, his hands on the smooth plaster, taking one step at a time. He knew he would have to go slowly or he risked tripping and falling, and at the same time he also knew he must hurry for soon the others would wonder what was taking him so long and send someone to find out what had happened to him. He moved faster, judging the length of the step and hopping as he went down. Then he saw a light. The stairway had ended and the ground was hard. It was moist and cold, and he smelled must and heard a faint trickling like running water. He continued ahead, his heartbeat picking up, his throat dry, conscious of an empty feeling in his stomach. The light cast a blue glow ahead. Greg hurried toward it. Then he was in the underground area, the crypt with its cobblestone floor. The stone coffin filled almost half the room. Greg lost no time. He kneeled and searched under it, finding what he was looking for almost immediately. It was a pistol, a little Beretta automatic, wrapped up in a cloth. He checked it quickly. It was loaded with six bullets. Greg returned the cloth. Slipping the Beretta into his back pocket, he went back along the dark passage, leaving much faster than he'd come, up the stairs, and emerged outside by the pool. He glanced around. He closed the gate. Then he stopped and stood stark still.

There was a noise above him, from the house. He looked up and saw a woman's figure in the window, illuminated brightly. It was Mrs. Masterson. She was looking down, directly at him. He was certain she had seen him. But she merely turned away, as if to let him pass.

Between calls, Mike reread the material Greg had left. The "will" had been brief: "I leave everything to the lady outside the Santa Monica Post Office, since there is little to leave and her needs are modest." What he'd called his memoirs was even briefer: "Man is born on Sunday, suffers the week, and dies on Friday." Obviously they were attempts at grim humor, but they only alarmed Mike, especially the "dies on Friday." This was Friday.

He called UPI, which was still following the Dodson case, and told the Los Angeles bureau chief he'd be in soon with some documents of interest. Then he called the city desk of the *Arizona Republic*.

"Jesus H on a crutch," said the editor.

"If I fax it to you, how soon can you print it?"

"Dunno. I'd have to show it to the fucking lawyers."

"I'm giving it to UPI, too."

"I always like that, gun at my head."

The editor called back at noon. The story would be bannered in the morning, under Dodson's by-line. Before the weekend was over it would be international.

Mike had been trying without success to reach Marie, but her husband finally responded to a page message. "You haven't heard about Rob," the doctor said, and told him.

"Oh, good Lord," Mike said. He felt a weight inside, cold in his gut, and at the same time he wanted to weep. "Greg was here last night and he didn't even mention it. Is Marie there?"

"She wants to speak to you."

Marie's voice was calm, controlled by effort. "I saw Greg last night, at the hospital. Oh, Mike, he loved Rob so, so dearly!"

"I know, I know. The boy was loved. You loved the boy as well."

"Greg is not in his right mind about it. He said something about getting even, an eye for an eye."

"Do you have any idea where he might be?"

"I'm afraid I have no idea."

"Well, I'll find him."

He hung up. Damn it, *damn* it! He'd let Greg leave, run off like a hurt animal, and now he sensed disaster. And he felt helpless. He grabbed the ringing phone. A secretary primly announced that Maureen Crawford was calling.

"You took your time getting back," Mike said. He was angry and didn't want to spare her. "Did you know that Rob died last night? The boy o.d.'d."

He heard her gasp. "Oh," she said. "Oh, dear."

"Greg is using again."

"Well, don't talk as if I'm to blame."

"I'm not blaming anybody. Have you seen him?"

"Yes, just recently. He was talking funny, but I certainly didn't realize it was because of his son."

"What did he say?"

"Oh, something about unfinished business. He said he was going to Masterson's for dinner tonight in San Marino."

"That's a help, a big help. Thank you."

"Will you let me know about him? I am concerned, you know."

"Sure you are."

"I don't think I deserve that tone of voice, or innuendo."

"That's right. You deserve nothing."

"I beg your pardon?"

He paused and then said, "You're right, Maureen. I'm half here today. It was unnecessary and I apologize."

"Greg is in danger, isn't he?"

"Yes."

"What can I do?"

"Be available, that's all. I'll be out so you can't call me, but I want to keep in touch with you, in case he calls."

"I'll be right here."

"Good."

"I *do* love him, the goddamn fool."

Mike hung up and sat on the bed, pondering. His fingers drummed idly on the phone. He was trying to decide whom to call next— the cops or sheriff or the feds—when his mind was made up for him. Lambert of the federal Drug Enforcement Agency called. He knew Lambert from his AP days—nights, actually, since he'd never gotten off the graveyard shift.

"What you up to?" Lambert asked.

"What d'you mean, up to? You have a tap on my phone?"

"Yeah," Lambert said. "Suppose you meet me in an hour or so."

"Meet you where?"

"Say, Santa Anita. Big place, Santa Anita, and it's close to San Marino."

417

"Why San Marino?"

"You know," Lambert said.

Mike called the UPI bureau chief again and said he'd have to back out on the exclusive he had promised about Dodson. But he hinted there might be something big coming down locally that evening. The bureau chief didn't know whether to be grateful or furious.

"While I got you, gimme a quote on that kid that o.d.'d. You know Arthur Gregory, so gimme a quote on how awful drugs are. Like that."

"I'd rather not."

"Okay, thought I'd ask."

An hour later, Mike was in a black Ford beside Lambert, parked in the darkness around the corner from the gate to the Masterson house. "Are we going in?" he asked.

"Going in? How can we? No crime, no warrant. No, all we can do is snoop. I got a dozen snoopers around, but that's all they can do."

"I have a friend in there who's in danger."

"You mean Gregory. The red Porsche."

"You're way ahead of me."

"Well, if I'd waited for you to call we might not be here yet. We rolled just after you sent that fax to Phoenix."

"I suppose you have a copy of that, too."

"I suppose," Lambert said.

"Well, I'm not going to sit on my ass here,"

Mike said. He moved to open the door. "I'm going to look around."

Lambert held him back, restraining him like a gentle bear. "We might get a warrant when that story breaks. Meanwhile, we sit. We've sat a long time. See, he's been in our sights, Masterson, but some big boys hold us back, I mean big like in that white house back East. But now maybe he's overstepped."

"Then he had Dodson killed?"

"He started the ball rolling and couldn't stop it."

Mike felt his heart squeeze. There was a quiet chill in the air. It had built up to this, rising starkly, and now it seemed to be playing out to its finish on a momentum of its own. His dread, he knew, was his helplessness.

Masterson made his appearance just before the butler announced dinner, entering the room quietly and shaking hands with his guests. His hand was cold. He looked much older than when Greg had last seen him, his gray face criss-crossed with tiny wrinkles and his eyes deep-set and hollow. He moved with catlike silence, and when he smiled it was not reflected in his eyes, which lacked the verve they had shown before. His thin shoulders slumped roundly. He was an old man, white-haired and benign looking, gentle in manner and soft of voice.

Greg felt the Beretta in his back pocket,

hard against the chair, as he sat down in the dining room.

Could this be a dream? A hallucination? No. It was real. He was here. Chair, table, host, guests, butler and aide, trays, carpet, murals on the wall, twin lighting fixtures tinkling faintly—all that existed in its solidity and flesh, the atoms of it, before and about him. An onion soup was served.

He felt the Beretta.

Masterson looked up. "My apologies for the guard outside. It's rather foolish, I realize, but the police received a threat against me so they advised that everyone who enters be searched."

"Hope you frisked the butler," cracked the Frog.

He got no reaction, not even an elite sniff from the butler, although the comment had been delivered for reaction, to ease the tension that seemed to hang in the air. Colin Webster was flushed and sweating. Norwine, next to Webster, suffered a palsylike trembling of his hands. Once he dropped his fork. The Frog, his joke fallen flat, looked flat himself, grim and twitching his mouth. He never twitched. Norwine never trembled.

Masterson seemed to be making a board meeting of it. "We anticipate the production of at least eight feature films a year, in addition to television work, which is as ambitious a schedule as that of any other studio," he said calmly, in businesslike tones. "This represents significant opportunity for all of you, gentle-men. I have asked you here tonight, in fact, to assure you that your futures with Videoscope are secure and very promising.''

The Frog applauded lightly, but no one else joined. Webster wiped his forehead, and Norwine's spoon tapped faintly on his plate. It seemed to Greg that Masterson spoke to him. And spoke more, silently. Come to me and never worry. Bow to me and that which you want is yours. You need not ask. Just beckon and it shall be yours—cars, homes, women, prestige and honor and friends, the good life of roses and honey, of melodious sounds and security and warmth. See with my eyes, touch with my hands, the hands and the eyes of Mr. Hyde, strong hands and benign eyes.

Greg was tempted. He felt the Beretta, poking him.

It was false prestige, false honor, false friends. He knew that. Yet did it really matter if a man like Masterson were erased? There were others, many of them. And the Mastersons themselves went on, their anointed scions prevailing after they were gone. They couldn't be caught, or destroyed; they had too much money, too much power. The Dodson papers could make them uncomfortable for a while, but not very long. Men like Greg in Gucci shoes and tailored suits would present effective counteracting propaganda to the press, mitigating against the charges—Masterson the philanthropist,

Masterson the war hero, Masterson the immigrant's idol and cherished dream, Masterson the patriot.

What did the old man know? The old man knew all.

Masterson had used him, yes, but Greg now knew that others also had used him. He had been read and used. Mother had used him, she a prophet who had discerned the future and seemed to know he would do as he had done at a time when it was most appropriate. Denise Stevens also had somehow known, and used. She couldn't merely testify against Masterson, for that would be the breaking of a code, a betrayal. But she could act as the instrument of betrayal and revenge. And what of Mrs. Masterson, the vaguest of these shadow figures? She, too, knew; dead sons linked her and Greg.

He sought Masterson's eyes, but could not fix upon them. He was as elusive and impalpable as ever. If so, how could he be condemned? Little of him was known, so could he not be innocent? Multiple doubts now assailed Greg. Who really was this old man? Had he arranged the Dodson killing? Was he the drug king of the West Coast? Was he scum? Child-slayer? Inhuman? He had spoken calmly before of hundreds, thousands, killed horribly in war. Had he enjoyed that? And what about you? Who are you? Can you kill? You did in war. Can you now? Is this another war? Perhaps it was.

Greg knew what he would do.

It was silent in the room. Norwine trembled. Webster sweated. The Frog then made a sound with his lips, appreciating the soup. Masterson sat calmly, regal and serene.

The butler entered, his obsequious assistant trailing. He pushed a tray with the salad in a huge, gold-fringed bowl of gilded crystal.

Greg stood up. He had a vision of Rob on a merry-go-round.

His eyes swept the room, taking it all in— pepper grinder, the salad spotted with red tomato chunks, dressings in matched bowls, the dark dour butler, Norwine and Webster and Frog. And, again, Cyrus Masterson.

Greg kicked the salad tray. As the bowl shattered on the floor, he drew the Beretta. And then at last Masterson's eyes met his. The look was not begging or asking, not astonishment or disbelief. It was a look of relief. Greg aimed carefully and pulled the trigger. It was only then that he knew he understood Cyrus Masterson, and he felt immense relief and release in himself.

"What was that?" Mike asked.

"Car backfire," Lambert said.

"Backfire, my ass."

Lambert was on the radio. "We're going up to take a look. You stay put."

"Oh, no. This is my party, too."

"Then stick to me like skin. Promise?"

Lambert drew his pistol. A rain was falling,

slanting in the glow of the streetlights. Ahead, the iron gate thrust its spear points into a ring of light like a halo.

Masterson sat back against his chair, blood oozing from a red hole in his forehead, dead with his eyes and mouth open.

"Dear boy," Webster said, and fainted into his soup.

Norwine screamed, a shrill woman's scream, his hands over his ears, and sank to his knees. His trousers were wet. Greg pointed the Beretta at him, but he didn't fire it. Let him live, this O. Norwine the Sniveler, seeing himself; he deserved the agony of life, its truths. The Frog got up and kicked Norwine under the table, glared at Greg, slowly shook his head, and waddled away. He looked more disgusted than surprised. The butler cringed behind his assistant, offering him for sacrifice.

Greg backed away. He ran in the hallway, his shoes clanking. The quickest way out was through the French windows and over the balcony to the pool area. As he slipped down to the grassy area under the balcony, bright lights flashed on. He heard shouts. A man appeared in front of him, by the pool. There he stopped for a long second. Greg recognized the man; he'd been ahead of in the buffet line at the pool party, the one who said he was in real estate. He had a pistol, a snub .38, and he was dressed in black so that he merged with the night but stood out vividly in the floodlights. Greg pointed the Beretta and squeezed the trigger. The man slumped, but there was a crack and a flash of red from the .38. Greg felt the hit; it seemed to pick him up and send him reeling back. It was a hit near the midsection, and it knocked out his wind. He struggled for balance. There was no pain, but his hand over his stomach reddened and he felt a warm trickling down his legs. It then became a dream, one that wavered and pulsated surrealistically; he was running and there was a wetness in his face and he was on something that was spongy like grass. He wanted to find the Porsche. Maureen was waiting for him in the Porsche and they were going to pick up Rob and all of them were going to go to the fair. Then he saw the Porsche but it wasn't Maureen. It was Marie. He felt a surge of happiness. She looked very young. They were going to ride the merry-go-round and for a moment he thought he was already doing that, listening to the music and smelling popcorn and cotton candy and feeling the dizzy whirl as he reached out to grab the brass ring. But he wasn't there. He was lying on grass. He could hear the smell of rain. He felt fine. Someone kneeled beside him.

"Hey," Greg said. "You, old buddy?" He coughed. He tried to get up but couldn't move. "Mike?"

"Yeah," Mike said. "Sure it's me."

It was hard to talk. Blood choked him. He felt stuffed and swollen inside. But he knew where he was, what he had done. He knew his name. Greg. Legend. He knew it was Mike.

"Kicked Hyde," he said. "Kicked his ass, old buddy."

"You bet," Mike said.

"Hey," Greg said, his eyes opening wide.

He saw a field of green stretching before him to the horizon and beyond, a vastness interminable that brightened as it ran swiftly to a far, far distant point, where the brightest light of all burned and beckoned.

"Hey, Rob," he said.

Mike was crying. Someone touched his shoulder. Mike pushed the big hand away.

"Okay," Lambert said.

They left them alone.

TWENTY-SIX

Mike called Pam from a booth in San Marino. It was still raining and he was soaked and shivering. He noticed for the first time there was blood on his shirt.

"Oh, no, God," Pam said when he told her.

She was silent for a while and then he heard sounds of her crying. Usually the full effect of bad news took a while before it hit her, stunning her to a long silence. Now she broke immediately.

"I'll be home as soon as I can," Mike said. "I don't want you to wait up."

"I will though. Hurry, please."

"I'll try."

"But be safe."

He cleaned up at the DEA offices, downtown on Figueroa. He gave a statement to a male stenographer and was out by midnight. The rain was gone; the air was crisp and cool. He'd read Dodson's article in the *Arizona Republic*, faxed to DEA from Phoenix. The *Times* was out early and played last night's shootings in San Marino on page 1 of the bulldog, but they didn't get it right. Yet that wasn't their fault; it was DEA disinformation. The article said Masterson had taken a professional hit, and Greg and one of the old man's bodyguards had been killed in the melee. It was probably the best way for now, until it could all be sorted out. Masterson had been receiving death threats, the *Times* said, but the mystifying part about it was that none had come directly to him, but instead to his wife.

Mike had a stop to make before he went home. He'd called Maureen, telling her about it, and she'd said she would wait in her office until he came—no matter how long it took. She wanted more details, she said. When he got there, he found her behind her desk, wearing glasses and studying papers.

"I had to work," she said. "Takes your mind off it." She paused, taking off the glasses, and added: "A drink?"

"Thanks. I need a drink."

"Brandy, as I remember."

She brought out a decanter of Courvoisier XO cognac and poured a liberal amount into a gold-fringed glass. "You take it straight up, as I remember."

"You have a good memory."

"For things," Maureen said, pouring a little for herself. "Tell me now, please."

He did, seated before her desk, she behind it, and as he spoke her expression didn't change. She gazed at him, her large dark eyes impassive, almost incurious. He told her what actually had occurred, not the *Times*'s version.

"I see," she said. She rose and paced briefly, her hands behind her back, and then returned to the chair. "The poor fool."

"That's how you sum him up?"

"I guess it is. He had foolish ideals. He was a misfit, in a way. The society doesn't allow for people like Greg. Sooner or later they get run over. And I don't think they really care if they do."

"You imply they get run over because that's what they really want."

"Am I a guinea pig for your next book? A type?"

"Perhaps."

"I'd like to know what you think of me."

"Intelligent," he said. He paused and went on. "Attractive, efficient, personable. All of those. You're also ambitious, opportunistic, unfeeling."

She sniffed. "Sounds heinous."

"I'm sorry that it does."

"I care for myself. I admit it. Others care for themselves, too, but they won't admit it. Tell me. Do you think Greg was ambitious?"

"Well, yes."

"And opportunistic?"

"I suppose so."

"But not callous or unfeeling."

"No. Not at all."

"Why wasn't he?"

"You tell me why, Maureen."

"Because he didn't have to be. He had a head start, a good education, and natural charm. He didn't have to scratch and step."

"And you did."

She looked at him, her eyes hard and her lip curled. "I learned very early in life that if you let your guard down somebody hits at you. Your guard is down when you fall for somebody."

"I suppose that's right."

"When a man is nasty, it's called sophistication, lack of naivete. When a woman is nasty, she's a bitch."

"I don't buy it. You're exaggerating."

Maureen issued a faint snarl. "Am I? Well, then I am. But you'd better get up to speed if you hope to become a writer. Don't you think Greg couldn't go for the jugular. He went for Ashley's."

"Why did he go for Ashley?"

"For a silly reason, like men do. He thought I slept with Ashley."

"Did you?"

"Is that any business of yours, my sex life?"

"No, of course not. I'm sorry. It just came out."

"Greg closed his eyes and saw no evil. He knew where Masterson was coming from, believe you me."

"I think you're right. But it was because of you. It was a fast way up, and you don't like the slow lane."

"It would be nice if all of us could know everything like you obviously do," she said, her voice calm. "I like money and I do not like losers. But Greg worked for Masterson before I met him. I think you might know that."

"Okay," Mike said. "Touché."

She shook back her hair and looked vacantly away, her features softening. "I did love him. It wasn't easy for me, but I did. Love isn't easy for everybody."

"Love means different things to different people."

"I really don't think I would have stayed with Greg much longer. Underneath, he was a lemming."

"I'll give you this. You're a frank one."

"Oh, we can be honest with each other, here. At least I know who I am. He didn't know me. You don't. What I am, you see, is a bastard, and I need a man who's a bastard, too."

"Now you're being too hard on yourself."

"I'm being honest. I'm the frank one."

"I think I'd better go now."

"Yes, you go. Go back to your bourgeois, smug little valley and write about things, because you understand everything. Think what you like about me."

"I notice you have a way of contradicting yourself."

"Well, I'll tell you this. I'm not as fast as you might like to think I am. The fact was Greg was too fast for me at times, his roller-coaster ups and downs. And then he was the baby a lot and I had to be the grown-up. That was all right. I'm not a child, thank goodness. I was born grown up. I wasn't brought up to go to Harvard or Yale or Stanford. I was brought up to scratch, by a drunken old man who beat us and tried to crawl into our beds. I didn't have time to cry about it then and I don't have time to cry now."

"Maureen, Pam and I will pick you up and take you to his service if you like."

"His funeral? Thanks but no thanks. I don't make the funeral circuit. I don't think the dead like the idea of us parading by, looking at them." She smiled, privately it seemed, mysteriously. "I'll see Greg in my own way."

"What do you mean?"

"In the mirror," she said.

"In the mirror?"

"My little foolishness. I'll see him when I see me."

"I think you're more upset than you want to admit."

"If I am, then I am. I don't like sad songs. I

don't sing them for others and I don't want them sung for me."

"Well, I'll leave you then. Back to my bourgeois little valley."

"I'm sorry about that crack." She tossed her head, a beautiful dusky animal with eyes that now looked distant, hurt. "I'm sorry I talked so much."

"I'm glad you did. I know you helped Greg. He needed love and you gave it to him at a critical time." Mike smiled. He touched her arm. "I know it's hard for you. But love is something we all need."

"Do we?" she said. "Well, he did."

She took a compact from her purse, turned away, and powdered her face. Mike left. Pausing in the hallway, he thought he heard her sobbing.

The sky lightened and a moon and stars appeared as he drove the freeway, heading home. He wasn't in a hurry; besides, the VW shook if he pushed past fifty. Mike tried not to think, but he did of course. He thought about love, a word with no definition; like a poem, it was merely there, inexpressible. Nothing was so absolute yet so fragile. Greg had loved intensely and possessively. Maureen had loved without commitment or sacrifice. Nothing could come of such love, and it could be described, articulated, so perhaps it really had not been love.

Mike didn't know. He knew so little.

Perhaps it was true that Greg had never

surrendered his childhood, as Maureen had suggested, making him vulnerable. What he'd avidly sought he hadn't really wanted, not at its price; what he'd yearned for deep in the soul he didn't quite know how to find or hold. His real need was every man's need, love. There was that word again. Maybe Greg had found what he'd searched for in the end, a microsecond of resurrection.

Mike turned off the freeway. Feeling anxious, he coaxed the VW ahead. The porch light was shining. The door opened and Pam came out. Light glistened on her hair. The twins peeked out and swooped past her, squealing. Pepper yipped and danced in tight circles. Mike stood in the after-rain mist, the clean right rain, knowing quite fully the meaning of love.